Protecting the Truth

ANNIE BOON

ISBN-10: 1507620403
ISBN-13: 978-1507620403

DEDICATION

For my family.

CONTENTS

1

'Hi.'

Nicola didn't bother turning round. 'I'll have about twenty clean glasses in a minute,' she said from the depths of the dishwasher.

No reply. Surely someone had just come in to the kitchen? She tossed the steam out of her hair and looked round.

A guy she'd never seen before was leaning nonchalantly against the Aga looking slightly amused.

'The party is through there,' Nicola said helpfully indicating the door leading to the hall while trying to pass over a tray of clean glasses.

'I didn't come for the glasses. I came to find out what could possibly be so exciting that you wanted to spend the whole party in here.'

Nicola blushed and screwed her hands up in the tea towel. Her heart was pumping and her skin was prickling.

'I'm Julian.' An outstretched hand was offered and taken. 'Coffee?' Expertly he reached behind her to fill a kettle. That close. Nicola was sure he must be able to feel her prickly heat but he wasn't fazed. They sat opposite each other smiling awkwardly.

'And you are?'

'Nicola. Nicola Cowan. I live in Frampton. Just down the road.'

'I've just moved here. Well my parents have. To Mulberry Cottage which is also just down the road, so we must be neighbours.'

The kitchen door swung open swirling the room with music, chatter and party atmosphere.

'Julian,' screeched a wild shock of blond hair. 'There you are. Come on, it's my party so you have to dance with me. We've found some more fizz.' She moved over to the kitchen table and looked possessive. 'I thought you were sorting the glasses,' she said to Nicola.

Before she could open her mouth, Julian grabbed Nicola's hand and dragged her towards the door.

'Too late, Jocelyn. Nicola and I are just longing for a dance, several in fact. And I do think it's rude to expect guests to slave away in the kitchen like Cinderella. Are you afraid of the competition? Nicola is very attractive.' He gave Nicola a squeeze pushed her through the door which banged decisively behind them.

Nicola giggled. 'Jocelyn won't like that,' she said, flinging the tea towel aside. She'd been clutching it like a talisman.

'Doesn't bother me. We're dancing,' was the reply.

Hours later, or so it seemed, the disco finally played the last track and people started to drift off. Julian and Nicola unwound themselves and an awkward silence lumped between them.

'I'll walk you home,' said Julian just as Nicola caught sight of her father edging towards them.

'Ready, Nicola?' said her father totally ignoring Julian and looking pleased with himself. 'I was just having a drink with the Willstones so I can offer you lift.' With that he took her arm and steered her towards the front door. Nicola turned and looked desperately over her shoulder. Julian gave her slight wave, grinned and mouthed 'I'll phone you.'

Back home, as she climbed the stairs, reluctant for the night to be over, Nicola paused to listen to her parent's conversation seeping out under the sitting room door.

'Dee Willstone told me that the new people in Mulberry Cottage are Caroline and Dermot Smith Owen. Old friends of theirs from Kenya. Dermot is retiring soon and they're going to move here permanently, when they come back from Saudi Arabia. They've got two boys, both at university. I think she said one was called Julian. I wonder if they've registered at the surgery yet?'

Nicola slid down the stairs towards the door but she didn't catch her mother's reply.

The next morning as Nicola was carrying a bowl of cereal past the front door on her way to the sitting room, a comfy sofa and some ghastly morning reality TV show, the doorbell rang. Not looking her best in baggy pull ons and an old T-shirt, Nicola dragged the door open expecting some delivery man with a parcel since it was so near Christmas. Squinting into the morning sunshine she nearly died.

'You're invited for brunch. Ready?' inquired a voice dressed in amusement.

Julian stood relaxed on her door step in well pressed jeans, a light blue cashmere sweater; it could only be cashmere, and expensive cologne.

'Brunch,' he repeated. 'Jocelyn had so many friends staying over last night, a brunch party has been organized and we're invited.'

Nicola was rescued by her mother who'd come to find out who was at the door.

'Mum, this is Julian, Julian Smith Owen.' said Nicola by way of stunned explanation. 'He needs a coffee and I need to change.'

'Hello, I'm Monica Cowan…' was all she heard as she fled upstairs.

'Whoa! What's happening?' Maggie, pesky younger sister, was lolling on a bean bag in Nicola's half of their shared bedroom wearing what looked suspiciously like one of Nicola's last presentable white shirts.

'Maggie how could you,' snarled Nicola looking at her shirt.

'Chill big sister and explain. What's the national crisis?'

Briefly Nicola tried to explain Julian but kept tripping over her emotions and any way what was there to explain as they'd only just met.

'Major emergency. I need to look stunning like five minutes ago.'

Nicola paused halfway down the stairs. Low voices seeped out of the kitchen on a raft of fresh coffee. Julian must be making a good impression if her mother had used real beans. They were sitting cosily at the kitchen table like old friends. Julian stood up and grinned.

'Your mother has just been filling me in on all the Frampton gossip. I feel I've been living here for ages.'

Julian slipped his hand into hers as they turned out of the gate and headed up the hill to The Grange.

'Your Mum is really nice,' he commented.

Nicola smiled happily. On a day like today she could be generous. Her Mum was nice.

When they reached the entrance to The Grange, Nicola pulled Julian round to face her.

'Are you sure Jocelyn invited me for brunch?'

'Well, not exactly. She invited me and I didn't want to go on my own so I invited you. Is there a problem?'

They walked on in silence as Nicola considered her nemesis, Jocelyn Willstone. A couple of years older than Nicola, Jocelyn was strident like her mother, Dee, a bully at primary school and a queen bee at Pony Club. It was entirely due to Jocelyn and her cronies that Nicola's secret imaginary friend, Jamie, had come into her life for protection. To make matters worse, from Nicola's perspective, Jocelyn was tall, model thin and perfectly groomed.

'So what's it with Jocelyn?' asked Julian, intrigued. 'I've known her for ages, since we were all small kids in Africa. I know she can be a real pain, very bossy like her mother, but she's manageable. I see her as an annoying little sister.'

Nicola let it rest at that and steered the conversation to Frampton village gossip regarding which her mother was somewhat of an expert.

The Grange preened its Cotswold stone façade in the winter sunshine. A log fire crackled and spat contributing a background sound to the casual crowd gathered in the hall. Charlie Willstone, Jocelyn's father, ever the generous host was pouring drinks and handing them round with a large dose of good cheer. He had just hailed them as long lost friends when Dee emerged from the kitchen looking harassed.

'Should we serve the food in the kitchen or the dining room, Charlie. And where is Jocelyn?'

Spotting Nicola, Dee rushed over.

'Nicola, could you be a star and help in the kitchen just until I find Jocelyn?'

Julian stepped in. 'Nicola is a guest just like everyone else. We'll help you find Jocelyn.'

With that he gripped Nicola's arm and muttering something about enormous cheek, steered her in the direction of the drawing room. Nicola smiled at Julian. It was lovely that she mattered.

Being a newbie in the area and like Nicola not really knowing any of Jocelyn's Oxford Brookes Uni friends, Julian spent most of the afternoon talking to her without really noticing the rest of the crowd.

Julian explained that he was reading PPE at Lincoln College, Oxford. He was in his third year and had absolutely no idea what to do after graduation. Nicola was too shy to ask what PPE was but it sounded really academic.

'I'm hoping my future will become blindingly obvious when I wake up one morning but it better be soon. All my mates are getting jobs and the parental pressure is on.' His parents were currently living abroad but were intent on returning to England permanently. His brother had gone out to Saudi to visit for Christmas but Julian preferred to stay in England to study.

'My aunt Gellie is house sitting at Mulberry Cottage so she is looking after me. She's great. Very bohemian. Her real name is Angela but we've always called her Gellie.'

'To be quite honest,' continued Julian. 'I feel that my roots are back in Africa, in Kilifi in Kenya because that is where I was brought up and that is where I first went to school. Then I was sent back to England to boarding school and that was when Gellie took over as a sort of honorary stepmother. You must meet her. She's coming down from London tomorrow and will be around for Christmas.'

Julian smiled at her and looked into her eyes. Nicola felt herself going scarlet. Julian's life sounded so exotic. What was he going to think about her boring life? Well better 'fess up' and get it over with.

'I'm taking my 'A' Levels in the summer and I hope to go to London to UCL, chemistry, if I get the grades. Until then its Stanton High School in Cheltenham, boarding.'

'You'll be fine and London will be great. You never know, I might end up working there.'

That lovely smile again and Nicola was sure he would have kissed her if there hadn't been a bacon butty in the way.

'Why don't you come and hang out at mine on Friday? You can get to meet Gellie and we can have lunch?'

What a lovely idea. Nicola almost hugged herself.

Walking slowly down the lane and up the hill, Nicola savoured every minute of anticipation. The cold air brought colour to her cheeks and messed up her hair but for once it didn't seem to matter. She had never felt this way before about anything, about anyone. She pushed open the wooden gate and walked up the gravel path towards Mulberry Cottage. Before she reached the front door Julian appeared and grabbed her hand.

'It's so good to see you again,' he said. 'Come on in. Gellie is dying to meet you.'

He ushered her into the warm cooking filled kitchen to be welcomed first by a large black Labrador who looked remarkably like the Willstones' dog, and secondly by Aunt Gellie.

'Hi, Nicola. How nice to meet you. I'm Julian's aunt but please just call me Gellie.' A strong floury hand grasped Nicola's. 'Oh dear, I'm sorry,' Gellie wiped her hands on her apron. 'I was just about to put some soda farls in the oven for lunch.' And with that she turned round and whipped the baking trays off the table and into the oven. 'There,' she said triumphantly. 'Would you like tea or coffee?'

'Coffee would be lovely,' Nicola replied. Gellie was not at all as she imagined. For a start she was dressed in designer jeans, a T-shirt and cowboy boots, very un-aunt looking. Slim with a mass of wild black hair arguing with a scrunchie which was desperately trying to keep order. The curls were winning, escaping every which way round her face.

'Home Jake,' commanded Gellie, gently helping the dog out into the cold with her boot and shutting the door behind him. 'He's not ours,' she said by way of explanation. 'He belongs to the Willstones up the lane. I expect you've met Jake before since you know Jocelyn.'

Nicola had walked up to Julian's from the other end of the lane and had completely forgotten that the Willstones were near neighbours. Well a couple of acres separated the two properties but the The Grange was the nearest house. Jocelyn must have shown Jake the way to Mulberry Cottage. Nicola felt a wave of jealousy as a current of insecurity swept over her.

'Well,' said Gellie, wiping her hands on her apron, 'I'm not going to let the opportunity of some fit young people with nothing to do pass me by. Julian, will you go up to my studio and fetch the list on my work bench, please. We are going to unpack your father's books and stack them on the shelves. The books are all in boxes on the floor. They need to be arranged as per Dermot's lists. I'll finish making lunch and give you a call when it's ready.'

Nicola spent a very happy day sorting books with Julian. His father had a mammoth collection which had been in store for years. There were rare antiquities and hard back copies of children's classics and Julian and Nicola were soon embroiled in a competition to see who had read the most. After lunch Gellie took Nicola up to her temporary studio and showed her the knitwear she designed. Grabbing a couple of samples she put them on and sashayed up and down giggling happily. Then she let Nicola try on some of next season's samples. They were the nearest thing to a luxury item that Nicola had ever seen all hand knitted from the naturally dyed Peruvian alpaca wool hanging from long racks at the back of the room. Nicola knew nothing about fashion but she could tell that Gellie's work was something special.

'I use a really ancient 12 gauge knitting machine to try out patterns and designs using different weaves and from there I create my samples. When I'm happy with a result the sample goes to be made up and then to Wandsworth to the cutting room to be finished.' Gellie swirled round in a rainbow colour effect.

'I'm having a show in London just before Easter to introduce my designs to the more exclusive shops. My agent says it's time to make the move from selling direct. It's all a bit scary because I'm an artist not an entrepreneur. I'd love you to come. I'll give Julian a couple of tickets.'

Winter darkness started to creep slowly into the valleys chasing away the grey afternoon, cheating it out of its daylight hours. Nicola was loathed to leave the comfort of Mulberry Cottage, but it was only two days to Christmas Eve and her mother needed some help. 'I'll phone you, Nicola,' said Julian. He gave her a peck on both cheeks and held both her hands at the same time. 'Merry Christmas.'

Nicola's father, as the local doctor, was on call for part of Christmas so the Cowan household had the usual chaotic festive season with an agenda dictated by other people's maladies.

'Another Muddle Christmas,' declared Maggie.

The family made the morning church service together but then Andrew was called to an emergency at the local hospital so the turkey was put on hold. Maggie and Bundle, the Cowan's half greyhound/half something else dog shared a box of chocolates and were both sick. Henry, middle child and general disappointment, managed to watch an unsuitable video which his mother didn't catch up with until the credits were rolling and Nicola kept taking her mobile out of her pocket and putting it back. That failed to make it ring. Presents were rushed through so that the turkey would still be edible and Monica got into a panic writing down who had got what so that she could supervise Henry and Maggie's thank you letter writing. Nicola was relieved to snuggle into bed to carry out an endless debate with herself as to whether she should have rung Julian.

Boxing Day dawned bright, clear and frosty which Maggie described as a Christmas card day. To compensate for the dysfunctional yesterday, Andrew decreed that a brisk country walk was what they all needed and there would be no excuses. He expected everyone, including Bundle, on the terrace at 11.00 sharp dressed appropriately. Meanwhile he would be in his study with the OS map of the local area. As soon as he left the kitchen there was a communal groan. The lunch would have to be prepared at break neck speed even though it would only be leftovers. Nicola didn't want to leave the house in case her mobile rang. Reception in Frampton, other than in the Cowan's kitchen, was practically nonexistent. Henry was nursing a monstrous hangover. On Christmas morning his mother had asked him to fill the red wine and whisky decanters in the dining room. Henry had taken this to mean emptying and refilling the said decanters and since his mother was so dead set against waste he drank what remained in each decanter before washing and refilling. He thought he'd done an excellent job especially since the actual extent of his refilling task had largely gone unnoticed. Perhaps that is why the unsuitable video had seemed so funny. Maggie just didn't want any exercise at all especially if it meant going somewhere with her family. Bundle, on the other hand, was over the moon because the word 'walk' had been repeated several times. In fact the word had been uttered enough times in Bundle's book for it to be nigh on a certainty.

So at 11.00 the family assembled and, after Nicola had retrieved her favourite beanie from Maggie's head and Maggie had found a replacement, the family set off with Andrew and Bundle in the lead. Next in line was Monica jollying along Maggie who was still sulking over having to give up the beanie, followed by Henry in one of his Goth outfits. Nicola brought up the rear wondering how long she could lurk there before making a break for the front to chat happily to her father and keep up appearances of the family Christmas he felt duty bound to provide.

It was a lovely day for a walk and they passed several local families with relative attachments out exploring the countryside. On the way back they had just turned the corner of the wood which all but concealed their house from the rest of the village when they walked slap bang into the Willstone family also out for a walk with Julian and Gellie in tow. Following a plethora of air kissing 'Mwah, Mwah,' Gellie was introduced to the Cowans and Julian very publicly recalled that he had met Nicola at Jocelyn's party before Christmas. Henry and Maggie greeted the younger Willstones with the minimum amount of enthusiasm that can be generated by teenagers while Bundle and Jake pounced on each other with canine zeal. Monica couldn't believe her luck. They had run into The Willstones en masse and she wasn't about to let them get away.

'Come and have a drink. Festive cheer,' Monica said to Dee Willstone and at the same time managing to give Andrew a big dig in the ribs with her elbow. 'We're going to have mulled wine on the terrace and light the chiminea.'

'Please come,' said Andrew on cue, 'We're just round the corner and it would be great to make it a party.' Dee and Charlie exchanged a quick glance and without asking Gellie, accepted on everyone's behalf. Andrew was dispatched on the short cut across the field to 'get things going'. A hare got up in the field and shot off towards the wood. Bundle, who was by now very bored, the walk having stalled for some considerable time, claimed her 10% greyhound ancestry and raced after the hare followed by an enthusiastic Jake. Nicola was first to react and set off after Bundle thanking her lucky stars for the hours spent on the hockey pitch at school. Julian gave chase leaping the wall to gain some time advantage. By the time he reached the edge of the wood there was no sign of either the dogs or Nicola. Forcing his way in through the thick undergrowth he found an ecstatic Bundle who had found a rabbit and not the hare who was her first quarry and Nicola crying over a dead furry body.

Julian gently pulled Nicola to her feet and examined the rabbit. 'It's got mixy. It was going to die anyway. Probably best that Bundle got there first.'

They looked at each other. Slowly Julian's hand reached out and eased her beanie of her head. As it fell to the ground the fir cones at her feet buzzed and crackled. The static energy coursed painfully through her body setting her hair alive with anticipation. The space between the tick and tock of time stretched to accommodate their sense of each other in their first serious kiss.

'Mmmm,' said Julian pulling away gently 'We'd better get back. I think they're waiting for us. Have you got a lead?'

Nicola didn't have one. It was with Maggie but Julian had some rather old maltesers in his pocket which did the trick. Bundle trotted along to heel all the way back to the road. Monica was mighty glad to see Bundle back without any socially embarrassing mishap. Maggie was delighted to hear that Bundle had caught a rabbit 'Bloody vermin,' she said, much to her mother's discomfort. Jocelyn slid up to Julian. 'You must be so fit to catch the dog and the rabbit,' she said. 'Oh Nicola caught them,' he replied, 'I just got in there in time to clear up.' He looked round to catch Nicola's eye. Nicola blushed and tried to hide in her scarf. There was no sign of Jake but no one seemed at all worried.

'I expect he's curled up in the porch at Mulberry Cottage,' concluded Gellie.

Andrew, not ever having excelled in the domestic side of things had a bit of trouble setting up the 'party'. He got the chiminea going with the best part of a whole packet of firelighters and then worried about the black smoke and the chemical smell hovering around the terrace. He was damned if he was going to waste any good wine on either the mulling process or the Willstones and ended up in the pantry with Monica's cooking wine and the remains of the cheap French brandy used to fire up the Christmas pudding. The fruit was easy to find but the mulled wine sachets took a little longer. However he was ready and waiting at the door to welcome the guests much to Monica's surprise. 'Not a problem,' he said gleefully as though this was something he managed to throw together every week.

Nicola sorted some soft drinks for the younger members. She smiled to herself, happily. Boxing Day was turning out to be better than expected.

'Come and chat to Gellie,' said Charlie to Andrew with an infectious laugh. 'She's great fun and very talented with it'

Charlie liked nothing better than to be surrounded by people preferably in party mood. Tall with an angular frame that had filled out since his army days, Charlie had hung on to his foppish fair hair and boyish good looks. He was more than happy to let Dee run The Grange and family life as a minor dictatorship but he did enjoy conducting the occasional dalliance right under her nose. What better an ego boost than to have a lovely lady, preferably young, on one's arm? He kept in shape with village cricket and golf and the occasional session in a gym organized by Dee when she felt he needed taking in hand. Goodness knows how he would have turned out if Dee had not been around.

Dee was in almost every way, a complete opposite to Charlie. She had a definite code of practice which made her blind to everyone except those who she considered to be above her on the social scale and those who could assist her in elevating her status. Dr Andrew Cowan was visible because he was the local doctor respected by the great and the good in the area. Monica Cowan just about registered because she was the doctor's wife. Nicola was useful to have around as a 'friend' for Jocelyn when needed even though she was a bit younger. She was very good at being available last minute to exercise Jocelyn's ponies and was generally very biddable. Dee was unaware that there were two more Cowan siblings. Maggie didn't like Dee and likened her slightly pinched expression as 'looking like she had a bad smell under her nose.'

Squeezed out by adult conversation Nicola walked over to Julian. He was standing beside the sundial opposite Jocelyn. As Nicola approached Jocelyn slid her hands on top of Julian's at about nine and three o'clock.

'Great,' said Julian pulling his hands away. 'Here comes a scientist who can explain how this thing works.'

Jocelyn flung her hands in the air. 'I knew all the time,' she shouted to the sun and turned and stomped off.

'Phew,' said Julian as he placed Nicola's hands gently on the dial and interlocked his fingers with hers. 'If this weren't such a public place I'd kiss you again. And this time for much much longer.'

Nicola caught his blue eyes looking darkly into her very soul and quickly glanced back at the terrace. Charlie and Gellie were standing close together deep in conversation. Nicola heard his deep infectious laugh which seemed to occupy a bass octave all of its own. Charlie seems very happy she thought. Dee had collared Andrew and was asking in a roundabout way for all sorts of 'interesting' information about mutual friends who also happened to be patients. Andrew found this all a bit pathetic but also very amusing and played with Dee by only confiding, in very hushed tones, that which was common knowledge anyway.

Dee soon got the message and tired of playing games. She clapped her hands and announced that the Willstones had long outstayed the generous Cowan hospitality and that it was high time they left for home before the baked potatoes were completely ruined. Julian reluctantly let go of Nicola's hands.

'Gellie and I are invited for lunch,' he sighed leaning forward to give Nicola a peck on the cheek. 'Why don't we study together next week? You could come to Mulberry cottage?'

What a lovely idea.

'See ya,' Julian smiled broadly and trotted over to Gellie. 'Come on ole gal,' he said giving her a slap on her very trim velvet clad rear, 'Let's go and eat the Willstones out of house and home. Then we won't have to cook for a week.' Laughing the Willstones collected up hats, scarves and gloves and with much wishing of 'Happy New Year' they left.

Studying with Julian wasn't easy because there were so many distractions. Whilst he seemed quite capable of switching off and engaging in some all consuming philosophical abstraction, Nicola had great difficulty in peeling her eyes off him. Her gaze documented his eyes, his hair, the cleft in his chin and his lips which had proved able to jumble up her emotions by just touching her lightly on her cheek. Catching her off guard he suggested a coffee break and smirked when she went crimson.

'What are you doing on New Year's Eve?'

'Nothing.'

'Haven't you been invited to the Willstones?'

'No. My parents are going so I have to babysit Maggie.'

'I'll come and babysit Maggie with you. Much more exciting.'

'But hasn't Jocelyn invited you to the party?'

'Yes, but I rather spend the evening doing unimaginable things to you.'

'You'd better tell Jocelyn, then.'

Julian grabbed his phone and went in search of a signal.

'I'll give you and Dad a lift to the Willstones on New Year's Eve and then pick you up, if you like,' said Nicola to her mother the next day.

'Darling that would be wonderful,' replied Monica thinking she could really get stuck in to the Willstone's champagne, and it would be the real thing, for the entire evening.

'You sure? Haven't you got plans?'

'No plans,' said Nicola smiling sweetly, 'I'll be able to baby sit Maggie.'

Monica barely concealed her sigh of relief. NYE sorted then. Maggie safely at home with Nicola in charge.

'Thank you so much, sweetie,' she said 'We won't be late. I'll make you and Maggie a special supper and you can leave all the washing up. A real girlie night in. Just the two of you.'

That was Nicola's next problem. Maggie, and how to buy her silence and how to get her upstairs and in bed really early. Mission Impossible.

'Hey?'

Maggie and Bundle were lying sprawled across bean bags in their bedroom. Maggie was reading a book and didn't look up; Bundle did look up and slid to the floor dislodging a half eaten packet of chocolate biscuits that they had been sharing.

'Maggie,' said Nicola sitting down in the warm space vacated by Bundle. 'Maggie, can you keep a secret?' Now that got her attention. Maggie loved intrigue almost as much as she loved chocolate. She put her book down and swiveled round to look Nicola straight in the eye.

'You want to share a new secret or ask me to look after an old one? This will cost you dear and if you're not prepared to pay up then forget it. It's not going to happen.' Maggie stuck her nose back in her book in order to emphasise her point.

'New Year's Eve. The Ps are going to the Willstones, Henry is out with his mates so it's just you and me and Bundle to welcome in the new year.'

'Y-e-s,' said Maggie slowly.

'I've invited someone to join us and that's the secret.'

Maggie waited expectantly.

'Julian Smith Owen, from Mulberry Cottage.' There, she'd said it.

'Cool,' cried Maggie. 'I knew you had the hots for him.'

Nicola look shocked.

'Oh come on, Mum may be as blind as a bat but I'm not. No way.'

Nicola looked at Maggie long and hard.

'You're having a laugh. I'm a person you know. I may be thick and not clever and bright and fantastically attractive like you, but I am a person. You stalk round this house locked in your own private world. I'm your sister but to you I don't exist until now when you need me.'

Nicola opened her mouth but Maggie got there first.

'So now you're going to pay. My silence has a price and this is it. A Chinese take away, sweet and sour king prawns, fried rice and prawn crackers, three DVDs, 'I Loved a Zombie', 'Killer Four' and 'The Revenge of the Nightjar', and three alcopops. That's the deal.'

Nicola's mouth dropped open. Their mother would go mental over every single item on the list. Groaning inwardly at the expense but feeling hugely guilty about what Maggie had just told her, Nicola reached over and gave her sister a big hug.

'Done deal,' she told Maggie. After a moment's hesitation, not really believing what was happening, Maggie hugged Nicola back until they were rudely pushed apart by Bundle rooting for the remains of the packet of chocolate biscuits.

On New Year's Eve Monica took pains to explain supper to Nicola. She'd got all Maggie's favourites; Chicken nuggets, frozen peas and chocolate ice cream.

'I'd leave you a glass of champagne, Nicola, to celebrate but since you're driving I don't think that is a very good idea, darling. We'll have one together as a family when we get back.'

Julian was late. Maggie was splayed out on the sofa in the old playroom, sipping a banned alcopop waiting for her Chinese to arrive while Nicola paced up and down playing 'He loves me, he loves me not' across the limestone tiles in the hall. He arrived out of breath clutching a bottle of champagne, the Chinese take away order and a box of chocolates.

'Sorry,' he said, 'I had to drop Gellie off at the party, then get the takeaway, then take the car back to The Grange so that Gellie can get home and then run like the wind into your arms.' He gave Nicola a big hug.

'And?' called Maggie. Nicola grabbed the bag and rushed it into Maggie who was lying with her hand outstretched. 'Now, Maggie. A deal is a deal. You stay in here with Bundle, your food, drink and DVDs and we stay in the drawing room. If you want me ring my mobile and then come and knock on the door.'

'Cool,' said Maggie grinning from ear to ear.

If asked, Nicola would have described the evening as near perfect. She shared champagne from Julian's glass, nibbled chicken nuggets, threaded peas onto cocktail sticks and the person with the least number had to kiss the other for as many minutes as there were peas on the winning stick. Nicola fetched Monica's timer from the kitchen so that minutes were counted properly. Then Julian fed her chocolates from a huge box he'd brought while removing first her T-shirt and then her bra. 'You have the most gorgeous boobs,' he told her while gently playing with her nipples 'But do you know which bit of you I like best?' Nicola shook her head. 'The back of your neck. Just here,' he said caressing her with the tips of his fingers. I fell in love with this very bit when I saw you bending over the dishwasher at Jocelyn's party. Do you realise that I have been in love with you forever? It was just a question of when we'd find each other.'

He kissed her again passionately this time and Nicola just melted in his arms. For the first time in her life, ever, she gave herself up to another person. Happiness exploded within her and reached every nerve ending in her body.

'Happy New Year,' he murmured in her ear at midnight and then the kitchen timer blasted them back to earth at 12.30 am. Nicola jumped up and pulled on her T-shirt. Nothing had been heard from Maggie in the playroom. Nothing at all. Nicola raced in to find Bundle and Maggie in the same position as they had been earlier but now surrounded by empty cartons and bottles.

'Quick, quick. We must tidy up,' cried Nicola to Maggie and hastily threw open the window to get rid of the Chinese smell while liberally spraying the room with air freshener. With a howl Bundle shot off to cower in her basket in the kitchen.

'Calm down, Nicola, for God's sake,' said Maggie stuffing the debris into a bin bag. 'You go off and collect the party animals and when you get back I'll have cleared up here and be safely upstairs under my duvet. I've had a lovely evening. How was yours?' she said looking slyly at Nicola.

'Fine. I mean it was wonderful,' she replied feeling her face turning pink.

'Job well done, then,' said Maggie. 'Now go. Oh and Happy New Year.'

Nicola paused only to give Maggie a brief hug and a kiss on the cheek before running out of the room, grabbing the keys and letting Julian sweep her into his arms and carry her out to the car. She dropped him at the gate to Mulberry Cottage, and, after a very long goodbye, drove sedately to The Grange where the party looked in full swing.

The first person she bumped into was Jocelyn.

'Oh it's you. You haven't seen Julian, have you? He was here earlier with Gellie and then apparently dashed off to get a Chinese of all things. Their car is still here,' she said glancing over Nicola's shoulder.

'No, sorry, can't help you,' said Nicola 'I've just come to collect the parents.'

Jocelyn wandered off as though the encounter with Nicola hadn't happened.

Really. Thought Nicola, Jocelyn could be so like her mother. It wasn't necessary to be that rude especially since they'd all known each other for years. Dee Willstone had very kindly loaned Nicola the family pony when Jocelyn grew too big to ride him and she needed a smarter model altogether. Beetle, aka the Dartmoor Demon, taught Nicola more than how to ride. An expert tactician well versed in how to negotiate the mine field that was Pony Club, Beetle took no prisoners. He did everything his way but made exceptions when the chips were down. Then he would turn in a command performance and he and Nicola would walk off with a coveted prize. Of course, on those rare occasions, he was immediately reinstalled as the star of the Willstone stable. Nicola smiled at her memories. When Jocelyn left primary school for a smart boarding school she and Nicola drifted apart. Jocelyn didn't need her anymore as Dee had lined up new friends for her to play tennis with, to party with and to spend the summers with in Rock in Cornwall. Then uni in Oxford and the party venues switched to London. Now Dee Willstone had Julian Smith Owen, soon-to-be Oxford graduate, of impeccable parentage and eligible bachelor, in her sights.

Not if I can help it resolved Nicola and set off to find her partying parents.

'Oh my God.'

Without thinking Nicola said it out loud and sat bolt upright in bed. Her bra was somewhere in the drawing room and if her father had gone in there for his customary night cap, he was probably looking at it right now. Maggie's bedside light snapped on and a hand emerged from under her covers waving a pretty white lacy bra with pink edging.

'Lost something, Nicola?'

Ashen faced Nicola turned towards Maggie and then bounded across the room and bounced on top of her little sister.

'Where did you find that?' she hissed grabbing her bra.

'Careful,' Maggie replied 'You're squashing these very expensive chocolates,' she said producing the box that Julian had brought with him. 'I found your bra hanging from a wall light.'

Maggie giggled. 'Now calm down, come in here otherwise you'll catch cold. We'll have a drink and share the choccies.'

Expertly Maggie twisted the cap off the last bottle of alcopop and handed it to Nicola. Now it was Nicola's turn to giggle. They shared the drink and the chocolates while watching the New Year's moon track across the bedroom carpet.

Amid the packing, assembling a food stash and the lost items panic, Nicola's mother tried to reach across to her daughter before she was swallowed up in her boarding school and her mock 'A' Level exams.

'I'm so pleased that you're friends with Jocelyn again and Julian seems a very pleasant lad,' and then she added 'even though he's a lot older.'

Trust her mother to throw in a dampener and what was four years anyway, thought Nicola to herself. She was longing to get back to school to discuss the entire Christmas holidays with her best friend, Kate.

Nicola and Kate Wasson had been best friends since Kate had turned up in Year 9 having been 'advised to leave' her two previous schools. The only child of an Oxford Professor (archaeology) and his professional musician wife, Kate had had an unconventional upbringing and was never going to conform. She arrived on the back of a music scholarship but the school had a hard time to keep her focused on her flute once Kate found jazz and a saxophone and more recently heavy rock and a bass guitar. Nicola loved visiting Kate's Oxford home in a rambling Victorian pile – open house to academic waifs and strays, former students, wannbe students and enough classical musicians to form an orchestra. Even though he wasn't in the same College and wasn't reading archaeology, Julian had certainly heard of Professor Wasson and was looking forward to meeting his daughter.

So when Kate fell in through the door of their shared study preceded by her beloved saxophone and clutching a new guitar, Nicola couldn't wait to tell her everything.

'And I do have to ask you a massive favour,' said Nicola once Kate had wrung every last detail from her. 'Julian has asked me to spend half term with him in Oxford and I just can't face explaining this to my mother. Could you please ask me to stay with you as cover?'

'Not a problem. I'm away skiing but consider it done.'

With consummate ease, Kate forged her mother's handwriting and signature on the requisite exeat forms. Nicola's mother was hardly over the moon at the arrangement as she'd always regarded Kate as slightly dubious company but Kate's mother had always come across as very sensible and down to earth. Kate, on the other hand, lived very much for the moment. Tall and athletic, dark blue eyes, framed by untamed hair, Kate was impetuous and impatient with everyone except Nicola. Since Day One of their friendship she'd been Nicola's self appointed guardian little realising that she shared duties with Nicola's secret imaginary friend, Jamie.

In the middle of February, Nicola found herself on the top deck of a bus in Oxford with Julian. The mock exams were over, the results excellent and this was her reward to herself for the hard work and not seeing Julian since the beginning of the year. Nicola had spent the train journey rehearsing meeting him again. Should she run up to him and hug and kiss him with sheer joy? That would depend on whether she saw him first and there was no one in the way. Would he rush up to her and should she wait for him to do that even if she saw him first? In the end he ran up to her and gave her a big hug, a kiss on her cheek and then swung her rucksack over his shoulder and grabbed her hand. They would take the bus he said to the house he shared with his brother, Lucas.

Julian chatted nonstop. How extraordinary thought Nicola, he's nervous. In fact it was quite sexy. Nicola and Kate had talked at some length about whether Nicola and Julian would take it to the next level and how they would get round to it. Nicola listened carefully to Kate, who was very worldly wise, trying to identify signals that might come from Julian so that she could anticipate and be ready. 'It will just happen,' said Kate 'and it will be wonderful,' she sighed. Nicola just had to take her word for it.

The pretty Victorian terrace was just a few minutes' walk from the

Banbury Road in north Oxford.

'The house has been the family's base in the UK and now we have Mulberry Cottage as well.' Julian turned and smiled affectionately at Nicola as he ran up the steps. The front door swung open and a welcoming face oulined by wild dark curls smiled down at Nicola. Heathcliffe-esque was how Nicola would describe her first glimpse of Lucas to Maggie, many years later. 'How corny,' commented Maggie, 'But how appropriate.'

'Julian,' the voice smiled, 'You never said, how absolutely gorgeous. Hi, I'm Lucas. Black sheep and younger brother. Come in.' Shouldering Julian aside, Lucas stepped forward and with the briefest of surfs across her cheek so that she hardly felt his designer stubble, he took her rucksack from Julian and herded them both inside.

'Don't worry Jules, I've cleaned your room up and put fresh straw down. Mum would be amazed at the level of domesticity I've managed to achieve in such a short space of time.'

They had arrived on the landing and Lucas, who appeared to have taken charge, pushed open a door and dumped the rucksack on the double bed.

'Lecture calls so I will have to leave you two to get to know each other better,' Lucas smiled wickedly and dodged his brother's fist as he ran down the stairs. Julian opened his mouth to shout something but he was too late. The front door closed with a bang.

Julian picked up both Nicola's hands which were hanging loosely by her sides. She wasn't quite sure what to do with them. Pulling her towards him he kissed her full on and she kissed him back. It lasted, on later reflection, a good four minutes.

Then he stood back and still holding her hands he pulled her towards the door. 'Come on,' he said, grinning from ear to ear, 'I only have a week to show you my Oxford. It's already lunch time on Day 1 so we'd better get going. Lincoln College is first on the list.'

'Oh and I'm living in College this year so this room is all yours.'

Nicola almost felt disappointed.

By Wednesday there was nothing to report to Kate. Nicola sent a text and the reply was that Nicola should make 'it' happen but no further advice as to how. They were having a great time exploring Oxford together even though it was February, cold and damp by the river and few tourist attractions open. But Nicola was seeing Oxford from the inside, from the student perspective and she was fascinated. She fervently hoped that uni in London would be like this and resolved to work even harder when she got back to school to make absolutely sure of a place there. Julian said she should take a gap year and apply for Oxford but Nicola found the academic atmosphere quite intimidating. Anyway Julian wouldn't be there next year. They were sitting drinking pints in the local pub, (Nicola had never had a pint of beer in her life before but needs must), when she asked Julian what his plans were after finals. She felt him hesitate. She felt a prepared speech imminent. She felt slightly shaky as though maybe she shouldn't have asked.

'Well, I think I'll probably end up at the Foreign Office in the diplomatic side of things, though I need to brush up my languages. (Slight hesitation). In August I am going back to Kenya, to Watamu, to teach in an orphanage my Dad helped to set up when we lived there. It is run by a convent, The Sisters of Mercy, but really by Sister Benedicta, we all call her Sister Benny, who has been there forever. It's sort of payback. I'll be there for about six months and then I'm going to Madrid to improve my Spanish.' Julian paused, and took one of Nicola's hands. He's a great hands on person thought Nicola rather bizarrely as Julian looked straight into her eyes. 'Nicola take a gap year. Come with me. We'd make a great team. If you go off to uni while I'm in Africa I'll lose you to someone else. I don't want that. Please, Nicola, please come with me. Come with me to Africa and Spain. When we come back you can go to uni and I'll be in London as well and we'll be together forever.'

Even though she knew that this is what she wanted more than anything else in the whole world at that very moment, Nicola knew it wouldn't happen quite like Julian wanted. Her parents had made it absolutely clear that there would be no gap years. Once her education was complete then it would be up to her but until then, while they were paying, she would carry on straight through. Nicola could not imagine going to either of her parents together or separately to explain that she'd fallen in love with a guy they hardly knew who was asking her to turn her life upside down by deferring her university place and running off to darkest Africa for six months. It just wasn't going to happen and her eyes filled with tears. Nicola closed her eyes for a moment and found herself standing in a flower-filled meadow, a breeze sifting through her hair and the sun warming her arms. Her parents were running towards her carrying black velvet cloaks. They ran up to her and wrapped her in the cloaks. Then they bound her into a parcel with golden braids knotted together with her childhood memories. As they worked they chanted mantras from her growing up years: 'We are spending a great deal of money on your education. You should be grateful: You must remember that you have your brother and sister coming on behind you and we must give them the same opportunities: We will spend money on your education just once and then it is up to you: You have always worked hard, Nicola, and we are very proud of you.' Nicola opened her eyes to find Julian looking at her thoughtfully. She shrank from the exposure.

'I can't. I want to come with you more than anything but I just can't. My parents would never agree to a gap year and to me delaying my uni course. I'll wait for you. If you go to Spain after Africa I'll come and visit. I promise.'

Julian grabbed her hand; they left their drinks and walked back to the house in a confused silence. The house was very cold.

'Damn, Lucas has turned the central heating off again. He must be really broke this time,' said Julian rummaging behind the boiler in the kitchen.

Not sure quite why, Nicola walked slowly upstairs. On the landing she turned slightly as her hand touched the door handle. Shocked she found Julian right behind her looking questioning into her eyes. She was the only thing that mattered; she was Julian's entire focus; she felt safe; she burned inside. If there wasn't one quite large problem in the way she would have felt very powerful. Julian slowly put his hand out and stroked her neck letting his hand drift up to her chin still holding her gaze.

'Nicola,' his voice was hoarse. 'Do you want this to happen? You must take the lead on this. I won't do anything unless you want me to.'

Nicola looked at him helplessly.

Without answering, she opened the door surprised to find the handle almost welded to her hand. Julian moved swiftly forward, lifted her up so that her legs wound round her hips, and started kissing her neck. The point of no return was when they reached the foot of the bed and she reached for his zipper.

Days later when Kate was pumping her for information, Nicola had to confess that her first time was not the magical moment she had expected.

'Like a surgical procedure without an anesthetic?' Kate was obviously in need of more information.

'That would be a bit harsh,' replied Nicola. 'My God I wanted him so much. My body was completely out of sync with my brain and I just let it take over. It didn't exactly hurt but I didn't have an orgasm or anything.'

Back in the moment, Julian rolled over propped himself up on a pillow.

'Nicola, Nicola. I'm so sorry.' He bent over and kissed both her tightly shut eyes.

'Look at me.'

Nicola squinted up at him.

'I didn't realise it was your first time. I mean I was trying to take things slowly but I was kind of overtaken. Forgive me. Why didn't you tell me?'

'And how on earth was I going to do that without sounding completely pathetic?' Nicola almost shouted in exasperation.

Leaning over her, Julian let his tongue trail over her spine.

'It is easy for you to see what pleases me so let's start over. There are some things I am going to ask you to do to me. You, however, are a mystery so in return I am going to ask you to show me what you would like me to do to you.' Julian was speaking very slowly his voice sounding sticky.

His mouth came down on hers and they started all over again but more slowly this time. Julian stayed that night and they spent the whole of the next day in bed and the following night amid take away pizza boxes. They talked forwards and backwards for hours, about their hopes and fears, what made them laugh and how they had somehow found each other. After a while they stopped asking each other how they felt or what they were thinking about because they knew.

'So Gellie was in charge of bringing us up for a lot of the time. Mind you, I just went to one boarding school. Lucas managed to go to four and had to leave three in disgrace,' he told Nicola. They listened to the house moving about in various ways, doors banged, the washing machine turned on and off but no one knocked on their door.

The next day Julian had to get up early for a tutorial in College. He was dining there that night and staying over so Nicola would not see him again until Saturday morning. He told her that he had arranged for Lucas to look after her but since there had been no sight of Lucas since she had arrived, Nicola was not hopeful. She'd be fine she told Julian. As soon as he'd left she slid out of bed and rummaged in her bag for her phone. There were six text messages from Kate and two from Maggie The most recent text from Kate threatened a long horrible death by chocolate if Nicola failed to reply. Nicola replied:

'It' happened on Wed. Wow. I'm soooo in love. N xx.

Looking round, Nicola decided to explore. Julian's room was very minimalistic: white walls, sanded floors, white curtains, stripped wood furniture. The room was dominated by the double bed and a huge sound system. The CDs were largely rock music with a bit of classical. It didn't look as though Julian spent much time in the house, probably because he had a room in college. The wardrobe was full of jeans, trainers and sports equipment. A very expensive suit shared a hanger with a shirt and tie, a sort of emergency smart dressing combo. The chest of drawers revealed boxer shorts, socks, polo shirts but nothing interesting. Two photographs stood on the top; one of Julian surrounded by what looked like an African boys soccer team and the other of Julian, Lucas and another guy in safari gear carrying guns. The walls boasted a couple of African spears and shields and a zebra skin adorned the floor. A philosophy text book beside the bed snuggled up to an alarm clock. Somebody had done a sweep of the room to remove all the personal details that might satisfy Nicola's curiosity, apart from an old school trunk wedged into a corner which was securely locked. Above the bed hung a rather incongruous poster of Martin Luther King 'I have a dream'. I have a dream too thought Nicola but we're not quite on the same page. It really told her nothing more except that Africa was a very important part of Julian's life. Served her right for being nosey. Nicola had already cased the shared bathroom. Lots of boys stuff and two definitely different tastes in toiletries. Julian was on the suave sophisticated end of the scale whereas Lucas inhabited the outdoor action man position. Concealed in the airing cupboard was a large (opened) box of condoms.

Nicola showered and found coffee and bread in the kitchen. The toaster didn't work and, as the bread was obviously of a certain age, she thought she'd leave breakfast until she got to town. It was a bright cold morning and Oxford was looking its best. Dressed in her warmest clothes with Julian's lovely soft woolly scarf, which she'd found on the floor, to keep her warm, Nicola set off on foot. She was quite surprised that none of the people she passed seemed to notice that she'd lost her virginity. It felt completely different and she felt sure it must show somewhere like her ears were now green instead of pink.

She never ceased to be surprised by the elegance and regal nature of the university buildings which lined St Giles. The stark winter light gave the colleges a hard cutting edge at odds with their soft stone colouring. It was amazing that so many people just walked up and down the road without giving them a second glance. Didn't they recognise such a precious landscape? Obviously not. Nicola paused at a shop and bought a post card for her parents. She sent a text to Maggie.

Having an amazing h/t in Oxford. N xx

And got an immediate reply

With JSO, I presume? M x

Nicola smiled and put her phone in her pocket. She wrapped Julian's scarf tightly round her neck and inhaled deeply. She could smell him so clearly that if she closed her eyes he might have been right beside her about to give her a big hug. Instead Jamie appeared looking very much the student in his long black coat with the collar pulled up round his ears. He was instantly recognisable by his red hair and freckles and the way he pushed his glasses up his nose to focus.

'I'm just so so happy,' Nicola told him and felt his smile brush her cheek in the morning breeze.

'I want everyone to know.' She threw her arms in the air and laughed making passersby smile.

Jamie kept her company until they reached Broad Street where he slipped easily through the closed gates of Trinity College.

She smiled to herself as she crossed the road and went into The Covered Market sort of on her way to Blackwell's Bookshop to indulge in some serious book browsing. The market was full of boutiquey type shops and Nicola was soon happily rummaging through clothes rather than books. She'd just tried on but rejected as too expensive a lovely pair of faded denim jeans when looking up she thought she saw Jamie lounging against a wall. She started to walk towards him when an arm snaked across her shoulders. Whipping round she found herself gazing into Lucas' dark, laughing eyes.

'There you are,' he said 'How can I possibly look after you when I don't know where you are? Now lunch. I know you haven't had any breakfast because there is never any food in the house. We'll go to Georgina's.'

With that he swung her round and they headed off down one of the Avenues and up some steep stairs to a little café hidden on the first floor. It was full of students and academic tourists but Lucas managed to find space for them to sit at one of the long tables.

'Coffee? And a stuffed baked potato, they are really good here.'

Nicola nodded happily. She studied Lucas as he stood in the queue. Taller and slimmer than Julian with black curls like Gellie's. Well she was his aunt after all. At one point he turned and smiled at her and she was instantly reminded of Charlie Willstone but then chastised herself. She hadn't met either of Julian's parents yet so this was no time for comparisons.

They chatted happily over lunch and Nicola welcomed the relaxed atmosphere after the intensity of the past few days. Later on in Blackwells, Nicola realised that she'd probably spent two hours hardly thinking about Julian let alone mentioning his name. After lunch Lucas told her to be back at the house and ready to go out about 7.30 as he was going to show her his Oxford and then he left. On her way back she remembered to call home. Her mother was delighted to hear from her, hoped she was not working the whole time and to be sure to thank Kate's parents for having her to stay. There were a couple of texts from Julian which piled in one after the other. Nicola blushed when she read one of them.

She wished she'd bought the jeans after all when trying to decide what to wear on a night out in Oxford. She'd never seen Lucas looking smart so she decided that casual was definitely the way to go.

'Right,' said Lucas 'First stop The Bricklayers for a drink. There is a live band playing so we'll see what they're like and maybe stay depending who we bump into. Then we'll get something to eat and then who knows?' He smiled at her. 'Welcome to Oxford a la Brookes.'

The pub was crowded and the music deafening. Lucas bought two pints and spotted a table where a crowd of friends were waving frantically. Lucas introduced Nicola to them all as she sat down next to a hunky rugby player. No one stood on ceremony, nobody seemed to care that she was still at school. They just wanted to chat, have fun and tease each other mercilessly. Nicola noticed that Lucas was in the middle of everything that was going on but equally on the outside. After about an hour or so of drinking and laughing they moved on to a nearby burger bar and had something to eat. Then the party split leaving Nicola with Lucas and a stranger

'Nicola, meet Sulei, Suleiman Abbas, my handsome Saudi prince and best friend ever. He lives in Oman but is studying French and IT at Brookes. Sulei meet Nicola, Julian's girlfriend. 'Now, 'Chico's'?' asked Lucas.

So they set off back into town on foot. Oxford seemed alive with young people all coming from somewhere on their way somewhere else. No one was rushing but they all walked with a sense of purpose and a sense of enjoyment at being out and about. The boys kept stopping to talk to people or to wave acknowledgements across the street. Lucas in particular seemed to know an awful lot of people and he introduced her to them all. But she was just Nicola. 'Here's Nicola; let me introduce you to Nicola; have you met Nicola?'

Chico's was a small nightclub down an alleyway. Everything about it was small except for the number of people packed in. After a couple of vodka shots, no pints here, Lucas suggested that they dance to the Latin American music on the small dance floor. As there wasn't much room, Lucas was dancing very close to Nicola, seemingly without touching, their bodies synchronised to the music. Whether it was because she had had far more to drink than usual or whether it was the music or the heady atmosphere in the club, Nicola managed to lose herself for several hours. She was very surprised when the club started to empty at 3.00am and the music faded. 'Home,' whispered Lucas in her ear and walked her back his arm draped protectively over her shoulder. As she turned to say thank you for a lovely evening he put a finger to her lips and gently kissed her on her cheek.

'You're lovely Nicola,' he said as he pulled away. 'Don't let Julian forget that.'

He bounced down the steps grinning with his eyes as well as his mouth and was gone. But he lives here thought Nicola as she shut the door behind her. Suddenly very tired she climbed the stairs. Lucas had only mentioned Julian's name once.

The next morning Nicola woke to the sound of the door being opened, a smell of fresh coffee and the rattle of a tray being inexpertly manhandled.

'Good Morning Sunshine,' cried Julian as he put the tray down on the floor, tore off his clothes and jumped in beside her.

Nicola shrieked as his cold body met hers. 'God you look fantastic in the mornings,' he said. 'I've missed you so much. Why don't you just stay in Oxford and we'll forget that the other world exists?' Nicola giggled with pleasure and wiggled down under the duvet, pulling off her T-shirt as she did so. Julian had no option, or so he said, but to make love to her.

The coffee was cold by the time they got round to eating breakfast. Julian hadn't asked her about her evening with Lucas and she hadn't asked about dinner in college. Instead he fumbled around in his coat which was lying on the floor and produced a parcel tied up with ribbon.

'Pressie,' he said 'But you have to open this first.' He fumbled around some more and came up with a very expensive looking thick white envelope. Nicola slit it open and read it.

The Directors and Trustees of the Sefton Institute of Art and Design
request the pleasure of your company at the launch of
'Angelica'
On Wednesday 19th April 2002 at 11.00am
St Barnabas Arts Centre, The Quadrangle, EC12 9NQ
RSVP: hospitality@sefton.org.uk

Scrawled on the bottom in ink was *'Please come, Nicola, and wear the pressie! Gellie x'*

Nicola looked at Julian for an explanation. He was grinning broadly.

'Gellie was awarded this grant from the Sefton Institute to develop her designs into a fashion range. This is her opportunity to showcase her designs to the industry. She had been working flat out for the last year and the final hurdle is launching her knits as *'Angelica'*. She would like us all be there for support helping backstage and being friendly faces so she doesn't get too stressed out. Now open the pressie.'

Nicola untied the ribbon and eased the tissue paper open. Inside was one of Gellie's designs. It was a long cashmere cardigan interlaced with ribbons. The collar dropped down the back as a hood but the best bit, felt Nicola, were the long inner sleeves which could be pulled down under the proper sleeve and over your hands with a loop for your thumb to keep the sleeves in place and your hands cosy.

'It's stunning,' Nicola said.

'It's yours. You're to wear it for the show,' said Julian. 'Now I have made all the arrangements. We'll stay with Gellie at her flat. We'll have to go up on the Monday to help with all the setting up and then stay to party and clear up – so that will be a whole week together at Easter before we have to start thinking about exams again.' He smiled at her excitedly and she gave him a big hug.

'This is far too generous a gift,' said Nicola 'But what am I going to say to my parents?'

'Gellie said that if you like she will write to your parents and ask if you could go to London and stay with her to help with the show. Dee and Charlie will be there with Jocelyn so there will be lots of people you'll know. Perhaps your Mum would like to come?'

It was all so much to take in so changing the subject slightly she said 'Lucas looked after me very well last night. Does he have a girlfriend?'

Julian mused for a moment and replied.

'There was Carla, a beautiful Italian who has run off back to Florence and her beloved art because Lucas would not commit to a relationship,' he paused, his voice dropped to a conspiratorial level 'Now you mustn't say anything to anyone about this. I don't think Lucas knows I know. He's been having an affair with a married woman in Saudi and it is all very embarrassing. Lucas met Leila in London and got completely besotted. Then she was hauled back to Saudi by her family for an arranged marriage. Of course with Dad out there Lucas has the perfect excuse to visit but he's not supposed to see her. I know he did over Christmas.'

'How sad,' thought Nicola but it did go some way to explain Lucas' somewhat bizarre behaviour, his appearances and disappearances like Alice in Wonderland's Cheshire Cat. They were in Oxford after all.

With promises to text 24/7 and to talk every day, Nicola caught the train back to school and Julian buried himself in college.

2

Thousands of miles away in Watamu, a small township on the East African coast, a colony of Arit Jinn were becoming restless in their parallel world in an ancient tree standing in the courtyard in front of a convent. Mischief-making opportunities had slowed to an all time low and they had become bored. The mention of Watamu by a person they knew well, Julian Smith Owen, flagged up on their radar. The signal, however, was coming from another country on another continent and, because of the distance, had taken a long time to arrive. To be any use the jinn would have to find a means of accessing the situation. They settled down to watch and wait.

Sister Benny stood at the window gazing at the Tree of Forgetfulness. Her convent needed more money and the time it was taking to search and find charitable institutions which might be able to help was submerging her in paperwork. She needed help.

Her thoughts returned to her first days at the Convent of Our Lady, newly arrived from the mother house in rural Ireland and bent on making a difference to the souls in Kenya.

'First of all,' a very young Sister Benny glanced down at her 'to do' list, 'I would like you to chop down that tree in the courtyard. It's old and rotten, probably dangerous, and it's taking too much light from the windows.' Actually she found the tree creepy, like it was watching her.

A very young Moses, gatekeeper and general handyman, looked down at the threadbare carpet and fiddled with his cap.

'You can't do that, Reverend Mother.'

Sister Benny raised her eyebrows. 'Why not? And it's Sister Benny, not Reverend Mother. I don't intend to stand on ceremony.' She drew herself up to her not very great height to emphasise the point.

Moses shifted and dragged his eyes from the floor. 'That tree is special. It's full of memories and you can't cut it down because the memories would be lost forever.'

Sister Benny inclined her head slightly and waited.

'It all started with the slaves. They left their memories there before they went down to the ships. People have been leaving memories in the tree ever since. The Arit Jinn who live in the tree guard the memories.'

Sister Benny wasn't quite sure she was hearing this. She sat down and directed Moses to sit opposite her.

'Tell me about the Jinn.'

'Jinn are spirits and they live in trees, walls sometimes in houses. You can't see them but you know they are there. Some jinn are really bad but the ones we have here are Arit Jinn. They're not bad but they can play mischievous tricks. We keep them under control by throwing open the chapel doors after Mass because they hate the smell of incense. And lemon grass,' Moses added helpfully.

Sister Benny absorbed this information. The whole concept of faith appeared to be a different ball game in Africa.

'You just can't cut the tree down,' said Moses. 'The Arit Jinn would have no home and they would run away with all the memories.'

That was then and this was now. The ancient Tree of Forgetfulness remained, sheltering the Arit Jinn who watched her every move.

Gellie picked up Nicola from Frampton after lunch on the Sunday before the show. 'I'm driving up to London with a car load of very special stuff I don't want to let out of my sight.' Gellie told her mother. 'It would be so useful to have Nicola to help me load, unload and sort everything out,' she explained and since Gellie had so very kindly provided an invitation to her show, Monica could hardly refuse such a practical request.

'I don't know what to wear with the very special knit you gave me,' wailed Nicola to Gellie as soon as they had turned out of the drive. 'I'll just have to go shopping tomorrow.'

'You'll be far too busy for any shopping trips,' smiled Gellie, 'So I've arranged for one of the dressers to kit you out. My treat. To say thank you.'

'Julian can't wait to see you,' she added lighting up the car with an electric smile.

The days before the show were a whirlwind of altering arrangements. Gellie would not get access to the arts centre until the morning of the show so the epicentre was her workshop and studio in Wandsworth. Jocelyn was strutting about giving ineffectual orders to anyone who was prepared to listen. Gellie was getting more and more annoyed with her and to reduce her stress levels gave her increasingly mundane tasks which involved Jocelyn being out of the way for much of the time. There was a morass of double bookings, cancelled commitments and overlooked possible buyers to be fitted in at the last minute. Nicola loved the frantic business of it all.

They got up early, grabbed sandwiches and went to bed late. And she was with Julian.

St Barnabas was a deconsecrated chapel turned arts centre. The exterior was definitely ecclesiastical but the inside had been stripped out just waiting for the next creative event. A huge wooden structure made of different lengths of hexagonal blocks had been erected on the site of the altar table. It reached up towards the high church windows capturing the natural light allowing it to stream in over a collection of glass, metal and mirror shards strategically placed on the hexagons. A raised catwalk led the way from the hexagons through the choir to the apron stage opening out in the chancel where chairs had been set out in a wide semi circle. At the western end a bank of stage lights were poised to direct a lighting programme onto the hexagons.

On the day of the show, Nicola was dressed along with the models and that included her hair and makeup. Then she was told to wander around front of house showing off the knitwear. Just before the start she was to take her seat in the choir between her mother and Julian. Nicola was very nervous. She had hardly started wandering around before Jocelyn appeared in front of her, clipboard at the ready.

'What do you think you're doing?' she hissed 'That jacket is for the show. You can't wear it. You're not a model.'

'Jocelyn,' said Gellie appearing as if by magic, 'I asked Nicola to model that jacket out here. In fact I gave her the entire outfit. Now please go and project manage back stage where you're supposed to be.'

Nicola felt a light touch on her elbow and turned to find her mother at her side looking quite shocked and it took Nicola a moment to realise that her mother had never seen Nicola looking quite as she did that morning.

'Nicola, you look quite different,' stumbled Monica. 'In fact you look amazing. Are you modelling or something? I thought Gellie said you'd be helping out.'

'I am helping, Mum,' replied Nicola feeling very grown up. 'This is one of Gellie's designs.' She didn't tell her that it was a present from Gellie because her mother was bound either to insist she gave it back, or, more likely, try to pay for it.

Slightly embarrassed they both turned to look towards the catwalk where Jocelyn was now having an argument with Julian about the seating arrangements. Julian had just put the names on the reserved seats and Jocelyn was busy swapping them round.

'They are a lovely couple, aren't they?' said her mother in a conversational manner. 'They're going to Africa in August to work together at an orphanage for six months after Julian graduates. Nice to see a young couple taking time to work for a worthy cause don't you think?'

Nicola looked aghast. Hadn't her mother remembered all those days she, not Jocelyn, had spent with Julian at Christmas? She felt herself being sucked down a dark narrow channel away from reality at a fast rate of knots. She felt faint. She felt sick and headed for the exit. Julian was instantly at her side.

'Nicola, what's wrong?' He said hugging her close. 'You've been working too hard, my fault.'

Nicola pushed him away and managed to stand upright. 'Why didn't you tell me you were seeing Jocelyn and that you're going to Africa with her?' Nicola was nearly in tears as she saw her world crumbling in front of her.

'Hang on a minute. One thing at a time. I am not seeing Jocelyn. Got it? I know Dee has been trying to match make for heaven knows how long but I am not interested. Got it? Jocelyn and I grew up together so she's like the sister I never had. I have never fancied her and never will. Our parents are very old friends so I see her like family. End of story. As for going to Africa together, well, this is the first time I've heard about it. I am going to sort her out right now. Don't cry you'll smudge your eye makeup. And, I haven't told you look absolutely fabulous today.'

With that Julian led her back into the hall and her seat in the choir. Just as she sat down, a fierce looking journalist stopped her to ask if she was wearing an *Angelica* design and then wanted Nicola's name and address. Really today was proving very stressful and the show hadn't even begun. She sat down next to her mother who was in deep conversation with a very attractive lady on her other side. Monica turned to Nicola and introduced her to Caroline Smith Owen. Julian slipped into the seat beside Nicola just as the lights dimmed in the hall, the spots shone on the hexagon and the commentary fought with rock music for supremacy. From the chaos of the last two days, the frantic activity from the early hours of the morning, you would never have believed that such a vibrant show could come together. Nicola felt very proud to have been part of it. In a raging storm of reflected and refracted lights bouncing back off the hexagons, the models sashayed down the catwalk onto the apron to explosive applause. As the music reached a crescendo the models were led down the catwalk for the last time by Gellie herself arm in arm with Lucas.

Nicola stiffened slightly. She hadn't seen Lucas since that night in Oxford and suddenly he had sprung into the centre of the show as if from nowhere. He walked purposively but sensuously down towards the audience and then almost lazily turned and directed the applause to Gellie.

The lights dimmed as the applause grew with demands for more. Suddenly in a barrage of the lights at full power, Gellie stood alone in front of the hexagons. Her hair had been teased out into a crowded halo, blusher gave her high cheeks precise definition contrasting with the paleness of the rest of her face. The soft mohair clung to her rangy figure and as she stepped forward with a huge smile, the jacket billowed out behind her. The audience leapt up to meet her.

'Wow,' was all Julian could say. Nicola was spellbound.

Flash bulbs went off like a glow worm frenzy and from the buzz of conversation and the way people crowded round Gellie, the whole show had been an enormous success.

'Let's hope the orders start rolling in now,' said Lucas appearing at Nicola's shoulder and lightly brushing his cheek against hers 'See you at lunch.'

Dee Willstone had organised several large tables in a nearby popular restaurant where she hoped the party would be the focus of attention. It was. A number of hangers on gate-crashed but since they were influential people in the fashion world, Dee graciously made room for them. Julian introduced Nicola to his father who was charming in a diplomatic way but slightly distant. Her mother was quite overcome by the occasion but Charlie saw to it that she was not left out by introducing her to some locals who'd travelled from Frampton for the day. Gellie flushed from the success was kissing everyone in sight and grinning from ear to ear. Dee was smiling graciously and accepting compliments like the show had been entirely her creation. There was no sign of Julian or Jocelyn.

Nicola suddenly felt all alone in a room crowded with people when Lucas appeared with two glasses of champagne.

'Now where were we. Ah, yes, did I remember to tell you...'

'Lucas,' cried Nicola. 'Where have you been? Were you here earlier in the week? I didn't see you around. How come you were escorting Gellie for the finale?'

Lucas raised his glass. Nicola raised hers and as she did so her eyes were drawn to his intense gaze. Their eyes met exchanging a confusing range of mixed messages. At least they were confusing for Nicola who had to look away hoping that Lucas could not feel her blood pressure rising rapidly.

'I only arrived back from Saudi last night with Mum and Dad,' he replied lightly. 'So I had no real job for today. No official clipboard for me. Not like Bossy Joce. I was just hanging around in the background being generally annoying and unhelpful until Gellie suddenly couldn't do the last walk. She freaked. So I just grabbed this gorgeous sweater from one of the models, pulled these designer jeans from a hanger, linked my arm through Gellie's and set off down probably one of the longest walks in her life. How did we look?'

'Amazing,' replied Nicola

'Just as I thought,' said Lucas laughing, and rushed off to greet a very pretty girl with a big hug.

Dee was trying to get everyone to sit down for lunch. Not knowing where to sit, Nicola hung back but Julian appeared and pulled her to one side.

'All sorted,' he said. 'I've spoken to Sister Benny in Watamu and she is going to send me up to Lamu to work on some building project and keep Jocelyn back at base under her watchful eye. That means there will be several hundred African miles, and in Africa those will be very long miles, between us, and no direct transport. Will you be happy now?'

Nicola was astonished that Julian had gone to so much trouble and so quickly. She just couldn't have asked for more and she slipped her hand shyly into his as they made their way to the table and sat down for lunch. After coffee everyone started to mix again and Gellie took Nicola over to talk to Caroline.

'Here's the girl I wanted you to meet,' said Gellie. 'Julian's latest squeeze. You've met her mother, Monica Cowan. They live at Lower Hill Cottage just down the road from where you are in Frampton. Nicola has been a brilliant help this week.'

'Hello Nicola,' Caroline extended a manicured hand. 'We met just before the show started, didn't we?'

Nicola smiled shyly. Well at least she'd been remembered. That was something.

'Julian tells me you have been a tremendous help getting him settled in Frampton. He's just dying to have somewhere to call home because we've moved around so much. I hope we'll be seeing you around in the summer when we move into Mulberry Cottage permanently.'

Nicola smiled and nodded noting that Caroline had the most beautiful brown liquid eyes just like Gellie and Lucas. Julian had his father's blue eyes which could change in intensity to match his thinking. Just then as Nicola was wondering what to say in reply, her mother appeared at her side.

'You are coming home tonight?'

The question mark hung in the air between mother and daughter.

Nicola explained carefully that she had to stay for another couple days to help Gellie sort out the post show chaos and restore some order in her studio. What she really meant was that she had two more days with Julian before school started.

Monica was rather reluctant to leave Nicola in such a highly charged heady atmosphere which she personally found quite scary. But it wasn't the time to make a scene and drag her home. At least Nicola would be safely tucked away back at school in Cheltenham next week and Gellie did seem to be keeping an eye on her.

That evening everyone partied like there was no tomorrow. Julian wickedly introduced Jocelyn to one of the set designers who'd been eyeing her from a distance and they seemed to hit it off immediately much to Dee's annoyance. Charlie was in very high spirits in the middle of the dance floor, Gellie couldn't stop smiling, Lucas was wound round several of the models at once. When they got back to Gellie's flat, Nicola and Julian fell into bed exhausted. She must have had far too much to drink because a couple of hours later Nicola awoke with a raging thirst. Slipping carefully out of bed so as not to wake Julian, Nicola tiptoed out onto the landing and closed the door. There was a faint light from under Gellie's door and the soft sound of whispering. So who had come home with Gellie wondered Nicola. As she turned towards the stairs, Nicola heard a deep chuckle which sounded very familiar but she couldn't place it. Shaking her head she went carefully downstairs and raided the fridge. The next morning they woke up to Gellie singing in the kitchen and a delicious aroma of cooked breakfast seeping under the door. Gellie said nothing about how or with whom she had come back home, Nicola didn't tell Julian and normal life was resumed at the pre show hectic pace. The next night Gellie didn't come back at all and they didn't catch up with her until the following day.

It was very sad saying goodbye to all their new friends. It felt almost like the breakup of a very close family even though it had only been a week. With promises to keep in touch and see you all very soon, Julian and Nicola left for Frampton but Gellie stayed in London with a big fat order book. Her mother was relieved to get Nicola back under her wing apparently unscathed. Maggie was not so easily convinced and demanded the whole truth but in the end had to make do with an edited version. Maggie did, however, pounce on Nicola's *Angelica* original.

'How on earth did you get this? It's awesome,' Maggie was examining the reverse stitching on the pockets and the hidden sleeves. 'Look at the ribbon work. It's so soft it must be cashmere. Is it? Can I wear it tomorrow, please, please?'

'Yes it is cashmere. No you can't borrow it. It's mine,' replied Nicola laughing at Maggie.

'I have to learn to knit.' She yelled downstairs 'Mum can you teach me how to knit, like right now?'

Nicola smiled at her impetuous sister who was currently suffering from at least three Life Defining Moments a day.

Back at school, Nicola's world was reduced once more to the school environs but at least there was light at the end of the tunnel. Julian's final exams started at the beginning of June and lasted a week. Nicola's 'A' Levels were more spread out and she didn't take her last exam until the end of the month. Julian's parents had arranged for him to fly out to Saudi as soon as he had finished so that the family could spend their last two weeks at the official residency together but he'd be back to meet Nicola as she walked out from her last exam. He promised. And before their exams started, Julian had invited Nicola to his College May Ball which luckily coincided with half term.

Nicola and Kate scoured all the dress shops in Cheltenham for a ball gown and found a slinky grey straight one with no back. Kate did the alterations and lent her a pair of shoes. By the time the last weekend in May arrived, Nicola's nerves were at screaming point. She'd taken her chemistry and physics practicals and she just wanted to get the rest of the exams over and done with. Kate's mother had written again with an invitation to stay so Nicola spent a couple of days at home over half term and then took a bus to Oxford. Her mother was pleased she was taking some time off. A College May Ball would be just the right event to raise Nicola's spirits. So nice of Julian to ask her and so convenient that Nicola could stay with Kate. Maggie saw through it all and begged for the full story threatening to tell all. Nicola relented and was actually relieved to share her excitement.

The smell of newly mown grass hung in the evening air mixed with the delicate rose fragrance drifting in from the Fellows' garden. The leaded windows in the mellow buildings dozed in the evening light anticipating a hectic night ahead. The College had been transformed into a Caribbean island complete with beach and beach volley ball. Julian and his friends held a champagne reception at the Oxford house and everyone was up for a night of serious partying. Exam fever, the end of an era, beginning of new lives spread far and wide following farewells to old friends rolled into a heady atmosphere. At ten o'clock they all gathered for a Caribbean barbeque and then danced to steel bands in the marquee. In the early hours after a particularly slow dance outside in the Fellows' garden, Julian took Nicola's hand and pulled her towards a secluded staircase. They didn't make it to his room at the top. Julian pushed her up against a door, pulled up her dress and yanked her knickers off. His hands caressed her body searching for her breasts. Is that why Kate said no bra when she tried on the dress wondered Nicola in an abstract fashion. With Julian's tongue massaging the back of her throat, Nicola responded with a low moan wrapping her legs round his hips. Nothing was going to stop what was happening to her and as he pushed her hard against the door, Nicola felt a pain shoot up through her and spread out in a glow of satisfaction. It was hot, fast and very sexy. Nicola could hardly stand when her feet finally found the floor and she shakily rearranged her dress. Julian was leaning back against the wall with his eyes closed. 'Nicola my love, promise never to leave me, promise always to love me,' and he buried his head in the nape of her neck.

They did manage to make breakfast by which time the beautiful college stone work was being washed by the early morning sunlight. Nicola could not remember feeling so happy, so complete. How could she hang onto these moments? How could she wrap herself up in this wallpaper and live inside it forever?

With promises to meet for lunch at Georgina's, Nicola and Julian finally tore themselves away from the party, stumbled back to bed. Later as she pulled on her jeans and a T-shirt and stuffed her dress into her rucksack, Nicola felt an aching grey cloud of depression settle around her. It had all been so perfect. Sensing her mood, Julian reached out for her and pulled her close to him. 'Very, very soon we'll be together forever.'

Disappointed people were filing back down the narrow staircase and the noise was quite frantic as Julian and Nicola squeezed inside Georgina's. 'You hungry?' Julian mouthed at Nicola as he found a small space at a crowded table. She shook her head. 'Over here,' called a voice from the crowd and Nicola turned to see Lucas, Sulei and Jocelyn waving from a table in the corner. It was a very happy group. Lucas and Sulei had finished their exams at Oxford Brookes on the Friday and were still celebrating. Jocelyn only had course work but all that had now been submitted. They were all chatting idly about summer and Oxford when Nicola's mobile went off. The reception was terrible so she went down to the market street to take a call from her mother wondering how half term was going. If she knew even half of it thought Nicola as she chatted about revision. When she got back to the table, Lucas and Sulei had gone. Julian was sitting opposite Jocelyn who was leaning towards him as he held her hand.

'He's mine: he's mine,' exploded through Nicola. Instantly she envisaged Julian kissing Jocelyn and Jocelyn getting that very special charge of excitement that belonged to her and her alone. Seized by the green eyed monster of jealousy and feeling her tower of happiness crumbling at its foundations, Nicola marched over to them, retrieved her rucksack from under the table and left. She had crossed the road by the traffic lights and was heading towards the bus station by the time Julian caught up with her.

'Nicola,' he cried catching her elbow and spinning her round to face him 'What the hell are you doing?' She looked straight at him tears spilling down her cheeks.

'You said she meant nothing. I believed you. I don't believe you any more.'

'Oh for Christ sake! Nicola just grow up. Jocelyn is virtually my sister.' Julian's eyes grew dark and intense. He grabbed both her arms and shouted 'I'm not going to fuck my sister, ever.' With that he turned round and marched down Broad Street and disappeared into College. Nicola searched for her rucksack which had fallen onto the pavement and made her way unsteadily to catch her bus. People gave her odd looks but she didn't stop to find a tissue, just wiped her face on her sleeve. Before she realised where she was she was speeding away from Oxford and Julian.

Jamie was waiting for her when she reached Cheltenham.

'Should I have chased after him? Was he telling the truth? Am I so totally lacking in self confidence that I never believe anyone? What should I do now?'

Jamie wiped his glasses and then stared straight ahead leaving Nicola wallowing in the depths of her dilemmas.

Julian's exams started the day after tomorrow. The 'Good Luck' card at the bottom of her bag was beginning to rustle to remind her to post it. But what if it was all over just like that because she acted like a child? Nicola posted the card anyway on her way back into school.

She told Kate everything, well most of everything, and felt a bit better. Kate said to wait and see if he phoned. The card would arrive tomorrow and that should prompt a reaction.

The next day was spent in revision classes. Nicola couldn't concentrate and just drew hearts intertwined in complicated patterns all over her work. She checked the battery on her mobile and then decided it would probably not receive calls because it was overcharged and phoned Kate in the next building to release some of the battery power. Kate said she was an idiot. At lunch time she got a text:

I'm at the Mocha Café, High Street. Meet me. J xx

Nicola dumped her books on Kate and rushed out of the back gates and into town. Julian wasn't in the café. He was outside in the bus shelter huddled in a hoodie looking miserable. He gave her a quick hug and bundled her into the cafe before he spoke.

'I can't do this Nicola. I'm so unhappy. I can't work, I can't eat, I can't sleep. I'm so so sorry I behaved so badly. Please forgive me.' He looked up at her from sleep deprived blue eyes.

Nicola slowly took first one of his hands and then the other and then dropped them when she remembered how all this mess started. 'I'm the one who should be saying sorry,' she said. 'I should have trusted you. I do trust you. I do believe what you say. I love you so much.'

Julian's face lit up with a sunny smile. 'Friends? Lovers?' he asked

Nicola leaned over and kissed him and they sat with their heads together until the coffee arrived.

'Lucas told me you got back safely,' Julian said, 'so I didn't have to worry about you being lost but I just had to come and see you to sort this out. I was afraid that if I phoned you'd tell me to go and jump in the river. And then I thought that if I actually turn up you'll have to speak to me,' he smiled.

He continued with his prepared speech. 'I should have told you before but I just lost my temper completely. When you saw Jocelyn holding my hands and you thought the very worst of me, it wasn't like that at all. Apparently Jocelyn's got the hots for Torin, one of Gellie's set builders. The one I introduced her to after the show. Dee is going to be so mad when she finds out as a carpenter is nothing like what she had in mind for her beloved daughter. Here's the problem. Torin is off to Florida, to Orlando to build a set for Disneyworld. This is his big break and he will be away for six months. Jocelyn has cancelled her trip to Watamu and is going with him. Her problem is she hasn't exactly told Dee about her change of plan. Watch this space for an eruption of volcanic proportions.'

'And I thought you'd just want to disappear out of my life because I was behaving like a child.'

It wasn't until much later that Nicola remembered to ask herself how Lucas knew she was safely back at school.

As Julian turned yet again to wave goodbye, Nicola shivered and went to call him back for one last hug, one last kiss. But she didn't and went back to school a very happy bunny. Kate was very relieved that everything had worked out. A depressed suicidal Nicola was the last thing either of them needed.

Julian's exams finished as Nicola's began and she got a very cheery text saying he thought he'd done well and wishing her the very best of luck. He had her exam timetable and would be thinking about her all the way to Saudi, all the time he was there and all the way back to her school gates.

Physics was over, chemistry was over and there was a lull of about a week before the last two biology exams. It had been a long hard road and Kate was busy planning to party nonstop for at least two weeks because when the results came out she'd probably be dead meat. Nicola felt very calm about it all. Her mother had rung her a couple of times to check she was fine and Maggie had sent a card she'd made at school saying she was knitting for Britain. The morning of the last day of exams was warm and sunny. Only seven and a half hours and she'd be flinging herself into Julian's arms outside the school gates and she wouldn't have a care in the world about who saw her. She imagined him suntanned from his break in Saudi, his blond hair bleached almost white, his eyes a brighter blue than before. She looked at her watch. He must be back in London by now so why hadn't he been in touch? Nicola hugged herself anyway as she ate her breakfast.

Kate had already finished her exams and left school and the two of them had planned to meet up in Oxford very soon. It was strange walking over to the examinations hall that morning on her own, without her best friend. The drive was crowded with kids dashing wildly to various parts of the school but Nicola felt dislocated from all the activity. The Zoology paper had been straightforward, only an afternoon of Botany to go. As she crossed the road she saw Jamie coming towards her, his shoulders hunched up and his long black coat wrapped tightly even though it was June. As he came closer she could see that his glasses were smashed and there was blood trickling down his cheek. Her phone rang just as Jamie walked straight through her piercing her body. She winced as she reached into her pocket. It was Gellie: Jamie had disappeared.

'Nicola? Nicola? I'm so glad I've caught you. Can you speak?'

'Yes, yes, I'm just on my way into school.' Didn't Gellie realise she was in the middle of her exams. Really!

'Nicola. I've got some terrible news. I didn't want you to hear it from anyone else.'

There was a pause.

'Julian died in hospital early this morning in Riyad. He was in an RTA last night on the way to the airport. He never regained consciousness. I'm so sorry...Nicola, are you still there?'

'Yes.'

'I'm at Heathrow, flying out to be with Caroline and Dermot. You're breaking up. Nicola. I can't hear you.'

Nicola turned her phone off, sank onto a seat by the tennis courts and buried her head in her rucksack. She sat there for a couple of minutes and then walked off to the school gates. Trying not to look at the low wall where Julian was supposed to be sitting in four hours time she caught a bus into town, a train to Stroud and a bus out to Frampton. As she walked the long way home so as to avoid Mulberry Cottage she was met by her frantic mother just leaving in her car.

'Darling. What's happened? What's gone wrong?'

No reply. Nicola stared straight ahead.

Her mother scooped her up in her arms and held her very tight. 'The school phoned to say you didn't turn up for your last exam and nobody knew where you were. I'm so glad I found you.'

No reply. Monica bundled her into the car. As she was struggling with the seat belt, Nicola turned her tear soaked face towards her.

'Julian's dead, Mum. He was killed last night in Saudi. Gellie phoned me. I want to be dead too.'

Monica straightened up in a daze. Had she heard right? Julian was just a friend, surely, not someone to get this distressed about. They had known each other for a very short time. One look at her daughter's face told her she'd got that one all wrong. This was going to take some sorting. Meanwhile Nicola had started crying deep rasping sobs that shook her hunched up frame. Monica could only wrap her arms around her to try to hold her together.

Her father was striding round the front of the house when they pulled into the drive. One look from his wife told him to keep his mouth shut, so he took cover in his study.

Settled in the kitchen wrapped in her *Angelica* knit, Nicola hugged her cup of warm sweet tea. Her mother sat down in front of her looking for answers.

'Tell me.' She commanded trying not to sound too stern. Nicola had always been such a good biddable child. Dramas from Maggie were to be expected but not Nicola.

'Gellie phoned me just as I was on my way to my last exam. She thought

I'd finished which is why she waited until the afternoon. Julian was killed in a car crash in Riyadh on the way to the airport. He was flying back to see me.'

Nicola gave a great gulp. 'I like him, Mum, I really, really like him.' Then she realised it was all in the past tense now, gave a rasping sob and broke down into another bout of crying that tugged at her mother's heart strings.

The kitchen door pushed open and her father came in.

'I've just been on the phone to The Grange' he said. He'd obviously been eavesdropping through the closed door.

'The crash happened late last night. A lorry driver lost control of his vehicle on the road out to the airport, crossed the central reservation and hit Julian's car. Julian and his driver never had a chance and there are doubts as to whether the lorry driver will make it. Gellie Crawford and the Willstones flew out this afternoon. That's all I know.' He ended rather lamely.

Nicola thought she was going to be sick.

'Just tell me it isn't true. Tell me Julian is still alive.' She whispered.

'I can't do that sweetie.' Andrew paused. As a local doctor his working life had been threaded with life and death situations and it never got any easier. The one thing he thought he had got right was never to let death be all consuming for those that were left behind. Putting living back into perspective was his prescribed antidote. He proceeded to try to apply it. Monica saw what was coming and tried to intervene by taking control of the situation.

'Darling, you've had a huge shock. Take things very slowly for the next couple of days and then I'm sure you'll start to feel better.' She wanted to tell Nicola that Julian wouldn't want her moping round the house for months but it didn't seem right.

'Nicola, listen to me.' Andrew was unrolling his prescription. 'You must phone the school and explain. They need to contact the Examinations Board to put forward your extenuating circumstances so that we can try to retrieve something from all of this. As it stands you will fail the exam and not get the grade you need for uni.'

Unwittingly he then let the self abuse genie out of the bottle.

'You've let everyone down by letting this get all out of perspective. I know it is awful losing a friend in such tragic circumstances but your priorities are to get the grades.'

Something made him turn round to look at Monica and her expression sent him fleeing back to the sanctuary of his study.

Nicola sought refuge under her duvet. Her grief seeped out and piled itself on the floor in stacks relating to everything she'd shared with Julian. At night she'd move between the stacks reliving all the precious moments.

She had intended to slash her wrists, dramatically in the bath wearing a white nightdress and a garland of flowers in her hair. There were a couple of problems with this arrangement. For a start she didn't have a white nightdress only an old T-shirt and a pair of trackie Bs and she had no idea how to weave a garland. Maggie would have known but Maggie was away. At midnight Nicola crept off to the bathroom with a razor blade, so light, so cold and so small. Hard to imagine that something so everyday could do something so major as detach a life from its existence. She put the blade on the inside of her arm and pressed gently to see what it felt like. The blade sliced into her flesh and blood rose up out of the faint red line. Nicola stared mesmerised as the blood ran down her arm and dripped onto her knee. In one slash she'd discovered the meaning of cathartic. It felt like the final throws of an orgasm but she was in control. She made two more cuts just to confirm what it felt like and then held her arm under the cold tap to stop the bleeding. Having bound her arm in a towel, Nicola crept back to bed and finally slipped into a deep much needed sleep.

The following morning, Nicola got up early, had a shower, washed her hair and was in the kitchen ready for breakfast much to her mother's surprise. Perhaps Andrew's theories about dispelling grief were right after all. She took Bundle out for a long walk carefully avoiding the lane up to Mulberry Cottage and The Grange. It was a lovely day. Nicola felt the sun on her legs and the breeze in her hair. Her arms were covered by long sleeves. She'd kept her phone switched off so once carefully hidden behind a stone wall she sat down to check her texts. There was one from Kate:

What the hell is going on?

A longer text from Gellie told her that everyone was devastated and that Julian had been buried in the European Cemetery in Riyadh two days after he died. So he had gone, really gone and she felt that the old Nicola, the one with all the plans for the future, had gone with him. What the new Nicola was going to do now was really anyone's guess. However, one thing was certain. Nicola carefully wrapped her soul tightly in cling film so that nothing and no one could ever get close enough to her ever again. She needed Jamie. She hadn't needed him when she had Julian, in fact she'd hardly given him a second thought. Walking up the hill with Bundle she noticed that Jamie waiting for her on the other side of the stone wall. She begged for his help but he just kept looking straight ahead focused on the horizon. He didn't even turn round when she yelled at him.

Kate came rushing over from Oxford as soon as she could. She listened patiently to Nicola eulogizing over Julian and was careful not to be judgmental. Maggie came back from her school trip and was overawed that her sister was experiencing such a drama and disappointed that Nicola seemed unable to explain how it felt. Then she got tired of the melancholy, general inertia and a life that didn't seem to extend beyond walking the dog. She made a plan.

It had only taken her a couple of weeks to master knitting basics so it wasn't long before Maggie was experimenting with different materials. The house was soon festooned with shapes knitted from scraps of material, strips of ribbon, string, elastic and anything that Maggie thought would work. Some did, some didn't. Her art and design teacher was soon pumped dry of ideas so Maggie had to turn elsewhere for inspiration. She went to Gellie. Unable to afford really trendy outfits in the local shops, Maggie's friends started asking her to make them unusual outfits. In a moment of inspirational clarity, she came up with a portfolio of designs to show Gellie. It was to be the start of a new teen range called *Gellateens*. Gellie was too busy with her bulging order book so Maggie decided she had to get right under Gellie's nose and her plan was work experience in Gellie's studio. The plan was destined to failure as no way would her parents sanction her living on her own in London without a chaperone. Nicola was the obvious solution. Playing on Gellie's obvious concerns for Nicola, Maggie put her plan into action.

'I wanted to ask you if you would like to come and work for me over the summer, Nicola. I need someone like you with an organised mind to sort out my office so that I can get a new project up and running. What are you doing? When do your exam results come out?'

Gellie had appeared for coffee with Monica one morning. She hadn't spoken to Nicola since the disastrous phone call.

No answer.

Gellie tried again. 'I need someone I can trust, Nicola. The fashion industry is so cut throat you never know who is stealing what.'

Gellie leaned over and looked at Nicola with those so like Lucas eyes.

Nicola went cold. She'd forgotten about her 'A' Levels filed away deep at the back of her mind. She remembered not turning up for her last exam paper. The exam board had been less than sympathetic so there was absolutely no way she was going to get her university place. She'd be lucky if she even passed the subject. Horror about the fallout from the results threatened to strangle her. To describe it as nuclear would be an understatement. She cleared her throat.

'That is a very kind offer,' Nicola muttered without much enthusiasm. It wasn't until she heard her mother thanking Gellie for offering Nicola a summer job so that she could keep an eye on Maggie while she did some work experience, that she realised how easily she'd been conned.

At the *Angelica* headquarters in London, Nicola was put in charge of the day to day cash book and it was soon clear that Gellie was the sort of imaginative artiste who had no real idea how to manage cash flow. She introduced Nicola to Oliver Sanders, an accountant recommended by

Charlie Willstone, who had been trying to sort out her mess.

'The main problem has been that Miss Crawford has taken creative accounting to a level that would surprise the city wise boys. Last month when I asked for her invoices so that I could file her VAT return she gave me this beautifully embroidered bag stuffed full of the receipts.' Oliver shivered when he recalled the lack of systematic order. He looked round the tiny office and smiled with satisfaction when he noted that Nicola had already set out a number of files in the correct order and tidied the one and only desk so that at least you could now see its surface. He had been on the point of telling Mr Willstone that the task of bringing Miss Crawford to financial heel was beyond even his capabilities. But now he could see a light at the end of this textile tunnel. Having spent the morning explaining to Nicola exactly how he wanted things to be done, he left the office a happy man. Nicola was delighted to have a real task to get stuck into. It was the nights that were the problem. She had devised this process of remembering everything important about Julian, images of him laughing, the way he said her name, which she played over to herself before she went to sleep, scared that she might forget even a small detail. The nightmares started when grief metamorphosed into guilt. Would Julian still be alive if she hadn't insisted he caught that plane so that he could be back as soon as her exams finished? Was his death in some way her fault? Maggie, completely oblivious to Nicola's suffering, was Gellie's work shadow and her diligence paid off when Gellie finally agreed to help her with her *Gellateens* project.

Then came a phone call from Kate. Would Nicola like to come over to Oxford and then they could both travel to Cheltenham to get their exam results? Not that Kate thought there would be much to celebrate with hers, but she would enjoy cashing in on Nicola's predictable success. As it would be so much better than going on her own, Nicola agreed.

Kate picked Nicola up from Oxford station. 'This is not going to be a good day,' Kate said as they drove in through the school gates and parked in the staff car park. Nicola agreed because in her sleep deprived world there were no good days. Kate's results were actually better than she thought and would get her into Kingston Uni, her second choice. Nicola scraped a pass in Biology. Goodbye London and Bath. Hello UCAS Clearing. Her teachers gave her the forms and offered to support her through the process. Nicola rang home. Her father was out and her mother burst into tears and told Nicola to come home immediately so that they could sort this mess out. How about a re-mark? Surely there must be a mistake? No mistake Nicola told her mother.

'You have been predicted three 'A' grades all the way through sixth form and now you've thrown away your place at a prestigious university and ruined your entire future.' Her father was incandescent with rage.

'You are being too harsh, Andrew.' Her mother came to the rescue. 'We need to sit down and look at the clearing process and salvage what we can. Nicola needs our support right now not a forensic investigation.'

Her father had made a list of possible universities for Nicola to phone the next day. She wasn't sure she even wanted to go to any of the places he was suggesting or university at all, but she dutifully took the list away and promised to look up the course requirements and to identify which ones could be possibilities. Her father wanted the amendments back by supper time.

Jamie slipped into the study looking helpful.

'So, where would you like to visit? Wales? No. Not far enough away to be different. Ireland is the opposite. Too far with that sea bit in between. So that leaves Scotland or the north of England. That's quite foreign really.'

'Why do I want to go miles away Jamie?'

'You need space and something new in your life.'

Nicola made a list of universities a suitable distance from home. Newcastle fitted the bill. She didn't make the grades for Chemistry but it might be worth a try. Nicola phoned and gave her details to a member of staff who filled in the clearing form there and then. Someone would get back to her tomorrow.

Before she could explain her selection process to her father the next morning, the phone rang. It was a tutor from the chemistry department at Newcastle Uni who were very sorry but they couldn't offer her a place as her grades were not good enough. Perhaps she should consider a re-sit? However there was a Professor Boyd who would like to speak to her if she could just hang on for a moment. Nicola told her rather surprised father that she was about to speak to Professor Boyd at Newcastle Uni.

'Miss Cowan? Ah, Professor Boyd speaking from Environmental Sciences. Your clearing forms were passed to me this morning. I have a grant to set up an undergrad course in environmental science starting October next year. It is too late to get the course into the undergraduate prospectus for this year's applicants so I'm looking for candidates by whatever route and your application interests me.'

Nicola felt a surge of relief and a right feeling about this as Prof. Boyd went on to outline his course and to explain that he was looking for a broad breadth of talent across his first year undergraduates. Would she consider applying for his course through UCAS for October the following year? Without really thinking Nicola said she was considering going to Kenya, to Watamu to work for about eight months, well, at least until next summer. Prof. Boyd was delighted. He had a group of post graduate research students working at the marine nature reserve in Watamu and he was sure that Nicola could visit and learn something about the department's research work. If she was offered a place, would she consider accepting? Nicola was overwhelmed. Yes of course she would. Course details would be in the post shortly but if she needed any more information she should get in touch.

Nicola leaned back in her father's office chair amazed with the way in which her life had been sorted for the next three years. A lifetime. An hour ago she had no university place, now she had had an offer for a course that sounded so much better than chemistry and a gap year as well. The latter might be a bit of a problem. What on earth had possessed her? What could have possessed her to think that the Mother Superior at the convent in Watamu, about which she knew very little, would possibly want her in her orphanage when she didn't know the first thing about her or her family? The Cowans weren't even Catholics for a start. Before she had time to think about that the door opened framing her parents.

'Nicola, perhaps you could tell us what is going on? We are doing our best to help you through this difficult phase by giving advice and support. You, however, seem to be running with a different agenda?' Her father glared at her.

Nicola took in a gulp of air. 'I've been chatting to a Professor Boyd at Newcastle Uni who is starting a new undergrad course in Environmental Science in October next year. He would like me to apply for his course through UCAS and I'm pretty certain he'll offer me a place.'

Nicola looked defiantly at her parents.

Her parents exchanged an unfathomable knowing look and then gazed at Nicola. Her mother rushed forward with a big hug.

'That is absolutely marvelous darling. Well done. I knew things would work out for you. That all your hard work would pay off. Hasn't she done well?'

'Yes, yes. Well done you, Nicola.' A little forced but her father did manage a smile. 'But what about your Chemistry? After all you've studied it to quite a high level. It would be a pity to waste all that hard work.'

'That's OK,' replied Nicola. 'I can do modules in Chemistry and Bio-chemistry. Professor Boyd wants to have students from a whole lot of different backgrounds and some with non cognate subjects.' Nicola wasn't quite sure what that meant but she hoped to impress her parents with her knowledge about the course she'd just signed up for. It was such a mammoth leap into the dark she felt quite sick.

The phone rang again. It was Gellie wanting to know about her exam results.

'I'll be down at Mulberry Cottage this weekend,' Gellie told Nicola. 'You couldn't possibly just finish off this month's accounts for me if I bring all the stuff with me? Please? That nasty Mr Sanders is coming on Monday to collect them for a financial audit or something. Charlie did explain it all to me. Anyway I want an opportunity to impress him.'

'Of course I will,' replied Nicola. 'Oliver isn't nasty; he just likes things done properly.'

On Saturday morning Nicola walked over to Mulberry Cottage. It was a lovely day and she was looking forward to spending it with Gellie. The front door was ajar so Nicola pushed it open and called out to Gellie. The kitchen door opened and Caroline Smith Owen appeared wiping her hands on a towel.

'Hello Nicola. Come in and have a coffee. Gellie has just popped over to see Charlie to pick up some more forms.' As Caroline gave her a very Julian smile, Nicola felt herself wobble. Luckily she composed herself on the way to the kitchen.

Gellie noticed Nicola's white face when she came back but a warning glance from Caroline stopped her from saying anything. Instead she explained where the problems lay and Nicola was relieved to get down to work. By lunch time everything was in an order that Nicola was sure would satisfy even Mr Oliver Sanders' high standards and after stacking the records neatly in their box she wandered into the kitchen. Something smelt really good.

'What perfect timing,' said Caroline. 'Come and sit down and have lunch and tell us all about your university plans.'

After explaining about the new course, Nicola bit the bullet. 'The problem is, I have to take a gap year and the professor asked me what I intended to do. Well that was a bit difficult and before I thought about what I was going to say I told him I was going to Watamu to work in an orphanage, you know, like Julian.' Nicola felt really embarrassed but rushed on 'By sheer coincidence the Prof. has research students working on a marine reserve there and he expects me to visit. So I'm stuck.' Nicola looked helplessly at Gellie for support.

Caroline and Gellie exchanged glances. There was a silence.

'Well,' said Caroline, 'Now neither Julian or Jocelyn are going, no doubt Sister Benny could do with some extra help. How much do you actually know about Our Lady's Orphanage in Watamu and The Sisters of Mercy who run it?'

Nicola explained that Julian had told her quite a bit. 'He was very enthusiastic and supportive of the whole project.'

'Are you sure this is something you'd like to do? asked Gellie. 'Living is quite primitive there. Sister Benny and her team are lovely but the children can be hard work … and fun of course.'

'Yes,' said Nicola firmly. 'I really want to do this. I need to get right away from here to somewhere different and I'm not afraid of hard work.'

'So how can we help? Shall I phone Sister Benny right now?' Caroline consulted her watch. 'I should be able to catch her.'

Gellie and Nicola sat and waited, listening to Caroline's low authoritative voice on the phone but unable to catch what she was saying. She came back smiling. 'Sister Benny would love to have you work for her but not without your parent's approval. You must get their agreement and then we can chat again and make arrangements.'

In their tree in the courtyard outside Our Lady's Convent in Watamu the Arit Jinn raised their heads and eavesdropped on the telephone conversation. Suddenly things looked a whole lot more interesting. Fragments of past events at the convent were retrieved and the Arit Jinn settled down to piece them together. The prospect of further mischief-making with a new subject bound up with old adversaries was irresistible. The Tree of Forgetfulness shimmered with their expectations. Sister Benny, glancing out of her study window, noticed how the leaves were trembling in the still air.

'It has nothing to do with your mischief-making and scheming.' Sister Benny addressed the tree and then turned back to the ever increasing mountain of paper work. She sighed deeply. At least a solution might be on its way.

On the way home Nicola paused and leant against a stone wall warmed by the sun to think through what she'd just done. Somehow everything had fallen into place with such electric speed that her brain was having difficulty keeping up. She closed her eyes and then opened them when she sensed someone approaching. Jamie was next to her.

'Jamie, have I gone mad or have I done the right thing? Everything happened so quickly without me really thinking about it. I just needed to do something.'

'Nicola, it's all right. You'll be well looked after in the convent. They know the Smith Owens and Gellie so you'll be fine. It will do you the world of good to get away somewhere completely different.'

Nicola smiled happily. Jamie usually managed to say the right things.

In reply, Jamie turned away and sauntered off.

There was a family supper at the Cowan's house that night which had been planned to celebrate Nicola's exam results. Monica insisted on going ahead because Nicola had been so positive in turning round her disaster. Over coffee, her father cleared his throat.

'And I have some very special news for Nicola,' he announced. 'We, that is your mother and I, have arranged for you to work in the pharmacy at the surgery for six months. With your chemistry 'A' level you will be a great asset and you can live here, at home and save your money because you're going to need it.'

Andrew looked very pleased with himself; Monica smiled indulgently thinking that things really had turned out quite well, in the end. Maggie looked horror struck as she had made plans for Nicola that involved *Gellateens* and Nicola stared at the face of history repeating itself with her parents back in control. Nicola drew a breath in sharply. She knew she was at a crossroads. No, more like a major intersection. If she turned left the road led back into her old life as Nicola Cowan, an appendage of Cowan Inc. with every move supervised and debated by her parents. If, on the other hand she turned right she could joyously embrace the newly released Nicola Cowan. She remembered that Kate had had a failsafe strategy when they were being hauled before authority at school: 'Keep talking and eventually the get-out words will come to you.'

Her father was looking at her expectantly. Nicola cleared her throat.

'Thank you. Thank you both so much for such a kind and generous offer. For sorting out the huge mess I've made. I really stuffed up. I was thinking the other day, while I was walking Bundle, about what you have always told us, Dad, about what a privileged childhood we've had living here in the country and going to good schools, having such supportive parents.'

Nicola hoped she wasn't laying it on too thick.

'But it was only in the last day or two that I have realised the enormity of all this. So much so I felt I could not go much further without giving something back. So I have been speaking to Gellie Crawford about the possibility of spending six months in Africa working at an orphanage in Watamu. Jocelyn Willstone was supposed to go and do this but she changed her mind at the last minute so the orphanage have been let down. Dee and Charlie know the orphanage very well and the Mother Superior who runs it. The Smith Owens set it up years ago so it's not like I'm going to the middle of nowhere. It would only be for six months and then I will be back to work maybe at the surgery to get some money together for Uni'.

'Well done Nicola,' Maggie cried. Andrew and Monica exchanged worried glances. This was not what they had had in mind at all. But what could they say?

Her father cleared his throat again. 'I must say,' he said, 'in this day and age it is admirable to hear a young person actually say that they would like to give some of their time to helping those less fortunate than themselves.'

He's stalling for time thought Nicola and crossed her fingers under the table.

Andrew turned to his wife and asked for her thoughts. Monica was actually thinking that it must have been Jocelyn Willstone who'd put this crazy idea in Nicola's head as a sort of compensation for Jocelyn no longer going herself. If only it were that easy. She couldn't say 'no' straight off. One look at Nicola's face flushed with anticipation and expectation told her that this was the first real direction in her life that Nicola had made for herself. She couldn't, just couldn't, put her down.

'I think that is such a good idea. Now that you have a place at Newcastle practically signed and sealed, this is a marvellous opportunity to do something different. And choosing to help children get a better start in life. Darling,' she said reaching over the table to give her daughter a hug, 'I think that your idea is wonderful. We'll talk to Gellie and the Willstones tomorrow and see if it is possible to get it all sorted.'

Nicola grinned in relief that it had been that easy. On their own in the kitchen Andrew turned to Monica.

'Well that was a turn up for the books. Nicola, who has always been so biddable, turning round with a plan completely out of the blue. You obviously feel it is the right thing for her to do, so help me understand why.'

'It feels right,' replied Monica. 'I know we don't really know the Smith Owens well but they did set up this orphanage when they lived in Kenya. Charlie and Dee were involved and Jocelyn was going to work out there this summer but she changed her mind because of the Smith Owens tragic loss. Jocelyn and Julian were very close according to Dee.'

'Anyway,' continued Monica, 'It means that Nicola won't be going off into darkest Africa to some unknown project run by god knows who. We will have ways and means to keep checking on her without her knowing. I think she should go. The debacle over her exam results and losing Julian so tragically really hit her hard and she needs to get away. To do something completely different on her own.'

Meanwhile, upstairs, Nicola and Maggie were reliving the evening with a couple of vodka shots under Maggie's duvet.

'Have you ever considered that you might, at the tender age of fifteen, have a problem with alcohol, Maggie?' asked Nicola.

'No way,' replied Maggie. 'I merely represent the product, and I am proud to say this, of the excellent local school. Cheers.'

'Seriously Nicola,' Maggie propped herself up on her elbow, 'This is your one big chance to get your life back. Get away from here. Leave your memories behind stashed in one of those boxes under your bed. Go and have fun. And stop cutting yourself. It's beginning to show.'

Maggie felt Nicola stiffen but she had to say it. Maggie rattled on. 'I'm sure Mum hasn't noticed — yet. Lots of people at school cut themselves that's how I can recognise it. But it has to stop.'

'Now that I've got my life sorted for the next two years, I feel really different. I think I can put all that behind me and start again.' Nicola did not add that she'd decided that this new Nicola would never ever give so much of herself to another person having found out how little was left if everything went pear shaped.

'Maggie, how come you're so street wise? You are far wiser than me and I'm four years older than you. And how come you're so supportive? You want this bedroom all to yourself, don't you? When I get back I won't be able to get a toe through the door let alone my rucksack.'

'Absolutely,' was the reply.

The next three weeks were consumed by frantic activity. Andrew and Monica duly interviewed the Smith Owens, the Willstones and Gellie about Nicola's plans which were welcomed with great enthusiasm. The Smith Owens's obvious deep commitment to the orphanage convinced Nicola's parents that it would be a safe and very worthwhile destination for their daughter. Dermot Smith Owen pulled massive strings inside the Foreign Office and a working visa arrived within days. Andrew organised enough immunisation to keep an army at bay and Dee advised on her packing list. The pace at which the events were all slotting into place was quite scary and Nicola sleeping badly was sick in the morning. Although she didn't say anything at the time, her mother put it all down to stress. Nicola had never been good at handling stress. She received a very cheery email from Sister Benedicta (please call me Sister Benny) saying how much they were all looking forward to welcoming her and could she please bring a large pot of Marmite with her.

Nicola sat and looked at her rucksack packed and ready to go. That afternoon she'd gone to Mulberry Cottage to say goodbye to Gellie and been welcomed by Caroline.

'I'm so glad to see you before you go,' Caroline said, 'as I have something to give you. Come with me.' She led Nicola into Dermot's study and handed her a parcel loosely covered in tissue paper. 'Open it,' commanded Caroline looking expectantly at Nicola. It was a complete collection of adventure stories. Julian's name in rather shaky handwriting was just inside the front cover.

'I thought you might read the book to the children at the orphanage,' said Caroline. 'They love listening to stories. It was one of Julian's favorite books and I would like you to have it.' 'Thank you. Thank you so much,' replied Nicola.

It was the first time Nicola had said goodbye to her family for anything longer than two weeks. She felt very detached from the emotional scenes as though she was floating along in parallel. It didn't stop her reaching for a large kitchen tissue to blow her nose more than once during the last few hours at home. She walked round the house saying farewell to all the rooms and telling them she'd be back in about six months. Her parents hugged her tightly as she waited for the bus to Heathrow and her mother held back her tears until they were nearly back in Frampton. It was all quite grown up in the end as they wished her luck and told her to take care as she heaved her rucksack over her shoulders.

ANNIE BOON

3

Nicola lay on her narrow bed encased in a mosquito net. The euphoria which engulfed her when her plane landed at Mombasa had leaked out on the journey to Watamu and the orphanage which was to be her home for the next six months. Six months, why had she agreed to such a long time in the first place? Nine days was an eternity from where she was coming from right now. The road trip had been interesting, different. She had never seen anything like the main highway from Mombasa north to Watamu. The road was crammed with toxic belching lorries; overflowing buses hogging the middle of the road and then veering suddenly to pick up even more passengers when the only available space was on the roof; improbably stacked unroadworthy bicycles; helmetless motorcycles with passengers riding sidesaddle and stall holders, risking life and limb, weaving through the traffic to tout their goods. It wasn't much better inside the convent van which Nicola shared with three hens, a goat, several sacks of flour and two small children who giggled every time she tried to talk to them. It was a million miles from her mother's pristine Volvo estate. Moses, the driver and also Sister Benny's right-hand man, according to Moses, chatted merrily as he negotiated bad drivers, more goats, children, potholes and stray dogs but Nicola could not hear a word because of the groans from the van's engines and simply fixed a smile on her mouth and tried not to think about being sick. The van windows were jammed wide open allowing Africa's signature smell: death, rotting stuff, wood smoke and drains, to permeate the vehicle. She had imagined that the convent and its orphanage would be a collection of imposing buildings offering protection whilst standing guard over Watamu. That was her first disappointment. The convent building and the chapel had been imposing but the salt blown from the sea blended with neglect over time had reduced it to a hollow shell. Clustered round an open courtyard dominated by an ancient tree were a collection of traditional mud huts and breeze block single storey buildings, mud rendered with thatch roofs. A high wall surrounded the compound and, where sections had crumbled away, bougainvillea laden with heavy flowers struggled to escape into the outside world. The gates were probably the least impressive. Made of corrugated iron of various ages and origins, patched and repatched, they had to be manually hauled open lopsidedly threatening to collapse on anyone trying to enter.

Sister Benny was not as she expected either. Nicola tried to think back to how she'd imagined the mother superior. Tall, angular with presence. What she found was small, round, glasses held together with bale twine – 'the new ones are on order, my dear but it takes an age' – as the glasses gathered speed on a predictable descent down her nose. Somehow, on reflection, it was Sister Benny and her alone that prevented Nicola from running away from Watamu and Africa that evening. She didn't have 'presence' but she had warmth and a personality that invaded the collection of bandas, roundels and shacks that had arranged themselves around the two storey stone convent building.

'We'll save the guided tour for tomorrow. Sister Maria will show you where you'll be staying and then bring you back here to me. A light supper before Eucharist and then I expect you'll want to sort yourself out and get some sleep.' Sister Benny smiled reassuringly at Nicola and Sister Maria, who could only be about fourteen years old, stepped forward from the shade of the old gnarled tree in the centre of the courtyard and took Nicola's hand. The air was still and heavy but something light moved through the tree's branches. The Arit Jinn were observing the new arrival.

Nicola gazed into the darkness and it was very dark. It was quiet outside but not silent. Nicola could hear the quietness of people and animals sleeping, lots of them very close. Suddenly she saw very clearly why she had come here. Why she had decided on Watamu without really thinking about it. The part of her that could not accept that Julian was dead thought that she would find him here. Her mind's eye saw him striding over to greet her, his suntanned face smothered in a big smile, to hold her close so that she could feel his heart beating through his white linen shirt. Nicola was angry now. She sat up in bed and hugged her knees to her chest to keep herself in one tight ball. Was this what had kept her going through all the emotional turmoil of his death, the exam failure, her perhaps university place at Newcastle – Newcastle for goodness sake, she had never been there in her life. It was miles away. Julian was dead. Julian was nowhere so looking for him was pointless. She should go home, now and face up to what had happened in her life, to pick up the pieces. Gellie would give her a job until she sorted herself out. Nicola rolled over and let the tears stream down her face. How was it possible to make such a mess of one's life? She missed her family, the security of the family home, she even missed Maggie. She would get up early, before breakfast, pack up her stuff and then go and tell Sister Benny she had made a mistake, and leave. Sister Benny. Sister Benny was going to be difficult. In the end Nicola could not face her and decided to give the convent a month's trial. She lay on her bed and considered the evening's events.

The imposing wooden doors at the entrance to the convent building opened into a wide hall lined with mahogany armoires, trunks and boxes, stacked as though the owners had only just arrived or were packing up ready to leave. They exuded an old smell of past dark things. Nicola shivered as she imagined secrets concealed in the folds of old sheets and blankets brought out from England, slept in by nobility, abandoned and then rescued by Sister Benny who could not abide waste. If they were feeling particularly restless, the Arit Jinn invoked their poltergeist talents and played jenga with the trunks. It was their secret game with Sister Benny as only she knew that they had been up to mischief.

In contrast to the creepy hall, Sister Benny's office, sitting room, whatever, was a large airy room on the ground floor. There was a expansive view across the courtyard to the main gates, the path to the school and the small clinic. Not much was going to be able to slip under Sister Benny's radar. A wide veranda ran the length of the west side of the convent giving Sister Benny another commanding view of her flock. She began by asking Nicola to tell her a bit about herself and why she wanted to come to Africa to work in an orphanage and particularly her orphanage. And then jumped in first herself.

'As you know, I have known Dermot and Caroline Smith Owen and Caroline's sister, Gellie Crawford, for a very long time.'

Nicola was sure she detected a slight hesitation from Sister Benny and a cool look to see if Nicola had reacted to the names. It was only a hint of a pause as Sister Benny rushed on.

'They were so supportive when I arrived here in Watamu, newly escaped from the mother house in Ireland, to a very unloved orphanage. Together they helped me get this place back on its feet and I will always be so grateful. And then Julian'…another slight inflection maybe, 'and Lucas have generously given time here during school and university holidays. Gellie and Lucas still come when they can but I haven't seen Dermot and Caroline for a long while.' Another pause and then Sister Benny decided to mention the previously unmentionable.

'It was quite the most terrible tragedy for Dermot and Caroline to lose Julian in such an awful accident. Gellie came here a couple of weeks ago and we talked for a long time about grief and bereavement and she spent time in solitude in the chapel. I gather that you had become very close to Julian?'

But Nicola had become a very adept at keeping her emotions locked away if anyone came looking for answers on the subject of Julian. She was ready with her much rehearsed speech.

'Yes. I really, really liked him. We had known each other for about six months. I know that is not long and as everybody keeps telling me we were so young but it was more than enough time for us to know that we would spend the rest of our lives together. Only that wasn't to be. I rejoice that we had that time together and that God has given me the strength to live on without him. That's why I wanted to come here to a place where Julian spent so much time and to repay God by doing something for other people.' Nicola hoped she sounded convincing. It had taken her hours to get the God versus good works balance right. Sister Benny nodded in approval but inside was not completely convinced she was hearing the truth. Time would tell.

'My dear. It is perfectly natural to grieve. It is perfectly natural to be angry. Sometimes you must let go in order to fully understand why. And don't forget God is all seeing and all knowing and you cannot hide from him.'

Another pause. Sister Benny reached out and squeezed Nicola's hand. Nicola felt her emotions rush up from her heart but before they could throw themselves on the floor for all to see she gained control. Rather like not being car sick earlier. Had she been able to fool Sister Benny? Nicola was fast gaining the impression that Sister Benny was more than equal to God in the all seeing all knowing stakes.

'Gellie was very complimentary about you which is why I agreed to have you here in what is, I suppose, what they call a gap year. This orphanage is a charitable institution and has no permanent income. We rely solely on God and the generosity of others. Recently that generosity has been more difficult to access and I am being called further away from my religious duties as I struggle to keep up with modern demands. And this is where you come in. I need someone to fast track me into the computer age, to sort out my filing and to set up a decent accounting system. But nothing too complicated as I must be able to understand it and run it myself when you leave. Gellie told me you would be marvellous. In return you will get what's called board and lodgings here and I do hope you would like to spend some time in our school helping the little ones to read, and maybe you know something about football? In other words we want you to feel part of our community. Our vision here for our primary school is to make education available to all who desire it irrespective of their cultural, political, religious and social backgrounds or academic abilities. These aspirations are the bedrock for our religious life here and I expect you to respect them. The community is very ecumenical and no child is ever turned away from our orphanage. But I have ranted on too long and it's getting dark. It is time you went to bed ready for your baptism of fire tomorrow when we go to the office.'

Sister Benny stood up and rang the bell on her table. Sister Maria appeared again from the darkness and took Nicola back to her hut.

Lying in the darkness going over all that had happened in the short space of time that she'd been in Africa, Nicola realised that there was nowhere else for her to go. She had to stick this one out to prove to herself that she could do it and to prove to Sister Benny that what she had told her earlier had been the absolute truth. Nicola resolved to start going to Mass. But what if that meant confession as well? Had she taken on more that she had bargained for in this hairbrained scheme? But at least it sounded as though Gellie might come and see her which was very comforting.

The next day dawned bright and clear. The community of the Sisters of Mercy at Our Lady's Covent rose early with sunrise and largely went to bed with the sunset completely at one with the earth's daily rhythms. Wearing khaki combat trousers and a white shirt Nicola sought to compliment Sister Benny's neat interpretation of a nun's habit adapted to an equatorial climate. She was rather surprised to find a young girl in a bright khanga with matching headgear but then thought it refreshing.

'Ah, good morning, Nicola. Let me introduce you to Anna who runs the convent.'

Anna smiled shyly. Grabbing a set of keys, Sister Benny came round her desk and signaled to Nicola to follow her.

'Now to my real office. This desk is for formal duties when I have to meet officials. My other place is where the work gets done.'

They crossed the corridor into another large airy room with a huge desk, two chairs and numerous cardboard and wooden boxes stacked in rows. Only one surface lay uncovered and that was a new looking table with an office chair tucked underneath it.

'You have arrived at exactly the right moment, Nicola. A computer and printer are due to arrive from a hotel down the road. They are updating their systems and we are going to benefit. Even better, the hotel is covering all our computer costs for two years.'

Sister Benny beamed at Nicola.

'Stephen is coming with the computer and he's going to install it and get it going and you will be the first person to use it. Does Microsoft and Windows sound familiar? Good. Now,' said Sister Benny throwing open a large walk-in cupboard. 'Here are my filing cabinets but they are as yet unused as I just can't seem to give up on my boxes. Gellie tried to set up a system when she was here but she didn't have enough time to get it going. Here are her notes.'

Nicola was handed a file of paper covered in Gellie's familiar scrawl and smiled at the drawings in the margin. Secretly, having firsthand knowledge of Gellie's 'filing', Nicola thought it might be better to start again from scratch.

'Right, shall we get going?'

'I think I'd better read through these notes first. Then if we could have a chat about your box system, I can get down to trying to devise a system we can both work with,' suggested Nicola surprised at how in control she sounded.

'Wonderful,' came the reply surrounded by a beaming smile. 'And in the afternoon, we'll visit the classrooms and you can meet the children and their teachers. They all know you've arrived.'

With that the door swung shut with a clump as Sister Benny sailed forth to address the rest of her day. Nicola pulled out the office chair and sat down at the table. She opened Gellie's file. At first glance she couldn't understand a word so she walked over to Sister Benny's filing system and started looking at the labels on the boxes. There was a hesitant knock on the door. Nicola walked over and pulled the door open to stare straight at yet another box. A voice from behind the box announced that it was Stephen and that this was the first part of the computer delivery.

'I wasn't expecting you quite so soon,' exclaimed Nicola.

'The new computers arrived early from Mombasa and we need the space,' replied a lilting African voice. 'The manager asked me to bring this over today and to do the installation. Is it OK?'

Pleased to have a diversion even though she had hardly started, Nicola stood to one side as Stephen staggered in.

'Phew,' said Stephen wiping his brow, 'Thanks. You must be Nicola. Welcome to Africa and welcome to Watamu.' He held out his hand. Smiling, Nicola shook hands.

From then on Nicola did not get a word in edgeways as Stephen gave her his life history, the convent's life history and his views on global economies about which he was an expert having studied Business and Management at Manchester Uni two years before. Having confirmed that Sister Benny would like Excel downloaded, for the new accounting system, Nicola mentioned that she was hoping to go to Newcastle Uni the following year.

'Ah well,' said Stephen, 'You must meet the marine biologists when they come back in the autumn. They come to the Field Centre for a couple of months to do research in the marine reserve. Some of them are environmental scientists as well. Nice crowd.'

Nicola let that one slide by and soon they were on to internet access and programme installation. Sister Benny was obviously a person who could charm people into helping her.

'There,' said Stephen straightening up and packing discs into his briefcase. 'All done. Your system is ready to rock and roll. I'll just pop in and tell Sister B on my way out. Nice to meet you, Nicola. See you again soon.' And with that he was gone.

Phew, thought Nicola and sat down in front on the screen. She was about to see if she could log onto her email account when Sister Benny breezed in.

'So you met Stephen. Nice lad. Came to school here you know before he went on to High School on a scholarship. Said he'd drop by if we have any problems and he sounded like he might like you to find some.' Sister Benny's eyes twinkled. 'Now a few things have come up and I'm needed in the Clinic. Are you all right on your own? Any problems ask Anna. She's here all day.' With that she was gone.

Nicola turned back to the computer and found two new messages in her in box. She almost opened the one from her mother first but chose Maggie's instead.

Jambo – I've been researching East Africa but there isn't much info on Watamu so you must tell me everything. Mum is over compensating for losing you by taking a sudden interest in my art work, even talking about me going to college! Talking to my art teacher about my portfolio too! It is all a bit too full on as I can't leave school until after GCSEs. My dream would be to leave school and work for Gellie full time but she says I would be more use to her if I'd been to art college first. Is it really creepy being surrounded by nuns? Are you doing lots of praying and if so say some for me. I need all the help I can get! Gellie and Bundle send their love. Maggie xx

Nicola smiled as she read Maggie's email missing her little sister. She would reply later and clicked on her mother's email.

My Dearest Nicola,
Hope you're settling into your new home. We had a message from Sister Benedicta, sorry, Sister Benny, via Gellie, saying that you'd arrived safely. I hope your decision to go to Newcastle was not made on the spur of the moment, that it was the right one and that Africa is proving worthwhile. I do know that you have always been interested in helping people ever since you were little. That's why I always thought you'd make a very good doctor. Dad sends his very best love and says remember not to drink the water. Bottled only. We all miss you. Looking forward to hearing from you very soon. All my love Mum x

Nicola looked up from the computer screen and sighed. Suddenly it all seemed so far away. The Convent's calming rhythm was beginning to soothe her broken heart. Hoping that Sister Benny was not going to shoot through the door, Nicola composed a reply.

Dear Everyone (Everyone was going to read it and that would mean she could keep it fairly light and not delve too far into deep and meaningfuls)

Hello from Africa! Or 'Jambo' as everyone says round here. It seems like I've been here ages because it is soooo different to home. No I'm not surrounded by nuns, Maggie. There are two kinds here – the enclosed nuns who stay in the convent and pray and sing (beautifully!) and then those who combine a contemplative life with an active one and who work in the orphanage, the school and the clinic. It is really quite difficult to tell who is a proper nun and who isn't because some dress like nuns, some have bits of nun dress like covering their hair and then there are those who are sort of nuns but have never taken their vows. Sister Benny tried to explain it all but I haven't quite got it yet. She's a really lovely person. She's definitely a nun who works on the outside but she has to play her part on the inside as well. But as she pointed out this is Africa and therefore several adaptations have had to be made in order for the convent, orphanage and all to work together to achieve God's wishes. So it isn't like a convent as we know it. But it is a very happy place. The kids are very smiley and I get to meet them this afternoon. No one is stressed even though life is very basic. If your school wants to do fundraising for good causes, Maggie, this is a definite candidate. I don't go into the convent. The chapel is as far as I've been allowed. Sister Benny's office is at the front of the main building which I would describe as tatty colonial but I would hate her to hear me say that! Her bookkeeping skills are far worse than Gellie's which I didn't think possible so I'm going to start by organising everything to do with accounts into a new system we can all understand. That is task number one. Then I have to sort out the charities who support the orphanage. I may be some time! But you know me I love to make order out of chaos.

I live in a makuti hut which means it has a palm thatch. I will take loads photographs to show you when I get back so that you can see exactly what it is like. I have my own primitive 'en suite', a chest of drawers and a bed with a mosquito net. The floor is covered with mats made from woven palm leaves, more makuti – see I'm learning the language - which I share with some very large insects which everyone has assured me are harmless. There are geckos who live behind the crucifix, green crickets sticking on the walls, bats in the roof and toads in the drains. So it is pretty crowded. There are four huts in this group. Next door is Sister Mina who is a nurse. She shares with Sister Aurelia who is away on a retreat at the moment. Then there is Mary, who teaches and is quiet and religious then Sarah and Katrina. They are all very friendly and kind so I'm being well looked after. I haven't dared enquire whether there is any night life round here! Watamu is a holiday resort but the convent is like on a different planet. But Stephen, who comes and helps with computer stuff, told me that a group of research students will be back at the Field Centre at the marine reserve next month. I think there are the ones from Newcastle Uni that Professor Boyd told me about so hopefully, I can get in touch with them.

Honestly, I want you all to know that I am really happy here. I have put all my

recent problems into perspective and I am ready to get on with the next part of my life. Julian was an amazing person
(Nicola paused to let two tears one from each eye slowly make their way down her cheeks. She was relieved that they were not part of the email.)
…who I will always remember with joy but he has gone out of my life (two more tears filled her eyes) *and I would not be doing his memory justice if I moped around thinking what if. He loved this place and he would have been here now so I'm doing my best to fill the enormous gap and trying to do some good. And it is working for me so please do not worry. I am not going to do a runner. I will be back in the summer ready to go to uni.*
I miss you all and Bundle. Lots of love Nicola xxxxx

Nicola sent the email and looked round. Where to start was problem number one. She rang Sister Benny's little bell and Moses stuck his head round the door.

'Moses, please can you help me move the filing cabinets over here and line them up against the wall. Then I think my desk will have to shift to this side so that we can get to the files without walking round my desk.'

'Yes Ma'am,' replied Moses rolling up his sleeves.

'And it's Nicola not Ma'am. Ma'am makes me feel ancient,' said Nicola.

'Yes, Miss Nicola,' Nicola gave up and started moving boxes to make way for the filing cabinets. Towards the middle of the afternoon, Anna came to enquire how things were going.

'Fine,' replied Nicola wiping the sweat from her forehead.

'Anything you need to know?' asked Anna.

'That tree in the middle of the courtyard is a bit creepy. It feels like it is looking at me. It's half dead anyway. Why doesn't someone cut it down?'

'That tree has been there forever. Sister Benny would love to chop it down but Moses won't hear of it. So it stays. Now, the children are waiting to meet you.'

Nicola was rather shocked to find them all lined up on parade under the ancient looking tree. Sister Benny appeared on cue and introduced Nicola and told them that she had come to visit from England where Manchester United play football. A ripple of approval ran thought the ranks. Six kids were invited to shake Nicola's hand to welcome her and then they broke into a gloriously lilting song in Swahili. Being African they swayed gently to the rhythms and clapped their hands in time. Nicola was so impressed. At the end of the song a group could contain themselves no longer and crowded round her shyly telling her their names.

'Here is your reading group for your first month,' explained Sister Benny. Eight eager children crowded round her shouting questions.

'Are you married?' 'Do you have children?' 'Can you play football?' 'What is England like?'

Sister Benny raised one hand and they hung their heads and fidgeted with their reading books.

'Good. I'm sure Nicola will answer all your questions presently. You are here to read with her so let's get started.'

Nicola sat down under the tree and her charges arranged themselves around her. Sister Benny smiled encouragingly and walked back to her office. The rest of the children had returned to their classrooms and Nicola could make out a restless sea of small dark heads tightly packed in rows moving with the low murmur of repetition. Every now and again one or two would peer out at her reading group eager to know what was going on.

The days slipped past as Nicola immersed herself first in Sister Benny's filing system and then, using the knowledge she'd gained from working with Gellie's Oliver, in establishing procedures she hoped Sister Benny would be able to use and understand. The light relief was reading stories to the nursery class and then working with her reading group in the shade of the ancient tree. She chose 'Wind in the Willows' as her first book but progress was slow as the children found it difficult to imagine a toad driving a motor car and kept asking her to explain how Toad did that. Nicola lost her haunted look, she put on weight, her skin gradually became lightly tanned and she started to find peace with herself. Maggie sent endless amusing emails and her mother carefully worded ones. Kate, who was somewhere in Australia, just couldn't imagine Nicola in Africa. 'If you are still there in April,' Kate emailed, 'I'll come home that way and track you down.'

At the beginning of October it was still warm and sunny. Nicola decided she didn't miss the English autumn one little bit. The accounts filing was going really well. She'd completed the historical records and moved onto current accounting activity. There weren't many regular donations. There was the odd legacy and monies from fundraising events in England and Ireland and, of course, payments from the Catholic diocese. But there was one regular payment which came in every quarter referenced CW 69519307. After about an hour's search in Sister Benny's files Nicola found the source. Charlie Willstone had been making regular payments to the Orphanage since May 1981.

That is just so generous, thought Nicola. And hardly in character. She wondered if he was trying to buy himself a place in heaven and then felt guilty at having such inappropriate thoughts.

Searching through Sister Benny's files had also uncovered some boxes hidden at the back of a cupboard and one afternoon curiosity got the better of her and she pulled one out and opened it up. There was a collection of neatly bound registers tied up with red ribbon. Thinking they must be old registers of attendance from the school, she was about to put the lid back on the box when a title on one caught her attention. 'The Book of Lost Souls' Nicola whispered to herself and sat down with the book on her desk in front of her. She was about to untie the ribbon when the door opened and Anna stuck her head round.

'There are some people to see you, Nicola. Shall I show them in?' said Anna glancing at the red ribbon on the desk and the about to be opened register.

Without stopping to wonder who had come to see her as she'd never had visitors before, Nicola hastily placed the book back in the box and the box in the cupboard. The room was a bit of a mess.

'I'll come with you, Anna,' Nicola replied. 'Who are they? Why do they want to see me?'

By the time Nicola had finished speaking, she'd reached the hall and was greeted by four faces all smiling hellos.

'Hi Nicola. Sister Benny said we'd find you here. I'm Joe. We're Newcastle Uni students and we've just arrived back at the Field Centre for a month's research in the marine park. Prof. Boyd said we should get in touch.'

Joe grinned very appealingly at Nicola who was completely taken aback.

'Hey,' said Joe 'Stephen said he told you all about us.'

'Yes, yes,' said Nicola 'He did. I just wasn't expecting you to turn up like this. It's really very nice as I don't know many people, you know students like me, here. In fact I don't know any.' She finished rather lamely.

'Well there are twenty of us in total. All the Prof's students. Some are final year, like us, but we also have a couple of PhD students, two post docs, and some American exchange students so a real mixed bag. How about joining us for a pizza? I'll pick you up around seven tomorrow. Sister Benny says it's fine in case you're worried.'

Nicola felt rather small at the last comment. She was nineteen after all and Sister Benny didn't have to mother hen her. She smiled at Joe.

'That sounds really great,' she said. 'Thank you.'

'See you then,' smiled Joe as they slouched out of the door. Nicola stared after them. 'Wow,' she muttered 'Talk about the unexpected,' and went back to her office. The cupboard door was firmly closed but Nicola was sure she'd left it open. She looked in and saw that the box she'd been delving into when Anna had come into the office had gone.

Sister Benny was all smiles the next day as though she'd pulled off some sort of coup.

'It'll be nice for you to get out with young people your own age,' she said, 'sometimes life here, if you're not one of the community, can get claustrophobic. And sometimes we forget that those of us who have not taken vows need to connect with life outside. So go and enjoy yourself. Make new friends, they are a nice bunch. Last time they were here they came over once a week to take some of the children swimming. One thing though.'

Nicola looked worried. Please, please not a curfew. That would be so embarrassing.

'Please bring me a take-away cheese and chilli pizza and don't tell anyone,' and with that Sister Benny disappeared to talk to the gardener.

On Wednesday afternoon, Nicola was consumed with the problem of what to wear, reflecting rather sadly that she hadn't had much experience of pizza nights out. She tried to remember what they had been wearing when Joe and his mates turned up so unexpectedly. Jeans, it must have been jeans because everyone wears jeans. Hers were rolled up under her bed as she found them a bit too hot and sticky for Africa. She pulled them on and was shocked to find that she couldn't do the zip up. She knew she'd put on weight recently, good plain honest food and no exercise must have done it. Maybe she could borrow a bicycle and go down to the beach for a swim. That would soon shift the unwanted weight. Eventually she settled on the combats and white shirt. The convent laundry meant that she never had a pile of dirty clothes on the floor of her hut.

Nicola had been surprised to find that there was no evening in Africa. Night followed day as easily as moving from one room to another or in the time it took her to walk from her hut to the main gates. The night watchman had just arrived and was closing the gates as Joe roared up on a motorbike. 'Hey, sorry about the transport but the others have the minibus,' he said as the bike swerved to a stop. 'Have you ridden on the back of one of these before? You haven't?' Joe swung his leg over. 'Just hop on behind me and hang on for dear life.'

Seeing Nicola's face he laughed and told her was only joking. 'I have passed my test,' he told her.

There was, of course neither sight nor sign of any helmets or protective gear, so Nicola just did her best to hop on like it was something she did every day. She wondered what her mother would think if she knew she was on a motorbike with a bloke she had only just met, riding along a dirt road without a helmet. She giggled. Actually this was fun.

'About five minutes,' shouted Joe as he revved up the engine and they roared off but not very far as the road was full of people and animals and with no street lights, Joe had to wind a very tortuous route into the main street in Watamu where, to Nicola's surprise, there was a western looking pizza restaurant.

It was a thoroughly good night out for Nicola. Once Joe had introduced her and told them she would be joining the department the following year, Nicola felt she had been accepted as one of them, a student already, and she was surprised to find that she actually understood some of the research projects especially the ones with a chemistry bias. By the end of the evening she'd been invited to go bird ringing at night on Mida creek, to watch a turtle nest hatch and to visit the Arabuko-Sokote Forest.

'We only have a month here to carry out our field work,' explained Joe, 'so we work hard and play hard and go back to Newcastle for a rest.' Everyone laughed. 'Then we try and come back again in June after our exams. But I guess you'll be gone by then. But if you're still around maybe we can give you a project to keep an eye on for us.'

The party didn't break up until the owner started sweeping round their feet and they were halfway out of the door when Nicola remembered the pizza. She turned round to find that Joe already had the box. 'Don't worry,' he said, 'It's a standing order for Sister Benny.'

The only light at the convent gates was the watchman's lantern. In the dark Nicola gave Joe her mobile number and he promised to remember it and give her a call very soon.

'Thank you for this evening, Joe. I really enjoyed meeting everyone and it was so good to talk seriously for a change.'

'My God, I hope we didn't bore you to death. We are quite wound up in our research when we're out here.'

'No, no, it was great. I mean it. I know now that I have absolutely chosen the right course to do at uni and I would like to help with projects out here, if I could. I mean if you'd like me to.'

'Only so long as they are not Ludo's. He is so lazy.' With that Joe waved his hand and shot off down the road. Nicola, standing clutching a pizza box, watched him go thinking the test Joe took must have had a very low pass mark and that he probably took it in Watamu last week.

As she pushed open the gate the watchman stirred in his hut and came towards her.

'Thank you, Miss Nicola. I'll take the pizza to Sister Benidicta.'

Well that solved the delivery problem thought Nicola. She smiled at the thought of Sister Benny being unaware that so many people knew about her midnight pizza feasts. But no, on reflection, Sister Benny was just playing the game.

The pizza was not mentioned the next day when Nicola explained her latest spreadsheet to Sister Benny and Anna. At least we're making progress, she thought as Anna caught on immediately and offered to start putting some of the cardboard box records onto computer files. 'Then we can test the systems,' Anna said as she selected a box and hurried off with it. Sister Benny stood up and stretched.

'Sister, can I ask you something?' Sister Benny sat down again and looked quizzically at Nicola.

'I mean it may sound stupid but why are the convent gates open all day so that anyone can come and go but at night they are locked and guarded? I ask because churches are open all the time, aren't they? So why not a convent? And why the locks as well as a night watchman?'

Sister Benny sat very still for a moment and looked at Nicola.

'Well, there are a great many people in Africa who have nothing and the temptation to take what they need when they are desperate is very great. I expect you've noticed that many of the buildings here are protected by gates and high wire fences. But as you so very rightly say we are a house of God and therefore should be open at all times to welcome his people and to do his work. However I do have to be realistic. We run an orphanage and there have been times, and there still are, despite our efforts, when newly born babies have been abandoned at our gates. A newborn's place is with its mother and we make every effort to keep the two together when we are asked to take them in. It is very unfortunate when we do not have the opportunity to do that as many of my lost souls have died as a result of being dumped when no one was around. Hence the locked gates and the night watchman and it has made a difference. Now does that answer your question?' Sister Benny got up to leave.

'Yes, thank you Sister. I understand now,' Nicola smiled and tuned back to the computer screen. Those words 'lost souls' had made her remember the disappearing register and she made a mental note to have a rummage in the cupboard when she was on her own.

With everything being different, getting used to Africa, the food, the people, convent life, time seemed to whizz by with each day creating its own challenges from computer technology to surviving in this strange but fascinating country. Nicola mused within her thoughts as she sat in the old cane chair in her favourite spot on the veranda outside her hut. From there she could just see across the courtyard towards the main convent building but the view was partly obscured by the large gnarled tree standing alone in the centre of the courtyard. She asked Anna again about the tree because it looked like it might topple over if there was a storm.

Anna told her that no one could touch the tree because it had magical powers.

'It's a Baobab but it is also a Tree of Forgetfulness and it has stood there for hundreds of years. Before slaves were shipped off to Europe or America the men were made to walk round the tree nine times and the women seven times to make them forget their names, their family and the life they once had. So the memories of hundreds of people are stored in the branches.' Anna's voice dropped to a whisper. 'Now we believe that Arit Jinn, mischievous spirits, live in the tree and look after the memories. They could get very angry if the tree was chopped down and they were made homeless. Jinn are held responsible for all sorts of bad luck and the way to avoid their mischief is to dose yourself in lemon grass, myrrh, frankincense or sandalwood. Anything so long as it smells pleasant. Arit Jinn hate that.'

Being all seeing and all knowing, the Arit Jinn stirred in the Tree of Forgetfulness. They had idly watched the young English girl and kept watch as she moved around the convent. Now she was asking questions; she knew of their existence; she knew people who had a long association with the convent and the jinn had had some relevant memories to play with. It could get interesting especially if they could make mischief.

The sun was setting behind the clinic where a young local girl was about to give birth. Nicola had watched the family arrive in a slow procession earlier in the afternoon and now they were all hunkered down by the main doors waiting for news. Darkness soon wrapped itself round the convent buildings and the day shift swapped with the night. It was never completely quiet and still within the compound, mirroring the continual uncomfortable restlessness that is Africa.

It was now nearly the end of October and the last month had been so completely different that Nicola found it hard to think about what she'd been like when she arrived. The sea change had occurred with the arrival of the research students from Newcastle. Somehow Nicola had slipped easily into their company and they had opened up a whole new world that she had no idea existed. For a start she hadn't needed to 'qualify' for entry into this group. Tightly knit, yes, but so diverse in their interests, personalities and backgrounds that everyone was welcome provided they could voice an opinion or declare deep knowledge. There was none of the intellectual competition or sexual pressures that she had found so difficult when with Jocelyn Willstone and her friends in the Cotswolds. That seemed so far away now. Was it because of Sister Benny, who everyone seemed to hold in high regard, or was it, well, was it, whatever? Nicola decided she would probably never know. But for whatever reason was no longer important. She was included in discussions about field work which all the students took very seriously. It was their one opportunity to test theory and to gather data before returning to uni to work on the next stage of their research. Outside the study framework, they all made the most of being in East Africa.

Several evenings a week Nicola would visit the Field Study Centre down beside the beach and share a meal of local African dishes with whoever was around. The research laboratory was adjacent to the centre so people could wander in an out at will. The covered flat roof with gorgeous views over the ocean was the main meeting area where they would discuss all manner of subjects well outside of their scientific remit with great intensity and obvious enjoyment. Nicola had been particularly fascinated by the previous evening's debate about the Egyptian king, Amenhotep IV who renamed himself Akenaten, and who replaced the sun god, Ra, with a deity visible only to himself and sacked 1500 priests. One of the students, who was a serious Egyptologist in his spare time, declared that modern politicians could learn a great deal from this behaviour likening Akenaten's 1500 priests to the staff on Capitol Hill in Washington. This of course prompted a long and heated argument. It massaged her brain and delighted her soul and she sparkled in a way that was not lost on Joe. This was her dream. Forget massive parties, music festivals and fashion. Nicola had found her Shangri-La on a beach in Kenya and she felt herself grow stronger and more confident.

At the weekends Nicola joined trips to explore the Arabuko-Sokoke Forest where they climbed tree platforms and walked the 260m suspended boardwalk through mangroves on Mida Creek. Not her favourite, Nicola decided. She found the mangroves a bit creepy especially when the tide sucked and pulled at the mangrove roots like Maggie trying to get the last drop out of her milkshake with a straw. Joe was working on the marine turtle conservation programme and one night he took her to watch green turtles hauling themselves out of the ocean and up the beach to dig nests in the sand and lay their eggs. Very carefully they sat down on the sand beside a mother turtle that was covering her eggs with rhythmic sweeps of her paddles. The turtle's eyes were open but empty as if she was dreaming about being back in a more normal environment swooping and turning between fish and coral and away from the tedious job of burying her eggs.

'She never sees her babies,' explained Joe. 'She lays her eggs, covers them up and her job is done. If we stay long enough we will see her make her way back to the ocean. All these little guys running past us to the sea have done it all on their own.'

Nicola put her hand on the damp sand and a tiny turtle struggled over it and headed onwards. Peering through the darkness, once her eyes had got used to the night, Nicola could see baby turtles everywhere.

'They will spend three weeks swimming on the surface before their lungs are developed enough to dive,' explained Joe. 'That is when they are very vulnerable to attack. It's like Nature has been peppering the sea with Smarties and all the creatures that can see them are going to come over and feast. You can see why so few turtles make it to big turtles.'

And so Joe and Nicola sat companionably on the damp sand surrounded by big turtles, little turtles and turtle eggs. The moon was sinking and the sky was changing colour in anticipation of a new day. The sand looked white where the moon had carved a track up to the mother turtle. Small waves dragged the white path back and forwards across the sea. Nicola shivered. What did the moon see that she could not. Somehow she felt that some bit of her was being pulled away into the ocean and she wanted it back. Whatever it was Nicola did not want to let go. She shook her head to get rid of the panic.

'Cold?' asked Joe. Concerned he put his arm round her shoulder. Nicola shivered again. It was only a friendly gesture but was it? It was all really confusing.

Beside them the mother turtle, satisfied that her eggs were buried and safe from predators, heaved herself out of the pit she had dug. It was a supreme effort by a creature not built for mountaineering but now her eyes were focused and she looked ahead at the ocean even when she paused for a brief rest.

'Look,' said Joe pointing at the far horizon. The darkness was being pushed away by the rising light in the east.

'The sun will be up in a minute. We'll stay and watch that and then I'll take you back. You just have to have an African sunrise moment because it is actually Nut, the Egyptian goddess of the night, giving birth to the sun having swallowed it up the previous evening at sunset.'

As they watched sunrise, Nicola thought the Egyptians had probably got it about right. With one last heave over the sand and into the surf the turtle made it back to her ocean.

And that was last week. On Monday the students left to go back to Newcastle. Nicola assured Joe that she had filled in her UCAS form before she'd left home and that her mother had promised to send it back to her old school for her headmistress' report. On Tuesday afternoon Nicola walked along the beach past the Field Studies Centre. Even though the manager gave her a cheery wave and offered her a mango juice, it felt empty and forlorn. They would be back again in June next year, they said and would get in touch if she was still in Watamu. If not they would all be looking out for her in Fresher's Week the following October. Email addresses and mobile numbers were exchanged and Joe gave her a kiss on both cheeks and told her to take care.

Nicola shifted slightly in the old cane chair and dragged her thoughts back to the present. It was still very dark on the veranda as she searched her inner mind as to what she thought about Joe. She had spent a great deal of time with him. He was a kind, gentle, thoughtful soul who had not tried to come on to her. There had been the occasional touch, a hand over a fence or to steady on a rickety bridge, an arm to keep her warm on the beach. Nothing more, nothing less. Still raw with the memories of Julian, Nicola decided she would not want it any other way.

The lights suddenly got brighter in the Clinic and a thin high scream carved through the darkness and hit Nicola hard. The shapes huddled around the Clinic main door shifted anxiously rearranging themselves in different patterns. Two figures rushed over from the convent carrying bags and the whole place seemed to be alert but quiet, watching and waiting in a tangible tensile form. Even the Tree of Forgetfulness seemed to be paying attention. Nicola stood up and felt the next scream hit her full on. She sat down suddenly and went cold as she started to think very seriously. She had been so careful to lock herself away where nothing would ever touch her again; nothing would hurt her; nobody would be allowed close. Now reality was pacing round her head picking up bits of information and clicking them together into a chain. It was only a matter of time before the chain would form a circle of knowledge. It would not go away however hard she tried. Reality was rattling at the door demanding entry, demanding to be heard. Nicola gave in. Her last period was before the May Ball. She had noticed she had not had one during her exams but she normally missed one when stressed. Then Julian died, more stress and she had lost interest in her life. But she had been sick quite regularly until she came to Africa and lost a lot of weight. Monica had noticed all this and told her it was normal to react to a crisis like failing to do well in exams with physical symptoms. Since she had been in Watamu, Nicola had stopped being sick and put on weight which she thought was all down to living in a lovely calm environment and happily enjoying her new life. Sex and dates ran round her head in a toxic mishmashed fruit machine until it came up trumps. Four strawberries; she was pregnant.

'Idiot. Idiot,' she said to herself half out loud. Nicola Grace Cowan was five months pregnant and the father, Julian Edward Smith Owen, was dead. This was the biggest mess she had ever been in.

Suddenly Nicola heard that special baby cry as another soul joined the world in Watamu. The group of anxious relatives moved to the door and were ushered in by one of the nurses. There was a gentle murmur of relieved voices and an aura of calm descended over the convent apart from on Nicola's veranda where she was anything but calm and serene. She needed Jamie to help her but Jamie was not going to suddenly materialise in darkest Africa. She decided to write to him.

Dearest Jamie,
I know I always ignore you until there comes a time when I need you. Well, I need you desperately now. I am working in a convent in Africa and I am pregnant. Julian is the father and he's dead. I am on my own in this. I can't have an abortion because this is a Roman Catholic convent and this is Africa. I suppose I could always try to find a witch doctor. But the staff at the clinic are always talking about what witch doctors do and some of their work ends up here. Many women die as a result of the witch doctor's administrations. I can't go home because my parents would kill me and make me have the baby adopted. I can hear them telling me I've ruined my life and what would their neighbours say and the effect on Dad's practice. Only one option left. To have the baby here and then go home with a fait a compli. I'm sure that somehow I could still go to uni and take the baby with me and get a part time job. Newcastle is far enough away from rural Gloucestershire and the gossip mongers.
The one big 'if' in all this is Sister Benny. She might throw me out onto the streets. Probably not as that wouldn't be a very Christian thing to do. The worst thing she could do is send me home.

A shiver ran down her back as though someone had gently stroked her neck and let a hand run down her spine. A sudden certainty hit her with a strange force of resolution.

I will keep the baby. It is all I have left of Julian and I couldn't throw that away. He wouldn't want me to.

Nicola put down her pen and sat back feeling an awful lot better. The next step was how exactly she was going to tell Sister Benny and when. She couldn't sleep so just before dawn she crept out onto her veranda to watch the sunrise. Jamie was sitting in her cane chair so she had to sit cross legged on the ground.

'I got your letter,' he said.

They sat in silence.

'Is it the right thing to do? You know, keep the baby?' Nicola was whispering hoping no one could hear.

'What do you want to do?'

'I don't know. I've never had a baby. I don't know anyone with a baby so how do I know what to do?'

'Well you can hardly go to a witch doctor. God knows what would happen to you and Sister Benny would be bound to find out and then you would be in deep shit.'

'Thanks. I already know that. And don't tell me to go home because I just can't do that.'

'Well then have the baby and get it adopted.'

'We're in black Africa, Jamie, in case you hadn't noticed. What demand do you think there is for white babies round here?'

'Your decision then.' Jamie got up and strolled towards the Tree of Forgetfulness neatly sidestepping round the trunk just as Nicola thought he might climb into its branches.

Really, Jamie could be so unhelpful at times.

The Arit Jinn were over the moon. An imaginary friend had almost walked into their clutches. Life just didn't get any better than this. Their leader sighed. The imaginary friend would be useless without English girl's memories. That task was still on their 'to-do' list.

Later, Nicola was feeling positively brighter. The sun was shining, as it did most days, as she put the last details on the charities file on the computer. She asked Sister Benny to write a list of the queries she would most frequently ask about the status of a charity's commitments so that she could test her system. As it was such a lovely day, Sister Benny suggested a walk in her garden before it got too hot.

Sister Benny led Nicola through the door that led into the convent which opened out into a cloistered inner court. Nicola had never been this far into the convent itself and was amazed at the beautiful inlaid arabesque columns supporting the vaulted roof. The smell of the flowering bougainvillea matched the richness of the mosaic floor and the tinkling of the fountain added to the headiness of the atmosphere. Nicola gasped. She had no idea that all this was hidden behind the heavy mahogany doors. Sister Benny smiled.

'Sister Eugenie and Sister Ignatius look after this garden. You won't have met them. In fact you will never meet them because they are part of the enclosed order. All the nuns are at prayer which I why I can bring you through here. It is lovely, isn't it? It had all gone to wrack and ruin before Sister Eugenie arrived. It has been her mission to restore it. She spent a long time researching how it should look and I think the results of her work are amazing. It has had such a positive effect on those in our community who never step outside the convent. But come with me and let me show you my kitchen garden.'

They walked companionably through a door on the other side of the garden and out to the small farmyard strewn with hens of all shapes, sizes and breeds.

'That's Chanticleer over there,' said Sister Benny pointing at a highly colourful cockerel standing proud over a rather dowdy harem. 'I expect he's guilty of waking you up in the mornings just as it is getting light.'

Moses was struggling out of a pen with an armful of straw and gave them a cheery wave. Sister Benny pushed open a small gate in a palm fence.

'This is my garden,' said Sister Benny as they settled themselves on a bench surrounded by gently waving lemon grass. 'This is where I escape to in times of stress and to find my mojo as one of my children explained to me yesterday. I'm not sure what that means but I have a fair idea. I love my vegetables. I love watching tiny seeds grow into useful plants that will feed my community.'

Sister Benny gazed out over her garden. 'Unquestioning faith enables the catholic church to continue undisturbed. I question that faith in Africa. I have learned that every question is worth asking even if the answer is not immediately obvious. Faith teaches you all the answers but it doesn't point out that some of those answers might be wrong.' Realising that she was talking more to herself than to Nicola, she glanced sideways and as there was no reaction, they sat together in a gentle silence entirely at peace. At least Sister Benny seemed to be at peace but Nicola sensed a growing unease.

'Now,' said Sister Benny 'How are you settling in? I must say how pleased I am with all the work you have been doing for us. We have to rely so heavily on our charities I am delighted that we are beginning to look a bit more professional. I was wondering whether it would be possible for you to extend your stay by another two months so that you'd be here when I do my first round of fundraising letters?'

'Oh Sister Benny, I'd love to, I am so happy here,' replied Nicola, without really thinking about it. 'It is so peaceful after all the chaos of exams and getting into uni. I love Africa. I know it is poor and it's dirty and life is hard but everything you do here is so rewarding.'

Sister Benny smiled. 'Is there anything else?'

At this point Nicola cracked and two tears burst from her eyes and ran down her cheeks. Sister Benny leant over and took Nicola's hand. She smelt of mothballs, kindness, security and lemon grass and Nicola knew she had reached a point of no return.

'I think I'm pregnant, Sister. No, I'm sure I am. Julian Smith Owen is the father and he isn't here anymore and I don't know what to do. I can't go home and you probably won't want me here any longer but I do want to have Julian's baby because it is all I have left. If he was still alive I know we would get married and everything would be fine but he isn't and it's not.' It all came out in a rush.

'My child,' said Sister Benny, 'You're not the first person to sit here with a story like this to tell and you probably won't be the last. I did have my suspicions but I felt that you had not realised your predicament and I was waiting for you to come to me. So this is not a shock to me and I am prepared. You are very welcome to stay and have your baby here if that is what you want. But think carefully about this. Your parents should know what has happened and even though you will expect them to be very hard and judgemental don't be so sure that that is how they will react. They may want you to come home so that you can all get through this as a family and it will bring you so much closer together. And you don't have to decide right now. We still have a little time before you won't be able to fly home. How many months do you reckon you are?'

'About five, I think,' replied Nicola. 'Oh Sister. I was thinking about this last night when I finally had to admit to myself I was pregnant. You know, I went through all the missing periods and things which I put down to Julian's death and my awful exam results and being sick which I thought was stress. You must think I'm really dumb and stupid. And I don't want to tell my parents, not yet anyway. And I would like to have the baby here in Africa because Julian lived in Kilifi and it just seems to be so right.'

'Nicola, two things here are really important. You and your baby. If that is what you'd like then we will do our best to look after you. I remember Julian's birth. In fact although Caroline and Dermot were living in Kilifi, Julian was born here in the clinic. The Smith Owens have always been our greatest supporters right from the start.' Sister Benny paused and reflected on events all those years ago and the subsequent ones which had somehow led to her sitting in her vegetable garden with a young girl carrying a baby whose father had had such close ties with her convent. She recalled, in particular, sitting on the self same bench not long after Julian had been born, beside a young girl just a bit older than Nicola having heard a very similar story and telling this young girl that everything would be all right and she had been correct. This time, although the circumstances were slightly different, she had faith that she could engineer a satisfactory outcome.

'And, of course, you can't possibly leave at least until all the computer systems are in place! I can't do without you which is a very selfish thought on my part. Now, action stations. We must visit the clinic right now as the obstetrician is here today and I'd like her to see you.'

They both stood up and Sister Benny led the way out of the peace and security of her vegetable garden and back to reality. Nicola mused that the smell of lemon grass would never be the same for her again. As they crossed the courtyard the Arit Jinn carefully marked their progress noting that both Sister Benny and Nicola had been immersed in the lemon grass. That was not good news.

At the clinic Sister Benny introduced Nicola to Francine, the obstetrician from Medecins sans Frontieres and they sat down to discuss Nicola's medical history. There were quite a few gaps in the form where Nicola couldn't remember the facts but as they talked through her recent history, events previously unexplained began to fall into place along with the realisation that she was actually pregnant.

'You are in the second trimester and probably halfway through your pregnancy and you should feel your baby move. Have you felt anything yet?'

Nicola shook her head. Why is she asking me she thought? I've hardly got used to being pregnant, I've hardly got a bump which I thought was just fat anyway and I don't know what a baby moving should feel like.

'Right,' said Francine. 'I'm going to run through a load of tests and listen to the baby's heartbeat. Then I'll advise you on diet and supplements you should be taking. Don't worry, you'll be fine. You're young, strong and healthy just the way we like our Mums to be and I'm going to take great care of both of you.'

Both of you. Nicola suddenly realised that not only was she pregnant, she was going to have a baby. Something that she and Julian had made together was growing inside her. Keeping the baby would be a way of hanging on to Julian for a little longer.

An hour later, she walked out into the sunshine clutching a load of advice notes and feeling scared, elated and not quite herself all at once. Sister Benny was sitting under a baobab tree surrounded by a group of small children all laughing and trying to climb onto her knee. She shooed them off like small birds and she and Nicola walked back to Nicola's hut.

'Take the rest of the day off and relax,' Sister Benny advised her. 'By tomorrow everyone will know you're pregnant. It is impossible to have secrets here but they will all be delighted. Birth is an everyday occurrence but each one is treated as special.'

Nicola walked slowly into the cool of her hut and let a blank world wrap itself around her as she fell fast asleep.

Christmas came and went as a colourful mishmash of Christian solemnity and African exuberance. Her mother telephoned to say that an official unconditional offer for a place to read environmental science at Newcastle University had arrived and should she accept on Nicola's behalf? This was followed by a text from Joe congratulating her on getting a place. In spite of the euphoria of settling her future for the next three years at least, Nicola missed her family celebrations. She missed the early darkness, the cold, frosty mornings and the traditional family walk on Boxing Day. Presents arrived, presents were sent, cards exchanged but it was not quite the same as being there. It was difficult to keep her pregnancy a secret as Nicola was expanding rapidly round her middle. Everyone associated with the convent was very happy for her and the absence of any father which would have been so difficult for her parents was never a problem.

And so January moved to February without a single hard frost or snowflake in sight. Anna took Nicola to the market and together they chose some bright khanga trousers and loose tops which made Nicola feel more comfortable. From some angles it was hard to tell that she was pregnant so Nicola sent some photographs home so that everyone could see how well and happy she was. Maggie emailed to say that the parents had finally given in and that she going to leave school after her GCSEs and go to art college. She was still working for Gellie helping her with a new project designing a *Gelliebabies* range, part of which would be her main art work for her college portfolio. How ironic thought Nicola. *Gellie's so pleased that she's thinking of actually doing a limited run to see how they sell in the shops!* emailed Maggie enthusiastically. *I saw the photos of you in your African outfits! Could you please send me some fabric samples as I have got a few ideas I'd like to try out? Maggie and Bundle* xx

It was the 10th of February and a lovely sunny day. By lunch time Nicola had a splitting headache just behind her eyes. It was impossible to look at the computer screen so she went to investigate a box of files Moses had put out for her. After about an hour of trying to concentrate, she gave up and told Anna she just had to go and lie down. Her hut was stifling making her feel nauseous so she put the fan on and lay down under the mosquito net. Too tired even to undress she fell asleep. Soon she was dreaming that she was walking through a blistering desert following a mirage, or was it? There was a figure dressed as an Arab in a white jubba over his dishdasha moving up over the dunes without leaving any footprints. She was getting hotter and hotter but she wanted to catch up with the figure hoping he had some water. There was no one else around.

Nicola was aware of someone standing beside her. She forced her eyes open and tried to focus in the gloom. It was Anna.

'How are you feeling Nicola? You weren't at supper so I've brought you some soup and a jug of water. Here I'll put them down beside your bed. You OK?' Anna was looking anxiously at Nicola.

'I'm fine,' replied Nicola automatically. 'My headache isn't as bad but my back aches. Probably spent too much time sitting at the computer today. I'll be fine after a good night's sleep. Thank you for the soup and the water.'

'Would you like me to call someone from the clinic? You are pregnant after all. Perhaps someone should come and check on you?'

'I've got ages to go yet and honestly I'm fine. Just need to rest. I'll be back in the office tomorrow,' mumbled Nicola.

'Well if you're sure you're OK?'

Nicola nodded.

'Call if you feel any worse. Just shout, someone will hear. Good night. Sleep well.'

Anna closed the door softly behind her. Nicola returned to the desert. Her Arab had disappeared. Damn, if Anna hadn't come in she would probably have caught up with him and his water. But, wait a minute, Anna brought some water with her. It was probably just on the other side of the crescent shaped sand dune in front of her. She just had to walk in a straight line up to the top and she would find it. It was hot, very hot. She was wearing too many clothes. If she took her shirt off and then her bra and put her shirt back on she would be cooler. It was quite long, down to her knees so she could take her trousers off too and still not get burned by the sun. In fact it would be a good idea to wrap her cotton trousers round her head to protect her from the sun and she would be able to move more quickly without her trousers round her ankles. Fighting with her clothes was exhausting but she felt better. Not far to go really.

With a thump Nicola hit the floor by her bed. She burst into tears when she found that she was lying in a pool of water. She was no longer in the desert but she felt awful. Her headache was worse, her back ached and she felt a stabbing pain in her stomach when she fell. And now she had spilt the precious water all over the floor. Tears poured down her cheeks. All her energy had been consumed chasing up a sand dune that didn't exist. But somehow it felt that she had caught up with her Arab mirage and that he had enclosed her within his jubba and she felt secure and safe.

This is crazy thought Nicola trying to sit up and disentangle herself from her mosquito net. She was very hot and thinking straight just wasn't working. One thing at a time and the first was to stand up, properly. She put out her hand and found the edge of the bed. She moved her hand along the bed searching for the torch that she kept on her bedside table. In doing so she knocked over the jug of water that Anna had left earlier and she could not find the torch.

Crazier and crazier thought Nicola. She had already knocked over the water. She had been lying in it and now the rug underneath her was soaked through. Suddenly a wave of pain scorched through her back and she let out a scream. She sank to the floor wondering what on earth was going to happen next.

The door of her hut opened and a torch shone in her face.

'Holy Mary,' exclaimed a voice from the darkness behind the light. 'Nicola, speak to me. How did you fall out of bed? Is there a snake in here?' The torch light did a quick assessment of the situation. Quickly disentangling Nicola from her sheets and the mosquito net, Sister Mina dashed over to the door and called for help.

'Someone, anyone, get right over here to Nicola's hut with a stretcher.'

Several people arrived all at once and Sister Mina explained the situation.

'She has a fever, could be dengue as we've had several cases this week. But the big worry is that her waters have broken and she is in the early stages of labour.' Pause, more unwinding, Sister Mina tried to help Nicola back onto her bed. 'I haven't asked about contractions as I think she's delirious. She keeps muttering about an Arab and sand dunes. Rapid pulse and I think she is going to vomit. Is Francine still at the clinic?'

The door pushed wide open and more people surrounded Nicola who was still lying on the floor. Hands skillfully maneuvered her onto a stretcher and as they carried her out Francine bent over her.

'Nicola it's Francine. Listen carefully. You have a fever and you have gone into labour. There is nothing to worry about but you are going to have your baby and I will be with you every step of the way. Squeeze my hand if you understand.'

Nicola squeezed Francine's hand as the stretcher swung into the delivery room and she was laid out on the bed. A bright light made her screw up her eyes, a needle went into the back of her hand and a bag of liquid swung into view and then out again. Many hands took off her clothes and encased her in a rough gown and her legs were eased into stirrups. Another excruciating pain grabbed her spine and cascaded over her tummy while people talked in low voices somewhere else. Her body felt like it was a spit on a barbeque with the heat from the coals beneath her being sprayed with a lighter fuel of pain.

'You are 7cm dilated and I am going to give you a shot in your arm for the pain,' said Francine as Nicola drifted away back to the desert.

Francine stood back, worried. Nicola had been drifting in and out of consciousness and when she was there she was very confused. This wasn't going to be easy. She called her team together.

'I think our patient has dengue fever but I won't know for sure until I run some tests. More immediately the baby is going to arrive and we won't have much cooperation from the patient so prepare for a forceps delivery and get the emergency pack ready. This baby is a couple of weeks early so we may be dealing with a prem. And get Dr Adole the pediatric guy at Mombasa on the phone for me.'

The wind blew in disorganised circles round Nicola's legs. At times it threatened to drag her to the ground at other times it seemed to caress her with a distant voice telling her that everything was fine and that she was doing well. Doing well at what, thought Nicola. She was not doing anything except trying to stand up right, trying to work out where she was and why she could not see the stars. Deserts always have stars. Desert people navigate by stars so how was she going to find her way out of the desert without them? A cool hand smoothed her burning forehead. Nicola struggled to talk but her tongue, which now filled her mouth like a large lump of jelly, refused to let her make words. Sister Benny would want to know why she had not finished her project that afternoon when she had promised her that it would be ready.

With the next contraction she really felt pain and the weight of it caused her to sink into the soft sand and almost suffocate as it threatened to close over her face. Someone a long way away told her to breathe and through the sand she inhaled sweet fresh air. Then a baby's cry cut through the desert, whipping away the sand which had been such a problem and she was lying on a bed staring at this red baby yelling its arrival in the world.

'You have a lovely daughter, Nicola,' said Francine smiling behind her mask. Carefully she placed the naked newborn on Nicola's tummy where the baby snuffled lightly and then looked straight at her mother.

'Hello Julia,' muttered Nicola with her thick tongue and then fell back over a waterfall and into nothingness.

Francine took Julia in her arms, handed her to Sister Mina and turned back to Nicola. Sister Mina took a hard look and called Francine back. There were problems.

'Pulse weak, heart rate slowing. She's changing colour...' Sister Mina's voice drained away swamped by concern. Francine yelled for the intensive care crib and stabbed Dr Adole's number into her mobile.

Back at the convent, Sister Benny was sitting on her verandah in the darkness with a visitor. Their heads were close together deep in conversation. A shaft of light fell across the courtyard catching the Tree of Forgetfulness in one corner as a Sister glided across to Sister Benny. She spoke so urgently that Sister Benny jumped up, abandoned her visitor and rushed over to the clinic. Grateful that the light had included them in this turn of events, the Arit Jinn were all eyes and ears. They had caught a certain tension in the air between Sister Benny and her visitor.

Sister Benny found Francine on the phone.

'Yes, I'm coming in now with a very sick baby on a ventilator. Mum won't be travelling with us as she has dengue fever. Yes, I think the two could be related. You'll have everything ready? I don't want to lose this one. Bye.' Francine stuffed her mobile in her pocket. Moses was standing by with the Jeep's engine running and they ran out with the baby in her crib and roared off into the night.

Sister Mina noticed Sister Benny's arrival.

'I hear that there has been some drama tonight, Sister. How is our patient?' asked Sister Benny bending carefully over Nicola's face and stroking her brow.

'Drama indeed, Sister Benny,' replied Sister Mina. 'Nicola has dengue fever which probably started yesterday with her headaches. Francine thinks that may have prompted her labour which certainly wasn't helped by her falling out of bed. The baby was delivered safely but has developed heart problems and breathing difficulties so Francine has rushed off to Aga Khan Hospital in Mombasa where Dr Adole, whom she knows personally, is a consultant pediatrician. So little Julia will be in safe hands.'

Sister Benny nodded. 'And where did the name Julia spring from?'

Sister Mina smiled. 'From Nicola. We gave Julia to her like we do with all newborns and she touched her and said Julia before she lost consciousness again. Francine has given her some shots and we've put a drip up to make her more comfortable. Now it is the wait and see game. But she's young and healthy. Once we get her temperature down she will be up and about in no time. I'll be around all night to keep an eye on her.'

Sister Benny looked down at Nicola and sighed. 'It's what to do for the best that is the most difficult decision,' she muttered as she quietly closed the door behind her and headed silently towards the chapel.

The abandoned visitor finished his cup of coffee and standing up, smoothed his Arab robes and glided off towards the convent gates. The ever watchful Arit Jinn caught a glimpse of a shadow shivering along the walls of the makuti huts heading for the clinic. They knew who the shadow was, they knew where he was going, they just needed to find out why.

Nicola awoke in a hospital bed feeling very disorientated, battered and bruised. The room was dimly lit and so it must have been the middle of the night. Then suddenly she remembered, not everything, but quite clearly that she had had her baby. Julia, she had to find Julia. As she struggled to sit up somewhat impeded by the drips in her arms, the door opened and Sister Mina hurried over to her.

'Sister, where's Julia?' Nicola croaked though a very dry throat.

'Hush, my child,' said Sister Mina stroking Nicola's damp hair from her forehead. 'Julia arrived a little early and has a few problems breathing on her own. Francine and Moses have taken her to Mombasa so that she can have the very best care and come back to you very soon. I'm sorry we couldn't let you go with her you've got dengue fever and the hospital is very strict about infections. Your job now is to get better as soon as you can then you and Julia can be together.'

Tears rolled down Nicola's face. 'You know, Sister, I didn't want her at first. I sort of knew I was, well might be pregnant but I didn't believe it. I didn't want to believe it. I only started to want her or him or a baby, whatever, when I realised that it was all I had left of Julian. She will be alright won't she? She won't die because I didn't want her and ate all the wrong things and drank beer, will she?' Nicola's hoarse voice was reaching a panic level.

'Hush,' replied Sister Mina hugging Nicola close and reaching for a box of tissues. 'She'll be doing just fine. She's one of God's children and he takes care of his own. You'll see.' Sister Mina gave one of the drips an extra pump and Nicola fell asleep.

It was still dark when Nicola woke again. The convent's morning sounds had yet to stumble awake so it was a very quiet half light from a single bulb that greeted her. There was someone in the room. A figure was standing by the door dressed in a long black hooded robe. Nicola shifted slightly to get a better view and the figure moved forward towards her. Was it the Arab she saw in her dreams when she went into labour or was it merely Jamie playing tricks on her?

'Jamie, Jamie is that you?' whispered Nicola. She sank back against her pillows. Jamie had come to help her. Why had he dressed up as an Arab? Sister Benny would not object to her friends visiting her so there was no need for an elaborate disguise. The Arab drifted up and sat on the edge of her bed. A sunburnt hand reached out and stroked her sweating forehead with infinite care. Nicola still could not see a face and she tried to raise a hand to move the hood out of the way but her arm was weighed down with drips and other lines.

'Jamie, I'm in an even greater mess. I have dengue fever and I am strapped to this bed when I really should be with her, with Julia, and...' Nicola's voice choked on her tears which started to run endlessly down her cheeks and along her arms. The Arab brought out a large white cloth and mopped up the tears and the sweat together. The cloth smelt of goat and lemon grass and its rough texture grated on her skin. Suddenly the convent came to life as Chanticleer heralded in another day and the light became more day than night. The Arab started at the noisy intrusions. As smoothly as he entered her room he left, leaving Nicola with just a rather damp piece of once white cloth.

In another part of the convent, Chanticleer's morning salutations brought a nun to her feet in the chapel. She paused in front of the carved wooden crucifix and crossed herself.

'My God, my Redeemer, grant me the courage to change the things I can and the wisdom to know the difference.'

Giving herself a few moments of reflection, she continued:

'Oh my God, my Redeemer, behold me here at Thy feet. From the bottom of my heart I am sorry for the sin I am about to commit because by doing so I will deeply offend Thee who art infinitely good.'

Frankincensed out, Sister Benny tucked her rosary into her belt, rubbed her knees and headed out to face another unscripted day. Having been up all night this was going to be a very long day indeed and the first person to attend to was Nicola. The Arit Jinn had been up all night too watching the comings and goings at the clinic. Their eavesdropping in the convent chapel had confirmed their suspicions that they were on the edge of something very big indeed. All they needed was the detail and then they could settle down to some good honest scheming. The problem was that the English girl had no history and until she walked seven times round their tree, the Tree of Forgetfulness, they would not be able to access her memory. There was a problem with the lone figure dressed as an Arab. The Arit Jinn definitely recognised him but his mother's memories, which would have unlocked his identity and his history, were lost when the branch in which they had been stored broke off the tree in a storm.

Three days later, Nicola was well enough to sit in a chair on the veranda outside the clinic. She was exhausted and the news about Julia had not been good. She had not responded to treatment and Dr Adole was talking about flying her to Nairobi which would take her even further away. That was how Sister Benny found Nicola, wrapped in a blanket of misery and self condemnation, her eyes half closed to shut out the world.

'My dear,' said Sister Benny sitting down on a bench beside Nicola. 'Francine tells me your health is much improved and that you should be able to move back to your own accommodation very soon where we can still keep an eye on you. Not back to work just yet of course though we do all miss you.' Two tears slid down Nicola's cheeks but she said nothing. Francine had warned Sister Benny that this would not be easy, that Nicola's psychological health was very fragile and that she was in danger of sinking into a deep depression. Sister Benny however believed in straight talking her way out of all situations and was not to be deterred. We will of course look after her, nurse her back to health and keep her here as long as she feels she needs to stay in order to heal, Sister Benny told Francine. Francine gave a very French shrug of her shoulders as if to say well you are the boss; I will back you in what you are about to do.

'Nicola, I am really so sorry to have to say this. Things went very wrong for Julia last night and she lost her fight for life just before dawn. I have just been speaking with Dr Adole and they did all they could for her. She will be brought back here for burial and I'm sorry but it will be a sealed coffin. Those are the rules. Oh my dear, I am just so so sorry.' Nicola slumped forward into Sister Benny's arms and cried for her baby and her baby's father and for everything else. Never would she allow herself to be exposed to such huge amounts of pain, sorrow and suffering ever again.

Nicola made a good recovery from the fever. She attended her daughter's funeral held at sunrise in the Convent's small private graveyard with her pale face held high and remote. She scattered bougainvillea petals over the grave and stood by while Moses hammered in a simple wooden cross with 'Julia' burnt into its centre. Nicola walked out of the graveyard and back into her old life with mechanical strength. Privately she wrapped another layer of cling film tightly round her soul. At Sister Mina's suggestion she went to the Clinic every day to express milk for the orphaned babies which gave the nurses an excuse to keep an eye on her. But her heart wasn't in it and her milk soon dried up.

Every evening she curled up on her verandah and watched the sun go down on her life. The darkness was the worst bit. Her thoughts became entangled with her memories of Julian and the emptiness left behind by the loss of her baby. One particularly still evening as she waited for the moon to rise, a faint breeze rolled across the courtyard from the old tree. It caressed the back of her neck, whispered in her ear and teasingly pulled at wisps of her hair. And then it hit her. The grief from losing Julian compounded by Julia's death came from nowhere to consume her. There were no tears just a deep life defining moment when she recalled Julia snuffling on her tummy. Before the birth, Nicola simply did not stop to imagine what it would be like to have a baby once it had arrived. She had been completely unprepared for the tsunami of emotions that rocked through her fever ravaged body when she heard Julia snuffle. She'd crossed a line and Julian was not there to share the moments with her. Unsure of what to do next, Nicola stood up and made her way across to the Chapel where the sanctuary lamp reached out beckoning her. She had intended to go and pray for Julia's soul ever since her funeral but somehow never had because it would mean she really had gone. But tonight she was ready. Slowly she eased herself onto one of the rickety chairs stacked against the walls and gazed at the carved screen that separated the enclosed order from the outside world. The stations of the cross, muralled along both walls, had long succumbed to the high humidity and salt laden sea winds mutating them into a modern art form made ghostly by the single flickering light from the sanctuary lamp. The heavy incensed infused air made her feel slightly woozy. Really, it wasn't necessary to use so much incense; particularly frankincense which she'd been told was very expensive. A creepy sensation told her she wasn't alone even though a quick glance showed that she had the main body of the chapel to herself. Quietly she edged up to the screen and peered into the dimly lit sanctuary. A pile of old clothes appeared to have been left beside the altar. Just as she stretched to get a better view, the pile of clothes stood up, genuflected and was absorbed into the blackness of the archway leading into the convent. But not before Nicola had caught sight of Sister Benny's unmasked face. What she couldn't read in the nun's expression was enough to send her running back to her makuti hut. Curled up on the floor hugging her knees to her chest, Nicola concentrated on remembering the part of what she'd just seen that really disturbed her. Finally it came to her. Sister Benny had been clutching a bunch of knotted cords close to her chest as she fled the chapel which meant one thing only. Sister Benny had been self-flagellating in front of Our Lady – Sister Benny was into self-harming. The Arit Jinn observed all this from the branches and were well pleased with their plan to show Nicola that all might not be as Sister Benny would like it to appear. Before falling into an uneasy sleep, Nicola crammed her grief into a small box. There was no lock so a simple catch would have to suffice.

At the end of March, Sister Benny came bounding into the office beaming a smile at Nicola. The work on the convent records had been going really well and at last Nicola felt confident enough to throw some of the old cardboard box filing system away, forever. That gave a whole lighter airier feel to the room that Anna remarked was very uplifting. Her little 'after hours' reading group as she called them because they always seemed to appear on her verandah at the end of the day, had reappeared yesterday on the pretext of reading aloud but really looking for a story from her. There was a strict rotation for sitting next to her but the special treat was tracing the words in the story. Nicola was sometimes quite shocked at how thin and scrawny the fingers were but she never said anything. At first the children were so shy they just giggled if she asked a question not related to the story but since the story sessions had resumed they were beginning to open up and tell her about their brothers and sisters and to ask about her family. It puzzled her that they never asked about her baby. Before Julia arrived one or two of the girls asked whether she wanted a boy or a girl but when she reappeared back at her hut nobody asked where the baby was. Julia marveled at their ability to live in the today. Yesterday had happened but somehow stayed disconnected from the present. Tomorrow was going to arrive but until it did, today was all important. Nicola so wished she could share this uncomplicated world.

'Well, Nicola,' said Sister Benny sitting down opposite. 'I have some really good news for you. Gellie Crawford is coming to visit next week. Dermot and Caroline Smith Owen have rented a house in Kilifi just up the road close to where they used to live and have planned a family reunion. I am so glad they are coming back to Kenya. Of all the places they have lived I have always thought they belonged in Africa. When I hear what Gellie's plans are I will let you know. I know she is looking forward to seeing you again.' With that Sister Benny was gone, off on her eternal orbit of her convent and her flock.

Nicola sat slightly stunned. The old world which she had so carefully consigned to the outer margins of her consciousness was threatening to invade with a whole array of armaments against which she had a weak defence. Her first reaction was to flee, anywhere would do. Not practical, there would have to be another way. But the only way she could think of was to patch up the old Nicola, to block out the last few months and to proceed as from say, Christmas, as if none of the events had occurred. It was going to have to be done sometime before the summer and better to have a dress rehearsal with Gellie before facing her family. It should not be too difficult as she had managed to keep up a cheery flow of emails back to England in spite of what had been happening to her in Watamu.

The following Friday Anna asked Nicola to go and meet Sister Benny in the visitor's room but before she got halfway across the corridor Gellie burst out of the door, spreading light and chaos before her, to fling her arms round Nicola.

'Hi there. My you're so thin and so brown and you look so good.' Gellie was all enthusiasm. 'Come, grab a coffee and then I want to hear all your news. I promised to remember everything for your parents and for Maggie.' Gellie steered Nicola into the room. No sign of Sister Benny which was a great relief. Although she was sure that Sister Benny would keep her word about not telling anyone about the recent events, Nicola would have found it very difficult to lie in front of her.

'Sister Benny says you have done a fabulous job on computerising the convent records. I'm not surprised. Oliver keeps singing your praises and asking when you can come back to sort me out again. Now your turn. Tell me all.' Gellie settled down beside Nicola on a worn sofa and looked at her expectantly.

Nicola found it very easy to chat about the Newcastle Uni students and what fun they'd been and how she was looking forward to catching up with them all in October. She would probably be home before they returned in June. She told Gellie how much she enjoyed reading to the little children, how funny Sister Benny could be but at the same time she had a great respect for her and how relieved she had been when the computerised accounts project had worked. She was not sure whether Sister Benny had fully grasped the intricacies but at least Anna was a back-up. Nicola paused wondering if she sounded insane speaking so quickly.

Gellie jumped in.

'And I hear you've had a dose of dengue fever. That's the problem with Africa. There is always something out there waiting to bite you or infect you.' Gellie stopped to have a good hard look at Nicola and thought she detected a fleeting shadow cross Nicola's face. Nothing she could put her finger on. 'I guess you didn't tell your parents because I have only just heard about it from Sister Benny. But you're right not to worry them. Dengue fever is nasty but you get over it and I must say you're looking good if a little thin. But that is Africa for you.'

Nicola was very relieved that Gellie had taken over with a rattling conversation so that she couldn't get a word in edgeways.

'And Maggie. I must tell you about Maggie. As well as *Gelliebabies* she has had this idea to make wall hangings out of knitted fabric and one of my missions while I'm here is to source African cotton fabrics and look into setting up a cooperative to knit Maggie's designs. She is just bursting with ideas I have a hard job trying to keep her on one thing at a time.'

'She really loves working for you, you know,' said Nicola glad that the focus was now on Maggie. 'It's great that she's going to go to art college next year rather than stay on at school. Maggie is awful to live with if she doesn't get her own way.'

'You know, for sisters you two are so different. I know Maggie can be difficult but so long as she's working she's great. I know you're very efficient and controlled, Nicola, but apart from that you're a bit of a mystery. I would love to get to know you better.'

Nicola didn't reply, afraid to give up something of her carefully locked up life.

'Dermot and Caroline are arriving tomorrow, the Willstones are here already and then Lucas and a friend and maybe some others will join us. I have to check with Caroline. Anyway Caroline is arranging for us all to spend a week at Kulalu Camp in Tsavo East and I'm inviting you to come too. You'll love the camp. It is on the banks of the Galana River, north of Malindi. I have told Sister Benny you need a holiday and she agreed immediately. So it is all arranged, you will come won't you?'

Before Nicola could answer she heard a male voice laugh from the direction of Sister Benny's office. She started because it was such an unusual sound in the convent. She could not remember hearing Moses laugh but he did smile often. Nicola turned back to Gellie.

'That sounds lovely. Are you sure Caroline and Dermot won't mind me gate crashing a family do? I feel a little nervous what with you know.' Nicola's voice trailed off.

'Don't be silly. Caroline will be delighted and you can mix with Lucas and his friends. It will be fun.' Just then the door opened and Charlie Willstone came in. Rather surprised, Nicola stood up and was immediately wrapped in a large somewhat sweaty and definitely unwanted hug.

'Nicola, great to see you,' breathed Charlie. 'How is the gap year going? Jocelyn is dying to hear all about it.' Bet she's not, thought Nicola darkly.

Pleasantries over Charlie turned to Gellie. 'Ready? We're meeting Tom,

Duckie and a couple of others for drinks at the yacht club in half an hour and we have to pick up Elodie on our way. Great to hear you're coming up to Kulalu with us, Nicola.'Another hug and then Gellie and Charlie left a rather stunned Nicola finishing a cold cup of coffee on her own. Under normal circumstances she would have been very excited at the prospect of a week at a safari camp but after Gellie and Charlie's brief visit she found she was out of practice at chatting socially and especially with Julian's parents, his brother and their friends.

The following week Nicola was sitting nervously under the Tree of Forgetfulness waiting for Lucas to come and pick her up. Above her the Arit Jinn were peering down from their branches wondering what was going on. They had consulted their calendar and noted that Nicola was not due to leave the convent for at least another month. And yet she had a bulging rucksack at her feet and was dressed for a safari. Then the gate swung open and Lucas came striding across the courtyard looking, Nicola was shocked, gorgeous. His dark curls were still damp and his white linen shirt flowed nonchalantly over his belted chinos.

'Hi Nicola, how are you?' he said confidently as he bent forwards and kissed her on both cheeks. 'I'd better pop in and say hi to Sister B otherwise I'll be in big trouble.' With that he headed off up to the big wooden doors and let himself in. Nicola was left standing wondering whether she should follow or wait. Meanwhile up in the branches the Arit Jinn were brimming with excitement. They recognised Lucas and detecting a certain tension in the air, they settled down to observe. This could develop into something very interesting.

Nicola was still deciding whether to go into the convent when Lucas emerged with Sister Benny who wished them both a safe journey and a great week away. Almost like a blessing mused Nicola as Lucas swung her rucksack over his shoulder and led the way out to his jeep. As they approached, the passenger door opened and Sulei Abbas jumped out all welcoming smiles. Perhaps this wasn't going to be so bad after all. As they left Watamu Lucas and Sulei started chattering away in Swahili which Nicola though was exceptionally rude. After her months at the orphanage she understood some Swahili but only if it was spoken very slowly and clearly. So she gazed pointedly out of the window as the ocean receded and the number of people, broken down transport and animals on or in the middle of the road increased. Out of the corner of her eye she saw Sulei dig Lucas hard in the ribs.

'Ni wewe kwenda kulala na wakiti huu?' (*Are you going to sleep with her this time?*) asked Sulei.

'Hakuna ahili effing yahoo mwenyewo biashara!' (*Mind your own effing business*) replied Lucas keeping his eyes firmly on the road.

'Kuja juu, unajua yeip ana hots nwa wewe.' (*Come on, you know she has the hots for you*).

'Sulei, ni fidhuli kuongea Swahili na mtu ambaye hasemi lugha.' (*Sulei it's rude to speak Swahili in front of someone who doesn't speak the language*), Lucas turned to take a swipe at Sulei.

'Kuangala barabara wewe idiot.' (*Watch the road you idiot*).

'I do apologise for speaking Swahili, Nicola, but I had to use some very strong words about Lucas' driving. Now we are going to drive to Malindi to pick up two more friends and then head west on the C103 to the Sala Gate where we'll enter Tsavo. You are wearing your seat belt aren't you? Good.' Sulei turned back to face the road.

The fishing club in Malindi looked decidedly worse for wear. In fact the whole town looked in need of a bit of care and attention. There were so many potholes in the road that Nicola reckoned their journey was almost half as long again as Lucas swerved from side to side to avoid the worst of them. Nicola was feeling very car sick when they pulled up beside a low wall. Lucas and Sulei jumped out to greet the couple sitting waiting for them as Nicola gingerly let her feet touch firm ground.

'Nicola,' shouted Lucas, 'Meet Josh and his sister, Belinda, who are coming with us.' Turning round he loaded two rucksacks into the back of the jeep leaving Nicola to step forward and shake hands. After loading some drinking water they were off again, everybody chatting away, often at cross purposes, against the engine noise, apart from Nicola who hadn't a clue who they were talking about. She was right. This was a big mistake.

Paperwork at the Sala Gate seemed to take forever as the vehicle and its passenger were given a thorough vetting. Thank goodness they all spoke Swahili thought Nicola otherwise they might have been there all day in the sweltering sun. The dirt road from the Sala Gate to the camp followed the Galana river through open grassland and acacia trees whose flat tops hyphenated the intense blue sky.

'Watch out for red elephants,' Sulei told Nicola. Seeing her looking mystified he added 'Look down at the road. See the red soil? The elephants have regular dustbaths and end up looking red. You'll see them at the camp when they come down to the river to drink. It's not far now.'

They came to Kulala Camp quite suddenly finding it nestling under doum palms and a couple of baobab trees on the river bank just below Lugard's Falls.

'Leave the bags,' Lucas said excitedly. 'They'll be picked up later.' Striding ahead, he led the way into a group of large, thatch shaded tents nestling between the boulders. Caroline, Dermot, the Willstones and Gellie were standing around the mess tent waiting for them and there were shouts of glee and hugs and kisses all round. While all this was going on Nicola took a moment to take in her surroundings. The mess tent was very much smarter than the Cowan's living room back in Frampton. Large, comfortable, inviting sofas piled with plumped up cushions relaxed on animal skin rugs. Behind the sofas were shelves of books, photographs and other bits of memorabilia giving the impression of home from home in the middle of nowhere. Nicola couldn't remember the last time she'd seen such luxury. At the far end of the tent was a long dining table set for lunch. She turned to look at the veranda which stretched out over the river taking in a fire pit on its way. To her right she spotted a very inviting swimming pool and then she heard her name being called.

'Nicola, we're so pleased you could join us,' said Caroline. 'Let me introduce you to Elodie, my god daughter. You've already met her brother and sister, Josh and Belinda. Now that we're all here I must go and check on the luggage.'

'It's so nice to meet you,' said Elodie. Her voice had a trace of a South African accent. 'I heard so much about you from Julian. We're all devastated about what happened. He loved this place so much. We've all been coming here since we were kids.' She paused for a moment and Nicola wasn't sure what to say in reply.

'Africa is so harsh and so beautiful,' continued Elodie looking round 'We just have to get on with life. Now tell me about Sister Benny. How is she? She must be getting quite old now.'

Before Nicola could reply, Gellie came rushing up to show them to their tents.

'Elodie, you're with Belinda and I'm on one side and Nicola's on the other. The tents have all been moved since last year because of the floods. The boys are on the other side of the pool and the others are just over there.'

After the mess tent Nicola was not surprised at the size of her double bed or the spacious bathroom with a flushing toilet. How long was it since she'd actually flushed a toilet?

'If you want a shower, just tell one of the house boys and they will fill up the tank with hot water for you,' said Gellie smiling. 'Nicola, I'm so glad you decided to come.' Nicola couldn't recall the 'deciding' bit remembering that it was more of a fait a compli on Gellie's part.

'I know you'll enjoy the week. Oh and one golden rule to remember. The camp is unfenced so when you come back to your tent or go anywhere around the camp at night, ask for an escort. Just to make sure everything you meet is friendly.'

Nicola smiled weakly and said she was sure she would have a great week in such a fantastic place. There was walking in the grasslands in the morning, riding, the possibility of bird shooting, swimming in the pool, siestas when the sun was too hot, sundowners on the top of the rocks. All very casual, a lot of laughter and a great deal of good food. Everyone was very careful to include Nicola in everything and yet she felt like an outsider peering in through an open window. Elodie and Belinda were very noisy and talked for hours at night. If they were sitting on their veranda they always called to Nicola to join them but she was very aware that the tone and subject of conversation changed when she was with them. One evening, needing desperately to find her own space, Nicola slipped out of the camp to a nearby termite mound to watch the sun gather its clouds together and slide away to light the other half of the world. It was empty time when the day noise goes to bed and the night has yet to wake up. The silence grew thickly round her until a light footstep broke in. She turned to see Lucas standing looking at her. Without speaking he sat down beside her and Nicola was shocked at the effect of his physical presence. It tore at her forcing her to look at him.

'I miss him too you know. It's hard coming back here knowing he'll never return. I never said sorry for throwing him in the river when he was eight when I knew it was infested with crocodiles. Dad nearly killed me for that. I never said sorry for borrowing his rifle and not cleaning it properly. In fact there are so many things I never said sorry for. He loved being out here in the bush.' Lucas' voice trailed away in emotion.

Holding back her tears, Nicola reached out for his hand and he squeezed her's hard. Nicola was about to tell Lucas about how much she still missed Julian and how she had no idea how to lay her memories to rest when he turned slowly towards her, Nicola was sure he was going to kiss her.

A discreet cough behind them brought Lucas instantly to his feet pulling Nicola up with him.

'The truck is leaving for sundowners, Mr Lucas.' reported one of the guides. With his arm loosely draped across her shoulder, Lucas walked her back into the camp.

Later that night, long after Elodie and Belinda had ceased chattering, Nicola crept out onto her veranda and eased herself onto her hammock. She was trying to work out how the Smith Owen/Gellie/Willstone dynamics worked. For a start, Julian was all around the camp. He was referred to, talked about and his face smiled at her from photographs in the mess tent. It seemed perfectly natural for him to be included but there were no references to Julian and Nicola as a couple. She was on the outside, a guest at a private memorial where she didn't really know anyone. The exclusion cut through her like a knife.

The next day the camp was up before sunrise to ride out for breakfast, Nicola was happily looking forward to an activity where she could be on a par with everyone else. Belinda, who worked occasionally for a horse riding Safari Company had rounded up the horses and was now organising everyone. Gellie wasn't going as she had managed never to learn to ride and had no intention of ever doing so: Charlie declined saying he had had enough of horses in the army. Everyone else duly mounted the horse assigned to them and Belinda went round unnecessarily checking girths and stirrups.

Giving Nicola an appraising eye, she said, 'Jester is a good horse so give him plenty of rein. He likes to be leader of the pack but once you let him know who's boss he will respond. Oh, and horses hate elephants but since the herd moved east last night and we're heading west there shouldn't be any trouble.'

Nicola was enjoying herself. Jester was behaving beautifully and it was wonderful to be galloping through wide spaces breathing open air after months of being closeted in the convent. Lucas caught her up as they slowed down to walk towards the river bank and breakfast.

'You ride very well, Nicola,' he said 'Did you have your own pony?'

'No. I learnt to ride at the local stables. Then Charlie bought Jocelyn a horse she couldn't handle so I kept that exercised for a few years. I even managed some hunting before the horse was sold. I've always wanted a horse of my own so maybe when I've been through uni and get a fantastically well paid job, I'll buy one.' Nicola hoped she wasn't gabbling and giving too much information.

'If it's something you really want, I'm sure you'll be successful.' Lucas dismounted and casually handed the reins over to a groom who had come with the horses. 'Mmm breakfast smells good.' He led the way down to the river where tables and chairs had been set out under the trees and food was being cooked over a roaring fire.

'Come and sit by me, Nicola,' called Caroline. Damn thought Nicola as she watched Elodie slip in beside Lucas at the other end of the table but managing to smile at Caroline at the same time.

Caroline wanted to know all about her plans for uni and asked after her parents and what was happening in Frampton. 'A lovely village but I doubt that we'll ever live permanently in Mulberry Cottage. Dermot's a nomad and I'll never change him now. Now that Julian's gone and Lucas seems bent on wandering around with Sulei it doesn't seem practical to keep it. I was rather looking forward to being part of a community, you know, part of a village. Everyone, like your parents, seem to be so friendly and of course having Dee and Charlie as neighbours again was perfect. Now have you tried these fresh mangoes? They are delicious.'

Dee rode beside Nicola for a while as they made their way back at a slightly slower pace. Dee rode like one of the Pony Club judges Nicola was always falling out with. Back straight, legs perfectly positioned, hands correct and of course her mount behaved beautifully. Nicola had always found Dee slightly scary, selfishly absorbed in herself and maintaining, and where possible enhancing, her social status. Even though the Willstones enjoyed a lifestyle suited to The Grange, Nicola felt that money was an issue otherwise Charlie would not be doing *Angelica's* accounts out of hours. According to Maggie he was rarely in Gellie's office during the working day. A close friendship with Caroline and Dermot was carefully nurtured as being associated with the Smith Owens added a certain exotic cache. Dee was also capable of using and abusing her cultivated friends and Monica probably fell somewhere near that category.

Having asked Nicola, briefly, about her work at the Convent, Dee spent some time talking up Jocelyn's carpenter boyfriend who had metamorphosed into a film set designer much in demand for his talented work. Then she switched seamlessly to Nicola's brother, Henry, and his career plans as a pilot. Nicola decided to go for it.

'Henry found it very hard to settle down at school,' (Nicola graciously left off the plural 's'), 'but his headmaster says he is very bright and needs to be challenged. Now he has decided to become a pilot and his goal is to be accepted for training with one the world's best airlines, (*you'd better deliver on this one Henry*) he is focused and working really hard.'

Dee was silent for a moment as she computed this information. She turned to Nicola with a steely smile.

'It is so interesting that you should think that.' Dee kicked her horse on to ride beside Belinda and her place was taken by Lucas.

'Enjoying yourself? I must say you look very good on a horse.' Lucas grinned broadly.

'I was bullied into shape by the Pony Club many years ago. Jocelyn won the rosettes and I got prizes for simply competing.'

'Do you still ride?'

'Not very often now that the Willstones have sold all their horses.'

I told you all this before thought Nicola. Am I so unimportant in your life that all you can think of to say to me is something you've said before?

They rode back together chatting lightly about non-committal subjects.

Friday night was party night. Steeped in tradition, friends from neighbouring lodges and camps were invited to the evening barbeque and the boys spent the morning shooting 'for the pot' on a ranch outside the Park. As she was not invited on the shoot Nicola visited local villages with Gellie who was on a fabric hunt.

'Maggie has been doing some really creative work with ethnic fabrics so I thought I'd try and source some in case I decide to go into production,' she told Nicola and they spent a very pleasant morning together. Nicola marveled at the way Gellie could just wind herself up in a piece of fabric and suddenly it became a fashion item. Beautiful, fashionable and slightly wildly eccentric. Nicola sighed inwardly. Anna had insisted on making her a dress in local material and she was so relieved she'd thought to bring it with her. She showed the dress to Gellie when they got back to camp and she seized on the material and wanted to know where it had come from as she absolutely had to have some for her collection. Nicola promised to ask Anna.

Belinda and Elodie were sprawled on their veranda and invited Nicola to join them. There had obviously been some sort of party going on as glasses and cushions were heaped on the floor.

'We've ordered tea,' Belinda giggled 'I'm sure there'll be enough for the three of us.'

'How was the shoot?' enquired Nicola.

'Good fun, if a bit chaotic. Not much control of the dogs but I think the boys shot enough to keep the cooks happy.' Elodie gave Belinda a conspiratorial look under her long eyelashes. Nicola felt excluded and exasperated at the same time. Belinda pushed a bowl of green leaves tied up in bundles towards Nicola.

'Khat,' she said. 'Have some. Sulei got it this morning so that he and Lucas can stay up all night and drive to Dar. They're flying back to the UK tomorrow to study for their finals. Ugh, imagine having to sit still for two hours and write intelligently at the same time. Quelle horreur.'

Nicola looked doubtful.

'Haven't you tried it? We've been chewing all afternoon,' Belinda giggled again. 'Look,' she opened her mouth and revealed a ball of chewed leaves stuck in her cheek. 'Come on, try it.' She selected a small twig and Nicola put it in her mouth, pulled off the leaves and started chewing.

'Ugh,' she cried 'It's hideous. It's so bitter.' She almost spat it out.

'That's why we've ordered tea and lots of sugar. Don't give up, you'll soon be feeling very happy and everything you think and say will be deliciously sharp.'

Nicola persevered and soon relaxed in the girl's company.

'Before you arrived we were talking about having a Brazilian.' Elodie giggled. 'Have you had one, Nicola?'

'Once.' Nicola recalled the emergency shaving she had at the clinic. 'It was very itchy about a week later.'

'That's why it's high maintenance. Did you have a landing strip?'

Thankfully, Elodie and Belinda collapsed into helpless laughter before they could discover that Nicola had no idea what they were talking about, in spite of the khat making her much more confident, making her feel part of everything instead of loitering on the outside.

'You look lovely, Nicola. African prints in those colours really do suit you. And so does living in Kenya. You've lost that awful British winter pallor. Come on, we must join the party.' Taking Nicola's arm Caroline walked with her to the veranda and the fire pit where a long table had been set out stretching out to embrace the river. Nicola was disappointed to find that she had been squashed between two guests that she had never met before and that further down the table out of earshot, Elodie was sitting next to Lucas. The guests were very polite and chatted away to her but it was quite a relief when the tables were cleared away and someone got the music going. By midnight only the young were left dancing and drinking beside the fire pit. Sulei had carefully danced with all the women and he did dance very well with a great deal of rhythm put together in a style of his own. Nicola was enjoying herself dancing under the stars. It must have been getting late because the music slowed right down and as many of the hurricane lamps hanging from the trees had run out of gas, only the fire was left to toss dancing images around in the inky night. Suddenly Nicola found herself swept up in Lucas arms and held very close and very tight. It seemed so natural to kiss passionately and the khat started playing with her mind letting her imagine everything she wanted Lucas to do to her. Someone threw another log on the fire and, as the new light tore the closeting darkness apart, Lucas pulled away from Nicola and led her, his arm draped over her shoulder, towards the fire. Sulei came over and told Lucas it was time to get ready to leave and the party folded. Sulei skillfully escorted Nicola back to her tent. Belinda and Elodie were chatting on their veranda and asked her to join them but Nicola just needed to be alone to calm all the feelings coursing through her mind which seemed to be completely at odds with what was going on in her body. She would never ever understand complicated Lucas.

The next day she found a bougainvillea flower with a note attached to it on her veranda.

Great to catch up with you, Nicola.
See you in UK sometime.
Lucas x

It was early but the sun was already up drying the dew on the spider's webs and the fronds of tall grasses round her tent. Despite the warmth Nicola shivered as her heart contracted into a cold place. Lucas didn't care for her, he was, oh, so obviously just playing with her and so would be best forgotten. She only had a couple of months left at the convent and then she could leave all this behind like a bad dream and start life again. Mentally she stuffed Julian, Julia and Lucas into a dark corner of her memory, wiped a smile onto her face and walked up to the mess tent for breakfast. Sulei and Lucas had already gone, Belinda, Josh and Elodie were saying their goodbyes as they were off home to Laikipia, taking Gellie and Dee with them. There was no sign of Charlie. Nicola found it hard to understand how they all moved seamlessly between each other's house, ranches, camps, whatever. Back home her parents would never have visited without proper invitations and due consideration. Dermot and Caroline were going to take

Nicola back to Watamu on their way down to Mombasa. The week was over.

The Arit Jinn were busy documenting the vibes they had been receiving from Tsavo East and logging the information in the trunk of the Tree of Forgetfulness. The problem was the lost memories about Lucas Smith Owen. At the time they hadn't been worried because they were having more fun playing with the present. Now a nagging feeling told them there was more to this unfolding story which went back a long way. But there was a small but significant breakthrough. Before she left, Nicola had stuffed a ragged piece of white cloth soaked with memories into the trunk of their tree. Now they could really get to work by sabotaging Nicola's dreams.

4

Remembering all the nights lying in her makuti thatched hut in Watamu just longing to be back home, Nicola wondered why she had had all those dreams because the reality had not lived up to expectations. It had been wonderful to see her family again. Henry was about to train as a pilot having achieved, in his parents view, the impossible; Maggie was very grown up and their bedroom had been completely redecorated as an art studio 'for inspiration'. Her father looked older and started talking about retirement and her mother, well she looked more relaxed and a lot better for it. Bundle had died in the spring but no one had told Nicola because they thought it would be too upsetting. She had died one night in her basket in the kitchen but everyone felt she had been too much of a character to replace just yet. They would wait until Nicola came back.

Nicola found it very difficult to settle back into family life. In Watamu there was so much to do, so much that never got done because of staff shortages and the children always came first, so that she never had a spare moment in a day. She missed the little group of children who collected on her veranda at the end of the day hoping for a story. One child in particular, Maria, who had been thrown out of her village, abandoned by her family because of her cleft pallet, stuck in her memory and she made a mental note to send her a copy of her favourite book. Back home Monica seemed to think Nicola needed rest in a calm atmosphere to recover properly from her bout of dengue fever so the house was very quiet and Nicola had nothing to do.

One lazy afternoon Nicola walked to the end of the garden and sat down under the apple tree close to Bundle's grave. She opened her notepad on her knees and started writing.

My Dearest Always Love,
It is nearly a year since you left forever without a moment to say goodbye and I
miss you so much that it aches. I miss the way you looked deeply into my eyes
when I spoke to you making everything I said seem very important to you. I loved
the way you stroked the back of my neck kind of absentmindedly when we woke
up together in your bed. We never got to sleep in my bed. I check my phone for
text messages that always made my heart jump but my message box is empty like
my heart. I listen to our special music on my iPod and remember smooching under
the stars at your College May Ball. I loved the way you believed in me and my
dreams when no one else was interested. It gave me such confidence and now I'm a
lost soul without your support, crying in my own wilderness. Another Nicola is
living my life in parallel as I spend my time catching our memories and trying to
hold them together to make my life bearable. I committed one of the most heinous
crimes ever in letting our beautiful daughter die in some hospital in Africa. The
last link between us snatched on my watch. I think about her every day. You
would be the first to tell me to 'get a grip' and start living for today instead of
wallowing in our yesterday but I can't do this without you. You are now a part of
me that I will never give up – you will be with me always. Thank you for those
desperately happy few months that changed me into the person I am now. I will try
to go on without you even though I can't see the way forward through my tears and
my grief.
All my love forever, Nicola x

Carefully folding the letter up and putting it in an envelope without a name, Nicola stashed it in a box in her room with all her other precious memories.

She was lying on her bed staring at the ceiling when Maggie burst in throwing her bag down in the floor. The contents spilled out over the room and arranged themselves in untidy piles. Nicola rolled over and sighed at this familial chaos.

'What are you doing today, Nicola? Honestly you can't lie around for the rest of your life. You never used to be like this.' Maggie stood looking aggressively at her sister.

Nicola sat up suddenly.

'Don't use that 'never' word. I am stuck in Never Land. My life is never going to be the same. I have lost the love of my life and I will never love again. I am lying here because I'm never going to be able to get my life together. I am destined to go to some remote uni where I can never see myself being happy. What is the point?' Nicola glared at Maggie.

'Well pardon me for even daring to inquire,' Maggie retorted. 'Just take a look at yourself. You've lost so much weight and you're so tanned you look fabulous. Apart from your face. Everything you've just said shows on your face. You've given up and I think that's really really bad.'

Maggie leant forward and grabbed Nicola's wrist. Nicola's sleeve fell back to reveal a line of fresh scars on her forearm.

'I thought as much,' Maggie said triumphantly. 'You're cutting. And don't try and hide it. Those marks were not made by a barbwire fence you struggled through taking Jake home. What really happened in Watamu? What are you not telling us? You can tell me. I'll be your father confessor and it will never go any further, I promise.'

But Nicola just turned her face to the wall and tears rolled down her cheeks. She could never ever tell anyone.

'Well, I'm not going to let you lie there and bleed to death. Whatever reasons you have for doing it, they are just not good enough. We are going to London next week to work for Gellie. I have just been on the phone to her and she has arranged for us to house sit for a friend just down the road from her new place. So we are off at the weekend. I need you to come and talk to the Parents. They need convincing but with you beside me they will cave in. Just watch this space.'

Nicola gave up and went to wash her face while Maggie worked on tactics. Sitting on the linen basket and holding a damp flannel over her eyes, Nicola felt she was hidden effectively enough from the world at large to confess her innermost thoughts to herself. She had enormous problems with Lucas. Julian was her first ever love and she did love him, she still loved him. But Lucas had got under her skin, right down under to depths she never realised she had and she could not get rid of him. She could not stop thinking about him. He was camping out in her brain. But she had to forget because it was never going to happen. But it just might if she was working for Gellie. Lucas just might drop in.

Maggie got her way as usual. They were going off to London to work for Gellie. Her mother was very worried about Nicola getting too tired, getting ill again. She raised the old idea of working locally for a chemist but that was given very short shrift by Maggie. Nicola just gave in. It was easy to sit back and let her little sister run around and organise everything.

'I thought that that you should have a suit. After all you will be working in the finance side,' Andrew said, keen to make a caring father contribution. When Maggie handed over the credit card bills, he hardly blinked.

'Nicola can't possibly wear any of the clothes she had in Africa,' Maggie had told Andrew. 'She can't work in the fashion industry looking like a refugee.'

Andrew resisted the temptation to tell Maggie that during Maggie's last year at school that was exactly how he would have described many of her outfits.

She would not have admitted it ever to anybody but Monica was very relieved that Nicola was going to London. Since her return from Africa a yawning crevasse seemed to have opened between them. Mind you it wasn't like they were ever that close before, but Monica sensed an impenetrable barricade. She tried to talk about Nicola's experiences at the convent about living in poverty in Africa but learned nothing new beyond the carefully scripted details Nicola had trotted out before. She offered to arrange a fundraising event with Frampton WI but Nicola was less than enthusiastic. She even, on a carefully designed spur-of-the-moment shopping trip, 'just the two of us', tried to talk about Julian only to be rewarded with a wall of silence. Maggie maintained the sisterhood law of the playground and Andrew was no help whatsoever.

Monica drove the girls up to London with all their stuff. Gellie had moved her premises to Spitalfields where she had a larger warehouse with her office and studio above the storage. Making up the garments was now all done by out workers or her designs were sold on to independent manufacturers but marketed under Gellie's various labels. Gellie's house was in Whitechapel and the girls would be living in the next road. Monica was slightly worried about the post code but the house they would be looking after was lovely. Every modern convenience in what could only initially be described as modest mid terrace from the outside done up with, as Monica told Andrew later, Vogue meets House & Garden flair. It was already occupied by a large ginger cat who looked at them with distain before stalking out through his cat flap onto the rear terrace from where he observed the invasion through half closed eyes.

They had supper with Gellie who spent most of the evening discussing a new range of *Gellateens* designs that Maggie would be working on. So much so that Nicola had all the time in the world to reconfirm her earlier suspicions that she was only there as Maggie's minder. She wondered whether she would actually have a real job at *Angelica's*; had this been another big mistake? Then she had to remind herself that she hadn't objected when Maggie was setting her up.

The next day, at Nicola's insistence, they unpacked, read all the house rules and went food shopping locally. They managed to set the burglar alarm off twice. Nicola hoped that that was merely the learning curve and that they would not end up on first name terms with the team at the call centre. Maggie decided that the cat had a CCTV camera behind one of his eyes so that his owners could monitor their activities.

'If he is that intelligent then perhaps he could help with the boiler controls,' said Nicola emerging from a dark recess in the utility room. 'Thank goodness all we need is hot water. I would hate to have to deal with the central heating.'

The next day Maggie rushed off to the studio as soon as they got to work leaving Nicola in the office. Gellie stuck her head round the door.

'Could you please take the phone calls Nicola?' she asked. 'Sophie my PA is away on a course for a couple of days. Just take messages and tell them I'll call back. Oliver is due in about an hour to get you started. In the meantime could you make four large cups of coffee and one for yourself? The kitchen is the other side of the corridor. We're up in the studio. Thanks so much.' With a grin, Gellie was gone charging the atmosphere with her enormous energy resources.

Nicola sighed, she'd been right. Only good for making coffee when she needed to be worked hard as a distraction. She looked round at the chaotic cramped office. Sophie must be as bad as Gellie, perhaps that is why she had gone on a course. Better make the coffee. There was probably a whole stack of washing up to do before she could get anywhere near a kettle.

Things improved when Oliver arrived. He was delighted to see her again. Nicola made more coffee.

'At last. Someone who can establish a sense of order and reality to this sinking ship,' he said by way of a greeting. 'Well it is not exactly sinking. Not yet anyway. Actually it is doing very well but we just can't see it. Now that Gellie has all these different design areas we need to separate them all out of the main accounting function. This is where I need your help. You and I are going to set up systems for *Gelliebabies, Gelliebeans* and *Gellateen* leaving *Angelica* as the main business operation. Then we can do P and L forecasts for each area and we will know where we are at any one time.'

Oliver cast his eyes round the office.

'Hmmm. Right, you need your own space and laptop. I happen to know that there is a spare desk lurking in the warehouse. I'll get someone to bring that up here and all this lot,' he said indicating a bank of files, 'can go up to the studio as they are full of designs, past and present, which is not our office function.'

Oliver handed Nicola a folder setting out his ideas for the new systems and the detail of how they were going to achieve it.

'Should be a doddle after all your experience with Sister Benny's systems in Watamu. Now, suggest you get out of here. Go downstairs and take a right out of the side door. There is a cafe there where you can sit and read this uninterrupted. Put your coffee on Gellie's bill. Don't worry about the phone. I'll deal with it.'

So she did have a proper job. Nicola decided things were looking up. But living in a big city took some getting used to. The noise all day and night; the people rushing everywhere; traffic; hard pavements to walk on; putting a burglar alarm on when you went out and remembering to lock all the doors and windows. Still she would have to go through all this in Newcastle in October.

Sophie was pleasant enough but Nicola got the impression she was only there because she was trying to break into the fashion industry. She was brisk with Nicola and no help when it came to office equipment. Nicola decided it was because Maggie was her sister and as far as Sophie was concerned, Maggie was taking Sophie's rightful place in Gellie's design studio. So when it came to taking a day off midweek, Nicola had no second thoughts. Gellie was taking Maggie to meet some alpaca wool suppliers in Surrey; Oliver was at his desk at Rock & Hendersons plc; Sophie was in the office at *Angelica's* and Nicola was on an early train to Oxford. She had not thought about this trip but something was drawing her towards Oxford, to sit in Georgina's with a cup of coffee and a croissant a year exactly since she had sat there with Julian the morning after the ball where, she was now convinced, Julia had been conceived.

Walking up New Road from the station it was all so familiar. Nicola took the entrance to the Covered Market from the High so that she did not have to walk past Lincoln College. That would have been too difficult. Georgina's was packed but Nicola managed to squeeze into a corner with her coffee and croissant and got out a book on Environmental Science which was tantamount to hanging up a 'Do Not Disturb' sign. It was very noisy; lots of students in black tie and evening dress who had obviously been up all night just like she and Julian had a year ago. Nicola inhaled the heady atmosphere while not really reading Professor Boyd's take on the importance of Environmental Science in the modern world. She became aware of someone trying to get her attention and looked up at a jammed table on the other side of the cafe. Sulei, looking devastating in his black tie was waving at her. Sitting next to him but facing the other way with his arm casually draped around a very pretty girl's shoulder, was Lucas. Sulei nudged him and pointed to Nicola who went very red. Now is the time to run away fast, but too late. Lucas was making his way towards her.

'Excuse me; Can I squeeze through?; Sorry, I just want to get to my friend over there; Would you mind just moving up one place so that I can sit there?' Eventually Lucas arrived in front of her.

'Hi!' Lucas smelt of aftershave, booze and fags. He had black circles under his eyes. His bow tie was missing and his shirt was open displaying a suntanned six pack. Nicola felt a wrenching pain in the pit of her stomach. She had not expected such an encounter. This was supposed to be a very quiet tribute to Julian and her memories not a reminder of all her darkest thoughts and wildest inappropriate dreams.

'Hi.' Nicola managed to spit out. Lucas was now sitting opposite her, his face level with hers. Perhaps he will lean forward and kiss me, thought Nicola. Instead she said, 'What are you doing here?' as if it was not obvious to everyone else in Georgina's.

'We've been to Brookes May Ball. Finals finished last Monday so here we are celebrating before we get our results and life gets really serious. What about you? I hear you're working for Gellie over the summer. Have you started yet?'

'Yes. This week but there isn't much to do until Oliver, her accountant, gets things sorted.' Lucas obviously has no idea about the significance of the date or place. How could he be so cold hearted about his brother, thought Nicola. 'What are you doing over the summer?'

'Get my results. Go and see Mum and Dad. They are in Paris at the moment so that should be fun. Then catch up with Sulei in Riyadh. Poor Sulei is being sucked into the family business so we'll probably nip down to Watamu for a while before he has to give up having a good time. And then find a proper job somewhere. I have no firm ideas but I expect Dad has a future all mapped out for me. We'll see.' Lucas smiled that brilliant captivating smile that creased up his face and made Nicola want to cry.

'And after the summer? What next for you, Nicola?' Nicola looked up directly into Lucas' brown eyes and felt their gaze lock for a moment and, though she would deny it afterwards, an understanding of a mutual attraction passed between them.

'I'm off to Newcastle Uni to read Environmental Science,' she said lamely.

'Where the hell is Newcastle?' asked Lucas quite seriously but added 'Must be somewhere miles away. Why there?'

Nicola noticed that Lucas' friends were getting ready to leave. 'It's a long story.' She looked directly at Lucas again hoping to reclaim that precious moment but it had passed and Lucas' eyes were not giving anything away. The girl he had been sitting next to before approached their table.

'Hey Lucas, we're leaving. We're going to punt up to the Vicky Arms for lunch. Come on, the others are waiting.'

Nicola felt Lucas hesitate before standing up and giving her a beautiful smile. 'Got to go, Nicola. Maybe catch up over the summer at Gellie's. Take care.' He was gone.

The atmosphere cooled as he ran down the stairs so Nicola gulped down the rest of her cold coffee and left too. Oxford suddenly lost its shine and as her memories piled in one on top of the other, Nicola beat a hasty retreat to the station, racing ahead of her past, worried that it was going to catch up and overwhelm her. She had thought of getting in touch with Kate if she was back in Oxford but suddenly she was very tired and the thought of the terrace house in Whitechapel where she could be alone with her thoughts was very attractive. However, when the train arrived in Paddington station and she was surrounded with swirls of humanity heading every which way, Nicola sought refuge in the nearest coffee shop. She had almost finished her cappuccino when to her surprise, Jamie slid into the seat opposite her. He always looked the same, serious, freckled face, smoky eyes behind, yes, they were new glasses, denim shirt but no scarf because it was summer. Nicola closed her eyes and a tear ran down her cheek as she remembered the last time she had seen him.

'Nicola, so good to see you.' Jamie's hand brushed lightly over hers.

'How are things?'

Be positive thought Nicola, smiling up at him. 'They're good. Yes just great. I'm working for Gellie Crawford for the summer and then off to uni in October. You see I've got my life back together again. Going forward.' Nicola nodded to herself but she was not convinced. After all Jamie knew all her secrets.

Nicola dropped her face into her hands.

'No it's not good at all. I'm not the same person who went to Africa. I'm different and I can't get the old me back. Maggie's driving me at the moment and I'm not doing anything. I can barely cope with just living.' Nicola's sleeve fell back and she hastily pulled it up over her scars. She felt Jamie looking at them.

'Show me,' he said.

Nicola stretched her arm towards Jamie and slowly pulled back her sleeve. There were four new semi-circular cuts standing out red and raw against the old ones. As Jamie's fingers reached towards the vicious lines Nicola stared at the table in shame.

'I can't help it when I'm stressed,' Nicola whispered. 'It makes me feel so much better. The pain is a relief in a kind of harsh way. As the blood oozes through the cut and drips onto a tissue it's like all the bad stuff draining out of me. I can then throw the tissue away and I am clean again. I'm calm, I can concentrate again and I can face the world.'

'It doesn't work like that, Nicola. You are harming yourself, punishing yourself for things that are not your fault. Life sometimes throws shit at us but you must be strong and fight back. Go and tell Maggie that part of the deal is that you share the household chores. Tell Gellie that unless she gives you a proper worthwhile project over the summer you are going home tomorrow. Finally start organising your move to Newcastle. Get the course details, find out where your hall of residence is. How far is the hall from your department? Start looking forward in small pieces. At the moment you are trying to move forwards by looking backwards and it won't work.'

Jamie smiled his shy grin at Nicola and his freckles joined together round his mouth.

'Remember in Hamlet what Polonius says to Laertes 'Above all to thy own self be true'. You have to start trusting yourself to make your own decisions.'

'What...what about Lucas?' asked Nicola.

'Lucas? Well it sounds like he's a pretty lost soul at the moment and the best thing you can do is let go of the memories and let him sort himself out in his own time. Hey is that the time? I have a train to catch! See yah, Nicola'

Before the cafe door closed behind him, Nicola felt the familiar Jamie light caress brush across her cheek. She looked round but he had gone, slipping away unnoticed by the other coffee drinkers shrink wrapped in their own problems with the world.

As she pushed open the door to the house in Whitechapel, Nicola found all Maggie's designs for the *Gellateen* range laid out across the living area. Ignoring Jamie's advice delivered less than an hour ago, Nicola picked them all up and automatically shuffled them into order glancing at one or two as she arranged them carefully in Maggie's portfolio folder. They were good. Bright clashing colour mixes with the different textures of wool, cotton and ribbon, seemingly woven together with wild abandon. So very Maggie shouting her personality from the roof tops and so different from the restrained elegance of the *Angelica* knitwear. Maggie's designs were meant to be worn now by people with confidence and a sense of fun. Not like me thought Nicola and sighed. There was a note from Maggie saying she would be late back and that there was food in the fridge. Really? Thought Nicola but there was, surprisingly.

The next morning Nicola found a police car outside the entrance to the warehouse and a great deal of shouting going on inside. As she climbed the stairs she could hear Charlie Willstone's angry voice and winced. Her little office was squashed full of two policemen, Charlie, Maggie, Gellie and Oliver. Everyone was talking at once but Charlie was by far the loudest.

'Ah, Nicola,' said Charlie turning round in the doorway 'Let's get some semblance of order here.' Taking Nicola's arm he guided her across the landing and into Gellie's office and closed the door.

'Major crisis,' Charlie told Nicola. 'Sophie has done a runner so I need you to sit in here and calmly answer the phone, take messages, do whatever while I sort out this mess.'

'But what is the mess? I do need to know something. Is Maggie OK?'

He was halfway out of the door but Charlie carefully closed it behind him again.

'There was a break in last night.' Charlie drew Nicola's attention to the half open filing cabinets, the contents of the in tray spread across the floor and the general disarray. 'We're talking to the police right now but it looks like they, whoever they are, were after the designs for the new *Gellateen* range which is going to be launched next month. Luckily, Maggie left them at home yesterday so they are safe.' Charlie wiped his head and looked at Nicola. 'I'm relying on you to just run things while we sort this. Won't be long but I know you can do it.' With that he was gone.

Nicola sat down rather suddenly in Gellie's office chair. Then she stood up and went towards the door. The mood in the office sounded calmer, so Nicola decided to leave them to it and turned her attention to the mess. By the time Maggie hurtled in, order had been restored and the desk was probably a great deal tidier than it had been in months.

'Phew.' Maggie plonked herself down in a chair. Nicola noticed she was wearing a new *Gellateen*.

'So what was all that about?' asked Nicola.

'Well all very exciting. The police think it was a case of industrial espionage – how exciting is that? And they think it was an inside job and Charlie thinks Sophie was involved. He never liked her much.'

'It's not exciting, Maggie, it's serious. What if designs had been stolen and someone managed to mass produce onto the market before the launch? What if loads of people suddenly appeared on the street wearing all the pirated designs just before Gellie's launch party? It would be a disaster for everyone. Had you thought of that?'

Maggie managed to look contrite. 'At least I had all the designs back at the house. Gellie always keeps hers at home under lock and key, the latest designs anyway. Hey, what do you think of this one?' Maggie stood up and twirled round in front of Nicola. 'Do you like the African print threading down the side?'

Nicola did rather fancy Maggie's jacket. 'It's beautiful,' she said. 'I seriously need one, no, loads to take to Newcastle to show off.'

'Oh, you'll have to have one well before that. Now you've got Sophie's job you'll get a couple to wear at the Summer Fever Festival launch. You will be the important person organising the show because Gellie always goes to pieces. She gets so nervous, even Charlie can't calm her down. You do remember about the Festival? I did tell you all about it. It's being held near Frampton this year and it's going to be massive.'

Nicola looked blank.

'Honestly, Nicola. Hello, this is earth is calling Nicola Grace Cowan. I told you all about the launch last week and how it's going to be at the Summer Fever Rock Festival. The parents wouldn't let me go to Fever last year because you weren't here to babysit me. So inconvenient of you to rush off to Africa. But I went anyway and Gellie covered for me. This year it's all legal as we'll both be working there. *Armageddon* are playing but sorry, I forgot, you have no idea who they are, do you?'

With that Maggie flounced out of the office to be replaced by a pale faced Gellie.

'Nicola, I can't believe you've stepped straight into Sophie's shoes. I'm so grateful.'

Well, it would have been nice to have been asked, thought Nicola. Too many people just seemed to assume 'good old Nicola' would step in and save the day.

'Launching *Gellateens* means so much to me but I'm so scared because *Angelica* is so conservative and now I have to go whacky. Driven by Maggie of course but she knows what teenagers will wear these days and I need to crack that market.'

Gellie dragged a chair over to Nicola and sat down. Nicola thought it was rather ironic that here she was sitting at Gellie's desk in Gellie's seat and Gellie was sitting opposite like a visitor in her own office.

'I'm getting you some help tomorrow, Nicola. Felicity, who has helped out before is coming in till after Fever so she'll be holding down the business. She doesn't get on that well with Oliver but the two of them will just have to muddle through. Oliver's world is like a Su Doku grid where everything must slot into the right square and add up to its total every which way.' Gellie sighed.

'Creative business is not like that but it helps having someone like Oliver around who can anchor the creativity to a financial rock. So, there you are, you're free to concentrate on Fever. I know you felt I had dreamed up your summer job so that I could have Maggie here, well, that's all changed now.' Gellie gave Nicola a tired smile. Her mobile rang and Gellie got up and walked towards the door.

'Leaving now…tired…yes now…bye Darling,' was all Nicola caught of the conversation.

'I'm off now. See you tomorrow, Nicola.' With another tired smile in a drawn face with contrasting glittering eyes, Gellie left and a calmness settled gratefully on the building.

Nicola sat and stared straight ahead. How had things managed to change so violently in the space of a few hours? Stepping over the strewn papers on the floor, Nicola went over to the filing cabinet and extracted a worryingly thin folder entitled *'Summer Fever Festival – Golden Valley Site – Gloucestershire'* and sat down at the desk before opening the folder with a heavy heart. A marquee had been booked for the Saturday night with lighting, makeup tables, electricity points and rails for the clothes. But that was about it. Nicola glanced at the programme. The clothes show was on just before *Armageddon,* one of the hottest new bands on the planet – Nicola didn't consider herself a complete nerd. Fever was going to be, as Maggie predicted, massive. Oh my God, thought Nicola in the quiet emptiness of the building I need some serious help here. Maggie had failed to return with the coffee so Nicola made herself a very large, very strong mug of instant and sat down again. Inspiration, even after being tempted by an overload of caffeine, was not forthcoming. She started to doodle on the pad in front of her. She wrote Fever forwards, backwards, with her left hand and vertically down the page. Then moved on to word associations.

Fever – Dengue. Well certainly don't want to go there again!

Saturday Night Fever – One of her mother's favourite DVDs.

Wasn't there an Elvis Presley song with 'Fever' in it?

Scarlet fever – Kate had that in Year 10 at school just before the exams. Kate was so determined to do the exams because she thought if she didn't she would have to repeat the year. So they all covered her in makeup but then she fainted in an exam and the truth was exposed. Kate had sent a text yesterday saying she was working in London for her cousin over the summer and that they should catch up.

Nicola suddenly sat up. Kate's cousin, worked for a company that organised events. Perfect, if she could pull this off.

Grabbing her mobile, Nicola called Kate. No reply, as usual, so she left a message and started to work on Plan B in case the brilliant Plan A didn't work.

Three hours later and several cups of coffee down the road little progress had been made. Nicola had found the budget for Gellie's show stuffed in a random file but it didn't make much sense. She made a note to tackle Oliver about it. With the help of a map and her own local knowledge she pinpointed the site in Chalford Valley. It was a brilliant location. All she needed was a brilliant plan to match it. With a sigh Nicola pushed her chair from her desk and walked down the stairs and into the fresh air. It was a lovely sunny day but all Nicola could smell was disaster coming her way. She leant back against the wall and closed her eyes.

A black taxi cab crunched to a halt ejecting Kate in front of her.

'What are you doing out in the road? Come on, there's work to be done,' cried Kate propelling Nicola back into the office while updating her on her, Kate's, most recent exploits in the world of event management.

'What's the crisis? I've got a couple of hours before I absolutely have to be on a river boat on the Thames. So start talking.' Kate got her notebook out and looked expectantly at Nicola.

Nicola explained briefly about *Gellateen*, the burglary and the launch at the Summer Fever Festival. Kate's face registered surprise, excitement and then horror when Nicola handed over the file.

Flicking through it Kate said 'Wow, this is a big one. I mean Fever but is this all that has been done so far? No models booked? No presenter? No launch party? Caterers? Music? I don't believe this mess. This is serious shit, Nicola.'

'I know. You don't have to point out the blindingly obvious. That's why I called you. You are my last chance, my only hope.' Nicola looked imploringly at Kate.

'Hmmmm. And what's in it for me?'

'Tickets to Fever?'

'How many and they must be for all three days and with access to the VIP areas.'

'Done. How many do you want? Let me know.'

'I want three of Maggie's best designs. One for each day.'

'Done.'

'Cool. I'll do it. I'll have to tell my cousin, but a couple of Fever tickets should do the trick. I'll work out of hours so I'll make 'to do' lists, you do the tasks and then we'll move on. It'll be fun. I enjoy working under pressure. What's the Fever budget?'

Nicola told her and the response was a sharp intake of breath. 'I could ask Charlie Willstone for an increase?' said Nicola scared that Kate would back out of the deal.

'No let's see if we can make this work. Now I'm taking you out for a drink and you're going to tell me exactly what happened in Africa!'

The next day Gellie's new PA was in the office before Nicola and seemed to have *Angelica* and all its organisational foibles well under control. It was such a relief to Nicola to find a sense of calm and control instead of the usual chronic chaos. There was no sign of Gellie. Maggie was visiting a group of outworkers but more worryingly nothing from Kate. Nicola got out all the files relating to previous launches and started trying to construct a framework for Fever.

Late in the afternoon Kate arrived by taxi clutching several bulging folders. Nicola did not recall transportation by taxi as part of the deal but kept quiet.

'Right. We have a plan and Helen is up for it provided Dart and Associates get some exposure. All the basics are booked with D&A's usual suppliers. One major problem is models. They are just so expensive. So I had this idea. On Friday we'll send Maggie out into the crowd to pull kids who would look good in her designs. No pay but they can keep what they wear.' Kate paused and looked thoughtful.

'Get Maggie to make up two of all the garments so that we have one complete collection back here under lock and key. Now my only gap is the presenter. Will Gellie do it?'

'No way. She'll be shivering with nerves in a heap somewhere. She never presents.'

'Well then. Any ideas? Not much cash left in the budget. What about Julian's gorgeous younger brother?'

Lucas. Nicola hoped she wasn't going to blush. She bent down and retrieved a stapler from the floor.

'A possibility I suppose. He can certainly do centre stage but I have no idea where he is.'

'Find him,' said Kate.

'Gellie's his aunt isn't she? So he'll do it for her. Must dash. I'm on my way to another client. Thank you for asking me to do this. It's fun. Good contrast to astro physics and nice to have my own account instead of having to mop up behind Helen all day. I'll be in touch. Find Lucas.' And with that Kate was gone.

So where was Lucas. London? Oxford? Saudi? Kenya? Anywhere really. In the end, Nicola decided to send a text to Lucas' mobile on the grounds that it would be cheaper than actually speaking to him. She found his number in Gellie's address book.

Hi Lucas. Big dramas at *Angelicas*. We need someone to present the *Gellateen* launch at the Summer Fever Festival at the end of August. Your name has been put forward. No idea where you are but hope you'll be in the UK for the Festival. Gellie would love it if you presented the show - she'll want it in safe hands. You'll be brilliant.

Nicola paused. Was she overdoing it?

Nicola x

Nicola pressed SEND and turned her mobile off.

The next few weeks were a whirl of activity as Nicola moved between Frampton, London and the Festival site. Her parents were delighted that Nicola had got her teeth into something positive which was keeping her busy. Kate was brilliant but not very good at the constant checking of the detail that Nicola felt was vital. Gellie told her how wonderful she was at least three times a day and how delighted she was that Lucas had agreed to front the show. So he had replied to Gellie but not to her but Nicola had no time to stress about that. More than anything she was relieved that her strategy of putting distance between Gellie and the event until the last moment was working.

On the Saturday evening Nicola stood with one hand in her mouth and the other clenched behind her back with her fingers crossed. The sun was pulling a grey cloak over the Summer Fever Festival as it finally slid back down behind the Cotswold Hills. It had been one awesome week. It started badly with Charlie Willstone marching into the office and demanding all the Fever files just as the cavalcade of vans and cars was about to set off for the Cotswolds. Charlie's efforts to take over and run the show were, however, thwarted by everyone turning to Nicola for answers. Once on site Nicola's careful attention to detail had everything falling neatly into place.

The crowd's attention had been captivated by the whirling kaleidoscope of colour on the stage during the show and for a final dance the teenage models, who had been a wild success, were joined by anyone connected with the *Gellateen* range. Anyone and everyone, that is apart from Nicola who was still standing in the shadow of the stage not quite believing that, with a great deal of help, she had managed to pull this one off. She tipped her head back and stood up straight half hoping that Jamie would appear and congratulate her on moving on from the quicksand of time that she had been trapped in at Paddington Station at the beginning of the summer.

Figures moved past her as the members of *Armageddon* got ready to go on stage. Nicola could see Lucas dancing with Gellie. There was a certain intimacy about the way they danced together, hip on hip, fluid rhythm and a synchronization which Nicola found puzzling. Lucas and Gellie were so alike in many ways, able to change moods in an instant. Both could be wildly excited and glittery but whereas Gellie could crumple into a mess of insecurities Lucas' alter ego was one of cold calculating, being completely in charge.

Nicola turned to go and find Kate to see if orders were coming in back at the marquee. She bumped straight into Lucas.

'There you are,' smiled Lucas at Nicola. 'I was looking for you on the stage. I wanted to dance with you and here you are hiding. It's been a great show. Gellie's over the moon. Maggie's done a great job and so have you. Gellie's looking for you now.'

Lucas took a step closer and Nicola thought she was going to crumble under the strength of the sexual attraction that was thundering round her. She could smell Lucas like a lioness in heat smells her mate and her body was out of control. Suddenly Lucas had his arms round her but his kiss was a gentle caress. He stepped back and cupped her face in his hands his eyes glittering like Gellie's. And then they crashed together again and Nicola could only moan softly in his arms. Lucas pulled slowly away and ran his hands over his face.

'I'm sorry, Nicola. I shouldn't have done that but I have wanted to do it for so long.' Lucas grinned at her. 'I've got to go and catch a plane now that I'm in the serious world of work. Good luck at uni, Aberdeen isn't it?'

'Newcastle, actually,' muttered Nicola swallowing hard.

'Well have a great time in Glasgow and say Hi to Jamie from me.'

With that Lucas was gone leaving Nicola red faced and totally confused. How the hell did Lucas know about Jamie? And what exactly did that amazing encounter with Lucas actually mean in the greater scheme of things? And why the hell was she going to Newcastle anyway?

But far greater things were happening right in front of her. Nicola climbed onto the roof of the security van parked beside the *Gellateen* marquee. The afternoon's preparations for the evening show had been quite exhausting. To start with there were far too many kids clamoring to be models which took quite a bit of careful sorting. Then the usual panic of getting everything to fit with safety pins and even duct tape as a last resort. She hadn't dare go near the hair and makeup. But it had worked and now the main attraction were on stage and ready to go.

A crash of drums lit up the stage as *Armageddon* launched into hard rock. Drums played live had a great deal more beat and rhythm than Nicola had imagined. The thrum of the bass guitar echoed down the valley, weaving pouring and spreading the music through the trees and along the hedgerows. The lead singer's deep caustic voice made words atmospheric as the crowd danced and sang in front of the stage. To Nicola it was pure magic. When the band moved to tracks from the new album, the music became more possessive of and personal to *Armageddon's* signature and the crowd became more ecstatic. Not too far away from her perch, Nicola spotted Kate standing absolutely mesmerized gazing fixedly at the band.

Then it was all over and the crowd settled down to party to music supplied by a local DJ. Letting the darkness wind itself tightly round her, Nicola pulled out her mobile and phoned for a taxi. Twenty minutes later she was back in her room in Frampton with her duvet pulled up over her head. But as soon as she fell asleep she found herself trapped in the dream which had been haunting her for weeks. It always started with the Tree of Forgetfulness winding its branches round her chest constricting her breathing and then, just as she was going to suffocate, releasing her into some weird fantasy where nothing was recognisable.

The incessant chime signalling new texts finally woke her and the streaming sun pulled her back to reality.

Maggie: **Nicola where are you? We're worried. Charlie has organised a Big Breakfast at The Grange. 10.00. Be There! M xx**

Kate: **Wow! Hooked up with Armageddon's drummer. Totally Amazing! C U at breakfast!**

There was a timid knock at the door and her mother's worried face peered round the door.

'We thought we heard you last night. Are you OK? You look terrible!'

'Thanks Mum. Just tired really. It's been a hectic six weeks.' Nicola ran her fingers through her hair.

'Want to join us for breakfast? There's fresh coffee?' Monica gave Maggie's empty bed a sidelong glance but she didn't say anything.

'Actually,' said Nicola sliding out of bed, 'Charlie's organising a big breakfast at The Grange and I said I'd be there. Coffee would be lovely, though. I'll just have a quick shower.'

The walk through the countryside preparing itself for autumn, but not quite ready to let go of summer, lifted Nicola's spirits so that she was almost smiling when she arrived to find that the party had seamlessly transferred itself from the Festival to the Grange. Charlie was walking round with a bottle filling glasses and shouting 'Marvellous!' at everyone. Gellie had collapsed into a hammock on the terrace and looked as white as a sheet. A couple were woven around a statue beside the fish pond staring into the sun. Nicola was just able to make out Kate's tousled hair messed up with a blond head she didn't recognise. She was about to go over to them when she was grabbed by an excited Maggie.

'Hey, there you are! Where on earth did you get to? You missed a fantastic party. Never mind, come into the study and see the figures. They are amazing.'

Nicola followed Maggie into the house stopping to grab a cup of coffee from Dee in the kitchen. Oliver was sitting at Charlie's desk beside a couple of ledgers, stuffing cash into bags. He looked up and Nicola nearly fell over when he actually smiled at her.

'Hi Nicola. You're never going to believe this. Charlie has just done the sums and we have an enormous profit after every expense we can think of has been subtracted. Gellie is going to be stoked.'

'And the order book. Tell Nicola about the orders for *Gellateen* and *Angelica*. They are huge.' Maggie was grinning from ear to ear and quite taken aback when Nicola gave her a big hug. In a split second everyone was hugging everyone and laughing.

Racing back to the terrace to give Gellie the news, Nicola bumped into Kate.

'Nicola,' screamed Kate. 'This is Archie Kenny – drummer for *Armageddon*, and just the greatest on this earth!' Nicola found herself shaking hands with a very tall blond guy who bent down and kissed her gently on the cheek.

'Hi Nicola. Thank you for bringing Kate to Fever. My search for the most beautiful woman in the world has now ended.' And with that Archie swung a delighted Kate over his shoulder and gently put her down beside Nicola.

Nicola smiled at Kate who knew exactly how pleased Nicola was for her. However too much loved up stuff moved Nicola on to see Gellie who had been extricated from the hammock and was smiling, slightly bemused as her friends crowded round to congratulate her. Job well done thought Nicola.

After the Fever Festival Nicola's summer was over. Maggie went off to art college to start her foundation year; Henry was embroiled in ground school training and Nicola went home to pack for Newcastle. She dutifully ploughed through the reading lists, went shopping for uni stuff, caught up with Kate who was still on fire about Festival and her drummer from *Armageddon*.

It was quiet and peaceful at home. Her parents were adjusting to a house without Maggie and Henry but also getting used to having Nicola around when they'd largely adjusted to operating without her. Nicola felt slightly miffed at being a kind of guest in her own home and embarrassed at her mother's attempts to over compensate. Luckily Jake was overjoyed at having someone to walk him home even if, after a decent interval, he would reappear on the Cowan's doorstep. Sometimes Nicola would walk Jake home past Mulberry Cottage. It was empty again. Gellie had said she needed a country retreat over the winter but as yet she hadn't put in an appearance. Nicola wondered if Caroline and Dermot would ever come back and live there. She wondered if Lucas had his stuff stored there in one of the attic rooms but Lucas did not strike her as a person who would have stuff. Nicola checked her phone for messages even though she knew that the likelihood of receiving a text from Lucas equated to her chance of winning the national lottery when she hadn't even bought a ticket. But he might just get in touch.

Nicola kicked herself hard. She had followed Jamie's advice and 'got a grip on herself'. She felt she'd moved forwards towards a new life and was starting to be positive about her three years at Newcastle Uni although she was still a little hesitant about moving so far away from familiar surroundings. If only she could cut the invisible umbilical cord which was tying her to Lucas. If it was necessary to dwell on the past, she really should be grieving for Julian and Julia and not lusting after Julian's younger brother. But Lucas was family so kind of a way of hanging on. Or perhaps it was because he seemed so virtually unobtainable and had no interest in her, but that was a lie. Nobody kisses someone like Lucas had kissed her if they are not attracted to them. Where was Jamie when she needed his advice and guidance?

Bags were packed and ready to go. Nicola could almost touch her mother's apprehension. No one asked Nicola for her thoughts on Newcastle, the course she'd chosen, or where she was going to be living. It was just accepted that she had made all her own choices and a kind of false gaiety splashed around in the house.

An excited Dee phoned Monica but not to enquire about Nicola. Jocelyn had just got engaged to the set designer in Los Angeles and they were flying home for a few days to talk about the wedding 'Just so exciting, Monica', exclaimed Dee. Charlie had gone overboard and organised a party on the Saturday and of course all the Cowans were invited. The Willstones will be having a gloat fest was Maggie reaction. Luckily they hadn't planned to set out for Newcastle until the following Wednesday, taking in a few friends on the way and giving themselves time to see Nicola properly settled in, much to Nicola's embarrassment.

'What's his name, anyway?' Maggie asked Nicola sprawling across her bed and mentally rearranging their bedroom back into her own studio space once Nicola had but one foot out of the door.

'We can't keep calling him 'the set builder' can we?'

'No idea. Anyway he's morphed into a 'designer',' replied Nicola.

Maggie grinned slyly. 'Are you looking forward to the party, Nicola? Should be fun seeing Jocelyn all loved up. I wonder if she'll ask me to design her dress?'

'Hardly. Especially since you're doing sculpture this term. The mind boggles. Could be fun. Will Gellie be coming? I've hardly seen her since Fever and I won't for ages if I'm off to Newcastle next week.'

Maggie sat up. 'What do you mean 'if' you're off to Newcastle! You are going aren't you?'

'Yes, of course. Just don't mess up my half of the room. I will be back!'

If there was one thing about The Grange, it did do parties really well. Nicola drove them up to the front door and then had to swing round and follow the parking signs pointing past the stables. The Grange was looking magnificent in the mellow light of the autumn evening. The soft Cotswold limestone glowed in a way that Nicola felt like running up to the house and giving it a big hug. Light and noise spilled out to greet them as they entered the massive stone porch.

Jocelyn was poised to pounce on arriving guests.

'Hey you all came. This is awesome. Come and meet Torin.' Jocelyn rushed off to the drawing room. Maggie mouthed 'Tor - what?' at Nicola. 'Shut up' mouthed Nicola back.

'Here he is.' Jocelyn was wrapped round her fiancé like a python. 'Torin, darling, meet our favourite neighbours, The Cowans'

Torin stepped forward to shake their hands as he smiled indulgently at Jocelyn. Nicola weighed him up. Torin looked suntanned, fit and relaxed. She vaguely remembered him at Gellie's launch all those months ago as rather thin and pasty looking. In fact you could easily overlook him in a crowd. Now he would stand out. Returning to the States must have been good for him or Dee had done a very good makeover job so that he would be an acceptable addition to the Willstone clan. Nicola moved her head slightly and overheard Dee talking to the vicar.

'...Torin's family are in real estate in California. They own some very valuable property in San Diego and the strip in LA where Torin and Jocelyn will be living. Torin is doing so well as a set designer that they will soon be able to live anywhere in the world. Isn't it lovely? Now let me get you another drink...'

Good luck to them, thought Nicola. Torin was obviously doing well and Jocelyn was looking happy and relaxed. She's lost that pinched rather mean look she wore when she thought no one was looking.

The rest of her family had been swallowed up in the party crowd and Nicola was left on her own by the front door. Now the sun had set there was a chill in the air and Nicola could feel the evening air seeping under the sleeves of her summer dress. Her *Angelica* top was in the car so she set off to find it. It was dark in the car park but she found the car and turning to close the door with her top over her arm, she caught sight of a shadowy figure walking slowly towards her. Screwing her eyes up it was difficult to see who it was.

'Jamie?' called Nicola softly 'Jamie is that you?' The figure swerved sharply and headed off towards the stables.

'Damn,' muttered Nicola. 'Who the hell was that?' No telling, so she made her way back to the house. Jamie usually turned up after she'd been thinking about him and he always spoke to her. Why was this time so different? She needed him to reassure her especially since she was so close to launching off into the unknown again.

The party noise level had doubled since Nicola had slipped out and so had the number of guests. Stopping to talk to people she knew vaguely, Nicola went searching for Maggie. She saw Gellie holding court to a crowd of admirers and acknowledged her wave. If Gellie was over there then Maggie must be somewhere close. She was. Impatiently she pulled at Nicola's sleeve.

'I've been looking for you. He's here. Come with me.' Maggie gave Nicola a push in the direction of the dining room.

'Who?'

'Lucas, you idiot.'

'But I don't want to see him.' Nicola dug her heels in and swung round to face Maggie. Too late. A beautiful brown hand slid over her shoulder sending a paralysing shiver down Nicola's back.

'Hey. I was looking for you earlier. How are you?' Lucas stepped back and ran his eyes over her. Nicola suppressed another shiver.

Maggie looked expectantly at Nicola. It was time she said something really meaningful, right now.

But Nicola was locked into Lucas' eyes. It could only actually be a brief moment before the contact was shattered but in that time Nicola saw a depth of passion in Lucas' brown eyes but there was also an aura of uncertain danger, of lack of trust, a wildness that was threatening to explode and a veil of secrets that mixed and remixed all the messages that were being sent. Transmission was instant and Nicola felt that all she was sending back was the one clear message that she loved him.

'Nicola! I've caught up with you at last. And you, dear boy, when did you arrive?' Gellie slipped an arm possessively around Lucas and glittered at Nicola in a whirl of energetic colour.

'Just now. I left the car at Mulberry and walked up in all this clean fresh country air.' Lucas smiled at Gellie.

'I'm moving down here for a couple of months. After all the frantic developments in London, I need space and peace to get back to being creative. I've had admin up to here. You must come and see me, Nicola. I've a couple of samples to take away with you to trial on the uni scene. I have a little project in Newcastle that I want to discuss with you. Will you be in Newcastle next summer? Mmm,' said Gellie standing back from Nicola and running her eyes over the *Angelica* top she was wearing. 'Yes I think I need to get back to basics. That was always one of my favourite designs. Yes come and see me very very soon. Lucas, are you here long?'

Nicola let out a tense sigh. Gellie was rattling on at a great pace as usual covering up her embarrassment.

Before Lucas could reply Gellie glanced over to the door and waved. 'Come on Lucas, we should catch up with Jocelyn and Torrid, must remember to call him Torin, mustn't I, and then duty done we can relax and enjoy ourselves.'

Nicola looked over to the door and just saw Charlie lounging there with a drink in one hand and a very satisfied smile in the other.

'Nicola, you should have seized the moment and grabbed Lucas yourself before Gellie did. Idiot.' muttered Maggie.

'And what should I have done with him then, Miss know-it-all?' asked Nicola.

'Well if you don't know by now there really is no hope. Come on let's mix and match with the crowd.'

It was a good party, the Willstone's were expensively hospitable. Dee was going back to the States with Jocelyn and Torin to stay with Torin's parents in San Diego to discuss wedding arrangements. As far as Nicola could make out there would have to be at least two ceremonies and several parties before Jocelyn would consider herself as Mrs T. Nicola finally caught up with Lucas.

'What are you doing now?'

'I'm working for Sulei's family in Oman. I've spent time in London but now I'm off back to Saudi to improve my Arabic' And you?'

'I'm off to Newcastle Uni next week. Three years of Environmental Science.'

'I thought you were going to do Chemistry?'

'I was until I messed up my 'A's.' Nicola's voice trailed off and she saw a flash of comprehension in Lucas' eyes.

'Did you say Newcastle Uni?' A guy Nicola vaguely remembered from primary school joined the conversation. 'My cousin is in his second year doing biology. Great place. Really good party atmosphere. You'll love it!'

Nicola glanced at Lucas in desperation and saw that he had already turned half away looking bored. As she opened her mouth Lucas stepped forward and kissed her gently on each cheek.

'Must go. Time to get Gellie home. Have a great time at Durham and keep in touch. Take Care.' Lucas walked off across the room and out of Nicola's life. Nicola muttered 'Newcastle not Durham' under her breath at Lucas' back.

Her mother couldn't understand how one minute Nicola had been really focused on going to Newcastle, getting her stuff ready and willing to share the experience. The next minute she had turned cranky and could hardly be bothered to get out of bed. It all happened after the Willstone's party and all Monica could think was that Nicola was jealous of Jocelyn and the fact that she and Torin were getting married when it should perhaps have been Nicola and Julian. Hopefully Nicola would meet someone nice at Newcastle. But Nicola was not at all jealous of Jocelyn. Nicola had crawled back inside herself. She was where no one could touch her and her life could progress out in the other world without her being touched by it.

Her last day at home was lovely and sunny so her mother suggested a trip to Cirencester, a bit of shopping and maybe a pub lunch, but Nicola said she'd rather take Jake home the long way so that she could enjoy her last few hours of fresh air before she was consumed by urban pollution. And it was glorious walking over the top of the Cotswold Hills. On her way back, Nicola sat down in the shelter of her stone wall to admire the familiar view. Suddenly she saw Jamie striding towards her across the field his long coat flapping round his ankles. A bit overdressed considering the warm sunshine thought Nicola. Jamie sat down beside her and pushed his glasses up his nose.

'How are things, Nicola?' he asked.

'Jamie, I'm so glad you've turned up. I've just been having such an argument with myself. Here I am at the start of a life's big adventure, a new life chosen by sticking a pin in a map, to do a course I accepted as a last resort. At no time have I been brave enough to stand my ground and say that is not for me. Not like Maggie who seems to know exactly where she's going and how she's going to get there.'

'Only you can decide what you want, Nicola. That's been your problem all along. You can't just drift through life letting other people push or pull you in whatever direction pleases them. You must be firm with yourself and all those around you. As for Newcastle, go, with an open mind. If it turns out not to be for you, you will know but don't just throw it away unless you have a better alternative, which you don't. You might be surprised. You might love it. You don't need a boyfriend right now; you need a life, your life. So go out there and find it. Maggie is a good example though perhaps a bit too driven.'

With that Jamie raised his hand in a high five and left.

'Bye, Jamie. And thanks,' said Nicola to the retreating back in its long flapping coat.

5

Having never been north of Birmingham, arriving in Newcastle after a long car journey was something of a shock to Nicola. She had never imagined that England was so thick north to south. She was sharing a flat with five other girls none of whom had ever met before but they had all had gap years. Her parents left her unpacking, but not without giving her the information about student health services in case she should get sick again. 'Oh Mum,' was Nicola's reaction.

There were only fifty students in the first year intake of Professor Boyd's new undergraduate degree course. Most of the lecturers came from other departments but there was a large collection of post graduate students around which gave the place an edgy air of activity and purpose. Nicola soon caught up with the research students she'd met in Watamu who told her that the Sports Bar on Friday nights was the place to be.

'There are always some of us around in the bar about six o'clock and you'll soon get to know the regulars. It is a good place to be to find out who's doing what field work and where and if there might be some paid assistant work at a weekend. Also where the parties are, which events everyone is planning to go to. You know a sort of what's on and where.'

Nicola wasn't sure about going, particularly on her own, but her class mates were keen and after a couple of Friday evenings, Nicola had the courage to turn up on her own and even to follow-up some of the invitations particularly to uni rugby matches. She was quite relieved not to run into Joe who, she found out, was back in Watamu for a couple of months. In fact she didn't run into him again until one very cold dark winter morning at the beginning of her second term.

Back home for Christmas Nicola found her bedroom unrecognisable. It was stripped bare apart from three ideas boards as Maggie went through a minimalist phase.

'Great to see you too,' hissed Maggie when Nicola complained that she had nowhere to put her stuff. 'You're only here for a few hours and listen to you. I can hardly be expected to alter my entire mind set in order to accommodate you while you're on holiday.' Nicola gave up.

Mulberry Cottage was shut up again as Gellie had got over her country phase and retreated back to the city. No one knew whether Dermot and Caroline would be there for the festive season, in fact, no one seemed to know where they were, or care, as the main topic of conversation was the wedding in April. Naturally enough, Jocelyn had not asked Maggie to design her wedding dress but Maggie was rather wickedly bending Jocelyn's sister's ear over her choice of bridesmaid's dress. She showed her sketches to Nicola who was appalled.

'You can't, Maggie, you simply can't. Dee will have an absolute fit if she sees these.'

'Job done,' smirked Maggie.

Christmas was a happy family affair. On Boxing Day there was the now annual walk and get together with the Willstones. No Bundle to bound round their legs just Jake, who took to pointing out the shorts cuts back to his place on the rug in front of the fire, but he was ignored. Gellie was with the Willstones well wrapped up in layers of *Angelica* with a *Gellateen* on top. Nicola inquired, politely about Dermot and Caroline and was told that they were staying in Kilifi for the winter and Lucas was spending Christmas with them.

January was bitter in Newcastle. Nicola decided to copy Gellie and took to wearing layers of *Gellateen* with her favourite *Angelica* on top. Her flat mates raved about the *Gellateen* and soon Nicola was emailing Gellie with orders. Gellie thought she might visit Newcastle and investigate the possibility of a pop up shop somewhere near the uni. The beginning of her second term was so much easier than the first. She had great flat mates and a wide circle of friends both in the Department and across the university. Her life had a sense of purpose and she felt happy again. There was just a very small problem labelled Joe which she was about to meet head on. Late for a nine o'clock lecture, Nicola raced round the corner of the building with her head down into the wind and ran smack into Joe. With her notes splayed across the path, she met Joe's eyes, the one bit of his face visible.

'Hey, Nicola,' said Joe as he pulled his scarf down to his collar. 'I was hoping to run into you, but not quite like this. How are you?'

'Fine,' replied Nicola hurriedly picking up her notes before they dissipated around the quad.

'And you?' she said squinting up at Joe. She had forgotten how smiley he was. Joe smiled with his whole face which made him such a warm engaging person.

'Got a first and now I'm back doing a PhD that is if I ever get the time as Prof. Boyd seems to have me lined up for every research project the Department is involved in.'

'Wow, that's amazing. Congratulations.'

The quad clock struck the quarter hour.

'God I'm going to be late again,' said Nicola glancing nervously at her watch.

'It's Friday so why don't we catch up at the Sports this evening?' said Joe. 'See you around six?'

'Yes, that would be great. Thanks.' Nicola said to Joe as he handed her the last of her pile of notes.

In the end Nicola didn't make it to the Sports bar. One of her flat mates, had come back from a weekend in tears because her boyfriend had dumped her. She was also angry because he had managed to get in first so why was she so upset mused Nicola. Anyway it was decided that the six of them just had to have a night in the flat together with ice cream, chocolate, vodka and DVDs. It was all organised and Nicola found herself quite relieved that she didn't have to go and meet Joe before she had had time to think herself round the Joe problem. Not that he was a problem of course. Joe was just a friend.

Nicola was next in the department on the following Tuesday and feeling bad about not even letting Joe know that she couldn't make the Sports bar, she went looking for him. There was a note pinned up on his office door saying that he had gone to the department's new Field Centre in County Galway in Ireland for a month. There was a mobile number and an email address.

The end of January marked the imminent arrival of the anniversary Nicola was dreading. She decided to remember the day Julia was born rather than the day she died, because it was more important to recall the small scrap of humanity in her arms rather than thinking about what she suffered trying to survive. It was a suitably grey day and very cold. Wrapped in her duvet, with a beanie pulled down over her ears, Nicola stayed in bed and miserably tried to recall the intense pain and anguish needed to bring Julia into the world and how her last link with Julian was so cruelly torn away. Just as it was getting dark, Nicola fell asleep and found herself fighting the Tree of Forgetfulness nightmares which had followed her to Newcastle. There was a faint rustle and peeping out into the gloom Nicola could just make out Sister Benny bending over her.

'My Dear, I felt I should come and visit you to offer you comfort at this difficult time,' said Sister Benny arranging herself at the bottom of Nicola's bed. 'I have been watching over you and you have, my dear, been coping remarkably well.'

'No I haven't,' hissed Nicola. 'I'm horribly depressed and feel like I'm sliding away from reality as I know it. Seeing you is not helping at all. I want to remember but need to forget and I don't know how to do both at the same time.'

'Nicola, it is not our place to question the fact that God needed Julia more than we did.'

'He didn't need her,' Nicola found herself almost shouting. 'What could God possibly want with a tiny baby?'

'Hush. We must not question God's wisdom. Just think about what your life would be like if you had Julia with you now. How would you cope with a baby and university? Take a walk down to the shopping mall and look at all the single mothers sitting on benches, pushing their kids aimlessly in strollers. Would you have been able to do that?'

'So Julia is better off dead in your view. Is that it?' Nicola was on the point of crying. She could not believe what she was hearing. It was almost as though Sister Benny was trying to salve her own conscience over Julia's death. 'Go away. I didn't ask you to come.'

Nicola pulled the duvet back over her head and sank to a place where no one to reach her.

Several hours later, someone lifted a corner of the duvet. Nicola stuck a hand out and switched on her bedside light. Jamie was standing in the shadows wrapped in his big black coat.

'Jamie?' said Nicola uncertainly. She hadn't expected today of all days to be big on visitors.

'Nicola,' said Jamie. 'I just came to see if you were all right. What's wrong?'

'Everything. Sister Benny was here earlier and I sent her away. She has gone hasn't she?' Nicola looked wildly round her room.

'Shhhh. You're on your own,' said Jamie settling down on the end of the bed. 'Now, Nicola, it is no good wrapping yourself in your misery even for one moment. You have a wonderful opportunity to start your life again. Don't waste it on constructing what might have been. Go forward and make Julia's memory proud of you.'

There was a knock at the door.

'Nicola. Are you OK? We didn't realise you've been in bed all day. Can I come in?' It was Iona sounding concerned.

Nicola looked round but Jamie had gone. She sunk back into bed.

'Yes. Come on in. I don't think I have anything catching.'

Iona pushed open the door and came into the room with tea, toast and marmite.

In early March Nicola signed up for a weekend away with the department's Social Club. The aim was to walk some of Hadrian's Wall and as it looked as though an early spring was going to chase the winter all the way back to Scotland, Nicola was looking forward to getting some real exercise and a load of fresh air. It was just as she expected and a bit more. A bright sunny frosty Saturday took the party high up on the Pennines. Looking down from the vantage point of an old Roman Fort and half expecting a marauding horde to breach the ramparts, Nicola suddenly felt better. Here she was in a beautiful part of Britain with friends who had no idea about her past life, well apart from Joe and he only knew a little, and no one was peering at her wondering if she was going to collapse with another bout of dengue fever. Nicola turned, threw her arms into the air and laughed at her friends who were so surprised at this spontaneous action from someone generally considered to be a control freak, that they laughed with her. It was a wonderful moment.

Later, on the coach on the way back to the hostel, Joe slipped into the seat beside her.

'I think I saw the Nicola I met in Watamu this afternoon,' said Joe smiling at Nicola. 'What happened back there?'

Nicola blushed slightly. 'Did I tell you that I had dengue fever last year in Watamu? Well it has taken me quite a long time to recover. Today in the sunshine and fresh air I felt just so much better.' Nicola hoped that sounded plausible.

'You poor thing,' replied Joe, looking concerned. He asked how Nicola was getting on with course, how was the workload and was she looking forward to the first year field trip to Galway. Then they switched to chatting about Joe's research in Watamu and his plans to go back there in the summer.

Back at the hostel the talk was all about the new research facility in Galway. Since he had been heavily involved in setting it up and the only person who had been there, Joe was centre stage. Nicola watched him from the back of the room, impressed by how fluently he spoke and his careful consideration of all the questions thrown at him. On two occasions he looked over at her and smiled. Nicola turned away embarrassed.

The Easter vacation was dominated by a trip home for Jocelyn's wedding and furious revision. Having approached her uni course slightly nonchalantly, unsure as to whether it was for her, Nicola found that she had not done nearly enough study to be selected for her preferred options the following year. She immediately decided on a punishing revision regime to rectify this. Without thinking about the consequences, Nicola went to ask Joe's advice. His response was to keep her supplied with the most recent research papers, some of them his own, which naturally required numerous coffees in the Post Graduate Common Room. Nicola found that she could be very relaxed in Joe's company and began sharing in his passion for marine biology which was her top option choice.

The temperature in Gloucestershire was positively tropical, pushed to those heights by the frantic activity in Frampton. Dee Willstone had very set ideas about the timetable for Jocelyn's wedding day and as host, thought she was in charge. Wedding etiquette is different in the United States and since that was to be her home, Jocelyn had equally strong ideas of her own. Monica found herself being used as referee by both sides and, in desperation, tried to bring in Gellie as an adjudicator. At least that move united Dee and Jocelyn who were both appalled by Gellie's whacky ideas.

The atmosphere at The Grange was too much for Nicola so she took her offer of help down to the church where Gellie and Caroline were arranging the flowers. As the heavy door creaked open a shaft of light caught Gellie's dark unruly curls and Caroline's controlled straight bob as they laughed together on their hands and knees amidst a pile of flowers and greenery.

With Gellie otherwise occupied, Nicola felt it was a good moment to ask Caroline her burning question.

'Caroline, is Lucas going to make it to the wedding?'

'I sincerely hope so. He's travelling back from Nairobi with Elodie, you met Elodie at Tsavo didn't you, and then they are meeting Suleiman off a plane at some ungodly hour and coming straight here tomorrow morning. Then he has to go straight back, pressure of work he said. But we did see quite a lot of him at Christmas which was lovely.'

Caroline walked off to the pulpit with an arm full of roses leaving Nicola with her thoughts. That evening with their parents invited to The Grange for supper, Nicola and Maggie stayed at home with the sewing machine running while Maggie altered Nicola's outfit.

'I mean your dress is fine but we need to do something with the top and I need to make your fascinator tone in,' said Maggie with her mouth bursting with pins. She leapt to her feet and went to find her fabric bag instructing Nicola to fetch the bottle of vodka kept under her bed for emergencies. When Nicola protested, Maggie explained that it was a true emergency as the mission was to make Nicola even more stunning than the bride.

'Why? Why Maggie?' wailed Nicola in despair.

'Because he is coming to the wedding and you have to make an impression,' replied Maggie.

'Who are we talking about here? What do you know that I don't, little sister?'

'Oh for Goodness sake, Nicola. Everyone knows that you've got a truly burning desire for Lucas and that he feels the same way. I heard Gellie talking to him last week and he's coming to the wedding. Arriving tomorrow morning but can't stay so you've only a small window of opportunity to impress, dear sister. And impress you will by the time I've finished with you.'

'Why are you doing this, Maggie?'

'Because you have a right to be completely happy again and you and Lucas are made for each other. Done Deal.'

'I seem to remember you saying that Julian and I were made for each other.' said Nicola rather tartly.

'That was before I met Lucas. Looking at the Smith Owen genes which obviously have some sort of magic for you, Lucas is my preferred option.'

Nicola was not totally convinced about Maggie's intentions but after a couple of vodka shots, she was beginning to look forward to Jocelyn's wedding.

The morning of Dee Willstone's big day dawned bright and clear. Panic number one is over sighed Monica at breakfast, as Andrew read out the weather forecast. Then there was a bang at the back door as Jake, who had managed to escape from The Grange for the day, demanded entry into his safe haven.

'Don't let him into the drawing room. Any of you,' worried Monica. 'My outfit is draped over the sofa and if there is even a hint of a muddy paw mark anywhere I'll, well, I'll be extremely annoyed.'

There were no emergency phone calls from The Grange so the Cowans settled down to a relaxed morning and a panic-free lunch. That is apart from Nicola who suddenly decided that Jake would probably prefer to be back at The Grange enjoying all the fun. Grabbing Bundle's old lead she led a rather reluctant Jake out onto the road and set off up the hill past Mulberry Cottage. There was no sign of life at the cottage though the windows were open and the curtains were flapping in the breeze. At The Grange there was plenty of activity around the marquee as Nicola walked round to the back of the house. But the house was practically empty except for the staff who informed her that the rest of the family were in the church rehearsing and that Lucas had taken Torin to the pub as it would be bad luck if he saw Jocelyn before the ceremony. So Nicola retraced her steps back home. She'd just reached the empty Mulberry Cottage when something heavy thundered into her back. An overjoyed Jake had escaped again. He trotted into Mulberry Cottage garden and made for the back door like he owned the place. How many safe heavens did Jake have in Gloucestershire wondered Nicola as she walked round to fetch him.

Nicola had her hand on Jake's collar ready to pull him away when she heard it. That low burbling baritone laugh that exuded happiness and contentment but no clues as to its origin. Nicola stood with her head on one side pondering the matter. She was sure she knew who it was but a name would not come to her. Then she heard the cottage's creaking stairs and without any more thought yanked Jake down to the gate and hurried home. Jake kept looking back but Nicola dared not in case the owner of the laugh was standing in the lane watching her.

Even Nicola, perhaps just a touch enviously, had to admit that Jocelyn

Willstone's late afternoon wedding to Torin Karanski was beautiful. The church looked very cool according to Maggie; the bride looked radiant; and the music was very traditional arranged by Charlie who liked proper order and procedure with regard to the ceremonial. Monica was very moved by the way Charlie's voice cracked slightly when he announced that he was going to give Jocelyn to Torin. The bride and groom processed through the village after the service, on foot followed by their guests. Dee tried not to imagine how the horribly expensive dress was going to look at the end of the day.

By the time the guests sat down for dinner, Nicola had only caught a couple of fleeting glimpses of Lucas. Was he deliberately avoiding her she wondered as she found her seat next to Suleiman Abbas. Sulei was as gracious and charming as ever and entertained Nicola with lively conversation which had nothing to do with Lucas. So she just had to ask the question.

'Do you see much of Lucas these days, Sulei?'

'Yes. I do. When he's working in Africa for my family's business he comes and spends leave with us in Muscat and he and I go off on safari sometimes. In fact we were in Watamu only a couple of weeks back. We called on Sister Benny like we always do.'

'How is Sister Benny?' asked Nicola.

'Fine. A bit older. She was asking when you were going to visit the convent. The children at the orphanage ask after you too.'

'And Lucas, Sulei. What did you say he was doing in Africa? I thought he worked in London.'

'Yes, he does.' Sulei looked serious. 'But he has been advising my brother-in-law with security matters.'

Further questioning was interrupted by the speeches and then everyone got up and moved around ready for the dancing. There was no sign of Lucas so Nicola presumed he had left to continue his mysterious life elsewhere. Nicola made her way to the bar seeking solace in Maggie's company. At least that would not be dull. A light tough on the back of her neck made her spin round and there he was.

'Lucas.' Nicola was all confused looking into his face for a clue that he had sought her out and that this was not a chance meeting.

'Nicola.' It was the way he said her name with the emphasis on all three syllables. 'Come and dance with me.'

The dance floor was naturally crowded but for Nicola it was a empty of anything that mattered bar one person. After a slightly awkward start the weight of numbers pushed them together and Nicola was in Lucas' arms, she could not believe this was happening after three days on tenterhooks just wanting a moment like this. Lucas pressed his cheek against hers and whispered in her ear.

'Nicola, you look absolutely fabulous tonight. I can't believe that you are here on your own.'

And who, thought Nicola, could have possibly told you that? Stuck for a reply, Nicola shifted her cheek ever so slightly so that Lucas' lips were ever so closer to hers. But before anything could happen, Lucas raised his head, kissed her cheek lightly and then took her hand and walked off the dance floor. They found Sulei holding Lucas' coat.

'I'm sorry Nicola,' said Sulei, 'but we have to leave now. The car is waiting.' Turning to Lucas he said 'Elodie is just getting her coat.'

With that a blonde bronzed body in a backless tight fitting dress rushed up to them.

'Hi Nicola. Good to see you again. Sorry to have to rush off but the spy here has to get back to London tonight.' Elodie squeezed Lucas' arm affectionately. 'We're off wedding dress shopping tomorrow. It's so exciting.'

Nicola looked at Lucas with a please-tell-me-you're-not-marrying-Elodie look.

Lucas' eyes had gone black and glittery and he was obviously amused at her distress. Elodie, quite oblivious to this exchange rushed on.

'Piers and I are getting married in Lamu in August and then we're going to live on our ranch near Nanuki. It's all so wonderful. Have you met Piers Mongomerie? Anyway that doesn't matter. You're invited to the wedding. Will you be in Kenya over the summer? I'll send you an invitation. All the Smith Owens are coming and Gellie and the Willstones so there will be plenty of people you know.'

Elodie stood arm in arm with Lucas looking heart breakingly happy. Without looking at Nicola, Lucas muttered that the car was waiting and sweeping up Elodie's coat he marched out of the marquee followed by Sulei and Elodie. Lucas did look back briefly but he didn't smile at Nicola. Back in cold organising mode.

The next day Nicola hurriedly packed up her stuff and explaining that with her exams only two weeks away, she just had to get back to Newcastle to revise. Her parents were concerned but pleased that she was focusing on her university. Maggie was not so easily convinced.

'So what about you and Lucas then? I saw you dancing together,' said Maggie lying on her bed watching Nicola stuff her rucksack in an haphazard fashion which was very unlike her.

'So what about telling Lucas I was on my own?' replied Nicola looking venomous.

Maggie had the decency to look slightly guilty.

'I was only trying to preempt the inevitable, you know, help things along, said Maggie looking smug.

'Margaret Cowan just stay out of my love life. In fact stay out of my life altogether. Please.' Nicola was near to tears. 'Lucas is horrible. And anyway my life isn't hopeless. I have a new boyfriend. Nobody you know so you can't interfere.' Nicola was very surprised she said that. Was Joe going to be her boyfriend? She hadn't really thought about it.

'You may have another boyfriend but it won't last because you love Lucas and Lucas loves you back. You can feel the nerve cutting vibes between the two of you when you just look at each other.' Maggie made a hasty dash for the door to avoid the hairbrush Nicola aimed at her.

Joe was pleased to see Nicola back in Newcastle and had a pile of new research papers to show her. He only had a week in Newcastle before he left for Galway and the field centre.

'You'll be fine, Nicola,' Joe told her. 'You're a good student and you'll do well. I'm looking forward to showing you Galway. You'll love it.'

Nicola was rather relieved to be able to study for her exams on her own without any distractions. The exams came and went with no awful surprises. The time spent with Joe had really paid off in terms of her appreciation of the depth and range of the subjects she was studying. She slipped a weekend at home before she left for Galway and Monica was pleased to see that Nicola had lost the slightly haunted look she had had at Jocelyn's wedding, which Monica put down to exam stress. Maggie, to Nicola's relief was safely tucked away at art school.

Nicola had never been to Ireland and found herself quite excited at the prospect of spending two weeks with her course mates in a remote part of the west coast. People had been telling her that it was absolutely beautiful and on a bright sunny day in the middle of May, Galway was just that. Joe and three other postgraduate students were there to meet them when they arrived at Roundstone Field Study Centre, a farmhouse and converted outbuildings. Nicola stood looking at the Connemara Mountains swathed in sunshine, the small fields with their precarious stone wall boundaries and sheep everywhere. It was not as wild as the Pennines and not as manicured as the Cotswolds. To Nicola it was a friendly intermediary and she smiled happily as she turned round and caught Joe looking at her intently.

'Welcome everyone to the Field Centre. You are the first group of undergrads to visit and we hope you will come to love this place as much as we do. The farmhouse behind me is the nerve centre that is where we meet, eat, and work. To the right are two accommodation blocks. The boys are in Barna and the girls are in Cashel. Showers and washrooms are behind each block. Go and get settled in and meet back at the farmhouse in about an hour to discuss your programme for the week.' Joe looked very officious with his clipboard and I'm-in-charge voice.

As Nicola bent down to retrieve her rucksack, Joe walked over to her.

'Hi Nicola. Did you have a good journey? I'm so relieved to see everyone made it,' he said tapping his clipboard. 'This is the first time I have been in charge of a course and I'm really nervous. Two weeks seems an awfully long time.'

'You'll be fine Joe,' replied Nicola. 'Everyone is very positive and looking forward to this. Brilliant that it's after the exams. We can all relax and have a good time.'

'That's what I'm worried about. The good time bit and my job is to make you work.' Joe laughed and turned to walk back to the farmhouse. Nicola slowly let out her breath and walked in the opposite direction to Cashel.

That evening Joe took charge of the group meeting to explain the field trip programme. The students would be divided into groups of five and would elect a leader who would be responsible for meeting Joe and his assistants each evening to report on progress and to be briefed on the next task. The tasks would be rotated so that by the end of the trip all the groups would have completed the same work and be able to write up their results for the final assessment.

'This is not simply a class exercise,' explained Joe. 'We'll be working with the Irish Whale and Dolphin Group, and this is Donal, and the Marine Biodiversity Group from GMIT, and this is Marie.' said Joe indicating his two assistants. 'With Donal we'll be monitoring sightings of whales and dolphins as part of his group's Constant Effort Scheme and managing live strandings along this section of the coast line. With Marie we'll be exploring the marine benthos that is studying the communities of organisms living on the foreshore and near the sea bed in and around Gurteen Beach. So all those of you who have PADI diving qualifications see me later. Work starts on Monday morning at eight o'clock and notices will go up about groups and tasks later this evening. Tomorrow is officially a day off so we're taking you trekking up Errisberg Mountain just round the back of Roundstone. It's only 300m high and the route back passes O'Dowd's pub which will soon be very familiar to you all.'

Joe paused for breath as questions started flowing from the floor.

'Just one more thing. Next weekend is your time off. From Friday evening till Sunday you are free to do whatever. I can get train times from Galway to Dublin, Donal will organise a surfing/body boarding party at Dog's Bay round the back of Gurteen if anyone is interested and Marie is planning a trek along the Benbaun Circuit from Glencorbet. Over to you guys.'

Joe sat down looking fairly exhausted. Nicola could see that he had put a great deal of effort into planning their trip and she hoped it would be appreciated. She took a furtive glance round the room and saw that Joe had certainly captured the students' attention. Donal and Marie were busy fielding eager questions and when she looked back, Joe had disappeared.

The first week flashed by. Nicola could not remember when she had been so cold, so wet and so exhausted at the end of a day but also so content, so satisfied and so happy. Joe and his assistants set very high research standards and had no qualms about throwing work back if it wasn't good enough. After an initial couple of days of grumbling everyone put their weight behind the projects and worked hard during the day and drank hard in O'Dowd's at night. Nicola found herself acquiring new skills left, right and centre.

On the Thursday morning she was helping Joe drag the sea kayaks down to the water's edge ready for the mornings sample collections.

'What are you doing at the week end?' asked Joe as they walked back up the beach.

'I'm not sure yet. Some of the girls are talking about going to Dublin but I don't fancy a weekend getting lathered at great expense. Donal's surfing sounds great but I'm not an expert swimmer. Bit scary really.' Nicola squinted up at Joe's face in the sunlight.

'Well, perhaps I can offer an alternative. I have been invited to a music festival at Aughnanure Castle just up the road near Oughterard. I've had a pretty full on week here and I just need a break. Go and do something different, y'know? I was wondering whether you'd like to come with me?' Joe paused and looked at Nicola. Then he rushed on 'I'm meeting some friends from GMIT so it wouldn't just be the two of us, I mean I'm just asking you to come as a friend. Someone to talk to like we did at Watamu. I'm not doing this very well, am I?' Joe smiled apologetically.

'It sounds wonderful. I'd love to come,' replied Nicola and bent down to lift another kayak.

'That's fantastic. We'll leave early on Saturday morning. Bring your sleeping bag and I'll get the rest.' Joe looked so happy. Nicola wondered what she was going to tell her mates.

At the first practical class at the beginning of the academic year, Nicola had found herself in a group with Will, Ed, Hannah and Daisy. None of them had met before uni; none of them lived together and they led very separate lives except when they were working together in the department. On the field trip they had been mixed up but on Friday they were together huddled behind a rock waiting for Donal to bring the rib round to the beach so that they could go out to one of the islands. The wracks of seaweed hissed and crackled in the drying sunlight eager for the tide to come back to flood them with the sea. Naturally thoughts turned to the weekend.

'Right,' said Ed propping himself up on his elbow. 'I'm going surfing, Will and Hannah are off to Dublin, Daisy is trekking. So what, Nicola, are you up to?'

'I'm staying here at Roundstone,' replied Nicola fiddling with her boots.

'No way,' said Ed. 'What are you going to do all by yourself? Go to

Dublin with Will and Hannah. They'll look after you.'

Nicola blushed. Daisy sat up and looked at Nicola.

'Come on out with it. What are you really up to? We're your mates. You can tell us,' said Daisy.

'OK. But you mustn't tell anyone.' They nodded and leaned in closer towards Nicola.

'I'm going to a music festival.'

'But not on your own,' said Ed. 'Who is it?'

Nicola paused really quite unwilling to tell them but realising that they would get the information out of her somehow.

'Joe. Joe Delaney.'

Hannah let out a long breath. 'You are a dark horse, Nicola. When did all this blow up?'

Nicola looked at the sand. 'It's not like that. I met Joe in Kenya when he was working at the Watamu Research Station and I was working in a local orphanage. That was nearly two years ago. There was a whole crowd of research students and we just hung out together and did stuff. He asked me to go to this festival as a mate. He needs to get away from all this for a couple of days. I think he's quite stressed.'

'Hmmm,' said Hannah. 'Do we believe this, guys?'

'Well it will have to do for now. Here's Donal so we have to get going.' said Daisy.

There were no further opportunities for discussion though Daisy did manage to ask late that afternoon, if Nicola knew what she was doing.

'What do you mean, know what I'm doing. I'm not doing anything except going somewhere with a friend, somewhere where we're going to be surrounded by people all the time. You have a very suspicious mind, Daisy.' said Nicola rather severely.

But Daisy had noticed the way Joe looked at Nicola when he thought no one was watching.

On Friday night Nicola went down to Ryan's Bar with the surfers. It was a good night with music and singing and Nicola felt quite exhausted when she flopped into bed. The next thing it was morning and having stuffed a few items into her rucksack, Nicola went in search of breakfast and Joe.

It was a beautiful morning but Nicola felt strange being in Joe's old VW camper van with just the two of them and being able to see the landscape clearly instead of through a fog created by piles of wet gear steaming sea water into the atmosphere. The view was quite wild but not in a scary way. The heather wasn't out but the hills had a purple sheen which contrasted softly with the blue sky. Sheep speckled the hills like bits of torn white paper and the turf cuts zigzagged between then giving groups of sheep their own little heather islands. Everyone waved at them whether it was from a car, a bicycle or a tractor. It was rather like travelling with royalty.

'Do you know all these people, Joe?' asked Nicola.

'No way,' replied Joe laughing 'But they all recognise the bus because we're always going backwards and forwards on this road. It's great. So many locals are behind the whale and dolphin project because they hope it will bring more tourists into the area. Have you done any stranding patrols yet?'

'No that's next week,' said Nicola. 'You know I'm really enjoying this. The area is gorgeous and the research is so interesting.'

Joe turned to smile at her narrowly missing a couple of lycra clad cyclists who were racing each other round a blind corner.

'They're all mad round here,' said Joe almost swearing at the cyclists. 'I'd better concentrate until we get over the hill to Lake Corrib.'

Joe parked the VW in the main street in Oughterard to pick up some supplies. Nicola wandered down to look at the river feeling pleasantly content in the warm sunshine surrounded by the bustle of a market town on a Saturday morning. She loved the way the Irish painted the fronts of their houses in seemingly random colours which clung together in a kind of unique harmony. As the sun caught their frontages the houses smiled at each other across the street. Maggie would love this colour co-ordination she thought.

Aughnanure Castle stood proudly aloof gazing out over the calm waters of Lough Corrib. Nicola had never seen an Irish tower house. It looked like an English castle with bits missing. Surrounding the tower were a number of courtyards which were buzzing with musicians rehearsing, stallholders setting out their wares and local people greeting each other like long lost friends. With Joe engrossed in conversation, Nicola wandered off to explore. It wasn't long before she wished Maggie could have had a stall. The new *Gellateen* range would go down a bomb here and she felt quite excited about Gellie's plans to open a pop up shop in Newcastle over the summer. Turning a corner Nicola found the castle casting a malicious patch of cold shade across the grass where a fortune teller was bending over her crystal ball. Seeing Nicola, the fortune teller looked up and motioned Nicola to come closer. The ball changed colour and glared red when Nicola stood in front of it.

'I see love before you but you haven't caught it yet,' muttered the old lady.

Nicola glanced up and saw Jamie in his long black coat standing a little way apart. Before she could approach the old lady or Jamie she heard Joe coming up behind her.

'What are you doing here all by yourself?' he asked. 'Come on I have got loads to show you.'

Twisting round again, there was no sign of either the fortune teller or Jamie, just a patch of white daisies waving at her. Nicola shook her head to get rid of the last few minutes and followed Joe back to the noise in the other courtyard.

In Watamu the Arit Jinn collapsed in a heap on a broad branch of their tree. They had worked very hard to create the fortune teller. Recent visits to the convent by Lucas had dragged them out of their boring routine to plan and execute some serious mischief. Transcendental transportation requires a great deal of organisation and its creation had used an enormous amount of their spiritual energy. As the fortune teller was talking to Nicola, Sister Benny crossed the courtyard at the orphanage exuding clouds of frankincense and lemon grass. This completely destroyed the jinn's concentration and the connections snapped. The fortune teller and Jamie faded away as Joe came looking for Nicola and the Arit Jinn fell into a sulk which lasted for weeks. The whole operation would have been so much stronger if they had had Nicola's memories to play with. The tattered piece of white cloth had not been strong enough and anyway, it didn't belong to Nicola. It had come from someone else.

The afternoon was filled with Irish music and dancing competitions and at the end of the day Nicola and Joe found themselves on the shore of Lough Corrib beside a camp fire enjoying an impromptu music session. Well after midnight Joe fetched their sleeping bags and they settled down to sleep under the stars. It had been a lovely day and it seemed quite natural to snuggle up to Joe and after a while the soft goodnight kiss turned more passionate. Was this what she wanted wondered Nicola as her body as though starved of physical contact started to respond. The impossibility of matters going any further, as they were separated by duckdown and layers of clothes, and surrounded by fellow campers, saved Nicola from having to address the question.

The next morning as they rolled up their sleeping bags and went to find breakfast Joe asked Nicola if she was going to Mass with him.

'Mass?' asked Nicola.

'Yes. The church is a short walk along the shoreline in the next village.'

Nicola looked up and could see groups of people already walking in that direction.

'You are a catholic, aren't you?' asked Joe. 'Which means you go to Mass regularly?'

'No. I'm C of E if pushed,' replied Nicola.

Joe looked disappointed for a moment. 'But I thought, you know, working at the orphanage for Sister Benny, that you were.'

'No. Sister Benny is very ecumenical. It was never an issue. But I would love to come to Mass with you, if you would like me to.'

So they walked hand in hand along the shore to Mass. On the way back

Joe asked Nicola about her plans for the summer. Nicola was vague.

'I'm going back to Watamu with the Masters students for three months,' said Joe. Turning to face Nicola he said.

'Come with me. I'm sure Sister Benny would have you at the orphanage if you didn't fancy spending the summer embroiled in marine research.' Reaching for Nicola's other hand Joe smiled down at her expectantly and almost bent to kiss her.

'Oh Joe.' Nicola hesitated. 'What a lovely idea.' She hoped she sounded enthusiastic.

Joe turned and they walked on back to the castle.

'Perhaps you need time to think about it,' said Joe. 'Sorry to spring this on you.'

'No. That's fine but I have a problem. Gellie and Maggie are planning to open a shop in Newcastle over the summer and I've promised to help them. So I'll be spending most of the summer in Newcastle. They want to have the shop up and running by Fresher's week.'

Joe looked disappointed and they walked on in silence.

As the sun started to sink over an afternoon of more music and storytelling, Joe said it was time to leave.

'I have to pick up some marine samples so I'll drop you off at O'Dowds where you can catch up with the trekkers. Then I have to go to Galway as I have a meeting with GMIT tomorrow and I won't get back to you lot until the middle of the week. This weekend has been fun. Thank you for coming with me, Nicola.' Joe gave her a wide open smile.

'Can I ask a favour, Nicola?'

'Of course. Ask away,' replied Nicola.

'Well, since you won't come to Kenya with me, perhaps you might consider house sitting my flat in Newcastle while I'm away. My flatmate is leaving at the end of the month and I don't really want the place empty over the summer. Think about it. You'd be doing me a big favour. Rent free, just pay the utilities.'

Somewhere to stay over the summer had been at the back of Nicola's mind but for the moment it was just a problem to be solved sometime.

'Would you mind if Gellie and Maggie stayed over occasionally? You know, when they're in Newcastle?'

'Not a problem. Plenty of room. You'll house sit for me then?'

Nicola felt that she couldn't really say no and anyway it did solve a problem.

O'Dowds was busy but then it always was on a Sunday evening. Nicola found the trekkers in a corner of the bar and slid into a space beside Daisy. The group fell silent as Nicola put her drink down on the table.

'Ah, welcome back, Nicola. How was your weekend?' asked Daisy making room for her.

'It was good. Very Irish. How was the trek?' replied Nicola. Everybody started talking at once about their weekend and then laughed nervously giving Nicola the impression that they had all been talking about her before she arrived. A couple of people looked round as though expecting to see Joe in the bar but no one said anything. Nicola wondered if she'd made the right choice going to the festival with Joe. She really needed to think about Joe. Was she slowly being sucked into something she didn't want?

'Well? Tell all.' said Daisy as they walked back to the Field Centre.

'There is absolutely nothing to tell, Daisy,' replied Nicola feeling her cheeks glow. 'Like I said, Joe and I are just mates. We had fun. Joe relaxed which was the reason for going.'

Lagging behind the others, Daisy turned to Nicola.

'There is something you need to know, Nicola. Joe has a long term girlfriend called Dervla who is away for a year in Japan doing research for her Masters.'

Nicola looked horrified.

'I thought probably he hadn't told you about Dervla. You see there are two opinions floating around. Apparently they had a big break up before Joe went to Kenya last year. Then they got back together in the summer but Joe broke up with her again last September before she left. According to some people it is all over but friends of Dervla maintain that it isn't and when she comes back Dervla expects it all to be back on again. So be warned Nicola. It's not that simple.'

Nicola didn't say anything but she was really glad that Joe would not be back until the middle of the following week. It would give her time to think. It explained why Joe had not come on to her full on when he'd had plenty of opportunity to do so. Perhaps Dervla would turn out to be a blessing in disguise but somehow Nicola started feeling that she was in competition with Dervla and she wanted to win. She was going to win.

Back at uni for the last few weeks of the summer term Nicola found herself in a maelstrom of finishing assignments, exam results, choosing modules for the second year and parties. Joe was still in Ireland so she was able to push the problem of Joe to the back of the queue and was only reminded about it when her phone pinged with a cheery text. At least the problem of accommodation for the summer was solved albeit she had never been to Joe's flat but as he was a fairly neat and tidy person she presumed it would be fine.

Gellie had made a couple of flying visits to Newcastle to look at shop premises and then grilled Nicola about location. Gellie's shortlist was down to three and the whole scenario was looking positive. Maggie was getting very excited about the project and even their parents were talking about coming to the grand opening in the autumn.

And then Joe came back. He sent a text:

Hey I'm back. Wanna have dinner 2night?
Pick you up about 8. Can't wait to CU :-D J xx

Nicola texted back:

Lovely. Looking forward to catching up. N xx

What to do about Joe. Nicola gazed into the bottom of her third cup of coffee wishing that Jamie would appear to give her some much needed advice. First she addressed the base line. Did she fancy Joe? The answer was yes. Physically he was a fit guy. He was kind, considerate and fun to be with. He was smart, clever and interested in things which she considered important. But now there was the problem with Dervla and this probably explained why she had no idea where she stood with Joe. Did he want a relationship or not. At the Irish Festival Nicola would have ticked the 'yes' box but he was quite cool and distant when he got back to the Field Centre, and when he said goodbye to them all at the end of the field trip. She would ask him straight up about Dervla.

They went to a small Italian restaurant and gazed at each other in the dim candlelight. Joe was full of his work in Galway and the links he'd forged with GMIT. It was all looking good for his trip to Watamu as well.

Reaching out across the table and taking her hand, Joe said

'And how are things with you, Nicola? Did you miss me?'

Nicola nodded and gently pulled her hand away.

'I did miss you Joe. But we need to talk about…your girlfriend. We need to talk about Dervla. Please, Joe. I need to know where I stand on this one.'

Joe sighed and looked away. Then he turned back, looked at her and held her gaze.

'I met Dervla in my first year at uni. She was my first serious girlfriend and, yes, I loved her. We were together for three years but the last year was not much fun. We drifted apart. Going away to Watamu for three months I saw my chance to break up and I did. She was so upset. I don't think she believed me. She just sat and waited for me to come back to Newcastle and to come back to her. But I met you in Watamu and everything looked different. When I got back to Newcastle I told Dervla it was still all over and she slit her wrists. I felt awful. All my friends, and my parents, told me I was making a huge mistake. I relented. We got back together but it didn't work for me and when Dervla went off to Japan I seized the opportunity to break up. I don't think she believed me this time either. What can I do? Nicola, I really want to be with you and I desperately hope that you want to be with me. I have tried to take things slowly to be sure. Dervla means nothing to me. But I need to know how you feel about me.'

Joe took a sip of wine and waited. No reply; so he continued.

'Nicola, being with you is so easy, so uncomplicated. I want to get to know you better.'

'Joe, you are a really lovely person and I have missed you since I got back from Ireland…' Nicola did not have time to finish her sentence because Joe leaned over the table and gave her a long kiss and Nicola kissed him back. Without speaking Joe paid the bill and they left the restaurant and walked back to Joe's flat. It was on the top floor of a Georgian building very close to the university.

While Joe was in the kitchen to making 'the best Irish coffee ever, care of Marie's grandmother's secret recipe', Nicola looked round the flat. Very minimalist: very Joe: very organised: very tidy. Nicola groaned when she thought how Maggie would transform the place into a complete mess within five minutes of arriving. There were two enormous black leather sofas, a complicated sound system and a huge TV and video. There were no signs that Dervla could have lived in such a male orientated establishment. Nicola relaxed.

The Irish coffees were very good but so strong. Suddenly Nicola felt herself retreating from the world and as her head went back she heard Joe speaking to her from a long way away. It was definitely time she went home.

Not another Irish coffee she thought as she struggled to open her eyes. The sun was shafting through the gaps in the blinds and trying to spread light through the room. She was wrapped up in a duvet, still fully dressed (thank goodness) but her boots were neatly together on the floor beside her. Yes, there was definitely a smell of coffee and then Joe was sitting beside her on the sofa.

Nicola blushed and pulled the duvet up round her face.

'I'm so sorry, Joe. I don't know what happened. I don't usually pass out…' Nicola's voice trailed away.

Joe looked faintly amused. 'No worries. It is the first time a woman has gone comatosed mid-sentence and just as I was looking forward to all sorts of things we could do together. Am I really that boring?'

Nicola wriggled in embarrassment. 'It's fine. I'll go right now. And you're not boring, you're lovely.'

Joe pulled her to her feet and kissed her gently. 'I said slowly and I meant it. Now what you need is breakfast.'

Much later, on her way back to her own flat, Nicola bumped into Daisy.

'Hey, not so fast,' said Daisy looking her up and down. 'You look fantastic. No don't tell me. Joe's back and you finally hooked up.' The colour that rushed up Nicola's face told Daisy all she thought she needed to know.

'Well I hope you know what you're doing,' said Daisy

'I do know. I've never been so sure about a relationship in my whole life.' Nicola surprised herself in replying.

'I'm so happy for you. Let's get a coffee.' Daisy took hold of Nicola's arm and dragged her off.

Saying goodbye to Joe for the summer was harder than she imagined but then Maggie arrived at the flat and Nicola became immersed in shop fitting, then cleaning and decorating before the stock arrived. Gellie turned up with Charlie Willstone in tow to help with the legal and business side of the venture. Gellie turned down the offer of accommodation at Joe's flat.

'There really is only room for one more in the flat and living with you two young things would wear me out in a couple of days.' She told Nicola. 'Don't worry, I'll find a quiet, staid luxurious hotel where I can retreat at night.'

Later, when the big crisis happened, Nicola remembered that she and Maggie never found out where Gellie stayed. There was no need as she was always glued to her mobile. And they did see a great deal of each other during the day.

It wasn't long before Daisy and Hannah got in on the act and so the news of the new shop right next door to campus spread. Nicola was so busy she didn't really have time to miss Joe but she did keep up with all his emails and texts. One night Nicola flopped into bed and pulled the duvet over her head. She'd taken to wearing Joe's old shirts because they helped her to get to sleep and made him feel close to her. She was just drifting off when she heard her door open and close softly.

'Go away, Maggie. I need my sleep,' Nicola muttered.

'Hello Nicola. It's Jamie.'

'Jamie? What are you doing here?' whispered Nicola dragging herself into a sitting position.

Jamie wrapped his long coat over his knees and sat down on the edge of Nicola's bed.

'I came to check up on you. You haven't called on me in a long time.'

'I have called you, Jamie,' replied Nicola 'But you don't get back to me.'

Jamie shrugged. 'I'm here now.'

Nicola paused to gather her thoughts.

'It's Joe, isn't it?' said Jamie reading her mind.

'Well it is and it isn't,' sighed Nicola. 'You see I must admit that I'm happier now than I have been for a long time. Joe is so easy to be with.' She was going to add especially when it is long distance like now which meant she was with him but did not have to make any effort with the relationship. Should she feel she had to make an effort, though?

'Nicola,' said Jamie rather severely. 'You should know that you shouldn't have to make an effort.' He was reading her thoughts again which Nicola found intensely annoying. 'What's the problem? Is it still Lucas?'

'It's not Lucas,' replied Nicola rather too quickly. 'Lucas is, I mean was, Julian's brother. Any feelings for him would be rather like incest. Anyway he's been horrible. He plays with me. He makes me want him and then I feel he's laughing at me. It is all a game to him. Joe is just the opposite. Joe makes me feel loved, wanted, needed, respected and at the same time protected. I feel very safe with Joe. And he's fun to be around.'

'It sounds to me like Joe is a protective shell you can hide in away from the harsh realities of the real world. Do you love him? Can you say you are totally in love with him? The two are not quite the same.'

Nicola thought for a moment. 'I do love Joe. I love him very much.'

'But you can't tell me that you're in love with him. Nicola, you have to think seriously about this otherwise Joe is going to get hurt.' With that and a high five Jamie stood up and left the room as quietly as he had arrived.

Nicola threw herself back onto the pillows exasperated. She had just got her life sorted when Jamie turns up and makes her address issues that she'd rather avoid. Really she had too much to think about right now and her future with Joe would have to wait until he came back.

Angelica's Pop Up Shop opened to rave reviews at the beginning of September. The shop was packed for the official opening and Gellie and Maggie were delighted. Gellie was just back from two weeks in Kenya which included Elodie's wedding to Piers in Lamu. She had come back looking relaxed and happy.

'Such a lovely wedding.' Gellie purred at Nicola. 'Elodie looked ravishing and I haven't seen Piers looking so happy in years. They are a very together couple.'

And Lucas? Nicola desperately wanted to ask the question.

Gellie rushed on. 'Oh Lucas sends his love. He and Sulei got to Lamu for about five days then disappeared again. I must say Lucas was looking good.'

Then Gellie's professional life took over and she was back on the design track. Maggie had seized the opportunity to make the whole project the subject of her summer assignment and spent the evening taking photographs of everyone who tried on her designs. Their parents came to Newcastle for the opening and they were slightly disappointed that Joe was still in Watamu.

'Maggie has told us all about Joe,' said her mother, slightly miffed that her younger daughter had broken the news and not Nicola herself. 'You must bring him down to see us for a weekend when he gets back.'

Nicola made a mental note to murder Maggie at the first opportunity. What a cheek considering Maggie had not even met Joe. Nicola was glad that Joe hadn't been able to make it. It would have been a baptism by fire.

When Gellie and Maggie and their entourage went back to London and the flat was hers again, Nicola's life calmed down to normal. She was able to turn her thoughts to the next academic year and moving into a shared house just down the road, conveniently, from Joe's flat.

She went to bed early only to be woken up by a strange sound just after midnight. Someone had come into the flat using a key and was moving around in the kitchen. It couldn't be Joe because he was not due back until the following week and she knew for a fact that he'd gone to Zanzibar to give a paper at a conference. Anyway if it had been Joe he would have burst into her room and swept her into his arms. Very quietly Nicola got out of bed and locked her door, slid back under her duvet and listened. Whoever it was left the kitchen and went into Joe's room shutting the door behind them. It was a fairly noisy journey as though the perpetrator had no idea that there was anyone else in the flat. Nicola slid out bed and carefully opening her door saw that there was a light on in Joe's room. Back in bed she searched for her mobile. She couldn't phone the police in case it was one of Joe's mates Joe had told could use his flat any time. She phoned Sam in the flat below and waited until a sleepy voice from the vine like grasp of the bedclothes answered.

'Uhh?'

'Sam. It's me Nicola.'

'Nicola? Have you any idea what time it is? Is this a social call? Are you in trouble?'

Nicola could hear a muttering behind Sam and more bed cover sounds. Damn, Sam had someone with him.

'Sam. I have a problem. I'm in bed in Joe's flat on my own. Someone has just come into the flat, presumably with a key, and they have gone into Joe's room and shut the door. The light is still on and I have no idea who it is and frankly I'm scared.'

'Not a problem. I'm on my way to rescue you. I'll use my key. I'll be with you in five.'

'Thanks Sam. You're a real star.'

Pulling on a random selection of clothes, Nicola grabbed a torch and her keys, crept along the passage to the front door and let herself gently out onto the landing.

Armed with a baseball bat, Sam materialised beside her.

'Hey, calm down Nicola and tell me exactly what is going on.'

As Sam pushed the door open, Nicola pointed to the door outlined by a thin white light. Sam shoved the door open and tumbled into the room followed by Nicola. Clothes and possession were strewn over the floor and in the middle of the bed sat a rather shocked tousled figure half undressed and certainly not ready to receive uninvited visitors in the middle of the night.

'Whoa, Dervla. What are you doing here?' asked Sam looking shocked and slightly embarrassed.

'Well I am Joe's girlfriend,' replied Dervla. 'Where's Joe? I rather expected him to be here in bed.'

There was a short silence as Sam looked at Nicola for an answer. Suddenly Nicola sprang into action and pushed her way forward. Maybe she was on an adrenalin high, or maybe like two lionesses fighting over the alpha male, Nicola was going to win this love tussle come what may. Whatever it was made Nicola's eyes glitter and her voice strong.

'I am house sitting this flat and the agreement specifically says no lodgers so I would like you to leave right now with your stuff. I am not interested in any informal arrangements you may have with the tenant. I am in charge and I want you out of here. Now.' Nicola drew herself up to her full height and looked Dervla in the eye. So this was the competition. Small, dark, rather grubby, big green eyes which had narrowed as they surveyed Nicola. Dervla gathered Joe's duvet possessively up round her shoulders.

'I don't think we've met, have we?' said Dervla is a strident voice. 'I'm Joe's girlfriend and I'm going to wait here until he gets back to sort this mess out.'

'Joe's in Zanzibar and won't be back until the end of next week. If you really are his girlfriend then you'd know that. So I'd like you to leave right now and then you can sort things out when he returns.' Nicola leaned forward and grabbed the pile of keys on the bed. Deftly she removed the flat keys and slung the rest back. 'Are you ready?'

'Aren't you being a bit harsh Nicola?' asked Sam.

'No, no it's fine. I'll go. I can't be bothered wasting time arguing with this harridan. God knows where Joe found her but she is obviously doing a good job looking after his stuff,' said Dervla stuffing her possessions randomly into a rucksack. 'Can one of you give me a lift to my sister's house, please? Now can I have a bit of privacy while I get dressed.'

'So you know Dervla?' hissed Nicola at Sam as they took refuge in the living room which now wore the rank odour of deception.

'Yes,' replied Sam. 'My flatmate is on old school friend of hers. She's not a bad person, Nicola, not when you get to know her.'

'Why didn't you tell me, Sam, that you knew her and that she's Joe's girlfriend?'

'You never asked,' replied Sam infuriatingly, 'and I'm sure you know as well as I do that it is over between them. Has been for quite some time. It's just that Dervla hasn't quite accepted it and I think you should appreciate what she's going through.'

Before Nicola could reply Dervla strode into the room and dumped two rucksacks at Sam's feet.

'I'm ready,' she announced and turning she ran her eyes over Nicola. 'When your landlord returns please ask him to get in touch with me immediately.'

With that they all left and Nicola carefully double locked the door behind them.

Feeling very hyped up and restless, she gazed out over Newcastle and its university chilled out in the urban darkness. Joe was hers and she was prepared to fight for him which rather surprised her. She hadn't been aware of the depths of her feelings for Joe until she was threatened with his loss. Now she felt much happier and settled. Joe was hers and she was going to make very sure she hung onto him.

It took Nicola two days to get the flat to sparkle with cleanliness and leaving a vase of red roses beside a bottle of Cava on the kitchen table, Nicola moved out of Joe's place and into her shared house ready for the next academic year. Joe was slightly disappointed that Nicola didn't want to move in with him but Nicola explained that it was early days in their relationship and that she did not feel quite ready. Actually Nicola was quite fond of her own space and wasn't prepared to sacrifice that just yet. Joe claimed to have sorted Dervla but she still gave Nicola evil stares if they passed on campus.

Under pressure from her parents Nicola agreed to bring Joe to Frampton for Christmas and then she would go to Cumbria to Joe's family for the New Year. Nicola was very relieved to hear that Dermot and Caroline were going to be away, which meant that Lucas would not be around. Nicola just didn't want Joe and Lucas to meet. Well not just yet.

Christmas was fun. Her parents got on very with Joe which was a great relief but Maggie was very standoffish. Nicola decided to ignore Maggie. Gellie suddenly appeared for the Boxing Day walk and bored everyone with her enthusiasm for her new *Angelica* range. 'Back to Basics' as she called it 'and loving it'. She promised to send Nicola a new jacket from the range as her original must be in tatters by now. Nicola didn't bother to tell her that the jacket was one important piece of clothing she'd never be parted from. Nicola was busy packing up her stuff when Maggie appeared and threw herself on her bed.

'So,' Maggie said by way of introduction to an important subject, 'Joe is 'The One' is he?'

'Not necessarily,' replied Nicola. 'I really like Joe but we're just taking things slowly.' Nicola told Maggie all about Dervla. Then she wished she hadn't.

'Are you sure you're not just loving having Joe when Dervla can't, Nicola?' asked Maggie with her usual in depth perception.

'No not at all,' replied Nicola.

'Well just as long as you are sure.' Maggie got up and walked round the room. 'Now there is something else. I know I'm only in my first year in textile design but I already have an idea for my own range of knits for students. I got my ideas from watching all the students coming into the shop in Newcastle. I really got a feel for their style and I want Gellie to open a shop in Camden in London. But Gellie isn't listening. She's gone all retro with her back to basics ideas. She just isn't looking forward.' Maggie looked frustrated.

Nicola put her packing to one side and sat down.

'Are you trying to tell me you need a backer?'

'Yes, I suppose I am. You see Gellie has always been so positive about my designs and now she seems to have lost interest. She owns all the Gellie spin offs and I need something that is totally mine. People at college are all over the place doing their own thing and I know I can make this work.'

'I'll back you Maggie, you know I will. I'll see if I can get your designs into one of the small independent fashion shops in Newcastle and you can put the money into a fund to start your shop. Perhaps Charlie will help you. He always seems to be investing in new stuff.'

'Charlie is always interested in backing Gellie but not much else,' said Maggie darkly.

'Are there any entrepreneurial competitions in College? Have you thought about that?'

'Yes I have but I need support. If you support me, you know, read my business plans and tell me how good I am, I'll feel much more confident.'

'OK, I can do that. I'll ask the nice Oliver, you know, Gellie's accountant. He'll help you with your business plan.' Nicola gave Maggie a big hug. 'What's your design label called?'

'*Magknits*, cool isn't it?' Nicola just had to smile.

New Year in Cumbria was something else. Joe's parents lived in a white stone cottage in the middle of the village and Joe had been right. The Lakes were stunning in winter particularly since it had snowed overnight. It was all fresh, crisp and clear but, in spite of the beauty, quite intimidating. Eskdale Green seemed to almost cower in the valley below the high peaks as though it expected to be consumed by an avalanche at any moment.

The wind howled round the Cumbrian fells so Nicola was so grateful that she had her *Angelica* original to keep her warm. Her reception from Joe's parents was about the same temperature as the dining room on the north side of the house.

'They were very fond of Dervla,' explained Joe. 'She was around for a long time. But now they've met you and can see how wonderful you are and how much we love each other, they'll be fine.'

Nicola was not anticipating an early spring thaw. But the Lake District was beautiful in the winter sunshine and she and Joe went for long walks in the snow. Everyone they met, including the neighbours at a New Year's Eve party, were charming. Nicola had a text from Maggie with New Year best wishes and news that Lucas had been at the Willstone's party with a beautiful Middle Eastern lady.

I expect you're pleased that Lucas has been able to move on, texted Maggie.

Nicola was not sure that she was. Had Lucas gone back to the married Saudi lady that Julian had eluded to all those years ago in Oxford?

Nicola's second year at Newcastle Uni flew by. She was happy and contented and so her studies went well. Joe promised her that he'd sorted things with Dervla and, although she often saw them chatting, Nicola felt no jealousy. In fact she took to giving Dervla a little wave of acknowledgement if she saw her on campus. For Nicola it reinforced the feeling of supremacy, that she Nicola had won and it was a good buzz. No field trip to Galway this year but Joe would be going back with the first year students.

'Please come to Watamu with me this summer, Nicola. You can stay at the orphanage and I can help you with your field work for your dissertation.'

Nicola looked thoughtful. Her research would be so much easier if Joe was there on hand. There was no reason to go back to Frampton for the whole summer and it would be nice to see Sister Benny again and to finally lay the Kenyan ghosts to rest.

'Yes, Joe. That would be lovely.'

Joe had repeatedly asked Nicola to move in with him but she had always managed to sidestep the issue. Now she'd taken to saying maybe in the autumn at the start of her final year. A summer in Watamu would be a good way to decide whether this would be the right move.

Thinking about spending the summer back at the orphanage prompted a spate of Tree of Forgetfulness nightmares. This time they lasted longer and were more detailed as the Arit Jinn perfected their techniques. Nicola was half running half being dragged across interconnecting flat roofs escaping unidentified danger. She knew who she was with but could never remember who it was when she woke up.

6

As darkness settled over the orphanage the night became quiet. Nicola sat on her old familiar verandah gazing out over the courtyard where the Tree of Forgetfulness stood proud. Was it a mistake to come back? It was lovely to see all the children again some of whom remembered her. She certainly remembered them and she was enjoying her new role as an assistant teacher. Spending weekends with Joe at the Field Studies centre on the beach were very happy times. And yet. Nicola gazed at the Tree and imagined its gnarled bark wrapped around all the secrets it held and maybe her own personal memories from her last visit.

It was the fact that the Tree of Forgetfulness was alleged to have magical powers that led the Arit Jinn to make their home in its branches. So far they had not been disappointed. The downside was Sister Benny's habit of immersing herself in the lemon grass in her garden and then sitting beneath their branches. The smell made the jinn feel tired, cross and ill and certainly diminished their powers. If that wasn't enough, Sister Benny would, on occasions, throw open the doors of the chapel so that their tree bore the full brunt of frankincense and sandal wood. Nicola smiled as she thought about Sister Benny's canny mix of Catholicism and African spititualism which underlined the inclusive mix with which the convent was run. Did Sister Benny have dark secrets concealed in branches of the Tree? Nicola would have been very surprised if she hadn't.

Pondering over the thought that at least some of Sister Benny's secrets would be grounded in an uneasy relationship between Christianity and jinn, Nicola was startled when the door of the convent swung open and a dark hooded figure was caught in the pool of light that spilled into the courtyard. Nicola shrank back against the door to her hut unable to catch the exchange of murmured voices. Just before the door closed and the light was extinguished, Nicola caught sight of the figure gliding across the courtyard towards the main gate which creaked open to allow the figure to exit. Moments later she heard a motorbike start up and leave. Companionable silence settled around the courtyard leaving Nicola to creep off to bed with more questions and no answers

The next morning as Nicola was making her way across the courtyard towards the classrooms she was intercepted by Sister Gabriel who told her that Sister Benny would like a word in her garden. Nicola found her bending over viciously attacking the weeds which were threatening to win the war of survival with the lemon grass.

'Ah there you are my dear,' said Sister Benny straightening up slowly. 'Come and sit with me.'

They sat together shaded by bougainvillea flowers as Sister Benny ranted about her weed problems.

'But I didn't ask you here to discuss the garden,' she said smiling at Nicola. 'I want to ask a favour.' Sister Benny arranged to folds of her habit and adjusted the knots on her cincture while Nicola waited for her to continue.

'I have just heard from the hospital in Mombasa that a visiting surgical team from the *Smile* charity have selected little Maria Khan for an operation on her hare lip. This is fantastic news and an opportunity we cannot afford to miss. The problem is that we are short staffed as always and I cannot afford a member of my staff go to Mombasa to look after her. I was wondering if you would like to take her? It would only be for a couple of days and you would be staying at the hospital.' Sister Benny turned and looked at Nicola expectantly.

'Of course I'll go,' replied Nicola smiling at Sister Benny.

'Wonderful. I will make the arrangements right away. Thank you.' Sister Benny leant over and squeezed Nicola's hand.

'There is just one thing. I have heard that Al-Shabab, the terrorist group, are planning an attack this month and that Mombasa may be the target. We have had these dire warnings before and nothing has come of them so I am not taking this too seriously but I felt I should warn you. You will of course be perfectly safe at the hospital and you must promise me that you will stay within the grounds. Will Joe be happy with your going?'

Nicola felt slightly put out that Joe should have a say in what she did or where she went. It wasn't any of his business. Joe however was away in Zanzibar at the Institute of Marine Science for two weeks. Mobile reception in Watamu was intermittent and patchy at the best of times so actually he need not know until she was safely back at the convent.

'I'm sure Joe will be fine. It's Maria we have to think about,' replied Nicola.

Sister Benny stood up to indicate that the meeting was at an end.

'Be ready to leave after breakfast tomorrow morning. And thank you again,' she said rather formally.

'There just something I would like to ask you Sister Benny,' said Nicola, almost on the spur of the moment. 'I would…I would really like to visit Julia's grave.' There she had said it.

'Of course, my dear. We look after a large number of orphans and many don't make it very far down life's hard road, so as you know we don't make too much of the graveyard. There aren't many visitors. Come with me.' Producing a large bunch of keys from the folds of her habit, Sister Benny led Nicola out of her garden, through the vegetables to a high wall. Unlocking a barred corrugated gate, Nicola gasped as the sunlight lit up the beautifully tended walled garden. Rows upon neat rows of wooden crosses gazed up at her.

'We can't have headstones here,' explained Sister Benny, 'because the local coral rock weathers away during the rainy season.' Nicola was quite shocked at how many small graves they had to pass before reaching Julia. It had only been two years but so many had died since then.

'Africa is very harsh. God takes too many children from us but we do our best to save as many as possible.' Sister Benny held back as Nicola walked up to the neatly carved cross.

Julia
12 February 2003.
God needed her more than we did.

Tears rolled down her cheeks as Nicola remembered she would never hear her daughter laugh; never touch her soft skin again; and never play with her at bath time. After a decent interval and seeing that Nicola was getting visibly upset, Sister Benny stepped forward. There wasn't much room for sentiment in her world as so much of her time was taken up with insuring all her flock survived into the next week.

'Sister Gabriel carved this one herself,' said Sister Benny proudly.

'It's so beautiful,' said Nicola bending down to let her fingers run over the writing wet with her tears. 'I'm so sorry, Julia'.

Sister Benny laid her hands gently on Nicola's shoulders.

'Come, my child. Turn around and look to the future. Julia is watching you and hoping that she will have a brother or sister sometime to make you happy. Come, there is work to be done.'

Together they walked back to reality.

News travels fast and the convent quivered in anticipation. As Nicola was packing her rucksack there was a tap on her door and Sister Gabriel slid in conspiratorially.

'It's wonderful news about Maria, isn't it? Such a sweet girl and she's had such a hard life. This will be a big change for her.'

Nicola stood waiting for the real reason behind Sister Gabriel's visit.

'I was wondering, but only if you have a free moment. I mean it's not absolutely essential but if you could just...I mean it would be such a great help to me, for my work, I mean.' Sister Gabriel gazed at Nicola.

Nicola smiled at the Convent's herbalist. 'Of course. What exactly would you like me to do? I hope you don't expect me to raid the hospital dispensary or anything like that.'

Sister Gabriel looked both horrified and relieved at the same time.

'Oh, no. Gosh nothing illegal. No, certainly not. I need some more herbs quite urgently. There is a herbalist in Mombasa who has been my mentor for a long time. He lives in the old town quite close to the hospital so I was wondering if you could collect some items for me. Quite small packets and not heavy at all.'

'Not a problem. I'd be delighted to help.' smiled Nicola.

Sister Gabriel produced a slip of paper and some money from the folds of her habit.

'Here is the list and the money. Don't let him charge you a shilling more. I have written his address on the back and directions on how to find him. And thank you.'

Putting the list and the money carefully into her bag, Nicola recalled Sister Benny's instructions to stay in the safety of the hospital confines. She's probably scaremongering, thought Nicola wondering when was the last time that Sister Benny actually ventured out into the real world.

In spite of being brought up in a medical family, Nicola hated hospitals. As she gazed at the small figure in the large bed attached to drips and tubes, Nicola had to keep reminding herself that Maria's need for her was far greater than her dislike of hospitals. The staff were all very kind and the young doctor who treated Maria courteous but with no time for small talk with a queue of needy patients lined up for him. Although she had come round after the operation and everything had gone well, Maria was now sedated again and Nicola was bored.

'Why don't you go for a walk in the grounds?' suggested a nurse who had come in to check on Maria. 'We're quite quiet at the moment so I can keep an eye on Maria and you look as though you could do with some fresh air.'

Gratefully Nicola picked up her shawl and her small bag and headed towards the stairs. She had a plan that extended beyond the hospital grounds which had not looked at all inviting from the hospital window.

The freedom of being out of the hospital, away from sickness and the tragedy of constant death, was quickly diminished by the smell of animal dung, wood fires and exhaust fumes, shouting on all sides and the call to prayer being broadcast to every nook and cranny. Vehicles of every shape size and condition jostled in four lane formation in a space designed for two. Risking everything Nicola took a short cut across the central square. The fountain was long dead and the few straggly trees had not long to live. A group of old men lay sleeping on the dried mud surrounded by a collection of emaciated dogs sniffing each other. An abandoned white police box raised on a dais for directing traffic watched silently as Mombasa awaited its fate. Eager to explore the old town, Nicola didn't notice a tall figure in black Arab dress slipping easily through the afternoon crowds, also heading for the market.

Within minutes Nicola was in the winding streets of the old town and the atmosphere changed dramatically. The streets became alleyways. Tall whitewashed buildings adorned with carved doors and ornately carved plaster shaded the streets from the afternoon sun. It was a mish mash of Arab and Swahili styles developed since the time the Arabs controlled the trade up and down the east African coastline. Houses leant towards each other across the narrow alleyways like old friends exchanging confidences. High up on the buildings were small sheltered balconies and covered lattice work windows designed to shield the women from the outside world. At shoulder height the white walls had been polished silver by legions of pedestrians squeezed to the edges of the streets by passing mules and loaded hand carts. Beside the huge carved doors, often a demonstration of the owner's wealth and status, were stone baraza, ledges just off the streets where the local men could meet without entering the private space of the merchant's house. It was early afternoon so the baraza were empty and the streets quiet as everyone took shelter from the heat and intense sun. Snatches of quaranic verses muttered by those at prayer played with dappled sunshine. Nicola drew her shawl over her head and pulled one corner over her face as a mark of respect. Her map showed one main street leading down to the spice market and the apothecary but on the ground Nicola found a tangle of alleys leading off in all directions making it impossible for her to decide which route she should take. She shivered in the warm sunshine. Perhaps this was not such a good idea after all and she hurried on to get back to Maria and the familiarity of the hospital as soon as possible.

Without warning the peace of the hot sleepy afternoon was shattered. A low menacing boom and the rhythmic slip slapping of leather sandals on the worn cobbles brought a rolling cloud of dust and debris laced with a tangled mass of people and animals hurtling towards her. Some of this flotsam and jetsam was crushed by the wayside while others, fitter and younger than the rest scrambled forwards in a vain attempt to outrun the monster. In moments a stunned Nicola was flattened against a wall unable to move and scared that she was going to be dragged under the fleeing crowd. Gasping for breath, her lungs filled with dust and unable to see in front of her, she thought she was going to die. Suddenly she was grabbed from behind and dragged into a baraza. Galvanising her last ounces of strength and determined to go out fighting, Nicola bit the hand covering her mouth as hard as she could. She heard a gasp of surprise and then a very familiar voice.

'Oh for God's sake, Nicola. I'm trying to help you. Stop fighting me.'

As she was manhandled around, Nicola came face to face with Lucas.

Gasping for air and with her throat feeling as though it had been cleaned with industrial sandpaper, Nicola could only croak.

'Shhhh. A terrorist bomb has just gone off in the old market. Explanations later. We have to get away from here,' said Lucas as he buried her in his long robe and half dragged her up steps to a wooden door which he tapped gently.

The door opened just wide enough to let them squeeze through and Lucas carried her quickly up two flights of steps to the private quarters. Setting her down gently Nicola only had time to gasp at the ornate decorations as Lucas pulled aside a curtain and dragged her up a steep flight of steps and out onto a roof. It seemed like only seconds ago that Nicola was walking through the winding streets of the old town on a shopping trip and now she was being hauled through someone's private property. They ran across at least two more roofs before Lucas dived down another staircase and stopped in front of a door. Fishing out a key, Lucas unlocked the door and pushed Nicola inside. With the lattice shutters tightly shut, the gloomy light threw the geometric wall friezes into wild relief and the heavy woven rugs on the floor deadened the sounds of their arrival. Lucas tore off his outer garment and shook his dark curls free. Nicola noticed a hand gun stuck in the belt of his jeans and shivered. He looked furious and for some reason Nicola had to put her hand over her mouth to stop herself from laughing at him.

'What the hell do you think you were doing, Nicola? You were supposed to stay in the hospital and there you are wandering off into the souk, a western girl, on her own, in a highly dangerous situation. Are you mad? Have you any idea how stupid, you've been?'

Realising that Lucas was deadly serious and that she had, perhaps, been a little rash, Nicola shivered again and handed Sister Gabriel's map to Lucas. After giving it a cursory glance, Lucas spoke.

'I suppose it is too much to expect a doddery old nun to have any idea about the outside world and the dangers it contains. And you were walking in completely the wrong direction when I caught up with you.'

Nicola was just about the reply that it was actually none of Lucas' business how she conducted her life and to enquire as to whether he was stalking her, when the sound of gun fire from across the street sent Lucas grabbing her and flattening both of them against the wall. Cautiously Lucas crept towards the window and easing one of the shutters open, took a brief look at the situation. Closing the shutter he slid carefully back to Nicola and guided her back to the bed.

'As I thought,' he said quietly. 'All the different factions are out taking pot shots at each other. You see the bomb that went off in the spice market was a mistake. It was actually being moved to another location because the authorities were onto it. Now there are going to be reprisals for days until things quieten down. But you are safe here.'

Nicola was about to ask about where 'here' was, when the shock of the afternoon's events caught up with her and she leant over the bed and was violently sick over what she later hoped had not been a vastly expensive rug.

Lucas was instantly holding her in his arms, gently rocking her with her head on his shoulder. Realising that this was exactly where she had wanted to be for years, Nicola was overcome by embarrassment. How could this have happened when she was in filthy dirty clothes and smelling of sick instead of Calvin Klein? Carefully Lucas laid her on the bed and surveyed the damage.

'I'm so sorry. I shouldn't have scared you like that. Let me get this mess cleaned up.'

With that he left the room, carefully locking the door behind him. Nicola gently slid off the bed and eased the shuttered window open. If the space had been any bigger she would have fallen out in shock. Just below her, spread eagled on a courtyard roof was a gunman pointing what looked like a Kalashnikov down the street in front of her. Carefully replacing the shutter Nicola crossed the room and tried the door. It was indeed firmly shut. Back on the bed she opened the top drawer of a cabinet and inspected the contents. A copy of the Koran, well, that was to be expected, a mobile phone which wouldn't work because she didn't have a password and three condoms. Interesting. Routing around in her own bag she pulled out her phone. No signal of course. Nicola was just contemplating what to do next when the door opened and a small girl entered with a bucket and mop followed by Lucas carrying mint tea.

'This is Jaswant. She lives here,' he said by way of explanation as the girl started to mop the rug and the floor. Nicola could smell lemon grass which was a vast improvement on vomit.

'Here drink this. It will make you feel much better.' Lucas handed her a cup of hot sweet tea. By the time Nicola had drained her cup, Jaswant had left giving her a slow shy smile as she closed the door. Lucas had not said a word while Jaswant had been cleaning.

'Lucas,' said Nicola, feeling much stronger. 'Who owns this house, why is it necessary to lock me in? I'm ready to leave now as I must get back to the hospital and Maria. Thank you for rescuing me,' she added as she slipped off the bed and stood up facing Lucas.

'I'm afraid you can't leave. It is too dangerous out on the streets. Here come and sit down.' Lucas replied indicating two chairs beside a carved table. The chairs seemed to swim round the room as Nicola approached and she was glad to sit down.

'This house is owned by Sulei's sister and I stay here whenever I'm in Mombasa. This is my room and you have just ruined one of my favourite rugs. Hopefully it will recover. You can't go back to the hospital tonight so I have arranged for someone to be with Maria and I will get you back to Watamu and relative safety tomorrow. I have to lock you in because this is a strict Muslim household and you are an attractive young woman. I would not want to embarrass my hosts by their finding you wandering around their apartments. I assume you've already tried to leave?' Lucas looked at her quizzically, his eyes dancing in amusement. 'I thought as much,' he said when Nicola didn't reply.

'Now the situation is such that I have to leave you for a while but I will be back as soon as I can. You look worn out so I suggest you get into bed and get some sleep. It will be dark soon and as there is no electricity in this part of the building, you will be sitting here in the moonlight with nothing to amuse you.'

Nicola looked up and noticed that the sun's slanting rays through the shutters had indeed got longer and then the Muezzin started calling the faithful to evening prayers. She stood up and felt woozy again. Lucas took her arm and guided her to the bed. Pulling his long black robe over his head, he bent down and kissed her before silently leaving the room. The key turned in the lock as Nicola mused that Lucas, dressed in traditional clothing would pass as a local anywhere. Struggling out of her clothes, Nicola slid gratefully between the cool cotton sheets and fell asleep.

Much later she woke aware that someone else was in the room. Easing herself into a sitting position she could just make out an Arab, presumably Lucas, trying to make himself comfortable on the two chairs on the other side of the room.

'Lucas,' she hissed. No reply. 'Lucas,' she whispered a little louder. This time he stirred and sat up.

'Lucas,' she said softly 'Come over here. It is your bed after all and there's plenty of room. I'll lie right over on the edge so that I won't disturb you.' Nicola held her breath.

Lucas moved fluently over to the other side of the bed. At least she hoped it was Lucas still dressed as an Arab. The figure pulled off his outer clothing revealing jeans and a T-shirt not the traditional kikoi which was very reassuring. Stripping down to his boxers Lucas slid into bed beside her carefully leaving a large gap between them. The air was electric with enough charge to run a Christmas tree full of neon lights. It was so intense that Nicola's arms and legs hurt right down to her finger tips and her toes.

Painful desire sliced through her guts and still she waited not sure of how she should react. The thought of not having sex with Lucas here, now, in his bed threatened to suffocate her.

With an agonised groan Lucas turned over and reached out for her. His hands, confident and strong, exuded an unstoppable power that pulled Nicola towards him. Rather expertly Lucas removed her bra and pants and his boxers so that their hands could explore each other like collectors lasciviously running their fingers over priceless artifacts for the first time. Nicola shivered in anticipation as Lucas ran his fingers through her hair and nibbled her ears.

Without warning he pushed her away and then leant forward so that he could breathe into her ear.

'Nicola, is this you want? Because if it isn't, if I have gone too far, I'm afraid I am going to have to sleep on the floor. I can't lie here beside you like this any longer.'

'Oh Lucas. I have wanted this for ages. I want you right now.' Nicola was almost appalled when she heard herself say all this from somewhere like the other side of the door. What was she doing? She had no answer but she knew she wasn't going to stop now whatever the consequences.

Lucas leant over and pulled open the drawer she had investigated earlier. There was a sound like the snap of an elastic band and a curse. 'I don't know where Sullie gets these army issue condoms from,' muttered Lucas as he leant over and pulled out another one.

That means only one more time left thought Nicola.

As he slid inside her, Nicola felt about to take off on the magic carpet.

She shivered as Lucas traced the curve of her spine. A delicious warmth flooded her body as he pressed hard into her. She lost all sense of her surroundings as Lucas led her down a path of previously unknown pleasures. He took her to the edge then drew her back until she got to the point where she thought she'd die if she could not release her body into the deep pool of ultimate satisfaction. Her body surrendered to Lucas' command. She would do anything for him as she succumbed to the raw animal desires which he used to dominate her. There was no awkwardness as they moved together as one. The latticed moonlight outlined two people hungry for each other without restraint, apology or pretense

As Nicola cascaded back down to the now rather tumbled sheets and blankets she reflected that it had never ever been that good before.

Lucas was pushing the hair off her face and kissing her deeply.

'I liked that,' he said smiling at her in the moon serrated darkness 'I liked that a lot. So much so I think we should start all over again.' Nicola wasn't going to argue.

Lust satisfied, strangeness banished, their bodies moved exquisitely in tune with one another. Nicola ran her hands over Lucas' body. Not an ounce of fat concealed his muscles as his hands gently caressed her eager body. Gently at first and then with increasing firmness he entered her once more murmuring his thoughts in her ear. Nicola relaxed as her body responded naturally to all the demanding sexual signals. It was amazing to feel so part of Lucas after waiting so long. Nicola fell asleep curled up in Lucas' arms and dreamt that she was sitting on her verandah back at the Convent looking at Jamie. Shrouded in his long black coat in spite of the intense African sun, he was leaning nonchalantly against the balustrade. Nicola was trying to explain how she came to be in bed with Lucas somewhere in the old Arab quarter of Mombasa.

'Jamie?' she called softly.

'I love Lucas. I know that now.'

'Nicola,' he replied. 'Love is not the same as lust. You are confusing the two and they are completely different.'

Nicola tried to protest.

'Lucas is dangerous. He lives by his own rules in a very unstable world dictated by his job. You are about to be very hurt by him.' With that Jamie turned and walked out through the wall.

Nicola woke up hot with no idea where she was until she felt Lucas' back stiff and unyielding beside her. Without speaking Lucas turned to face her and roughly pulled her towards him. He turned her over and took her violently from behind, spilling into her as though he was trying to wash her out of his soul. This is rape cried Nicola to herself but her body was wet with excitement and with Lucas every step of the way belied this. Only her brain rationalised this brutal approach, by recalling that Lucas was dangerous. Lucas pulled away from her and turned his back towards her once more. Nicola lay dazed, tears running down her cheeks, her body aching as though she'd just been flung out of the latticed window onto the flat roof below alongside the man with the Kalashnikov.

The sun was piercing the lattice shutters when Nicola next opened her sore eyes. A great emptiness filled the bed and the room. Lucas had gone. Nicola searched for her clothes. She found her bra and pants on the floor but no sign of her jeans and T-shirt. Searching under the bed Nicola found Lucas' T-shirt and quickly pulled it on as she tried the door. It was locked. Peering out of the shutters Nicola was relieved to see that the sniper had gone. Below her in the street two heavily laden mule carts were trying to pass each other in the narrow street. It wasn't going to happen but neither man was going to back down. With them as witnesses she could hardly try to escape by jumping down onto the roof below. Turning back to the room, she saw a large wooden chest standing in an alcove next to the bathroom. Walking over to it she found what she had expected. Like the door, it too was locked. Giving up she sat down on the bed with her head in her hands.

A gentle tap on the door and the sound of a key turning in the lock roused her. Jaswant entered with a tray of coffee and pastries and Nicola's clothes neatly folded over her arm. Nicola made a rush for freedom only to run into another person carrying a large pitcher of hot water who pushed her back into the room. Jaswant looked rather alarmed and quickly handed her a note as the two left locking the door behind them. With a sigh Nicola looked at the note.

> N
> *Sulei will come for you at 10.30 and escort you back to Watamu.*
> *Don't do anything dangerous ever again.*
> L

No love; no kisses; no reference to the night they had spent together. Fearing that she was on the point of disintegrating, Nicola picked up her clothes and found the bathroom where the hot water washed the grime and the memories into the sewers and out, far away into the Indian Ocean. Coffee and pastries were very welcome but Nicola soon found herself burying her head into Lucas' pillow inhaling the smell of lemon grass. As she picked up her bag and stuffed the T-shirt and note inside, Nicola found Sister Gabriel's shopping list. She hadn't had time to give it a second thought.

At 10.30 exactly Sulei arrived looking pristine in a white dishdasha. Nicola caught the smell of his Christian Dior after shave as he turned to her.

'Welcome to my family house, Nicola.'

Sulei's family live here mused Nicola. She thought they lived in Riyadh and Muscat. This was supposed to be his sister's property.

'I hope you have recovered from your unfortunate experience yesterday and that you have spent a comfortable night as our guest.'

Hardly, thought Nicola. How much does Sulei know? Does Lucas tell him everything? Nicola felt herself blushing at the possibility. She did actually spend the night in Lucas' room and the bed was a complete mess. Sulei wouldn't need much imagination

'A car is waiting for us outside the hospital so we will have to walk a short distance. There is a regrettable tension on the streets so to ensure your safety please put this on over your clothes.'

Sulei handed Nicola a black burka that would cover her from head to toe with just a slit for her eyes.

'You must walk behind me with your eyes on the ground. Please do not look up. I have fastened a red ribbon to the hem of my robe. Please keep your eyes on that marker. Should you lose sight of me do not panic as I will have a friend behind us looking out for you.'

Nicola looked rather unsure so Sulei smiled gently at her.

'Is there anything I can do for you?'

Rummaging in her bag Nicola found Sister Gabriel's note and money.

'I don't suppose we could walk past the apothecary?' she asked Sulei. 'I promised Sister Gabriel that I would pick up some things for her.'

Sulei nodded and turning back towards the door spoke quickly in Arabic. Jaswant entered and held her hand out for the package and quickly disappeared. Nicola dropped the burka over her head and with one last look round at Lucas' room followed Sulei down the stairs.

The streets were once more full of people, animals, carts and noise. With her eyes firmly on the red ribbon as it danced over the cobbled streets, Nicola followed Sulei out into the square in front of the hospital and the pandemonium of the unruly traffic system. She shrank from the shock of the contrast and the imminent possibility of being run over. A black limousine with diplomatic plates stood waiting with its engine running. A uniformed chauffeur leapt out and held the door open. As Sulei bundled Nicola into the back. Jaswant appeared from nowhere and handed over a small brown bag. Sulei slipped into the car beside Nicola and as the door closed on chaotic Mombasa, Nicola leaned back in air conditioned luxury. The car sped quickly out of the city towards Watamu.

'Sulei, I just wanted to ask…' Nicola's voice trailed away. Sulei put his fingers to his lips not wanting to share any conversation with the driver so the journey proceeded in companionable silence.

The main road ran out of tarmac as they drove into Watamu and drew close to the convent, to be replaced by holes and ruts. Fearing for the safety of the car, the driver indicated that he could go no further and that they would have to walk the last bit. Not far from the convent, Sulei led Nicola into a small cafe and ordered mint tea.

'You can take the burka off now and become Nicola again if you would like,' said Sulei as they waited for their drinks.

'Phew,' said Nicola 'It was quite hot in there.' She ran her fingers through her hair and turned to Sulei. He anticipated her.

'Nicola, I can't explain Lucas to you even though he is my best friend. All I can tell you is that he's working for British Intelligence at the moment. We both are. You must never tell anyone that you saw him in Mombasa. If you knew any more it could be very dangerous for you. Don't worry about Lucas. My family is taking great care of him. Now we should get you back to the safety of Sister Benny's empire. I have to warn you that there is a reception committee. Your friend, Joe, heard about the bomb and Sister Benny has had a hard time preventing him from coming to Mombasa.'

Nicola sighed. That was all she needed. She wanted to be alone to be able to put some distance between Mombasa and Watamu and now, instead of being separate, they were going to be all joined up.

'Nicola. If you want to rest here for a while to compose yourself I can always say we have been delayed.'

He knows thought Nicola. Lucas has told him, the bastard, I'll show him I don't care.

Standing up, Nicola smiled at Sulei.

'No, I'm quite ready for this. Thank you so much for rescuing me and bringing me back. I hope I haven't caused any trouble. It will be lovely to see Joe.' Nicola had trouble adding meaning to the last few words.

'Nicola. It has been a pleasure. Come and visited us officially before you return to England. My sister would love to meet you. But wait a minute. Pass me your mobile and I'll put my contact details in your address book. Then if you need rescuing again you can get hold of me.'

Sulei's faced creased into his lovely smile.

With that they walked companionably towards the convent. As they slipped through the gates Joe came running and swept Nicola up in his arms.

'I've been so worried about you, Nicola,' he cried. 'I came back from Stone Town a couple of days early and heard that you'd gone to Mombasa with Maria. So kind of you to do that. And then the news about the bomb was everywhere and I couldn't get hold of you. No one knew where you were.' Joe was talking fast and holding onto her. Then he stopped and looked towards the gate.

'Who's that with Sister Benny?'

Nicola turned and saw Sulei standing by the gate. Their eyes met and he raised his hand slightly to say goodbye and was gone. Turning back to Joe, Nicola was at a complete loss as to how to explain Sulei. Luckily she was rescued by Sister Benny.

'So kind of Suleiman to look after you, Nicola and to escort you safely back to us,' said Sister Benny smiling in an almost conspiratorial fashion. Turning to Joe she added 'Suleiman's family are great benefactors of the orphanage and the work we do here. So rewarding when families of different faiths come together to help those worse off than themselves, don't you think? Now a cup of tea is in order.'

Nicola tried to focus on Sister Benny's face but her brain seemed to be going woolly and she was having trouble seeing clearly. Something Sister Benny had just said wasn't quite right but she couldn't remember why. Her head ached and she needed to find a patch of shade. Turning to Joe she saw his face rush away from her as she sank to ground unconscious.

Nicola came round that evening in the clinic. At first she thought she was back in the maternity suite but soon realised she was wrong. A drip in each arm made it impossible to sit up so she sank back and tried to work out why she was there. She remembered the hospital in Mombasa and Maria. Then she saw herself leaving to find the apothecary on Sister Gabriel's errand. The fleeing crowd, the dust, the debris, the noise and being grabbed from behind crowded in on her and she moaned audibly with fright. After that it was all blank until she was in a car with Sulei driving back to Watamu. Why was he there and surely that was the next day? The door opened and a doctor who looked vaguely familiar came in.

'Good, you're awake and back with us. How do you feel?' The doctor was checking the drips, Nicola's pulse and temperature. 'All normal which is great.'

Sitting herself comfortably on the edge of the bed, the doctor reached out for Nicola's hand.

'You're not to worry. Experiencing an extreme trauma, which you did, and then getting back to familiar surroundings can often cause the body to shut down as it were, in order to give it space to recover. You are going to be fine.' She smiled encouragingly at Nicola.

Nicola smiled back weakly.

'But I can't remember what happened after the bomb went off. There is nothing there. Maybe Suleiman told me but I just can't remember. Did he rescue me? Where did he take me?' Nicola was beginning to get distraught.

'Shush. Getting worked up won't help your recovery. Maybe you should ask Sister Benny later. But don't worry, the memories will return when you're ready. You're to stay here tonight so that we can keep an eye on you. If all goes well you can leave tomorrow.' The doctor stood up and made to leave.

'By the way,' she said, smiling as she reached the door, 'you have a visitor who is very keen to see you.' Then she was gone.

Nicola struggled to sit up as Joe's anxious face peeped round the door. He rushed towards her and did his best to give her a big hug.

'Nicola, I have been so worried but the doctor says you're going to be fine.' Joe held her at arms length and studied her face. 'What happened in Mombasa. What was so awful?'

He needs an answer right now but what can I say thought Nicola.

'Oh Joe, one minute I was walking along quite happily looking for the apothecary to get some things for Sister Gabriel and then there was dust and dirt and crowds of scared people rushing towards me. I was pushed back against the wall and grabbed from behind and I don't remember any more.' Two large tears made their way slowly down her cheeks.

'Hey, I don't want you to get all upset again. You should never have left the hospital especially since Sister Benny told you not to.'

'I know I was stupid. It was such a lovely day. Maria was still sedated and I just had to get some fresh air. I had to get out of that hospital. The garden was pathetic so I decided to go a bit further and find the apothecary. It was a lovely quiet afternoon when I left. I thought Sister Benny was just scaremongering to keep me at the hospital. I was wearing my scarf over my head so I was all covered up. I can't remember what happened next apart from the fact that a bomb went off. I think someone told me that but I'm not sure.' Nicola stopped suddenly aware that she was talking too quickly and gazed at Joe. Then she remembered the bomb went off in the wrong place but she wasn't ready to share that.

'The doctor said that you'd remember when the time is right. Let's just forget it and think about where we go from now,' replied Joe.

We? There is a 'we'? Nicola looked hopeful but underneath she wasn't quite sure if she wanted there to be a 'we' right now.

'I was talking to Sister Benny while I was waiting for you to wake up. She suggested that a break would be good for you. That is unless you want to go back to England to be with your family.' Joe looked enquiringly at Nicola.

Christ, thought Nicola. She hadn't given her family a second thought. Had they heard about the bomb? Surely they wouldn't come rushing out to Watamu to rescue her, would they?

Reading her thoughts, Joe said 'It's OK. Sister Benny phoned your parents and spoke to your Mum. She explained that you had been in Mombasa at the time the bomb went off, that you had a bit of a scare but that you were safely back at the Convent. You'd better speak to her as soon as you feel able. Just to reassure them.'

Nicola looked relieved. 'I don't want to go home just yet,' she said firmly. 'I'll stay as planned and go back at the end of the month. But a break would be really good.'

Joe smiled happily. 'Great,' he said. 'I have to go back to Stone Town next week to finalise a research project. I've been trying to get my hands on this one for months. We can stay in Stone Town for a couple of days and once everything is sorted, I'd like to take you to Ras Nungwi on the northern tip of the island. It is fabulous there. We can swim and just chill out together.'

So now it's 'we' and 'together' thought Nicola. 'Sounds wonderful,' she murmured.

Joe looked worried. 'I'm making you tired. That's against doctor's orders. I'll go now and make all the travel arrangements and come back tomorrow. Good night, Nicola.' Joe leant forward and kissed her very tenderly on her cheek. Nicola closed her eyes as he left.

As soon as she heard the door click shut, Nicola opened her eyes wide and stared at the opposite wall. Was she going mad? Remembering and not remembering, having Joe being all tender and loving when she needed to be on her own to put her life back in the proper order, it was all too much. If only she could fill the blank space that was yesterday.

As she was about to fall asleep Nicola did remember something. She remembered Sulei telling her that his family was looking after Lucas. Now, what on earth had Lucas got to do with what had happened in Mombasa?

And how did she come to be in a car with Sulei anyway? She had no answers. Feeling under the bed, Nicola searched for her bag. Surely someone would have brought here with her. It wasn't under the bed, it was inside the locker. Undoing the zip, the she found was a small brown paper package smelling of herbs and spices. Nicola threw it onto her bed as though it were alive and pushed the bag back into the locker. The package from the apothecary that she had set out to collect on the day of the bomb and yet she could not remember even finding the stall let alone picking anything up. Putting her head in her hands Nicola wept.

Meanwhile in the Tree of Forgetfulness the Arit Jinn were putting the final touches to their complete version of events. A true record they muttered in agreement. The ploy of sending the imaginary friend to Nicola in a dream sequence had worked and wound up Lucas, an old adversary. They would not forget how he used to stamp all over them when he climbed into their tree to retrieve his football when he was a small boy.

Nicola stood with Joe watching a crowd of passengers stream onto the ferry carrying parcels large and small, goats and even what looked like a dead body in a white shroud. Nicola shivered and shifted slightly to one side. She didn't like crowds and she didn't like people standing close behind her. They watched as Africa slid down into the Indian Ocean and then moved through the impossibly loaded ship to the bow to see Zanzibar rise up through the blue seas to welcome them. The hotel was modern, exclusive and perched just above the beach. Their room had a balcony overlooking the sea and for two days she slept, swam in the pool, ate copious amounts of western food and stopped wrestling with her memory. On their last day, with the contracts signed, Joe announced that they were going out for dinner to celebrate. Thoughtfully he took her to small restaurant just round the corner from the hotel so that she didn't have to go into the old part of Stone Town with its winding streets, crowds of people and polished whitewashed walls. Nicola felt slightly guilty that she hadn't seen any historic buildings or tried to absorb the culture around her.

They talked about Newcastle, Ras Nungwi, scuba diving and what Nicola was going to do when she graduated next year. They did not talk about the convent, Sister Benny or Mombasa. Nicola relaxed visibly as she felt she had suddenly been catapulted back to normality. Joe was good company. She liked his sense of humour, his laid back approach to life and the way he obviously cared about her. She wrapped his affection round her like a fleece blanket and luxuriated in loved and cared for feelings. The tension she felt when they were together in Newcastle where she had felt under scrutiny from her friends, the rest of her year and Joe's research mates was washed away by a good meal and champagne to celebrate. The

Newcastle goldfish bowl cracked into tiny pieces and she could be herself. The convent and its orphanage had begun to have a disturbing effect on her. Somehow Sister Benny's mix of Roman Catholicsm and African spiritualism created a feeling of unease under her skin. Things were not quite right and she was glad to have left that behind for a few days.

They walked slowly back to the hotel hand in hand with a sea breeze washing the warm night air across their shoulders and made love on the balcony under the stars. Hearing the Muezzin calling just before daybreak, Nicola turned to let her eyes roam over Joe lying naked beside her. He had a great body and last night it had been all hers. They had made love and not as pure lust or to achieve sexual gratification. Joe loved her but could she love him? Like an irritant, confused memories of a certain night in Mombasa kept creeping to the front of her brain. Quickly she looked out to sea hoping that the morning breeze would cool her flaming cheeks. Before she could answer all her questions, Joe stirred, looked for her and pulled her into his arms.

Ras Nungwi was just as beautiful as Joe said it would be. They were staying at Jim's Backpackers' Hostel beside the beach which was a far cry from the hotel in Stone Town. Tin roofs, communal showers and kitchens and a tiny bed with a very hard mattress but they seemed oblivious to the contrast. Joe took her scuba diving on the coral reefs, long walks along the beach and endless coffees in the local bars where they held hands across scrubbed wonky tables. On their last day as they paddled at the edge of the sea looking for shells, Joe put his hand in the water and pulled out a crab which he waved at Nicola laughing at the horrified look she gave him.

'Put that back. Now.' she screamed.

'No.'

'Now, Joe, or you'll regret it.'

'I think I'd rather like to regret it.' said Joe dropping the crab and running towards her.

They fell laughing into the sea. Nicola turned to Joe and gazing at him, without thinking, it came out.

'I love you, Joe Delaney.' Nicola blushed.

'I love you too, Nicola Cowan.' Joe leaned forward and they ended up kissing under water.

'Bet I love you more than you love me.' Joe stood up and started running towards the hostel.

'Bet you don't,' cried Nicola setting off in pursuit.

Back working in the orphanage, Nicola found a great peace had settled over her. She felt strong enough to walk past the Tree of Forgetfulness, the source of so many unsettling nightmares, with her head held high. Sister Benny noted the change in Nicola and was content that her plan was working nicely to its expected conclusion. There had been a few anxious moments but the plan was now back on track.

On her last night in Watamu, Nicola sat quietly on her verandah. Her rucksack was packed, she had said her goodbyes. Joe was picking her up first thing in the morning to take her to the airport in Malindi to start her long journey home. She would miss the children especially Maria who had drawn a picture of herself with her new smile. She would miss the nuns who had all been so kind to her but their unworldliness was beginning to irritate her. Those few days in Zanzibar had made her long for normality as she knew it. Suddenly she remembered the bag she had taken with her to Mombasa. She hadn't seen it when she was packing. A search of her hut revealed the bag under her bed a lifelong hiding place for very precious things or items she hated. Taking the bag out onto the balcony she decided to sort through it to see if there was anything worth saving and then bin the smell of spices and its memories. Right at the bottom of the bag she found a white T-shirt smelling very faintly of lemon grass. Pulling it out she found a small monogram and running a finger over the stitching she made out LSO.

Suddenly Nicola sat up very straight. Without any warning the memories of the night in Mombasa flooded back in turmoil. She remembered every detail of the sex with Lucas and his sudden disappearance into the night without a word. She blushed deeply at how much she had enjoyed every minute of it. Clutching wildly at his shirt she let her tears stream down and fall like monsoon raindrops on the floor. Damn Lucas, here he was back in her soul with a vengeance. She wiped her face with his shirt and as she did so the smell of lemon grass caused a more distant memory to rise to the surface. She was back in the clinic having just had Julia whisked away from her. A small nugget of doubt crept round the edge of her memories. Had the mysterious figure who had hovered round her bed really been Jamie, or someone else? Nicola was almost beside herself but knew she had to gain control otherwise she would be lost. No, she reasoned this was all too farfetched and anyway she'd been high on drugs. To make sure this went no further Nicola gathered up all the disturbing memories, tied them into a small parcel and walked slowly out into the courtyard. Carefully she pushed the packet as far as she could into the gnarled trunk of the Tree of Forgetfulness and then walked slowly round the tree seven times. She was leaving for England tomorrow and these memories would be lost forever. She didn't hear the Arit Jinn chuckling with delight. Now they had all Nicola's memories to play with and much more than they could possibly have dreamed of. The pieces of the jigsaw were falling into place along the branches of their tree. Nicola was so absorbed in this task that she didn't see Sister Benny standing in the shadow of the convent watching, her mouth twitching at the thought that her plan might yet again be in jeopardy. Damn Lucas Smith Own she thought, echoing Nicola's sentiments.

The next morning, Nicola was looking pale and tired when Joe picked her up. Mistakenly he thought it was because she was leaving while he still had another month of research to complete.

'The month will fly by, I promise" he said as he held her tight for their last goodbye.

For want of something to say Nicola muttered 'I'll pick you up from Heathrow. Come to Frampton and stay for a few days and before you go back to Newcastle.'

'I would love that,' replied Joe giving her one long last kiss.

As the plane banked away and headed for Nairobi, Nicola remembered that she had not got round to going back to Mombasa to meet Sulei's sister.

ANNIE BOON

7

At last. Nicola was curled up under her duvet in her own bedroom after an emotional home coming. Her parents very relieved to have her back; flowers from Gellie; Charlie and Dee Willstone called in for a drink and a very excited Maggie phoned from London. Nicola tried to play down the bomb incident in Mombasa but Maggie was having none of it.

'You were in a bomb attack for God's sake… Come on.'

Nicola had to explain several times how Sulei had rescued her and led her to shelter in his family home. Some of it truthful but how could she ever explain what really happened? Only her father looked slightly suspicious so Nicola hastily told him that the Abbas family had several homes including one in London.

'The family must have an enormous amount of money,' Andrew muttered.

After a couple of days spent recovering quietly at home, Nicola went to London. She may have left Watamu behind in a reality sense but nightmares continued to haunt her. She was quite surprised at how much she had missed her little sister who was delighted with the fabric samples Nicola had brought back from Watamu. They would be perfect for the summer range she was designing for *Magknits*.

'It all started as a College project and Gellie is really pleased with the way it is going.' Maggie was grinning from ear to ear. 'Of course I expect you to wear the whole range in Newcastle as a promotion.'

That evening they went out for supper together and Maggie's earlier euphoria suddenly evaporated.

'I have something I just have to tell you. I can't keep this to myself any longer and you're the only person I can share it with. Please don't interrupt. Just listen and wait till I've finished before you say anything.' Maggie looked appealingly at her big sister. Nicola nodded.

Gellie had not been very well at the start of the summer. Nothing specific, nothing the doctor was able to diagnose so he advised her to get much rest as possible. This left Maggie and the rest of the team to do the hard work to get the *Angelica* winter range off the ground. A crisis developed to the point where Gellie just had to be consulted but she wasn't answering her phone and no one knew where she was. Maggie decided to try Mulberry Cottage as that was one of Gellie's favourite bolt holes when things got too much. She arranged to spend the night with her rather surprised parents and then set off on foot to allegedly visit The Grange, but diverted to Mulberry Cottage. She knocked loudly on the door but the only response she got was loud barking from Jake. Peering through the tangle of climbing roses Maggie managed to see into the hall and up the stairs. Gellie and Charlie Willstone were standing naked on the landing whispering furiously. Maggie jumped back to the doorstep and stood in shock. She'd just about composed herself when the door opened and there was Gellie wrapped in a dressing gown running her hands through her hair as though she'd just woken up. Hastily trying to explain the crisis, Gellie led her into the sitting room and having grasped the problem, made a couple of phone calls as Maggie waited patiently trying to look nonchalant.

'All sorted, Maggie.' Gellie smiled gently, quite relaxed, at Maggie. 'Thank you for tracking me down, you did the right thing.'

'I'm so sorry for waking you,' said Maggie hoping she wasn't talking too quickly. 'You weren't answering your phone and we really getting quite desperate.'

'Don't worry, Maggie. I haven't been at all well this week but I feel much better now so I'll be back ready for anything next week.' Gellie moved to show Maggie out of the cottage.

'Almost like I was being swept out of the door with a big brush. Gellie has never done that before, kind of thrown me out. What am I going to do? I don't think they saw me at the window but I do know what I saw on the landing and it didn't look good. The whole time I was in the cottage it didn't feel empty. I was almost sure I could hear someone breathing above my head but perhaps that was just my over stretched imagination.' Maggie looked at Nicola appealing for help.

But Nicola was struggling with another download of long lost memories. Suddenly she saw it clearly and the bits of information that had been swirling around in her head, like an autumn breeze tossing dead leaves, tumbled into line. The key was Charlie Willstone's laugh which she could see now was quite distinctive. She remembered hearing it in Gellie's flat three years ago when she and Maggie were staying there for Maggie's work experience. Then all the other times she'd heard the laugh in what she had considered unusual circumstances became crystal clear. Gellie and Charlie had been having a clandestine affair for years which also explained why a woman as attractive and as talented as Angela Crawford had never married. Nicola was glad she was sitting down as the full force of what she had thought through hit her.

'Christ. That is quite something, Maggie.'

'But what do I do now?' Maggie was having difficulty coming to terms with the fact that the person whom she had held on a pedestal for so many years had fallen so dramatically from grace.

'Nothing. You can't do anything. And I think it has been going on for some time. What you saw was not just a one off.' replied Nicola and explained her thoughts. 'Think about the massive fall out if you went public on this. Or if we just told Charlie and Gellie what we know. Your job with Gellie would probably be over. What about the Willstones? Dee and Charlie might split,' Nicola paused, 'And the shock waves would go on and on.'

'Wow. I see your point. I had no idea. I don't think anyone has. So only the two of us know?'

'And that is how it is going to have to stay, Maggie. It is not our place to open this can of worms. God, I know it sounds stupid but I wish you hadn't looked. Secrets are so very dangerous.'

On her way back from London, Nicola went to Oxford to catch up with Kate. Nicola hadn't realised how much she'd missed her old friend being, as she had been, caught up in her own complicated world. Kate was now living with her *Armageddon* drummer, Archie Kenny, in the basement flat below her parent's house.

'I'm so happy.' Kate told Nicola as they struggled past the random drum kit and odd guitars littering the hall floor. 'My parents are delighted. They love Archie to bits. No one quite like him has ever come close to their academic world before.'

It was catch up time so Nicola told Kate all about Joe and how sure she was that he was The One.

'You're that sure?' Kate looked at Nicola quizzically.

'Absolutely,' replied Nicola. 'I never thought I'd find anyone after Julian but Joe took it all so slowly. We were kind of friends first, well for ages really and I never thought he'd make a move as there were all sorts of rumours flying around uni about a girlfriend, Dervla. Then suddenly it was different in Africa and it really all happened when we went to Zanzibar.' Nicola smiled happily.

'Hmmm,' said Kate. 'And I always thought you'd hook up with Lucas Smith Owen.'

Nicola jumped in hastily. 'Lucas is, I mean was Julian's brother. He's family and that makes it incest. I have to admit he is fantastically attractive and great fun but he's not my type and we haven't much in common apart from Julian.'

'More in love with love than love with Joe,' Kate misquoted quietly to herself.

'And Archie?' asked Nicola desperately trying to change the subject.

'Archie and I have absolutely nothing in common,' replied Kate. 'Apart from music. I've been allowed to play the sax on some the band's demo discs. But we're good together, no heavy commitments, just enjoying life.'

'What about the astrophysics?'

'That's going really well. I love the subject but I doubt that it will get me anywhere. After I graduate I'll probably have a massive career change though Archie thinks astrophysics is cool.'

A relaxing lunch with Kate's parents in the rambling North Oxford house that held so many happy memories for Nicola, was in complete contrast with the previous evening's conversation with Maggie. Nicola went back to Frampton and her nightmares.

Her mother decided it was time to spend some quality time with her daughter before she went back to Newcastle for her final year. So they went shopping, had their nails done, talked for hours over coffee. She tried to get Nicola to open up about Africa as she seemed to be distancing herself from the family. Sometimes she longed for the days when her children were small and always under her feet. At least she knew what they were up to. Nicola had spent a large part of the summer in Kenya, a place that she had never visited. Maggie was working hard at her fabric design and fashion course in London and when she wasn't in College she was working all hours for Gellie.

Nicola was getting very stressed about Joe's visit now that they were a couple. Her mother was going to a great deal of trouble cooking, cleaning and asking her interminable questions about Joe's like and dislikes. Her father was, as always, working all hours.

In the event Joe's visit went very smoothly. Nicola was surprised and pleased at the way in which he charmed both her parents. He asked a great many questions about the Cotswolds that he'd saved up from his last visit and her delighted parents paraded him round Frampton and took him to Cirencester. Andrew took him off to the pub for a 'boy's pint' before supper.

'They've shown you all the best bits,' grumbled Nicola when they at last found themselves spending a day on their own walking a stretch of the Cotswold Way.

'You are the best bit, Nicola,' replied Joe pulling her into his arms.

Maggie came for lunch on the Sunday and to Nicola's surprise was not overly impressed.

'He's not the one for you. Lucas is.' said Maggie as they were washing up the saucepans.

Nicola threw washing up bubbles at her.

'I've seen the way you look at Lucas and I've seen the way he looks at you,' hissed Maggie in her ear. 'Or is Lucas gay, is that the problem? He spends an awful lot of time with Sulei. They're such pretty boys.'

'Lucas is not gay.' Replied Nicola a little too quickly.

Maggie was onto that like a cat on a mouse. 'Aha! Got you. So what on earth did you get up to in Africa?'

'Shut up Maggie. You don't know anything.' Nicola hissed back as Joe came into the kitchen with another load of plates for the dishwasher.

A week later Nicola was back in Newcastle and her university world closed in around her.

In Watamu the Arit Jinn had practically given up on the Lucas/Joe competition with Sister Benny as nothing seemed to be moving on that front. So they reverted to being tiresome by pursuing their old poltergeist tricks like moving all the old trunks in the hall. Sister Benny found a wall of trunks barring her from entering her office particularly annoying. Waking the convent cockerel one hour earlier than normal was another favourite as it put the convent and the orphanage out of sync for a whole day.

Life, back in what would be her third year at university, was different. Joe had been promoted to Director of Research, a position he had been after for some time, so he was no longer involved in teaching undergraduates. This created a very satisfactory break between them in the department and Nicola's previous embarrassment regarding their relationship was thankfully resolved. She felt really proud when she walked past his office and read *Dr Joseph Delaney, Director of Research* on his door. Perhaps one day he'll be a Professor she thought.

Back in her shared house, life slipped back into the normality of student living. Joe did not like staying over at her place. The shower was overflowing with half empty girlie toiletries, the bathroom was never free and when it was he had to fight his way through dripping underwear. He preferred the serenity of his minimalist man flat with its huge TV and state of the art sound system. As his flatmate spent most of his time with his girlfriend, they had the place pretty much to themselves. That was when he was around as his new job took him away to conferences and when he wasn't presenting papers, he was pitching for contracts.

Christmas was difficult to negotiate but they finally decided that they should spend it with their respective parents and then Nicola would go to Cumbria to spend New Year with Joe.

It was wonderful to spend time back at Frampton. Both her brother and Maggie were home and it seemed like going back to their childhood as the arguing and banter soon became the normal way of life. On Boxing Day there was the annual walk with the Willstones, all of them, the Smith Owens, just the two of them and Gellie. Nicola was worried about seeing

Gellie again particularly as Charlie Willstone was with them, but with so many people around it was relatively easy to act naturally. Caroline asked Nicola if she was going to be around at New Year as Lucas was going to be there with a whole crowd of his friends. Nicola explained shyly that she was spending New Year with Joe, her boyfriend, in Cumbria. Caroline smiled gracefully, and told Nicola that she was pleased that she had moved on and wished her good luck in her finals.

They saw the New Year in at the pub in Eskdale Green where they partied well into the small hours. There was no threat of an early closure as the landlord had slyly invited the local policeman and his entire family and they were almost the last to leave. The next day, feeling that they needed fresh air and exercise in capitals, Joe and Nicola set off to climb Scafell Pike. At the summit they gazed down at the specks of Eskdale Green and Joe pointed out his house just to the left of the church spire. Kneeling down he produced a bottle of champagne and two glasses from his rucksack. Nicola thought it was the best way ever to start a new year and she was so busy trying to find Carlisle, which Joe had assured her would be visible, that she did not notice Joe rummaging in his pocket. As she turned round to tell him that Carlisle definitely wasn't to be found from the top of Scafell Pike, Joe went down on one knee.

'Nicola Grace Cowan, would you please marry me?'

With her brain in turmoil, random thoughts jostling to be heard, Nicola opened her mouth and said yes. Joe swept her up in his arms and champagne dripped down her neck from the open bottle.

'She said 'Yes',' yelled Joe into the open space. 'Nicola and I are going to get married.' He filled the glasses and they interlocked their arms and drank gazing into each other's eyes wondering at the enormity of what they had just agreed to do. Pulling her glove off, Joe slipped a single diamond onto the third finger of her left hand.

'There. Now it is official,' he said standing back admiring his purchase. The diamond flashed ominously between them so Nicola hastily moved her hand so that the sun could not send emergency Morse code with it.

'It is stunning, Joe. What can I say? Thank you so much. It's lovely. You're lovely.'

'And I love you too,' said Joe jumping into the moment hardly noticing that Nicola hadn't actually said to him that she loved him on such a momentous occasion.

Everybody was delighted with their news. Her mother wanted to know when they were planning to have their wedding. The experience with Dee and Jocelyn had shown her that you could never have too much notice for something like a wedding.

'December,' said Nicola without thinking and without consulting Joe. 'I would love a winter wedding with candles and holly in the church at

Frampton.' There was the small matter of Joe being a catholic but for the time being that did not seem to be important. As far as Nicola was concerned December was very far away. Practically next year and they had hardly started this one.

Maggie emailed;

Congrats! Hope you know what you're doing!
You missed a fab party on NYE at The Grange. Lucas came with a crowd of friends and flirted all night with his amazing 'Arabian Princess' called Leila Jamil. Pity Sulei couldn't make it as I quite fancy him.
Enjoy your new term and come and see me soon.
M xx

Nicola pressed the DELETE button.

The next person to question her engagement was Jamie whom she met out walking the day before she left for Newcastle.

'Be pleased for me, Jamie. I will never be alone again,' she said flashing her diamond in the sunshine.

'I am pleased, Nicola. But I hope you're not rushing in to this simply because you're afraid of being alone. Are you sure this is right?'

'Jamie. I think I am now old enough to make my own decisions, don't you?'

Leaving Nicola standing in the middle of the lane, Jamie sauntered off without a backward glance, tightly wrapped in his black coat.

Back in Watamu the Arit Jinn were desperately trying to pull Jaime's strings. They had noted the smug expression on Sister Benny's face when she had received Nicola's news. So the superior mother had the edge but the Arit Jinn were not giving up. They could sense an impending disaster in the wind which they might be able to work to their advantage if they could continue to focus on Nicola's nightmares.

The Lent term was frantic as everyone struggled to hand in coursework, to finish assignments, to revise for finals in May and to hunt for jobs. When Joe was away Nicola stayed at his flat where it was calm and quiet. The stress levels in her shared house were becoming unbearable. She had applied for a research scholarship to fund a PhD which Joe was confident she would get provided she made it to a 2:1 in her finals.

With that in mind Nicola worked flat out over the Easter break. She had had a couple of letters from Sister Benny updating her on general convent and orphanage news, and in particular about how Maria was making amazing progress after her operation, Nicola sent Maria a Newcastle Uni shirt and some photos of her with Joe.

The weekend before the exams were due to start, Nicola was struggling up the three flights of stairs to Joe's top floor flat thinking that he obviously had not thought about shopping and the number of flights of stairs when he signed the lease, when her mobile rang. As she opened the door and picked up her phone there was the 'ping' of announcing the arrival of a text message. The text was from Maggie.

Nicola, answer your fucking phone
This is an emergency.
M xx

Abandoning the supermarket bags on the floor, Nicola phoned Maggie who answered immediately.

'Maggie what's the crisis?'

'It's Gellie. One of her ovaries has burst and she's in hospital. The doctors want to operate but there is a problem. She has some strange blood group and Caroline isn't a match. They're seraching London for blood right now. Charlie is losing the plot, he was with Gellie when she collapsed and Dee is on her way. Remember the secret? This could get really messy. I need to do something so I thought maybe Lucas is the answer. Where's Lucas?'

Nicola could hear the break in Maggie's voice.

'I have no idea, Maggie,' she replied.

'Well, how about Sulei? He'll know where Lucas is. Look I've got to go. Find Lucas. This is an emergency.' The line went dead.

Nicola sat down on the sofa and put her head in her hands. She really didn't need this right now. She had no idea where Lucas was, she didn't really care but Gellie was in trouble. Picking up her phone she scrolled down her contact list. About to give up she suddenly came upon Sulei's contact details, the ones had had given her in Watamu in case she needed rescuing again. Well it was worth a try for Gellie's sake. She clicked on Sulei's mobile number.

'Suleiman Abbas.'

'Sulei? This is Nicola.'

The voice warmed instantly. 'Hi Nicola. How are you? Do you need rescuing again?'

Nicola ignored that. 'Sulei, do you know where Lucas is?'

'He's right here beside me. We're just on our way out. Would you like to speak to Lucas?'

'No. Just give him a message. Where are you?'

'We're in London at my flat in Knightsbridge.'

Nicola visibly relaxed. Maggie's plan might just work.

'Could you please tell Lucas that Gellie is seriously ill in hospital and she needs blood for an operation. She's some strange group and maybe Lucas might be a match. Caroline isn't.'

Nicola gave Sulei the name and address of the hospital.

'I'm calling for a car right now,' replied Sulei, 'and then we'll be on our way. I reckon ten minutes should do it.'

'Thank you, thank you Sulei,' replied Nicola and ended the call. Feeling really cold and shivery she pulled her *Angelica* jacket tighter around her shoulders. The flat didn't have central heating and Joe liked to live with the inside temperature the same as the outside one unless it was the depths of winter when he had been known to relent and put the gas fire on. Angrily Nicola pulled the jacket off and chucked it across the room. How dare the whole Lucas mess invade her world when she thought she had finally got rid of it? She went in search of one of Joe's sweaters twisting her engagement ring round her finger as she went.

Two hours later Maggie called again. It was getting dark but Joe would probably be in the pub having a post football practice drink with his mates. Nicola put the gas fire on for a brief spell.

'Nicola?'

'How's Gellie?'

'You're a star. I knew you'd do it. Lucas turned up with Sulei about twenty minutes after we spoke and he is a match and he has given loads of blood. Gellie has just come back from theatre and she's going to be fine. Charlie, Dee and Caroline are here and we're all waiting for her to wake up. I'll call later.'

The line went dead.

Nicola turned off the fire and sat in the gathering gloom watching the city lights burst into life. Newcastle was bracing itself for a night out on the town. But she hardly noticed the lights. She was trying to sort out everything Maggie had said and hoping with all her heart that chaos wasn't about to be vented on a group of her very old friends. If Charlie was with Gellie in hospital then, presumably, he was with her when she collapsed. That would be the worst case scenario. However that could all be salvaged because Charlie had always been Gellie's financial adviser so it could be possible that they were having a meeting. All Charlie had to do was to keep control of his emotions in front of Dee and everyone else and then the secret would be safe. Until the next time. It was a very heavy burden to carry. But Maggie had said that Charlie was on the point of losing it so the secret wasn't secure yet. The important thing was to keep everything in perspective.

She heard a key turn in the lock and Joe stumbled into the dark room. He flicked a light switch and came straight over and consumed her in his strong arms. His anxious eyes scanned her ashen face.

'Babe, what on earth is going on? What has happened?'

They sank back onto the sofa and Nicola wriggled round to face him.

'Maggie's been phoning. Gellie's just had an emergency operation in hospital. She's very sick. Everyone is there and they are just waiting for her to come out of the aneasthetic.'

Joe was relieved that Nicola hadn't collapsed from over revising. It was very important to him that she got a good degree and then the research scholarship. Although he had only met them a few times, Joe was of the opinion that the Willstones and the rest of them were very prone to the over dramatisation of events.

'I'm sure Gellie's getting the best care possible,' he said soothingly. 'Do you want to go to London to see her?' desperately hoping that she would say no.

'No. I wouldn't be much use. I hate hospitals, all those tubes and the smell of disinfectant.' Nicola smiled weakly at Joe. That wasn't the real reason at all if she was honest with herself. It was the possibility of meeting Lucas that worried her most.

Her phone went. Picking it up she saw that it was Maggie again.

'I'll go and make supper,' said Joe, diplomatically, heading off for the kitchen.

'Maggie?'

'Oh Nicola, the worst possible thing has happened.' Maggie burst into tears.

'Where are you Maggie?' Nicola fervently hoped that Maggie wasn't walking the streets on her own in this distressed state.

'I'm with Caroline at their flat. She's making up a bed for me,' replied Maggie, 'and some hot chocolate.'

'Just tell me what happened. I'll listen for as long as it takes.'

Maggie blew her nose loudly and then sniffed down the phone.

'Charlie and Caroline were sitting with Gellie holding her hands and Dee and I were sitting outside by the door. Dee went off to get some coffee and sarnies and then Lucas suddenly arrived. He rushed down the ward and gave me a hug and then Caroline came out and he fell into her arms. He looked absolutely shattered but no surprise as he gave gallons of blood. Anyway then Charlie came out and just then Dee came back Charlie jumped at Lucas and gave him a huge hug. He didn't see Dee who was behind him but she was close enough. Lucas looked quite shocked and then Charlie steps back with big grin on his face. Honestly, I didn't know what was coming next but it was far far worse that we could ever have imagined.'

'What was Maggie?'

'Charlie said 'I can't thank you enough son. You saved your mother's life. Come in and see her, she's just coming round.' Well we all just stood there. Then Lucas gave Charlie a venomous stare and slammed straight into Dee as he ran for the door. Charlie turned with a what-have-I-said expression and saw Dee scrapping coffee and sarnie bits of her clothes. Dee just turned and walked off which left Charlie, Caroline and me. Caroline took a long hard look at Charlie and said 'Well I suppose it was bound to happen. You're a fool Charlie Willstone. This should have finished years ago but you couldn't see that could you. You have effectively destroyed a good many lives in a couple of minutes. Go and take care of my sister and I'll talk to you tomorrow when we've all calmed down a bit. Come with me Maggie.'

We walked in silence out of the hospital and there was Sulei with his diplomatic car parked on red lines. We got into the back and Sulei sat in the front with the driver. All Caroline said was that she was taking me back to her place for the night. When we arrived she gave me the keys and shooed me in while she spent ages talking to Sulei in the car. Then she came in looking thunderous and Sulei left. I feel really quite ill, Nicola.'

'Maggie, I'm coming straight down to London to see you.'

'You can't,' Maggie was horrified. 'You're finals start on Monday and I'm not going to be responsible for you messing up important exams again. I'll be fine. Caroline's coming back. I'll have to go. Speak tomorrow.'

Nicola sat very still as part of the foundations of her world crumbled and dissolved around her. Was it possible that all this was happening in London as she sat in her familiar surroundings in Newcastle? Had the secret really turned out to be so much bigger than she and Maggie could ever have imagined?

'Supper?' said Joe coming back into the room. One look at Nicola made him reached for the bottle of medicinal brandy.

'What's happened now, Babe?' he said tenderly but thinking he would kill Maggie if she'd gone off and done something stupid and then felt it was the right thing to do to confess to Nicola.

'Charlie Willstone lost it at the hospital and it turns out that he is Lucas' father and Gellie, not Caroline, is Lucas' mother.' Nicola shook her head as though she was having trouble understanding this. 'Really Joe, this is all too much.' As she stood up, Nicola went pale and wavered as the room tilted to the left and then back to the right. Remembering what happened at the orphanage after the Mombasa incident, Joe sat her down and forced her head between her knees.

'Stay there,' he commanded and went off to find blankets and sleeping bags to pile on top of their duvet. Filling two hot water bottles, he carried Nicola into his bedroom. She hardly resisted as he struggled to get her into his climbing thermal underwear remarking to himself that these were probably the biggest passion killers ever. When she was safely tucked up he gave her a large tumbler full of brandy and told her to lie still. Fetching his now, almost cold supper, he sat beside her until he was sure she was asleep before going to his lap top to Google 'shock'. He seemed to be doing everything right apart from the brandy. That might have been a bit over the top.

Nicola woke in the middle of the night to find herself in a thermal straight jacket and covered in sleeping bags. Was this a camping trip gone wrong? Couldn't be Joe's flat as it was far too warm. Moving slightly she felt Joe fast asleep beside her. She needed a wee quite desperately so that must have been what had woken her up. Struggling to sit up she accidentally kicked Joe who was instantly awake.

'What's wrong? Are you OK?'

'I'm fine apart from a monstrous headache and I need a wee.'

Joe put on the light which illuminated not only the room but all her memories of the events that had got her into this state.

'Oh Joe,' she cried and fell back into his arms in tears.

The next morning Joe insisted that she ate an enormous breakfast while he took her mobile and made a couple of phone calls. He called Maggie and told her not to phone Nicola again until her exams had finished. 'You can email but you mustn't upset her,' he told Maggie and to emphasise his point he told her that Nicola had been in shock the night before. Maggie agreed but thought darkly that Joe had no idea of the far reaching implications of the previous evening's events. Then he phoned Caroline to inquire about Gellie.

'Gellie's making a good recovery. Nobody has told her about Charlie's outburst and I am going to keep it that way until I think she's ready. I have banned Charlie from the hospital.' Caroline told Joe.

'How's Nicola?'

Joe told Caroline about Nicola going into shock.

'I would like to explain the whole story about Gellie and Lucas and how he came to be brought up by Dermot and myself as our son. I think Nicola needs to hear this from me before the rumours, conjecture and gossip starts flying around. I have told Maggie the whole story. It would have been sensible if we'd all been honest from the start and not wasted our lives protecting the truth.'

Joe thought it would probably be a good idea but only if Caroline was prepared to write it down in an email and send it to him so that he could choose the best time to show it to Nicola.

'Her finals start tomorrow,' he explained 'so I'm just trying to keep her as calm as possible. It's difficult because she takes everything so seriously.'

Caroline agreed and told Joe to be sure to wish Nicola the very best of luck. Joe failed to pick up the fact that no one had mentioned how Lucas was coping.

'Gellie is making great progress and Caroline is looking after her.' Joe detected a slight relaxation in Nicola but her face was still outlined in anxiousness.

'Now, no arguments. Revision is finished and we're going out. The sun is shining and it is just a perfect day. Get your boots and a warm jacket. Let's go.'

Nicola was about to open her mouth and recite the last part of her revision timetable but Joe didn't give her a chance. He grabbed her hand, pulled her down the stairs and bundled her into his battered Ford Fiesta. They were heading south out of Newcastle on the motorway before Joe turned to Nicola and gave her hand a squeeze.

Getting out of the flat, out of Newcastle and away from all the angst that had wrapped its tentacles round her in a deathly embrace was just what Nicola needed. She wound down the window and let the country air tug at her hair thinking about Frampton. They were heading towards the North York Moors and Nicola was delighted when they abandoned their car at the top of the cliff above Robin Hood Bay. Nature had produced her colouring pens for this spring day. The sandstone houses with their red tiled roofs stood proud against their background of dark brooding cliffs. The occasional whitewashed building became a punctuation mark in the statement the village made about being permanent despite its precarious position tumbling down towards the sea.

Stopping to check the tide timetable, they set off at a smart pace along the beach towards Ravenscar. They soon slowed down as the pull of searching for fossils along the extensive rock reefs at the sea's edge became hard to resist. There was soon a competition as to who could find the biggest and the best. It was a very happy day which ended with a cream tea at the Laurel Inn back at Robin Hood Bay.

'Thank you, Joe. That was a really special day. Just what I needed but I couldn't see it.' Nicola was trying to pull the knots out of her sea spangled hair as they climbed the stairs back up to Joe's flat.

'Go and have a shower and then I'll cook supper. It's an early night for you.'

Nicola smiled at Joe grateful for the way in which he had taken over her life. If she could just get through the next week, she could then get to grips with claiming it back again.

While Nicola was in the shower Joe switched on his lap top and checked his emails. There was one from Caroline in his inbox which he printed out. As water was still flowing noisily in the shower, Joe took the email over to the window to read it

Joe, please give this to Nicola when her exams are over. Thank you. Cx

My Dearest Nicola,
I am writing to you because you need to know the full story before gossip distorts the truth. It is difficult for me to write this as so many of the events happened a

long time ago and those involved have practically come to believe fabrication as the truth.

In early 1979 Dermot was appointed to the High Commission in Nairobi and I went with him as an excited young bride. We had a holiday home in Kilifi and I much preferred to live there rather than our flat in the capital. Dermot had a great time travelling round the country meeting people and making friends so in no time at all we had a wide social circle. That's how we met Charlie and Dee Willstone. When they heard we had a house in Kilifi they moved there too. In 1980 I had Julian. I was determined to have a natural birth but things went wrong and in a panic Dermot whisked me off to the nearest clinic at Our Sisters of Mercy Convent in Watamu. Julian arrived safely after a very protracted labour and I was sent back to Nairobi to have the damage repaired but it meant that I would never have any more children. I sank into post natal depression to the point where I was neglecting Julian so Dermot asked Gellie, who had just finished her art college course, to come and help. Gellie bounced into our lives and took over to the point where I think Julian loved her more than he loved me. That summer we partied furiously. Dee was expecting Jocelyn and went back to England to have her baby in what she saw as relative safety after my experiences. In the autumn I decided to give up the rather fruitless life I'd been enjoying over the summer and started looking for something meaningful to do. I ended up back at the convent as an assistant teacher to the little ones. Sister Benny had just arrived from the mother house in Ireland determined, like they all are, to make a difference in Africa. I dragged Gellie along one day and it didn't take Sister Benny long to spot an opportunity. Gellie started teaching art and knitting, Gellie loved to knit. We were sitting planning Christmas parties early in November. I was so much better that I started wondering whether it was time Gellie went home to find herself what our mother used to call 'a proper job'. Suddenly she turned to me and told me she was pregnant, four months to be exact, and that she had only decided to tell me because her bump was beginning to show. She wasn't going to have an abortion and anyway she'd left it too late, probably deliberately. She was going to have the baby but she didn't want to keep it. She wasn't prepared to tell me who the father was.

We hatched a plot. I was desperate for another child and Dermot and I had talked about adopting but Gellie had presented us with the perfect opportunity. Gellie would allegedly go back to England to find a job but really she would go and hide out in the Convent with the sisters. I would meanwhile announce that I was pregnant but to get away from the heat on the coast I would go and stay with Elodie's parents, on their ranch on the Laipikia Plateau near Nanyuki. When Gellie's baby was born I would go to the Convent and return to Kilifi with a baby and Gellie would go back to England. Sister Benny wasn't easy to convince until Gellie produced a fairly generous cheque which, she said would be followed up by a regular payment to the Convent. Dermot thought it was mad but was eager for me to be happy and I was at the thought of a brother or sister for Julian. Gellie was the main problem as she refused to leave her lover and go back home. I found out who it was quite by accident. Gellie had to go to Nairobi to renew her passport and I arranged for her to stay at the Muthaiga Club. Dermot had to rush back to Nairobi for a meeting so I went too and called to see Gellie. The club manager told me she had gone out but that Mr Crawford was in their room and they could ask him to come and see me. You can imagine my surprise when Charlie Willstone turned up. He was just as surprised to see me. I really launched into him and told him this ridiculous affair had to stop. He agreed as Dee was due back shortly and Gellie would be 'disappearing' and then going back to England. Honestly, he was so casual about it. I could have hit him.

Anyway, the plan worked and I returned joyfully to Kilifi with a baby boy, Lucas. Julian was delighted to have a brother and Gellie returned sulkily to England to throw her energies into knitwear design. We moved back to England when the boys went to boarding school along with the Willstones. They bought The Grange at Frampton and settled down but Dermot and I continued to travel. Gellie was so fond of the boys. She never differentiated between them and was the most perfect aunt and substitute mother. They both adored her.

When Charlie started acting as Gellie's financial adviser I did wonder if there was anything going on between them. Gellie promised that there wasn't and that she had to have Charlie working for her because she needed someone she could trust completely. I didn't think Charlie would do anything to jeopardise his marriage as Dee is the one with the money.

Nicola, I was so wrong. I saw it immediately I got to the hospital and saw them together. I had a dreadful feeling that it would all come tumbling out if Charlie lost it. The rest, as they say, is history. I fear we have not reached the end of the fallout from all this. I have told Maggie the whole story as well as she was witness to so much.

As for Lucas, he will be badly affected. He will see it as a betrayal by the ones he loves most and coming after losing his soul mate, Julian, three years ago so he will be hurting. Sulei is looking after him.

Take care my dear. Joe has promised to give you this when he thinks the time is right for you as I know you have important exams starting very soon. Please come and see me when you feel able to talk.
With all my love
Caroline xx

Joe carefully folded the printed email in half and slid the paper into his desk drawer. The time to show Nicola its contents was definitely not now particularly since a day away from Newcastle seemed to have successfully buried all this stupid drama. Anyway, Nicola knew most of this already and she didn't need the detail, well not just yet. In Joe's opinion the Willstones and the Smith Owens conducted their lives like a TV soap opera.

Nicola appeared in the doorway with her hair wrapped in a towel.

'I thought you said supper would be ready.' She said smiling cheerfully at Joe.

'Of course, it is,' replied Joe striding towards her.

Whether it was Robin Hood Bay or a hot shower, Nicola suddenly felt different. She felt in control of her destiny and ready for her final exams. Wow, it was amazing. She just wasn't going to do any more revision. She was completely ready.

However in Watamu the Arit Jinn had been indulging in a little spring cleaning in their tree home and had turned up the package of memories that Nicola had concealed in the branches. Chattering with glee, they spilled the contents out over the bark. This, together with the news Sister Benny had received recently from London, was indeed a special find. Giggling furiously they stapled everything together and stored it carefully in the tree trunk.

The next morning Nicola walked down to the Sports Centre ready to sit her first exam. Her bag bulged with Good Luck cards and her phone buzzed with text messages. The drama with Gellie and Charlie suddenly didn't seem important any more. She was quite happy to ditch all connections with the Willstones, she had never liked them very much anyway, and the Smith Owens, well, it was time to move on to her life with Joe who could give her all the love and security she craved.

The exam week passed in a fast blur and ended with wild celebrations. Joe had to leave for Galway and a series of field trips. He would be away for two months as he had factored in a research project with the university out on remote Innisboffin.

'Come with me, Nicola, please.'

'I can't Joe,' replied Nicola twisting her engagement ring round her finger letting the sun snatch maliciously at the cut surface of the diamond. 'You know I find it very awkward when we're together in front of the department crowd,' she smiled shyly at Joe hoping he understood. 'And I've got to move out of the house and that will need a mammoth clean. And I should go back to Frampton and catch up.' Nicola paused as though she was downloading her memory. The drama which has been neatly sidetracked by her exams was looming larger in her brain every minute.

'God, Joe,' Nicola brought her hands up to her face. 'Maggie. I must speak to Maggie.'

Joe sighed. The moment he had been avoiding had arrived.

'Sit down Nicola,' he said and went over to his desk and retrieved Caroline's email.

'Caroline sent this email. It's for you but she sent it to me so that I could keep it until the time was right and I think that that time is now.' Joe handed the email to Nicola and left her to it.

An hour later Nicola found Joe working on his lap top in the kitchen. He looked up trying to gauge her reaction as Nicola sat down opposite him.

'Phew,' she said. 'That is some weird story but it does put much of what I know into context. It really helps that it all makes kind of sense now, you know, between Charlie and Gellie. I should go home and see Mum and Dad because they must be hurting. Frampton is such a small village. But I don't want to be involved in the mess so I'll go to London and catch up with Maggie, then I'll go to Oxford and stay with Kate for a while, well, until the results come out and then, well who knows?' Nicola hoped that would be enough information to keep Joe happy. She felt very unsettled.

Joe smiled with relief. Thank goodness Nicola wasn't going to start out on a crusade to make everything better. By the time he got back from Galway, Nicola would have her results and most probably the research scholarship and then they could plan their wedding and the rest of their lives together.

Nicola phoned Maggie and chattered excitedly about her exams being over and the parties that seemed to run into each other for days.

'…and the last thing I want to see right now is a bottle of vodka and a shot glass. Maggie are you still there?' Anxiously Nicola suddenly realised that she had done all the talking and normally it was the other way round.

'I'm here, Nicola, sitting in a dark pearshaped world in Frampton and if you want to see me you'd better get down here. I'm leaving for Rome next week.'

'Maggie. What on earth is going on? Why haven't you been in touch?'

'I told you. I didn't want to mess up your exams,' said Maggie flatly.

'This is really serious. Tell me.'

'Well after that night with Gellie nearly dying, Caroline told me the full story and I was gobsmacked, Nicola. I never realised that adults could behave so badly. I just couldn't go back to *Angelica*. It was so bad Caroline went and collected my stuff from the design studio. Honestly Caroline has been fantastic. She helped me work out a plan because I just wasn't thinking straight. At that point I hated Gellie more than anything. So I am going to sell *Magknits* to *Angelica* which should give me a pile of money for my year out from College next year and Caroline has arranged for me to work at a fashion house in Paris. It will be amazing.'

Nicola could tell from Maggie's voice that she was getting more animated about her plans so things couldn't be that bad.

'It is really strange how things work out. *Magknits,* won the College prize for best new fashion venture and the prize is a summer school in Rome. Aren't you impressed? So I'm off to Italy for two months to do unheard of stuff like classical drawing and oil painting. It will be awesome. Then I'll move straight to Paris which will put a lot of space between me and Gellie.

And the parents are impressed – at last.'

Maggie had cheered up considerably and Nicola was so happy for her.

'Look Maggie. I have to spend a couple of days cleaning the house out. I can't leave it to my flatmates, then I'll be home. Love you, little sister.'

Back in Frampton, Nicola and Maggie spent hours talking well into the dark nights in their bedroom. They sorted out the Willstone/Smith Owen saga hoping they had the facts in the right order and banished the secret they'd shared.

'Dee. Dee must have known about Gellie's affair with Charlie,' said Nicola.

'According to Caroline she did. But she thought it all started after they all got back to England. Dee had no idea the affair started in Kilifi so, of course, she didn't know anything about Lucas. She accepted the affair providing they were discreet so that no one would know.'

Memories from Watamu that she couldn't possibly share with Maggie kept interrupting the story but some of them were so cloudy and indistinct Nicola pushed them away hurriedly. She was not to know that the Arit Jinn in Watamu had found her memories and were busy knitting them together in their own pattern. They weren't ready for Nicola to understand so they fudged some of the stitches on purpose.

'Maggie?' Nicola turned to face her little sister just after they had agreed to turn out the light and go to sleep. 'Will you be my chief bridesmaid?'

Nicola practically suffered a chest injury as Maggie barreled her way into Nicola's arms.

'Yes, yes,' she cried. 'I thought you'd never ask. Any other bridesmaids?'

'I thought I'd ask Kate Wasson.'

And that lead to another hour of excited chatter.

Andrew and Monica were at a loss as to how to deal with the fallout from Charlie Willstones' outburst. Dee had immediately demanded a divorce and wouldn't let Charlie into The Grange which she owned outright anyway. Jocelyn was in the States so the great distance between her and the dramas in Frampton acted as a mild anaesthetic. The village was pulsating with whispered updates, most of them wildly exaggerated as Frampton had never seen anything like this before. Andrew hid behind his shield of professional confidentiality leaving Monica to walk round the village doing normal things with a poker face. Neither Nicola or Maggie mentioned the Willstones or the Smith Owens in front of their parents, they simply didn't want to go there. It was less hurtful to try and pretend it never happened. Mulberry Cottage was all shut up leaving the climbing roses to spiral skywards and claim the cottage as their own.

As soon as Maggie left for Rome, Nicola went to Oxford to catch up with Kate. The Oxford house was in a state of vast upheaval. Kate's parents had suddenly decided to move out of Oxford and had bought a vineyard in a village about twenty miles away. Kate was moving upstairs into the house and her parents would keep the basement flat on for the time being in case they got homesick.

Totally mad, was how Kate described it. 'They know nothing about wine except how to drink it but it will keep Dad amused and out of mischief. They aren't taking much of the furniture because the cottage is tiny, so I'm left with this jungle of brown furniture. I'd like to dump it all and replace it with IKEA but I'd be dead.'

Nicola thought Kate was secretly delighted to be moving into her old home where there would be room for the band members to stay over for as long as they liked. Kate, like her parents, loved a full house.

'So exams finished, what plans now, Nicola?'

Nicola explained about how she hoped to get a research scholarship so that she and Joe could stay in Newcastle.

'And the wedding?'

'December. At Frampton.' Hell, thought Nicola, it just got that much closer. 'Mum is getting really excited and uptight about organising it all, I really didn't think that there were that many minutiae to worry about.' Nicola turned to Kate.

'Maggie's going to be my chief bridesmaid. Will you be my bridesmaid too, Kate?'

'I would be absolutely delighted,' replied Kate solemnly.

'Hey, I don't know what your plans are but can you get back to Oxford the week after next? *Armageddon* are playing at Emmanuel College May Ball and it is going to be massive. Bring your ball gown and we can get in free as groupies. It will be like the old days and we can have such fun. Champagne all night long.' Kate looked hopefully at Nicola.

'I have to go back to Newcastle next week for the results and then I guess I'll just be sitting at home until graduation unless I get a job. Joe is in Galway running field study programmes and doing project work until the end of July so I'm on my own.'

'Fantastic,' cried Kate. 'Come for the May Ball and then we can find you a job or you can help sort out the house mess. Archie and the boys will be in the recording studio for three weeks and then they have a couple of rock festivals lined up over the summer so I guess I'll be on my own too.'

Kate gave Nicola big hug to seal the deal.

Back in Newcastle, Nicola sat on the grass in the quad with her friends waiting for an academically gowned figure to emerge from the Examinations office to make the short stroll over to the glass fronted boards where the results were posted. There had been a couple of false starts and now everyone was chattering nervously about their plans for the summer. They all fell silent as another figure exited the office and walked to the boards unlocking the glass front with a set of jangling keys. Having rearranged a few of the posted papers and secured the latest with drawing pins, produced slowly from the depths of his gown, the figure looked up and turned to wave at the group on the lawn. The rush for the January sales had nothing on the undignified scramble to the notice board. Nicola hung back slightly basking in the last few precious moments of not knowing what the future held for her until she was dragged forward by her fellow students. Not only had she got her 2:1 in Environmental Science, she had been awarded the Wentworth Scholarship for Research which would fund her doctorate. Brushing away tears of relief Nicola phoned Joe and was rather miffed that he already knew her results but he did sound very pleased for her and promised a massive celebration at her graduation in July. Her parents were delighted particularly with the news about the scholarship. Then Professor Boyd joined the happy group of graduates, relieved that the first year of undergraduates within his department had made it through the three years.

After another round of parties and celebrations, Nicola gathered up the last of her belongings and moved them to Joe's flat which felt very bare and unlived in. After a few days back in Frampton she set off, with a sense of relief, for Oxford. She hadn't got a dress for the ball so Kate took her shopping and they found a lovely slippery grey silk dress in Oxfam for practically nothing. They cycled down to Emmanuel College in the afternoon to watch the roadies set up and then spent ages changing and doing their hair. There was no sign of Archie.

'Archie likes to spend time on his own, playing his guitar, running through songs and twirling his drumsticks. He calls it getting in the groove or something like that,' explained Kate. 'The band takes performing really seriously even though they like to appear relaxed and chilled in front of their fans.'

Kate called a taxi and they arrived at the College just as dinner was finishing and the dancing and serious drinking was getting underway. Kate led the way to the Common Room where *Armageddon* were getting ready and introduced Nicola all round. Ben, the lead singer was missing.

'Ben's going to make an entrance from the river in a punt,' whispered Kate as they hurriedly tucked into beef wellington and strawberries and cream. The band left for the stage and a huge crowd gathered by the river bank. Kate and Nicola hung out of one of the windows and watched as Ben was punted slowly into view heralded by a string quartet on the bank. Once ashore Ben ran to the Marquee as *Armageddon* crashed into life with a dramatic drum solo. Nobody in Oxford could possibly be planning on getting any sleep in the next few hours. Kate and Nicola moved to the back of the Marquee where they stood swigging champagne from a bottle with the roadies and watched the performance. *Armageddon* had come a long way since Nicola had first heard them at the Summer Fever Festival. They were so much more professional and the music was even better. Kate looked on smiling proudly. After several encores, with their manager looking at his watch and the roadies shifting nervously as they wanted to get the kit packed up safely, the band left the stage and joined the crowd. Archie found Kate and the two of them dragged Nicola off to the bar. Just as she thought she might end up as a gooseberry at a ball as Kate and Archie had disappeared, Nicola was grabbed by the bass guitarist, Ethan, and pulled onto the dance floor.

'Dance with me, Nicola Cowan. Let's have some fun.'

Ethan was a great dancer, probably, mused Nicola because his life was so full of musical rhythm. Once on the dance floor, he refused to leave. They danced to rock music, indie, hip hop and managed to catch their breath during the slow numbers. People kept coming up and asking Ethan for his autograph and he obligingly wrote his name on dress shirt sleeves, on bare arms and sweaty backs. Occasionally the DJ would shine his spotlight onto the dance floor to pick out individuals or couples.

'And here, ladies and gentlemen, we have Ethan Blake, amazing bass guitarist with *Armageddon*. He's dancing with the beautiful Nicola Cowan from Newcastle.'

Nicola blushed furiously as the crowd clapped and cheered. She just caught sight of Kate diving away from the stage. Ethan and Nicola went on dancing until dawn broke and Kate and Archie summoned them to breakfast. As the sun rose speckling the soft beige of the college walls the four walked up the High in the middle of the road singing the words from Kate's favourite *Armageddon* track.

Back at the house Kate and Archie went to the kitchen to make coffee. Ethan took Nicola's hand and pulled her close. Nicola started at her reaction to his sexy male aura and the smell of Giorgio Armani 'After Shock'. Ethan breathed gently in her ear 'Thank you for a grand night out, Nicola,' and kissed her on both cheeks. Before Nicola could react he went into the drawing room shutting the door firmly behind him. Nicola stood listening to the Morgan's battered sofa groan as its upholstery was stretched heavily over its springs and then silence. She stumbled into the kitchen looking for Kate's coffee.

'Wasn't that a great evening, Nicola? Did you enjoy yourself?' asked Kate who looked as though she could party on. 'Hey, don't look so bemused.'

Nicola looked at Kate through tired unfocusing eyes.

'Ethan's gay, Nicola. Didn't you realise? I knew you'd be very safe with him. He just loves to dance and party and he's a really nice guy.'

Embarrassed, Nicola stumbled out of the kitchen, up the stairs to her room where she wriggled out of her now-a-little-worse-for-wear dress. Throwing herself down on the bed she decided that sleep was the only way out of this one. But the thin curtains and a dog barking over the wall would have none of it. Giving in, Nicola had a quick shower, pulled on her jeans and a white shirt, paused to consider emailing Joe but decided later would be better. The house was still relaxed around its sleeping occupants as Nicola crept out and, borrowing a bicycle from the rack, set off for the centre of Oxford. It was the fourth anniversary of that fateful coffee at Georgina's and, as she was in Oxford, Nicola felt pulled towards the covered market cafe. Maybe, just maybe, fate would wind time back and Julian would be there and they could start again. As she drew near Nicola knew that this was ridiculous but it didn't stop her.

As she walked up the stairs, Nicola could hear the chatter of conversation and happy laughter. The place was full but she managed to squeeze into a corner with a cappuccino hoping to wrap herself up in her own thoughts and memories. The couple sitting opposite decided to take their wrapped up in themselves elsewhere and as they got up to leave, Sulei slid in front of her.

'Hi Nicola,' he said reaching over the table to kiss her on both cheeks. 'You look lovely,' he added smiling at her. How come Sulei always said the right things even if they were hopelessly wrong? Nicola knew she didn't look lovely: she felt like dying from a massive hangover and no sleep. Sulei was, on the other hand, looking amazing. Fresh inquisitive brown eyes gazed at her and the just detectable smell of Christian Dior after shave was having an unsettling effect. His white cotton shirt still had the ironing creases down the sleeves.

'Nicola?' Sulei sounded anxious.

'Sorry, sorry Sulei. Late night,' replied Nicola shaking her head to establish some order in her brain. 'Great to see you too. What are you doing here?'

'It's difficult, Nicola. I thought of sending you an email or a text but really I needed to see you, to talk to you. I'm afraid that you might not want to be involved but I have run out of options. I thought that if you were here today, of all days, then you would still remember and maybe there was a chance.' Sulei looked into Nicola's eyes looking for an unspoken answer.

'Sulei, I don't understand. What are you saying?'

Sulei inhaled deeply and then held his breath for a moment.

'It's Lucas.' An invisible force tore at her guts as Nicola tried to keep an uninterested expression nailed to her face.

'Lucas?'

'Yes. After that dreadful night when Gellie was so ill and Charlie shouted out the truth, Lucas fled to Oman and he has been hiding in my sister's house in Muscat ever since. He has no plans; he won't speak to anyone; he's on PlayStation for hours; he won't go out and we're all at our wits end. My brother-in-law has had enough and has decided Lucas must leave. Lucas won't come back to England and he definitely won't go to either Kilifi or Watamu. Nicola, you are our last hope. Please will you go to Muscat and talk to Lucas?'

Nicola really didn't believe this was happening. Yes, in an earlier moment of madness on her way to Georgina's she had hoped Fate would drag the clock back but something had gone wrong. The clock had wound back but only as far as Mombasa and now it was threatening to fast forward out of control. The Aritt jinn were playing with a time machine.

'Sulei,' she managed to say, rather severely she hoped. 'What on earth makes you think that Lucas would listen to anything I might have to say to him? I expect you realise that he abandoned me in Mombasa and then instructed you to sort me out.'

'Nicola,' replied Sulei softly, taking one of Nicola's hands. 'You know that you two have been crazy about each other for years. The chemistry between you is astronomical when you're in the same room. Lucas knows but he won't admit it and I have never understood why. As for you Nicola…well?'

Nicola blushed. 'You were the one who told me Lucas is dangerous, Sulei. I listened and ran away and now I'm going to marry someone who really loves me.'

Nicola watched as Sulei backed off. Then he tried again.

'Nicola. Please. Just talk to Lucas. Stay with my sister who really would like to meet you. You never took up her invitation to visit when she was in Mombasa. You can stay as long as you like or just leave after you've spoken to Lucas. It will be your decision.'

Nicola felt herself being seduced by Sulei's softly spoken words on to some sort of path carved from destiny and the bark of a rather old tree in Watamu. How could she refuse to help Sulei and it would be helping Sulei not Lucas who sounded like he was behaving like a spoilt child. It was at least six weeks to graduation and Joe was away on Innisboffin with no satellite signals. Anyway she could text from anywhere in the world and he was not to know it wasn't Oxford. Nicola reeled from all these decisions that had fallen into place so easily.

'I'll go.'

Sulei looked relieved. 'Can you fly out on say, Wednesday? I'll book flights and make arrangements. I'm afraid I must return to Muscat tomorrow but I'll meet you at the airport after you've landed. Thank you Nicola. Now, can I buy you lunch?'

ANNIE BOON

8

Kate had been incredulous when Nicola had told her the whole story.

'You are kidding,' Kate exclaimed. 'You're not trying to tell me that you're tearing off to Oman to rescue some guy you owe nothing because he can't man up to a family situation?'

Actually, thought Nicola, Kate is absolutely right, as usual.

'I'm doing this for Sulei, Kate. I owe him and this is the least I can do to repay my debts.'

'Believe me, you're playing with fire. Don't forget you're going to marry a hell of a nice guy who loves you to bits. Meanwhile you're hung up on some useless idiot.' Nicola winced as Kate laid out the truth in front of her.

'OK. Go. I can see that you've made up your mind and nothing I can say will change anything.'

'Can I leave some of my stuff with you, Kate? I'll only be gone a couple of days, a week at the very most. I'll take my phone but could you please fend off my parents and anyone else who comes looking until I get back?'

Kate agreed to everything little realising that one of the last items Nicola put away at the back of a drawer was her engagement ring, nestled back in its box. She certainly didn't want to lose that far away on another continent.

It was late afternoon, Omani time, and the setting sun hung like a magnificent red ball of fire as the plane landed at Muscat. Sulei was waiting for her. He wasn't sure whether I'd actually come thought Nicola during the short drive to Sulei's sister's house in the new part of Muscat close to the sea. The huge gates swung silently open as the car approached the compound and as they swung shut behind them Nicola felt panic rising in her throat. A prisoner in Oman and only Kate knew vaguely where she was. A svelte figure in designer jeans was standing waiting for them on the steps of what appeared to be, in the now gloomy night sky, a huge mansion. Nicola had forgotten how quickly night followed day as you got closer to the equator.

'Nicola, I'd like you to meet my sister, Leila Jamil. Leila this is Nicola Cowan.'

Nicola's brain went into fast reverse as she remembered Maggie's email reporting on the Willstones New Year party. Standing in front of her was the 'arabian princess' that had spent the night dancing and flirting with Lucas. Another rewind buzzed loudly. This time it was Julian telling Nicola about Lucas' perchance for a married woman. She shook her head as she tried to reconcile the married woman with Lucas' soul mate Sulei. Nicola felt the complicated knots of the Smith Owen/Willstone saga tighten round her chest. Leila held out her hand towards Nicola.

'Nicola, I am delighted to meet you at last. I was so sorry that you were unable to visit us properly in Mombasa last summer. I hope we can make amends on this visit.' Leila turned and led Nicola into a high ceilinged entrance hall which opened out on to an enclosed courtyard brimming with exotic flowers whose scent was layered heavily on the still air. A fountain burbled water into a square pond laughing at Nicola's discomfort.

'Would you like some tea, Nicola? I will have your bag taken to your room.' Nicola was to discover that quantities of tea were consumed in the Jamil household.

Sitting cross legged on a highly decorative carpet, her back supported by soft silk cushions, Nicola reflected that Maggie and Gellie would love this riot of colour mixed in a rich harmony. She was alone with Leila who thanked her, graciously, for making the long journey out to Oman.

'Since Lucas arrived he hasn't left his room. He seems lost; scared of his own demons… My husband was understanding at first but his patience is running out.' Leila paused and waited for a reaction from Nicola.

Nicola sat up and placed her delicate china cup onto a low table. The lemon grass tea was delicious and very refreshing.

'But what can I do Leila?'

Perhaps she had been too hasty in rushing off to Oman to sort out a lost cause. She should have listened to Kate. The African heat was exhausting her even though the ceiling fan was doing its monotonous best to keep the frankincense soaked air moving.

'I haven't seen Lucas since last summer.' Nicola paused and managed to say 'Mombasa' before looking hard at Leila. 'We weren't actually speaking when he left. He asked Sulei to pick up the pieces.'

'Nicola, you're our last hope. I'm worried that if Kalan puts his foot down and makes Lucas leave he'll just drift off and be gone forever.' Leila stood up gracefully.

'I'll take you to his room so that you can say hello and arrange to talk to him tomorrow. He doesn't know you're here.'

Together they walked across the courtyard, watched by a shadowy figure, to a low white building where a light burned dimly in one of the windows. Nicola stepped gingerly over the threshold and gazed into the room blinking in the half light. Lucas sat huddled over his PlayStation at the far end of the room. Leila stepped back towards the door leaving Nicola out on her own. She cleared her throat.

Startled, Lucas looked up. Nicola was shocked at the dark circles round his eyes, his pale cheeks and his matted unkempt hair.

'Nicola?' Lucas took a minute to work out whether it was her. 'What the fuck are you doing here?'

Struggling to his feet, Lucas took a couple of steps towards her. She could smell khat on his breath.

'Why have you come, Nicola? This is no place for you, Mrs Soon-to-be-some-funny-Irish-name,' he said caustically. Taking a step back he threw his hands into the air.

'Have you come to rescue Lucas Smith Owen, because if you have you're wasting your time, he doesn't exist. Have you come...' Lucas waited to see if he had had any effect, 'to rescue Lucas Crawford because he may, genetically speaking, exist. As for Lucas Willstone...' Lucas spat the last word out with slow venomous emphasis, 'he never ever did exist and never ever will.' Standing up as straight as possible, Lucas stared at Nicola, daring her to reply.

Nicola pulled her shoulders back and returned Lucas' steady gaze.

'I came because I owe Sulei, to repay a debt by finding the real Lucas Smith Owen. The one we all used to know, the one who needs to stop acting like a spoilt child and start growing up.'

Lucas looked at her petulantly. 'You have no idea how it feels to be in the centre of a mess that you did not create. I have, allegedly, four parents who I hold responsible and none of them are doing anything to help me out of it.'

'Your mother, Caroline, the one who brought you up as her own, remember her? Well, she cares about you. We all care about you, you're the one with the problem.'

'You're absolutely correct. I don't care any more. I don't care about anything or anyone.'

Nicola turned to look at Leila and shrugged her shoulders as if to signify that here was a hopeless case. As she started to walk towards the door Nicola heard Lucas take a couple of steps towards her. She hesitated but did not look round.

'Nicola, I'm sorry. I know you've come a long way on a wasted journey. Please can we just talk tomorrow morning before you go back?'

Nicola turned and gazed at Lucas taking in his long black curls, designer stubble and sheer helplessness. She shook her head back to reality and found herself saying.

'Yes that would be good.'

She turned sharply and followed Leila and the shadowy figure out into the cool courtyard.

'Thank you, Nicola. That he wants to talk to you is a huge step forward. We'll meet again tomorrow. Tesbaheena ala kheer. Good night.'

The sun was already well on its way up its skyward track when Nicola woke the next day. Opening the shutters Nicola found the sea at the Ghubra beach reaching towards her on an inward tide. She took a really deep breath of the invigorating ocean air and got dressed. No one had mentioned breakfast but as she reached the courtyard at the bottom of the stairs a figure glided towards her and led her into a smaller, more intimate courtyard. Leila rose from a small bistro table.

'Nicola. Good morning. I hope you slept well. Your room was comfortable? You had everything you need?' Without waiting for a reply, Leila asked for breakfast and they both sat down.

Yoghurt with olives, pastries, flat bread with hummus and tea was quickly arranged on the table. Rather confused, Nicola smiled at Leila and murmured thank you as that seemed appropriate.

'I have instructed Lucas to meet you in about an hour's time,' Leila consulted her watch. 'I hope that suits. I have a rather busy day. Kalan will be back tonight and he would like a family dinner with you and Lucas as our guests.'

Wow thought Nicola. I hope Leila doesn't expect me to have sorted Lucas by tonight. That is a really big ask. Nicola was not sure that she could deliver, she could only give it her best shot.

Nicola found Lucas sitting beside the fountain in the main courtyard. He looked more alive in the morning light. He had shaved, washed his hair and put on a clean shirt and jeans. And he'd scrubbed his teeth so that he no longer smelt of khat. Seeing her walking towards him, Lucas stood up and motioned her to sit on the stone bench. Out of the corner of her eye Nicola spied a white robed figure hesitate beside a stone column and then slide down to a squatting position from where it was possible to keep an eye on them. The fountain's bouncing drops of water filled the silence between.

'Thank you for coming all this way to see me, Nicola,' whispered Lucas. 'I didn't mean to be rude last night.'

Nicola shrugged and waited for Lucas to collect his thoughts. Taking a deep breath and sounding unsure Lucas addressed a large white flower in the opposite border.

'I've thought hard about what you said to me last night. You're right. My mother is Caroline and Dermot is my Dad and nothing can change that. I should tell them that they are and always will be my real parents.' Lucas smiled. 'I feel so much better now I've decided I'm really Lucas Smith

Owen.' Lucas looked at Nicola for confirmation. She nodded.

Lucas' face tightened. 'I can't face Gellie yet. I love her to bits, she's always been special and now I can see why. But Charlie Willstone? I never ever liked that total loser and now I find out he's my real, no, biological father. I never ever want to see him again.'

Nicola said flatly 'Dee's left Charlie, they are getting divorced. The Grange is up for sale. I think Gellie is in London but I've no idea where Charlie is.'

'It's OK. I don't want to know. I'm not ready to go back to England. It still hurts too much.'

'You can't stay here, Lucas.'

'I know.'

'What about your job?'

'I'm on compassionate leave and as I'm due a holiday I can stay away as long as I like.'

Nicola thought this was probably an exaggeration.

'And what is this job that seems to allow you to do exactly what you want?'

'I work for British Intelligence. I infiltrate terrorist cells, especially Arabic ones, though I may have to move soon because my cover is getting thin. Your escapade in Mombasa didn't help. I was so angry with you. I know you didn't realise and you weren't to know but when you left the hospital, you were walking behind one of the most hunted leaders of Al Shabab who was in the city to enjoy his terrorist attack. I was following him and then suddenly you were in the way and I had to follow you instead. Then the bomb went off. Sulei feels it's time for us to get out. As far as the rest of the world is concerned we're second hand car salesmen. We import and export Ferraris, Masserartis, Jaguars you name it. It's all part of Sulei's family's business, the Abbas empire.'

Nicola didn't know what to believe; some of it, all of it, none of it.

Lucas turned to Nicola, his face alight and animated.

'I know I have really outstayed my welcome with Kalan and Leila so I'm leaving in a couple of days. Will you come with me, Nicola? Come with me on holiday! Come with me to Piers and Elodie's ranch in Kenya. Come to Swala.'

Nicola was too taken aback to speak. Her first reaction was that it would be impossible. But then she did have a couple of weeks to fill before graduation and her research contract didn't start until August, a good six weeks away. All she planned to do in between was find a job in Oxford to earn some money. Joe was away in a remote part of Galway and enjoying himself with students and dolphins. A trip to Kenya was very enticing.

Nervously she stood up. Without looking at Lucas she asked him to show her the courtyards and gardens. Slowly they started to walk, not too close together, mindful of being observed from every angle. It was hard to tell how it started but very soon they were talking in low solemn voices about the everythings and nothings that had happened in their lives so far.

They didn't talk about Julian even though it would have been the most natural subject to draw them together. Two hours went by in five minutes. Nicola had still not accepted Lucas' invitation when she was told that Leila was expecting her to join her for lunch.

Nicola dressed carefully for dinner that night. She tied her hair up and put on some light makeup. The soft red silk of the outfit borrowed from Leila highlighted the remnants of exam pallor and she dismissed the two unusual pinks spots on her cheeks as being a reaction to the Omani heat conveniently forgetting that the air con system was working on overtime. Kalan was in charge of the evening and was the first to greet Nicola, introducing her to members of his extended family. In turn they spoke politely to Nicola in excellent English. When she caught sight of Lucas her heart thumped hard and she gasped for air. He had swapped his slouched jeans for traditional Arab dress and he looked amazing. Sulei touched her arm and guided her in to dinner. 'It is rude to stare,' he whispered in her ear and smiled with satisfaction when he noticed how red she had gone.

Later that night, alone in her room, Nicola opened her wallet and carefully removed a copy of the email from Caroline which Joe had given her after her exams had finished. Spreading it out on her bed she reread what Caroline had written. There were a couple of points that Lucas had made when he was explaining his situation that she wanted to verify with her own memories of her first visit to the convent at Watamu. It had always troubled her that Sister Benny had just accepted her pregnancy without much surprise and had so readily agreed to her staying on at the convent to have her baby. Coupled with what she now knew it must have seemed to Sister Benny that history was almost repeating itself, though this time there was no Dermot and Caroline to rescue the situation once the baby was born. Another thought emerged from her recollections. The regular payments from Charlie Willstone that she had unearthed in one of the ledgers were now easily explained. Hush money paid to Sister Benny. The 'Lost Souls' ledger had disappeared from the office as soon as she had discovered it, probably so that her eagle eyes would not spot the details of Lucas' birth and his parents' true identity. Sister Benny was well and truly implicated in the sorry saga. Nicola fell asleep wondering if there were any more secrets buried in Sister Benny's records.

The next day she met Lucas again in the courtyard with their chaperone. Without hesitating, because if she did pause she wouldn't do it, she told Lucas she would go to Laikipia with him. It was probably the wrong thing to do but, after all, it would only be for a few days holiday and she needed to get some things sorted out.

'But only for a week, Lucas. I have to get back to England. I have to graduate and get a job for the summer.'

She spun round as she felt Jamie creep up behind her.

'Don't do this, Nicola,' he breathed in her ear. 'Remember it is Joe that you love.'

She was about to assure him that she was completely in control and that this was just a holiday but he was gone as quickly as he'd arrived.

As the Laikipia Plateau slewed into view, the small plane from Nairobi touched down on the grass runway at Nanyuki airport. Nicola gasped at the enormous expanse of baobab and acaia studded savannah with views opening up towards the distant Mount Kenya. It was a shocking contrast to the dry rocky deserts of Oman and the seeming endless townships of Nairobi which they had left that morning. It was appreciably cooler in Nanyuki than it has been in Muscat and Nicola gulped down mouthfuls of fresh air as they waited for the pilot to complete his paper work and then to metamorphose into baggage handler. As they walked towards the car park a young boy leapt over the fence and rushed towards them.

'Hey, Stanley. You old enough to drive? I don't believe it,' cried Lucas flinging his arms round the small taught body.

'Mr Lucas. You haven't visited for ages. I have grown up waiting for you to come back to see us.'

As they loaded their bags into the back of the truck, Lucas introduced Nicola to Stanley and they set off on their journey to Swala. Lucas was sitting in the front chatting in Swahili so Nicola was left to watch the Laikipia's savannah unfold in front of her. In some ways it reminded her of the safari trip she took with Lucas and Sulei to the game reserve north of Malindi on her first visit to Kenya but Laikipia was much larger and wilder than any place she had visited before.

She thought about her conversation with Kate before she left Oxford. She was fine. Everything was under her control.

A light breeze danced through the sparse grass bouncing rays of sunlight off the spikes on the bent acacia trees and the silver grey trunks of the baobabs. As she gazed out over the landscape Nicola sat up straight and screwed up her eyes to find the point where the sun blanched grasslands met the hard blue sky. It was difficult because the point was so far away and the vista kept changing. Suddenly Nicola found that magical essence that was Africa. Suddenly she understood the Smith Owen and Willstone's addiction to the country. It was the stark colour displayed with unpredictable, shifting movement. As the truck sped round a sharp bend, a small herd of Grevy's zebra crossed the road in front of them and settled down to graze by the roadside flicking their tales unsynchronised with the general shifting of the landscape. It was like being at a concert with the orchestra at odds with the score despite the conductor's efforts to bring them into line. Nicola sighed contentedly. The noise alerted Lucas who turned round to ask if she was OK and noted her happy relaxed smile.

Stanley pulled up outside a general store when they reached the small town of Rumuruti and disappeared with a long shopping list. Lucas and Nicola walked along the main street gazing at the unfamiliar fruit and vegetables on display in market stalls. Neither said much, Lucas because he was drinking in the rich atmosphere of a familiar place and Nicola because it was so new and exciting. A jangle of hardware shops strung up with galvanized buckets winking in the sunlight, white string headed mops, wooden stools, saffron coloured sponges and ginger tinted coconut mats crowded next to pharmacists with green crosses above their doors. Shoe shops displayed bunches of flip flops and plastic shoes like bananas. The chaotic scene was punctuated by diffident shopkeepers leaning on door posts watching the world drift by.

Once Stanley had loaded the stores they left the tarmac road behind and headed North East on dirt tracks. The landscape changed to wilder unpredictable rocky outcrops and denser bush though much was obscured by the mini sandstorm thrown up by the truck. A sharp left hand turn past a battered sign announced they had reached the edge of the Swala property and another two miles of dirt and dust brought them up to the ranch house and a welcoming party of three dogs who jumped enthusiastically on board to greet them.

Disentangling herself from the canine welcome, Nicola saw Piers and Elodie walking towards them all smiles. Behind them a low rambling ranch house built of pinkish orange bricks surrounded by a wide verandah relaxed in a tropical garden overflowing with bougainvillea doing battle with nandi flame trees.

Elodie came forward and shyly kissed Nicola on both cheeks.

'It's lovely to see you again, Nicola. We're so pleased you could come with Lucas. Welcome to Swala,' she said rather formally. Turning round she threw her arms round Lucas and hugged him.

'Lucas, we haven't seen you since our wedding and that is way too long,' she said severely. 'Now come out onto the verandah for tea and cakes while Stanley deals with the luggage,' and taking Lucas' arm she led the way.

Piers meanwhile came up to Nicola and held out a large bear sized hand which took hers surprisingly gently and gave it a squeeze.

'Welcome to Swala, Nicola. Nice to meet you at last.'

Once settled on the verandah, Nicola was taken aback by the magnificent views of the three snow topped peaks of Mount Kenya, 30kms to the east.

'Wow,' she exclaimed, 'This is an amazing view. You're so lucky.'

'I know,' replied Elodie. 'I should remember to be grateful every day. My parents built this ranch back in the 1940s and I grew up here. I guess

I've just got a bit complacent about it all.'

Piers and Lucas were deep in conversation about renovations, conservation and cattle ranching.

'We have to find another source of income if we are going to keep our horses as well as the cattle so Piers has this idea about building a few guest cottages so that we can offer bush experience stays. Here on the Laikipia Plateau we're not restricted by park and reserve rules so we can offer riding, walking and shooting safaris.'

'Sounds wonderful,' replied Nicola.

After tea, Elodie took Nicola round their guest suite. Nicola was slightly apprehensive about the arrangements but Elodie quickly put her at ease.

'There are two bedrooms here, one either side of a sitting area. The bathroom is through that door to the back. There is a shower and a bath. Any laundry that needs doing just put it into the basket and it will be back the next day. I'll leave you to settle in. Lucas will be ages now he's talking to Piers. They will have rebuilt the entire place by dinner.'

Nicola sank gratefully onto one of the beds. It was fine for Lucas as he was obviously completely at home on the ranch. But it was all new to Nicola. Light years away from a flat on the top floor of a Victorian building in Newcastle or a Cotswold stone cottage which had never had the money that was needed spent on it. She got up and padded round the building in her bare feet. Simply furnished, it lacked nothing. The pile of soft white fluffy towels in the bathroom was so inviting Nicola decided to have a shower as soon as she had unpacked. She separated the two rucksacks that Stanley had left coupled together and carried hers into the room she had chosen, spreading her few possessions around to claim ownership. Just to make her point clear she put Lucas' bag in the other room. Laying out a pair of safari trousers and a white shirt she went off to have a long cleansing shower.

With no sign of Lucas, Nicola walked over to the ranch house. The verandah was empty apart from a sleeping dog that wagged its tail but didn't bother getting up. Hearing some voices at the other end of the building, Nicola wound her way through an invitingly comfortable drawing room, trying not to be waylaid by a well stocked bookcase, then a wide airy hall adorned with horns, tusks and other African trophies. Just before she reached what she presumed was the kitchen, Elodie emerged from an office.

'Ah there you are, Nicola. Lucas is looking for you. We'll find him out at the front.'

No sign of Lucas anywhere as they stood beside the heavy wooden doors at the entrance to the house. The dogs appeared from nowhere and looked expectantly at Elodie. Just when she thought that standing out in the late afternoon sun waiting for the mercurial Lucas, who could actually be anywhere, was on the point of being embarrassing, there was a thunder of hooves and Lucas screeched to a dusty halt in front of her. Chucking the reins of the horse he was leading at her, Lucas yelled 'Come on. I'm taking you out for dinner.'

Nicola glanced at Elodie but she was smiling broadly. Catching up the horse she held the reins and a stirrup so that Nicola could mount. Lucas had, by this time, disappeared ahead of her down a track in a cloud of yellow dust. As Nicola was about to say that she wasn't sure about this and how she hadn't ridden for years, Elodie gave her horse a gentle thump on its rear and Nicola was racing off down the track. Hurriedly she pulled her horse up and gathered the reins and her thoughts. Gingerly she walked her horse forward, then kicked into a trot and nudged into a controlled canter. That felt much better. Like a whirlwind Lucas appeared by her side and reined his horse back to Nicola's sedate canter. Nicola steadied back to a walk.

'Lucas, where are we going? And can we not gallop off into distant Africa, please? I haven't ridden since Tsavo and nothing as well bred as this.'

'Don't worry. Mistral will look after you. She belongs to Elodie and she is very well behaved. But you're right, we should be enjoying the ride. We're going to the Swala bush lodge and you're going to love it. Be careful if we come up to some game and be prepared to canter out of trouble.'

The bush lodge overlooked the Ewaso Narok river at the point where the river plunged over a rocky outcrop into a deep pool below. Central to the lodge was a huge baobab tree. Two platforms had been built round the trunk and the branches had been incorporated as supports. The canvas walls had been fashioned out of redundant safari tents but one side had been left open over the pool. Outside extensions included a kitchen and a washroom with a bucket shower. The sun was slipping towards the rocks changing their colour from yellow to blue and pink to purple, throwing the lodge into stark relief.

'Definitely time for a sundowner before dinner,' said Lucas as they took the tack off their horses and turned them out into the safety of a fenced corral. Taking her hand, Lucas led Nicola round the lodge and along the edge of the pool. From there they scrambled up a rocky path which opened out into a wide ledge with the most spectacular view out over the plain towards the sinking sun. Reaching under a rock, Lucas pulled out two glasses.

'Gin and Tonic?'

'That would be perfect,' replied Nicola thinking that this must all be a dream and that she was about to be rudely awakened somewhere hundreds of miles away.

Settling themselves down on the rocks they gazed out as the huge red sun started its gentle slip below the horizon. The savannah was empty and silent as the animals sought shelter before the night predators emerged looking for food.

'Julian and I along with Elodie's brother, Josh, built a den here when we were kids,' said Lucas quietly. 'We spent holidays swimming in the pool, diving over the waterfall, building dams and fly camping. We cooked on camp fires, slept out under the stars and listened to the lions hunting. Later Elodie's Dad built a tree house and then Piers converted it into the lodge. I just had to bring you here to share the magic.'

They sat together in silence lost in their thoughts letting Africa's nympholepsy cast a spell over them.

'Ah, the gin,' said Lucas getting to his feet. It only took a moment for the sun to slip over the horizon pulling a sheet of darkness up behind it.

'Come down beside the pool and I'll fetch a couple of lanterns. We need some light.'

Clutching the two glasses Nicola made her way carefully down to a level piece of rock beside the pool while Lucas raced ahead. Being so alone with Lucas in the darkness of the African night, god-knows-where out on the Laikipia Plateau was not exactly as she had envisaged her trip to visit Piers and Elodie on their ranch. She shivered but not because she was cold.

Two lanterns weaved their way out of the lodge and then Lucas jumped effortlessly down beside her. As he turned towards her, soft Latin American music crept up to where they were standing.

'Dance with me, Nicola,' Lucas held out his hand.

No, No, No screamed Nicola's good resolutions, bouncing through her brain. But Nicola wasn't listening. She stepped towards Lucas and his hand circled her waist, drawing her slowly into his arms, closer and closer till they were inseparable. Then he started to dance, his hips swaying hers to the compelling rhythm of the music taking her back to when they first danced the Samba at Chico's in Oxford. Back then they had danced close but far apart: this time it had become very obvious exactly where Lucas was leading her.

During the second track, Lucas nuzzled her ear and bent towards her.

'No analysis, no discussion, no recriminations. Let's just enjoy being together.'

Their climax was so natural; so complete; so meant to be.

Later, wrapped in Lucas' damp shirt, a newly reconstructed Nicola wondered if it had really happened. Jumping up, she turned anxiously to Lucas.

'Lucas,' she hissed. 'Someone's here. Someone has set a table for supper.'

Lucas pulled her down beside him and laughed gently.

'I promised to take you out for dinner. And now we're probably a little late for the first course, or maybe we just had it?' He ruffled her hair. 'Honestly, did you actually expect me to cook as well?'

Feeling awkward and embarrassed that someone could have witnessed what had just happened, Nicola was lost for words.

Lucas grinned at her in the darkness. 'It's fine. Stanley brought dinner out from Swala for us.'

'Stanley? Stanley's here?'

'Yes. He's put the horses to bed. He's going to serve dinner and then we're going to stay here sleeping out under the stars.'

As if on cue, there was a discreet cough and Stanley materialised with a lantern, hovering at a suitable distance.

After dinner they stood together and watched the moon weave crazy patterns on the surface of the pool below them. Stanley came and bid them goodnight grinning from ear to ear which convinced Nicola that he knew exactly what had happened after sunset. And, an awful thought crossed her mind, how many other secret trysts involving Lucas had he witnessed?

'Lucas,' she said sternly.

'Hush, my love,' said Lucas putting a finger on her lips. Nicola was aware that he was stroking the bare third finger on her left hand and felt massively guilty.

Think of this as a gap week and take time out whispered Nicola's conscience on a salvage operation.

Lucas guided her up the spiral staircase by the pool to the next floor where an enormous double bed had been pushed out so that they could sleep under the stars. Lucas fell asleep quite easily wrapping her protectively in his arms. Nicola couldn't sleep. She had been feasting on forbidden fruits at the table of deception and now her conscience was fighting to win her back.

A deep low guttural cough startled her and she stared round trying to adjust to the complete darkness. Lucas grunted sleepily as she tried to nudge him awake.

'Lucas, wake up. There's someone wandering around outside,' she hissed hoping desperately that it wasn't Stanley with some ludicrous plans for an early breakfast.

Lucas sat up and they both listened to the night. There is was again, closer now. Lucas flung himself down and pulled Nicola into his arms.

'It's only a lion calling his mate. Now let's go back to sleep.'

Nicola sat up straight. 'A lion? A lion loose out there? Shouldn't we be worried?'

'No. If he decides to visit I have a rifle beside the bed. Go back to sleep.'

Nicola had forgotten that guns were as much a part of Lucas as his clothes but it wasn't a very comfortable thought.

'Anyway,' added Lucas reaching for her 'Stanley is first in line and he is armed to the teeth.'

Well, thought Nicola, at least there is some point in having Stanley around. Distracted by Lucas she forgot all about the lion roaming around in the darkness.

Dawn arrived with immediate effect and within moments they were far too hot under the loose sheet and blanket. Lucas announced he was going for a shower and with that he walked to the edge of the platform and dived off into the pool below. By the time Nicola reached the edge, with the sheet wrapped round her, Lucas was splashing around under the waterfall.

'Come and join me,' he called 'It's lovely in here.' Cautiously, Nicola went down the stairs and jumped in from the safety of a three foot drop. Lucas was right, it was fun. By the time they got back to the lodge a pile of white fluffy towels had arrived and Lucas laughed at her embarrassment as he wrapped her up like a parcel.

'It's OK. Stanley is out at the back getting the horses ready. Come on we've got to get dressed otherwise we'll be late for breakfast.'

Stanley helped Nicola mount Mistral still grinning widely. If he asks if I slept well, I'll kill him thought Nicola. Stanley, however, was too busy talking very fast to Lucas in Swahili and soon they were riding off through the bush.

'We're going to meet up with Piers and Elodie and have breakfast. Piers is inspecting his cattle,' shouted Lucas as they cantered along a dirt track. This is going to be so embarrassing thought Nicola but in the end it wasn't as nobody mentioned the lodge. The talk was all about calves and a programme for ear tagging and dehorning back at the ranch.

The herdsmen sat in a circle with their dogs and guns and listened intently to Piers, Lucas busied himself separating a group of heifers from the rest of the herd while Nicola was left to help Elodie supervise breakfast.

Elodie glanced at Nicola as they were packing the remains of breakfast into hampers to stack in the back of the truck.

'You look absolutely exhausted, Nicola' she said kindly. 'I'll give you lift back to the ranch if you like. Lucas can bring Mistral back.' Nicola nodded gratefully. The bright hot sun was giving her a headache.

'This is the best view of Swala,' said Elodie as they drove up to the top of a rocky outcrop.

The ranch house gazed back at them from its position slightly above the savannah and, caught full frontal by the morning sun, glistened its reply.

'Nicola,' said Elodie, 'Tell me, how's Lucas? Caroline, you know she's my godmother, wrote me a long letter about the appalling scenes with Gellie at the hospital. She said that Lucas had run off and disappeared but that's what Lucas does when things go wrong and everybody expects Sulei to pick up the pieces and put him back together again. But it looks like you did the putting back together this time.'

Nicola blushed furiously and hid her face in her hands. 'Elodie, it's complicated. Lucas is complicated and my life is a mess.'

'Nicola, everyone can see that Lucas is in love with you. At Jocelyn's engagement party at The Grange even I could see that. How can that be complicated?'

'I'm engaged to someone else. I'm going to marry Joe in December. How can that not be complicated?'

'Don't for heaven's sake marry someone you're not in love with just because you feel you have to.'

'Tell me I'm wrong. Tell me that you're not in love with Lucas.'

Nicola didn't reply. She'd heard all that before.

'I suppose living out here away from the complexities of life back in England we tend to look at the world in a very direct fashion. Things are what they are and I'm just telling you how I see it. But we must get back.'

Nicola decided to check her emails so Elodie left her alone in the office. Her inbox was stuffed with messages about parties she was missing and general chat about jobs, finding places to live and new housemates. There was one from her mother asking if Nicola and Joe were absolutely certain that they wanted a marquee in the garden in the middle of December because it was going to be so difficult to heat. An email from Kate asking when she was coming back as it was tiresome trying to explain that she, Nicola, was out all the time. A long email from Joe. He was in his element in Innishboffin – the field trip had been a great success – the research with colleagues from Galway was going really well but he was missing her dreadfully. He could hardly wait for July to arrive when they could be together again in Newcastle 'and finally be able plan the rest of their lives together.'

Nicola found herself typing a reply that Joe wanted to hear and, before she could stop herself, pressed 'send'.

A sound made her turn round and she saw Lucas standing in the doorway. In an instant she knew that he knew exactly who she had been emailing but it was only a second and then he was smiling at her.

'I'm going for a shower and then I'm going to lie in a hammock until lunch. Coming?'

Although they'd hoped to shower alone they found they had to share the water with a fat frog who refused to move even when Lucas threw soap at him.

'I hope we're not going to give him any ideas about expanding the frog population,' said Lucas as he pulled her close to him under the cascading water.

Exhausted, Nicola and Lucas settled themselves in hammocks on the verandah outside their rooms. Lucas fell asleep instantly with one arm thrown carelessly out of the hammock. Unable to sleep Nicola gazed at Lucas and wondered how long she'd been in love with him. She'd always known she loved him but couldn't admit it whilst he was Julian's brother. It was too close and she didn't think he loved her in return. Every time they got close something happened and he'd push her away. Now he was only Julian's cousin and she could look at him as a person on his own. Pulling her eyes away, Nicola turned over and looked at the sky searching for answers. She loved Joe but she wasn't in love with him. That was the stark difference. Joe was easy to love but she'd let him love her and confused it with being safe and not wanting to get hurt again. It was clear, after how she felt last night at the lodge, that whatever happened she would have to let Joe go. There was no way she could marry him now, ever.

Having made that decision, Nicola felt a whole lot better and allowed herself to gaze uninterrupted at Lucas trying to map his face, his hands so that she would never forget him. Lucas opened his eyes and grinned when he saw how Nicola was looking at him.

'Have you no shame? That is a very direct stare,' he said expertly leaving his hammock and tipping Nicola out of hers. 'Lunch?'

'I really couldn't eat any more,' smiled Nicola.

'Fine. Just a sandwich then, but we ought to catch up with our hosts.'

Elodie noted how much more relaxed Nicola looked when she arrived hand in hand with Lucas for lunch. She watched as Lucas slid his hand over Nicola's shoulder with the intimacy shared between two people who are committed to each other.

'We have a guest tonight,' She told them. 'Myles Creighton. He is going to the Laikipia Wildlife Forum with Piers tomorrow.'

'Would you like to come with us, Lucas?' asked Piers

'Love to,' said Lucas.

'Don't worry Nicola,' Elodie cut in 'We can go for a ride round the ranch and see if we can spot the pack of wild dogs. Stanley said he thought he heard them last night down by the lodge.' This time Nicola managed not to blush.

Myles Creighton was a tall rangy looking guy with thick blond hair which looked as though it had a very relaxed relationship with a hair brush. He and Piers chatted happily about playing polo and hosting shooting parties which had often included Julian and Lucas.

'Come and see us at Doleraine, Lucas. You've been away far too long. Bring Nicola. You can ride, can't you?' Nicola found herself been assessed by a pair of enquiring sky blue eyes. She hoped she was being passed as fit.

'We'd love to come, Myles. Thank you,' replied Lucas happily. What's with the 'we' wondered Nicola.

The next morning Lucas left early and after a leisurely breakfast, Elodie took Nicola round to the stables. As they passed the cattle pens Elodie explained that they had a stud herd of nearly 1000 Boran cattle in addition to the herd of Sahiwal Nicola had already met.

'Today we're going to ride out to the south where the bush is thicker. There's plenty of acacia woodland so we'll probably spy some elephant,' said Elodie as they were greeted at the stables by a groom who had already tacked up three horses. Elodie was going to ride Mistral and Nicola was introduced to Sirocco, Mistral's half brother. Nicola was slightly alarmed to see a large shotgun slotted behind one of the saddles.

'All the horses here are thoroughbred crosses. We have six horses being ridden at the moment, another six being broken or schooled and three brood mares and one riding stallion. The horses are my responsibility and I have a team of five grooms to help me. The gun is just a precaution. Don't worry, we've never had to shoot anything yet. Oh, we're riding into elephant country and horses don't like elephants. So be prepared to canter away if we spot a herd.'

It was the silence that impressed Nicola most. She had never been in a place where the absence of noise was so emphatic. As they rode up onto a ridge they looked down over the plain and saw a herd of Grevy's zebra eating their way through the savannah with their tails swishing away the flies. Further along the trail they came across a herdsman singing gently to his cattle. Elodie dismounted for a chat leaving Nicola to watch a stork come in to land awkwardly on a precarious bough. Remounting, Elodie reported that that one of the cows had wandered off the previous day and had not been seen since. The herdsman was very anxious but Elodie said that the cow had probably been killed and eaten by lions and the remains disposed of by hyenas.

'All part of the Laikipia ecosystem I'm afraid. This herd will be coming back to the ranch at the end of the week so we'll have a head count. Some of our lions wear head collars so that we can track their movements so maybe tomorrow evening we'll do a night drive to check up on them.'

Although they didn't spot any elephant there was plenty of evidence that they had been on the trail earlier. Dead acacia branches were strewn across the track and Elodie made a mental note to get some staff out to cut up the wood for the open fires on the ranch.

On the edge of the woodland, the grassland opened out onto the Ewaso Narok river which they followed up to the lodge. Here they dismounted to look for signs of wild dog. Elodie confirmed that they had been there but probably not since Lucas and Nicola had spent the night.

'Did Lucas tell you how we used to fly camp here as children before my father started building the lodge? Piers and I often escape here to spend the night on our own with the stars.' She smiled shyly at Nicola trying to gauge her reaction.

'Elodie. It is all so beautiful, you're so lucky to live here,' said Nicola mentally contrasting the view in front of her with a grey winter's afternoon in Newcastle and the constant noise of traffic and the pressure of people crammed into urban space. 'I feel like I'm cocooned in a dream world and I can't get a grip on reality.' Actually, if she was honest, Nicola was becoming increasingly scared of returning to real life.

That evening at dinner Lucas was full of the Wildlife Forum and what it hoped to achieve.

'You should have been with us, Nicola' he said. 'You must be an expert on ecosystems and their environments now you've finished your degree.'

Piers pricked up his ears at this remark. Although he'd welcomed Nicola when they arrived, he seemed far more at ease with Lucas talking about the ranch leaving Nicola feeling rather intimidated by him.

'Come with me to the office after dinner. I'll get the maps out and show you what we hope to do. I'd really like to hear your comments,' Piers said thoughtfully. Nicola didn't like to tell her host that her degree had focused largely on marine ecology and so went off with Piers in great trepidation.

Some of the maps Piers spread out over the table were yellow with age and complicated with lines drawn in pencil and ineffectively erased in places. Nicola listened intently as Piers outlined his five year plan for the ranch and then matched it against the latest aims and objectives of the Wildlife Forum. As his voice became more resonate with his passion for wildlife and the ranch, Nicola found herself recalling Professor Boyd's second year lectures on ecosystems analysis. Suddenly her brain woke up and in no time she and Piers were having a fascinating discussion with Nicola providing the theory and them both of them talking through the practice at Swala. Neither of them noticed Lucas standing in the shadows watching them intently.

'Did you enjoy talking to Piers?' Lucas asked later as they lay together in one of the hammocks wrapped up tightly in fleece blankets to fend of the cold night air.

'Yes,' replied Nicola enthusiastically. 'I've never had to translate theory into practice with the practice rolled out in front of me. At first I didn't think it would make sense but the more I found out about ranching and indigenous wildlife the more it all made sense. I hope Piers didn't think I was talking academic rubbish.'

'I doubt that very much. I think Piers learnt a great deal tonight.'

They swung gently under the pinprick stars in the dark velvet sky, listening to the night sounds.

'Can you feel it?'

'Feel what?'

'Africa. Can you feel Africa?'

'No, not really.' Nicola felt Lucas' disappointment.

'I can't feel Africa but when I'm in Watamu I can feel the old tree at the

Convent.'

'The Tree of Forgetfulness?'

'Yes, that's the one. It's so creepy like it is watching you.'

Lucas was quiet for a moment.

'I gave that tree a really hard time when I was little. We used to climb it because Sister Benny told us not to. I carved my name on one of the branches and the sap oozed like blood. I kicked footballs at it to see how many leaves I could bring down.'

'I did that thing, you know, walking round it seven times so that I could leave my memories locked up in it.'

'Wow. That's brave,' Lucas paused. 'Any particular memories?'

'Ones I wanted to forget, obviously.'

'About me?' Lucas persisted but Nicola was silent. 'Do you think those spirits Sister Benny calls Arit Jinn are watching us now? Can you feel them?'

Nicola shivered.

'Yes,' cried Lucas triumphantly. 'There I knew you could feel Africa.'

'I don't think spirits are quite the same as a continent.'

'Maybe, but you can feel something. Why is it that the only time we've been together is in Africa?'

In Watamu the Arit Jinn were jubilant. Their plans seemed to be falling nicely into place. They smiled benevolently as Sister Benny emerged from the convent and paused in their shade. She was looking at a small group of her children knitting long trails of printed fabric. Their teacher was totally absorbed in her task pausing only to brush aside the black curls which kept escaping from her scarf. Sister Benny was seriously worried about Charlie Winstone's continuing generous donations so in sheltering Gellie she'd agreed to keep Charlie informed about Gellie's health and general wellbeing. She was not entirely happy with this duplicity but needs must. Above her head the Tree of Forgetfulness was looking pretty sparky and confident in the sunshine. The Arit Jinn resolved to rearrange Sister Benny's trunks in her favourite configuration as they felt they could be generous being in such a winning position.

But what on earth was Nicola doing with Lucas in Laikipia? Hardly part of the rescue mission as described to her by Sulei, in strictest confidence of course. Sister Benny had her suspicions and she was not pleased. Nicola was engaged to a lovely guy who would cherish and support her for the rest of their lives. Whatever was going on at Swala was not part of the plan.

Back at Swala, Nicola wriggled round to face Lucas.

'I think there are more obvious reasons than a tree, allegedly, full of spirits.'

'Name one.' Lucas challenged her.

'I'm engaged to be married to someone else. Back in England.'

'Because I'm so madly in love with you I'd forgotten your minor complication.' Lucas was grinning confidently. 'And Jamie, is he one of your obvious reasons? He's often around when I've tried to get close to you. Who is Jamie, Nicola?'

Nicola would have sat bolt upright if that had been possible. It wasn't possible when two people are squashed in a hammock. Instead she let a cold chill ripple down her back dragging waves of memories from her head.

'Why do you want to know?' she replied stalling for time and wondering whether she was really ready to explain Jamie to anyone let alone Lucas.

'Well, in all the time I've known you, Jamie has been there. Well not actually there because I don't remember ever meeting him but sort of there, coming between us. I'd just like to know that's all.'

Oh my God, thought Nicola. She'd forgotten how she often used to say Jamie's name out loud when she wanted to speak to him. Embarrassed, she addressed the dark outline of a tree in the night darkness.

'Jamie is my imaginary friend from my primary school days. Jamie just doesn't exist,' Nicola said in a small voice. Then she added 'I talk to him when I get really stressed. It helps me cope, you know, with difficult stuff.'

'Whoa,' replied Lucas. 'That's why Sulei couldn't find him. He simply doesn't exist. Wait till I tell him.'

Nicola tried to look cross. 'Have you been stalking me, Lucas and don't you dare say anything to Sulei?'

'No, not exactly. Just trying to understand why this Jamie person was, no, is, so important to you. More important than me. We need to sort this.'

'Why? What needs sorting if Jamie doesn't exist?'

'Because if we're going to move forward this is something we must sort out now.'

'I can't Lucas, I just can't. It's all about things I can't talk about.'

Lucas shifted round in the hammock so that his face was close to Nicola's and he wrapped his arms around her.

'There, you're safe now. Nicola I love you. Please talk to me.'

He's told you he loves you Nicola's brain screamed at her. Far away in their Tree of Forgetfulness the Arit Jinn put their game of quoits on hold to listen to Lucas' conversation as it was broadcast on the night breeze.

'Just start talking to me Nicola,' Lucas whispered in her ear.

'Like I said, Jamie was, is, my imaginary friend. When I was being bullied in primary school he helped me stand up for myself. He helped me be strong and somehow he stayed around.'

'Was he with you in the clinic at the convent the night your baby was born?'

Nicola drew in her breath sharply. My God, how does Lucas know about Julia?

'How do you know about Julia?' she asked.

'Julia,' said Lucas very slowly and paused. 'I was at the convent that night. I was working in Mombasa and I just called in to see Sister Benny like I always did when I was around. She was like a second, no third, mother to me,' he added rather bitterly.

'There seemed to be a bit of a commotion in the Clinic and Sister Benny kind of shooed me out of the door. I was curious so I slipped over to find out what was going on. I recognised the doctor, Francine. There was talk of heart problems and calling the hospital in Mombasa which was unusual because if a baby wasn't going to make it then they usually let nature take its course. Life is tough enough in Africa without having to start living coming from behind. I wandered off down the corridor and saw your name on the door of one of the rooms and stopped to read your notes. I had absolutely no idea that you were pregnant, Nicola. Standing there I put two and two together and worked out that it must be Julian's. I was completely overwhelmed at the thought that I might be an uncle and that there was something of Julian that would go on living so I slipped into your room. You were very restless and as I approached your bed you called out Jamie's name. I was horrified that you had found someone else so quickly and that maybe he was the father and if so the maths told me that you'd been sleeping with him while you were with Julian.'

Lucas paused and brushed an errant tear from Nicola's cheek.

'I stayed for a while, hoping you'd wake up again but then it started to get light. I rushed down the corridor and bumped straight into Sister Benny. She was very angry with me and told me to get the hell out of there. I retreated back to Mombasa and it wasn't till a few weeks later when I'd made my peace with Sister Benny that she told me that the baby didn't make it. I'm so sorry, Nicola.' Lucas quietly kissed away the tears that were now streaming down Nicola's face.

'I only held her once,' said Nicola. 'I carry this cold empty space inside me that will always be Julia. I hate saying her name because my head floods with her loss. I suppose in England I would have been wrapped in after care but in Africa life seamlessly moves into tomorrow and then the next day. I thought I could leave her behind at the Convent, in the Tree of Forgetfulness, but she's always with me. I try to be practical. How on earth would I have coped with a baby, for God's sake? My life would have ended up so differently. I though time would heal but it hasn't. Only if I don't think about her. All this baggage stops me from getting too close to people because I can't explain it to anyone until now and I can't quite believe I'm telling you. In fact I'm so relieved that you know. Up until this moment I only shared my thoughts with Jamie.'

'I was so angry with you,' replied Lucas. 'I was angry that you had found someone else so quickly after Julian died. I wanted to be very nasty to you because I was jealous. I tried to get over it and then at Jocelyn's engagement party I saw you in the car park after I'd dropped Gellie and Elodie off at the house. It was getting dark and you called out to Jamie. I got mad again and spent the rest of the evening flirting with Elodie to make you jealous. I knew you were attracted to me and I had hoped that we could get together but I just got mad again.'

'Then in Mombasa I just couldn't believe my eyes when you walked out of the hospital right behind the guy I was tailing. There you were sauntering along behind one of the most dangerous terrorists in Kenya. I got hold of Sulei and asked him to take over and just managed to find you as the bomb went off. God, Nicola, I thought I was going to lose you right in front of my eyes. It hurt so much. And then making love that night it was like all my Christmases rolled into one until you cried out to Jamie in your sleep. That did it. I was back to being mad again. I can't believe I was so jealous of a guy who didn't even exist, a guy who'd never existed. After all the mess with Gellie and Charlie I did what I always do. I ran away to hide. When you came to rescue me I began to hope beyond hope that this time we'd end up together. And we have, haven't we? We are together forever now aren't we?'

Now it was Nicola's turn to hide. It was altogether far too complicated to sort out so she leant forward and kissed Lucas and they fell out of the hammock locked together and ran into their room and into bed.

'Talk to me Nicola,' Lucas' curls cut a hard outline in the moonshine. 'I want to hear your voice. I love the way it gets low and sticky when you want me so much you'd die if I stopped.'

The moon smiled along the lines of the half open door as he went down on her and Nicola shamelessly arched up to meet him.

Back in Watamu the Arit Jinn sighed and went back to their game of quoits in the tree. They just had to play the waiting game. Sister Benny sought sanctuary in the convent chapel.

The next two days passed in a whirl of riding, herding cattle, laughing and being at peace with one another. All too soon it was time for Nicola to leave and head back to England.

'Please stay here forever, Nicola,' said Lucas as they lay on the huge sofa beside the fire in the drawing room. Piers and Elodie had gone to bed but Nicola was acutely aware that they were not alone. Staff were moving silently round the ranch house restoring order after another busy day. She thought she could never get used to being looked after by staff even though Lucas had tried to explain that the local population relied on this type of employment to feed and look after their own families. She looked at Lucas lying idly among the cushions looking totally relaxed on the outside but slightly sprung on the inside. He reminded her of a leopard seemingly dozing, draped along the branch of a tree, but ready to react to any sound or movement in his sphere. Africa suits Lucas, she thought, this is his country.

'I have to go back,' she said firmly. 'I have to graduate next week and start work and...' her voice trailed away.

Lucas suddenly sat up straight. 'Nicola,' he said very seriously, 'Stay here in Africa, in Swala, stay with me forever. You know I love you to bits.'

'Oh Lucas, Lucas. I love you so much but I have promised to marry someone else. You know that. He's a really good person.' Nicola couldn't quite bring herself to actually say Joe's name in front of Lucas. It was too painful to spit the word out.

'You may love him, Nicola but you're not in love with him. You can't be because you know what we have together. Look at me.'

Nicola gazed up at the adoring face that she loved so much.

'I know. I have decided I can't marry Joe.' There she had actually said his name. It was real now. 'And you know, right now I really hate myself.'

'Nicola you're not a bad person. You're kind, generous and honourable. Go home and sort things out. I'll wait for you. I'll wait forever.'

A light hand slid over her shoulder and turned her round. Nicola felt her body betray her as Lucas folded his arms round her.

'Don't wait for me, Lucas. It just isn't going to happen. I'm not free to love you.'

Seeing that the conversation was going nowhere and not wanting to lose Nicola, Lucas swept her up in his arms and carried her off to bed where he did everything he could think of to make sure Nicola would not forget him.

The next day Nicola woke to bright sunshine pouring in through the shutters and no Lucas. Wearily she got dressed and packed up her few belongings in her rucksack. How could her life have changed so much in just a few days? Elodie was sitting have breakfast on the verandah and making a shopping list. She smiled brightly at Nicola.

'All ready to go? I'm just making a list of stuff to pick up in Nanyuki after I've dropped you at the airstrip. It's been such fun having you to stay and having some female company. You will come back and visit again very soon, won't you? And thank you for rescuing Lucas. I think you're probably the only person in the world who could have banished his demons so effectively.'

Sitting waiting for Elodie to bring the jeep round to the house, Nicola wondered if she could possibly live in Africa. It was so foreign but at the same time so peaceful. There was a gentle background hum of idle chatter laced with the occasional snatch of a song. Flowers tumbled out over the lawn in front of her, strange colourful birds ventured out to comb the grass and then a giraffe strolled past the fence down by the pool. Nicola shook her head almost in disbelief.

Nicola didn't dare ask Elodie where Lucas was because that would mean telling her sorry story. As the jeep swung out onto the main road heading for Nanyuki, Nicola took one last look at Swala. She saw a horse and rider on a rocky promontory watching them leave. When she turned again the space was empty.

In Watamu the Arit Jinn shifted uneasily in the Tree of Forgetfulness. Things had not gone exactly to plan. In her study Sister Benny relaxed in an aura of calm.

ANNIE BOON

9

Not knowing where to go after her plane landed at Heathrow, Nicola headed for Oxford and Kate.

'Hey, Hello you?'

Kate looked both surprised and relieved as Nicola threw her rucksack on the floor in Kate's hallway. Nicola looked up at her friend and for a moment was at a loss for words to explain her sudden reappearance.

'Oh no. Tell me what's going on and don't fudge anything because I can see you're suffering much more than jetlag.'

'Complete bloody mess. I've told Lucas I can't be with him and he's done what Lucas always does and gone off in a sulk so nothing is really resolved.'

'You've slept with Lucas?' Kate always went for the jugular. 'I thought you went to sort him out?'

'I need a coffee,' replied Nicola heading for the kitchen hoping that they had the house to themselves.

Not knowing where to begin, Nicola told her friend everything as they sat at the kitchen table with their coffee growing cold.

'So you see I can't marry Joe now and I don't think, if I'm honest that I want to anymore. But I have to tell him before graduation next week. My parents are coming to the ceremony and then heading off to Cumbria to meet Joe's parents to talk wedding arrangements so I have to tell them that it's all off.'

'This is some major mess,' observed Kate.

'It gets worse. There is my research post with Prof. Boyd. I can't possibly do that now with Joe just down the corridor so I'll have to see the Prof. next week and turn down the research scholarship and everything. So by the end of next week I'll be all alone, homeless and jobless.'

'There is no plan B,' Nicola added.

'Have you heard from Joe recently?'

'I had a text this morning saying he would be back on Sunday and he'd booked a table for supper; couldn't wait to see me, you know all that stuff.'

'And you replied?'

'Well, yes I had to. Said I was looking forward to seeing him and that we had lots to talk about.' Nicola's voice trailed away.

They sat in silence and drank cold coffee. Nicola wasn't thinking at all in contrast with Kate whose brain had gone into overdrive.

'Let's start by working backwards. You can have the flat downstairs for as long as you want. No rent but please could you house sit for Archie and me when we go off on gigs or whatever and feed my cat. I never know who is going to turn up looking for somewhere to stay in Oxford. So many of Dad's old students seem unable to forget his address.'

'Are you sure Kate? That would be wonderful.'

Kate was gratified to see some colour flood back into Nicola's cheeks.

'As for a job, I was working on a few contacts before you disappeared to Africa. Some of them will definitely be worth following up.'

'Kate you're wonderful,' said Nicola flinging her arms round her friend.

'Newcastle will be more of a problem. First of all you have to tell Joe. When does he get back from Ireland?'

'Sunday. How do I tell him?'

'There is no perfect way to end a relationship. The important points are to keep it short and blame yourself. Go up to Newcastle on Saturday and move all your stuff out of Joe's flat and be there on Sunday when he gets back. Tell him it's over and leave. No last dinner, no last drink together. Listen to what he has to say and be prepared for him to be as mad as hell. Accept complete responsibility.'

Nicola looked doubtful.

'When your parents arrive in Newcastle explain the situation to them, go to graduation and then see your professor. Once you've cleaned up this mess come straight back here and move into the flat. Come on Nicola. You can do this. Now you've got a plan it will be much easier. Divide it up into the individual tasks and do them one at a time. This is all getting way too serious. Let's see if Ethan is in and go out to the pub.'

Alone in the little basement flat she was going to call home Nicola curled up under the duvet and tried to get warm. Her mind just wouldn't settle down in spite of Kate and Ethan's earlier efforts to get her to forget and relax. How could she have ever thought that marrying Joe would have been the safest way forward? How could she have let Lucas disappear again when she knew that she truly loved him above all else? A small voice incessant voice in the back of her head kept asking her if that was really true? How could she be sure that what she felt for Lucas wasn't a destructive lust that threatened her future with Joe? It was time to take ownership of her life and to stop living with half her mind preoccupied with fantasies. Her thoughts were interrupted by a text pinging into her message box.

Babe, I'm just sooo excited! I've got a wonderful surprise for you but I'm not going to tell you what it is. You have to wait till Sunday! J xx

Groaning, Nicola pulled her duvet right over her head and found herself lightly stroking the inside of her left arm just below her elbow. Slipping out of bed she fumbled for her makeup bag and tipped the contents out searching for the small red penknife. Two years ago she had deliberately thrown the penknife into her waste bin but her mother had rescued it and berated her for throwing away a present from her younger brother. Guided by the moonlight pouring into the room Nicola allowed the blade to trace a line across her arm. There was no blood just a faint red line that did nothing to salve the ache inside her. She made her way into the bathroom. It was all part of the ritual. Pressing harder the blade glinted in captured moonbeams and refracted a glowing message on the wall. 'Welcome back Nicola' it read in the watery light as she cut into her arm. The blood welled up and Nicola watched it, mesmerised, as it flowed down her arm and dripped onto the stark porcelain. It didn't hurt. Instead the soothing numbness she remembered from earlier years spread calm through her. Pulling her arm up towards her shoulder she was able to increase the sensation by pressing the wound hard against her upper arm. Cleaning up the sink and rubbing some antiseptic into the cut, Nicola knew she was back in control.

Far away in Watamu, the Arit Jinn were disturbed by a breeze rustling through the Tree of Forgetfulness. Their mischievous plans for Nicola were not quite on track. For Sister Benny sitting quietly on the other side of the wall in her lemon grass garden the breeze brought reassurance.

On Saturday morning Nicola drove up to Newcastle and spent the morning divesting the flat she'd recently shared with Joe of every single trace of their relationship. Then she cleaned the place and put fresh linen on the bed. She wanted to hang on to the happy memories that clung to the walls but they had come unstuck along with her relationship with Joe. A text dropped into her message box.

Just off to catch the ferry. I can't wait any longer to tell you about my surprise. Check out daft.ie and go to The Old Garda Station, Roundstone. I bought it yesterday as a surprise first home for us seeing as how we'll be spending so much time in

Galway. Isn't that the best news? See you in a couple of hours to celebrate. J xx

Nicola sat down and with a heavy heart found the website. Printing off the details she read them and put them down on the coffee table with a heavy heart.

'Roundstone' she read *'means 'the stone of the sea' in Gaelic. The oldest and most picturesque fishing village located amidst breathtaking mountain scenery and beautiful countryside…'* Things had just got so much more complicated. And yet in a way they hadn't. Nicola sat up and pulled her shoulders back. How dare Joe decide that they would spend most of their year in Galway and go as far as buying a house without even asking her if she wanted to live in Galway? Beautiful it undoubtedly was, but it sure as hell wouldn't be for even forty two weeks of the year. He would be dragging her, unwillingly into an academic backwater.

The late Sunday afternoon sun was trailing long rays across the living room floor as she waited. When she heard boots tramping up the stairs, she stood up and waited for his key to turn in the lock.

'Nicola? Nicola, darling, I'm back?' Joe fumbled for the light switch. Nicola blinked in the bright light. 'Why are you in the dark, Babe?' Nicola didn't move.

'Nicola, what's wrong? What's happened?' Joe moved towards her, his arms outstretched to give her a huge hug. Nicola took a step back and Joe hesitated. Alarm, consternation and bemusement crossed his face in waves.

Nicola took a sharp deep breath. 'Joe, it's over. I'm breaking off our engagement. I can't marry you.' There, she'd said it.

Joe stared at her in disbelief. 'What? I don't understand.' He reached forward and grabbed her left hand noticing at once that she wasn't wearing her ring. It was sitting on the coffee table glinting viciously.

'Nicola, what's happened? I can't believe what I'm hearing.'

'Joe, I'm so sorry. I never expected things to turn out this way.'

'You're damn right. You fucking bitch. I suppose you're going to give me all that crap about loving me but not enough to be in love with me. This is just so not happening.'

Joe was getting angry. 'Is there someone else?'

'No, not really.'

'That's such a crass answer. Tell me.'

Nicola flinched. 'You remember all that trouble between the Gellie and Charlie Willstone? Well, Sulei asked me to sort out Lucas who was having a kind of break down in Oman at Sulei's sister's house. I've been to Oman, to Muscat.'

'That Arab? You've been seeing him … have you?'

Resisting the temptation to spring to Sulei's defence, Nicola carried on.

'This has nothing to do with Sulei. I went to Oman to talk to Lucas last week and then we spent a few days together at the Mongomerie's ranch in Kenya. We had a fling. That's all it was and that's why I can't marry you.'

Joe let out a long breath whistling the air through his teeth. 'I always saw that predatory Lucas as a threat but then I thought so much better of you. Seems like I was wrong. How could you let me love you? How could you promise to marry me and then sleep with Lucas? I suppose you're going to go running back to Africa to be with him now?'

'No, Joe. It's over with Lucas. Ended. But I can't marry you. I don't deserve someone like you.'

'Damn right. That's the first honest thing you've said. You fucking bitch. You know what? You and that spy,' Joe spat the words out, 'deserve each other. Now take all your stuff and get out. I never ever want to see you again. Get right out of my life now.'

Joe had gone very red as he started to pronounce each word individually.

'In fact I'm going to walk out on you first and I want no trace of you left here when I get back. In an hour I will have forgotten all about you.'

As he turned to leave he picked up a framed photograph of the two of them on a beach in Zanzibar that Nicola had missed in her clear out and hurled it at the far wall where it shattered. Then, picking up the Galway house details, he very slowly tore them up into tiny pieces and threw them in her face. With a venomous last look at Nicola he ran off down the stairs slamming the front door so that the windows in the flat rattled with the stress of what they'd just witnessed.

On hearing Joe's car roar off, Nicola had a last look round the flat where she had had so many happy times and slowly made her way down the stairs. There was still much to sort out.

On the night before graduation Nicola had dinner with her parents at their hotel and told them an edited edition of her break up with Joe. Her father was sympathetic and muttered about what a good thing she'd realised she couldn't marry Joe before, rather than after, the wedding. Her mother was initially far more worried about the mechanics of dismantling the wedding arrangements and then contrite when she realised what a devastating effect the whole mess had had on her daughter.

'Who have you told, Nicola?' she asked gently.

'Well Joe of course and now you. No one else.' It wasn't necessary to drag Kate into the firing line.

'Leave it all to me, darling. I'll sort it all out. I suppose we'd better ring Joe's parents and cancel our visit as I expect they know by now.'

Nicola sniffed gratefully and then buried her face in her mother's proffered tissue.

At graduation there was a bit of a mix up when the platform party, robed in academic dress, processed onto the stage. Someone quietly tucked the card with the name *Dr Joseph Delaney* under a seat and the party all moved up one place. In the end Nicola was proud to accept her degree from the famous person invited for the day and was rewarded with a big smile from Prof. Boyd. The next day Nicola went to see him to explain that she was no longer able to take up the research scholarship and that she was going to leave Newcastle and look for a job in Oxford. The departmental bush telegraph system had obviously been working overtime so he showed no surprise but deep regret at the choice Nicola had made.

'Should you decide to return to research and to do a Masters degree please make sure it is here at Newcastle,' he said kindly and promised to write a glowing reference for her. Nicola noted that her research had been demoted from a PhD to a Masters. Back at her friend's house there was a message telling her that Joe had called to see her. Nicola looked at her phone and saw six missed messages from Joe. She opened the most recent text.

Nicola, please, please don't leave Newcastle without seeing me. I want to explain, I want to apologise for being so nasty to you. I love you Nicola and I'm sure we can work through this mess and get back together. Joe xx

Nicola pressed DELETE, packed her bags, left a note and some money for rent etc. and said goodbye to Newcastle forever.

Halfway down the motorway Nicola pulled in at a service station for a coffee. She deliberately chose one that she had never stopped at with Joe but it wasn't the answer. Everywhere she looked there were couples eating and drinking coffee wrapped up in togetherness. There was no one beside her to ask what sort of coffee she would like and whether she would like a chocolate brownie, her favourite. Grabbing her take out paper mug Nicola fled to her car and leant against its familiarity in the summer sunshine. When she slid into the driver's seat she found Jamie sitting beside her.

'Where were you when I needed you most?' Nicola asked him rather tartly.

'Waiting for you to start sorting things out on your own.'

'Well I have, thank you,' Nicola faltered. 'At least I think I'm getting there. It has been much harder than I thought. I know now for certain that although I loved Joe it wasn't enough to marry him. To be with him for the rest of my life. He offered me everything I wanted like security, a known future, unconditional love but it wasn't enough. I can see that now.'

'And what about Lucas?' Jamie seemed determined to make her face facts.

'Yes,' replied Nicola slowly, 'I think I'm in love with Lucas but I don't know for sure if he really loves me and I certainly can't cope with his ethereal attitude to life. At the moment the best thing for me is to focus on getting a job and putting my life back together.'

Jamie left as she reversed out of her parking space feeling a bit more confident about her future.

There was no sign of Kate, Archie or Ethan in Oxford so Nicola went food shopping and settled down to cast a critical eye over her new home. At least there were no ghosts here and as she sorted out and put away her stuff, grateful that she'd dumped everything that related to her previous life with Joe in a skip. What had happened in Newcastle, stayed in Newcastle.

But it wasn't that easy. That night on her own in the flat the night came and claimed her as its own. Under her duvet Nicola broke down and cried a grief that far outweighed the years she had known Joe. Had she loved him? Yes, she had loved Joe. But a large part of her had loved Joe for what he was and what he offered. He was a great guy with a proper job who offered her marriage, kids, a home, security, pets. Another part of her was desperate to make up for the mess she'd left behind in Watamu which she couldn't even begin to tell her parents about and marrying the right sort of guy i.e. Joe that they totally approved of, would have compensated for the mess and hidden the truth. Her mind slid towards Lucas and a fresh bout of tears. Would she be able to cope with a life like Lucas led embedded in an expat culture that you had to be practically born into? After two days of crying, living in her PJs and drinking coffee, Nicola emerged in a stalemate with herself and a plan to put her life back together by going at it one step at a time.

The first task was getting a job, which proved more difficult than she imagined. There were plenty of voluntary jobs but one that paid a decent wage that she could live on proved elusive. Maybe her car would have to go. Oxford was full of summer school students and kids learning languages which gave the city a pleasant buzz of activity. She took a job in a pub working behind the bar 'just until I get something more suitable,' she told her mother hoping that the something more suitable wouldn't be a long time coming. Kate surfed the internet and browsed the local papers trying to keep her spirits up.

'How about London?' she suggested. 'You could commute from here.'

Nicola just didn't have the energy to reply. She couldn't talk to her parents because she felt they thought she'd made the biggest mistake in her life and that it was up to her to get out of the mess. Maggie was away in Europe enjoying her art award and appeared to be disconnected from the rest of the world. No one appeared to know where Gellie was so she couldn't ask her for a job and anyway that would mean travelling to London. Nicola liked living in Oxford, it made her feel safe.

A couple of months dragged passed. The bar was very busy so Nicola worked extra shifts whenever she could but it just didn't feel like her life was going anywhere least of all forward. Maggie came back from Europe totally enthused about sculpture and the post impressionist artists she studied in Paris. Classical drawing had not curbed her love of knitting and Kate warned Nicola that she would get a knitted interpretation of Michelangelo's 'David' for Christmas. Maggie however had moved on from knitted fashion to soft furnishings and was now working on a new collection which would hit the market once she had wrestled her trade name, *Magknits*, from Gellie.

'It will be awesome,' she told Nicola as they sat having coffee. 'When I was in Rome I trailed my fingers across all these ancient friezes and the buzz I got from all the different textures was amazing. I am going to design knitted rugs, cushions and poufs to start with all in undyed, organic yarns and then move on to chair covers. What do you think?'

'Sounds really interesting. Have you seen Gellie?'

'No,' replied Maggie a brief shadow crossing her face dulling her eyes for a moment.

'Dad has some patient who's a solicitor working on the legal side sorting out the split from Gellie so that I'm not involved. But how are you? What's the news on the job front? The parents are really worried but trying desperately not to interfere. You know, Dad's standing on your own two feet mantra.'

'You haven't been sent to interrogate me?' Nicola asked 'Because if you have I'm not telling you anything.'

'No. Honest. They don't even know I'm here.'

Nicola explained how she was working in a bar to pay the bills.

'I hate the bar work. The other staff are great. It's the customers who talk at you as though you're not a person. And they are so quick to complain if something isn't perfect.'

The two sisters sat together in silence. Nicola pulled anxiously at her left sleeve hoping Maggie hadn't tuned into the fact she was wearing a long sleeved T-shirt on a fairly warm August day. But Maggie seemed to have other things on her mind.

Nicola was getting quite worried about her job prospects and there were new scars on her left arm. The university term would be starting in October and she couldn't bear the thought of standing behind the hateful bar serving drunken freshers.

She walked reluctantly back to her flat. Her new austerity regime dictated that she walked everywhere except in an emergency and then she could take a bus. The car had long gone. Ethan was sitting on the steps down to the flat.

'Ah there you are.' He said languidly uncurling himself.

Well, obviously, thought Nicola. Was this going to be a day peppered with idiots?

'I'm glad I caught you. I think I may have found you a job.'

Nicola sat down beside him. 'Really?' She couldn't quite believe Ethan.

'Yes. A mate of mine works for a publishing company in Summertown and the head honcho has gone into melt down. One of his editors has gone on sick leave in the middle of a crisis.' Ethan handed her a scrap of paper. 'Give them a ring. You never know.'

And with that he bounded off into Kate's house.

A rather intimidating voice told Nicola that she was Nigel Kilgour's PA and could Nicola email her CV ASAP to Mr Kilgour, Chief Executive of KS Publishing in Summertown, Oxford. Thanking God, and everyone else she could think of, that she had devoted time to updating and polishing her CV, Nicola dusted it down and pressed SEND. An anxious twenty-four hours later the PA phoned summoning her to an interview. It was right in the middle of a bar shift but meeting Mr Kilgour was way more important than an irate bar manager.

The PA was even more intimidating in the flesh than on the phone and made Nicola feel that her outfit was totally unsuitable by merely lifting one eyebrow. Nigel Kilgour was, thankfully, relaxed, a little dusty like the piles of manuscripts in his office, but he had a firm handshake and a warm smile. He explained that he had a current editing crisis made worse by one of his, well his only he had to admit, environmental science editor being laid low with a detached retina.

'Hardly convenient when I'm supposed to rush this manuscript through so that the book can be published in time for some UN Conference on the environment. The last people on earth to understand publishing are authors. Just because it has been written down doesn't make it brilliant.' Nigel paused and looked at Nicola over the top of his glasses. 'I read your CV and note that you know nothing about publishing but you've a degree in environmental science and I'm desperate.'

He went on to outline the terms and conditions of her employment emphasising that there would be no contract until she'd worked for him for six months and within that period either one of them could terminate their agreement without further notice. She had to start work immediately. In fact it would be very helpful if she could take the manuscript that had led to her employment, home with her and when she came back the next day there would be a desk ready for her.

Clutching the weighty document under one arm, Nicola treated herself to a bus trip down the Banbury Road and skipped into her flat. She phoned the bar manager, handed in her notice on the spot and made a large cup of coffee. Curling up on the sofa, she opened the package and read the title.

Environmental Science: Connecting the Voids
Dr Joe Delaney, University of Newcastle.

She couldn't do it. How could she possibly edit a manuscript written by someone who in the first instance had taught her all she knew and who came loaded with emotional baggage? In fact, if she closed her eyes and thought hard enough, she could see Joe sitting at his desk in the flat concentrating so hard on his writing making sure that everything was perfect. He had hardly known she was there.

But she had to do it. She had just thrown away her only source of cash without a backward glance. Cautiously she turned to the first page and it was well after midnight when she made it through to the last. Putting the manuscript into her rucksack along with her notes she crawled off to bed. Perhaps this had been a good exercise on the road to recovery, thinking about Joe standing in his academic field rather than tied up in an emotional package.

The next day the desk was waiting for her as promised and she hardly had time to sit down before Mr Kilgour called her into his office and looked at her expectantly.

Nicola had decided on the bus after a great deal of soul searching to be up front from the outset about Joe being one of her tutor's at Newcastle.

'I know, and please call me Nigel. I would not have considered employing you without a certain amount of research into your background. So what is your considered opinion about the book?'

'I think it's an excellent piece of work, well researched, expertly written and comprehensive in its outlook. I don't understand why you gave me a book that would appear to be ready to publish?'

'I just wanted to test your knowledge on the subject and to make sure you wouldn't bullshit about your knowing the author. You passed on both counts.' Nigel shifted slightly 'Now the real reason why I need you is this. A new GCSE in environmental science is about to be introduced along with, naturally enough, a rash of text books to go with it. We have a number of proposals, a number of draft outlines and a few sample chapters here at KS and I want you to look through the GCSE syllabus and then texts we have already received and give us, in the first instance, some guidelines on what we should be looking for. Miss Cowan, Nicola, welcome to KS Publishing.'

Over the next few months Nicola started to develop her new life. She had a job she loved, a flat in Oxford and friends living upstairs. She was still self-harming and although the cuts weren't as deep, she still had to wear long sleeves to cover her scars. Weekends back at Frampton at her parents became regular and she also caught up with Maggie in London.

One brilliantly sunny autumn afternoon, Nicola left KS and turned north up the Banbury Road instead of south back to her flat. The evenings would soon be drawing in making a walk after work impossible. Without really thinking about it she turned right down towards the river and as she crossed the road glanced quickly at the name. Tackley End Road. This was where Julian and Lucas lived when they were studying in Oxford. This was where she slept with Julian for the first time and lost her virginity. Blushing furiously she stopped to work out which house it was. It looked exactly the same but freshly painted and geraniums were still managing to bloom in the front garden. As she stood swirling in memories the door opened and a very familiar figure jumped down the two steps on the opposite side of the road, pulled a beanie over his head and headed off towards the Banbury Road. Nicola practically fell into road stumbling to stay upright. An old man walking towards her grabbed her arm and asked if she was okay.

'Are you sure, my dear? You look very white. You very nearly ended up in the gutter. Not a very safe place to be.'

Nicola assured him she was fine, just a little shaky and needing to get her breath back. She sank down onto the low wall beside her and the old man went on his way.

Nicola's thoughts were leapfrogging all round her head. How long had Lucas been in Oxford? Why hadn't he been in touch? Why was he in Oxford, anyway. Perhaps he lives in Oxford, here in Summertown when he's in the UK. Julian had said it was a family house. Nicola looked over her shoulder half expecting her next encounter to be with Lucas' parents. Escape seemed to be the best course of action. Nicola ran back to the Banbury Road and jumped on the first bus at the nearest bus stop.

A few days later Nicola was walking through the Botanical Gardens near Christ Church when her thoughts strayed out of control to Lucas. Should she get in touch? Hey, I've been thinking, now I've sorted out Joe and it's all over, I'd like to get back together. Crap statement. She could always call Sulei and see if he said anything. Not ask directly but listen for some clues. No, too embarrassing.

 She was having brunch with Kate when she blurted out the events in Tackley End Road.

'You idiot,' exclaimed Kate. 'You mean you haven't been back to knock on the door. You haven't looked for Lucas?'

Nicola replied that there was no point, that Lucas had probably disappeared again.

'But you should at least find out if he's there some of the time. I know you're aching for him. It's written all over your face. Come on we'll walk up there now.'

'No,' cried Nicola. The last thing she needed was an over enthusiastic Kate by her side. I'll go but on my own.'

'Promise?'

'Promise.'

The road was quiet and sleepy in the afternoon sun when Nicola stopped outside the house. Taking a deep breath she walked up the two steps, rang the bell and waited. There was a thump and then the door opened sort of halfway. Pushing her blonde hair off her face, two clear blues eyes peered at Nicola enquiringly. Why is it always a gorgeous blonde, leggy model type thought Nicola despairingly.

'Yes?'

'I'm looking for Lucas Smith Owen. Is he around?'

'Lucas? Oh you must mean Caroline's son. No, haven't seen him. I'm house sitting for the Smith Owens for a couple of months. Sorry. Can't help you.'

The door shut fast.

December arrived crisp and cold but at least there was no deep and even snow. On the first Saturday which should have been the happiest day of her life, Nicola padded around the flat in her dressing gown. If everything had gone to plan this would have been her wedding day. It hadn't, so it wasn't. What was the point she asked herself. There was no point. Kate and Archie were away, nobody had thought to phone to ask if she was alright, to enquire about whether she was miserable or lonely. Even Jamie didn't bother showing up. The world had moved on and so had she but not necessarily in a happy direction. But she knew now that Maggie had been right. Joe was not the one for her.

Spring in Oxford was always uplifting. The cherry blossom came out in a magnificent display and stuck all over the pavements in a brown, marmalade adhesive, mess. Students started cycling in sweatshirts rather than long thick coats. Nicola was beginning to find GCSE in Environmental Studies rather tedious and longed for something more academically challenging. Curled up on the sofa one evening with the latest bonk buster laundering her brain, she heard a soft knock at her door. Kate, Archie and Ethan were away at a gig in Liverpool and as far as she knew there were no waifs and strays upstairs. Perhaps this was another aimless backpacker looking for somewhere to crash for the night. Wearily she grabbed the house keys and went to the door. A shadowy figure was just climbing the steps up to the house and there was a car parked in the drive with its engine running. The figure turned round and jumped back down beside her and Nicola found herself wrapped in Lucas' arms.

'Oh, Nicola, Nicola,' breathed Lucas into her neck and she inhaled the sweet nostalgic scent of lemon grass. His lips closed passionately on hers and she was lost in memories and love for this man who had haunted her for years.

There was a discreet cough behind them and Lucas pulled gently away holding her tightly at arm's length searching her face.

'I have to go. There's a plane waiting for me at Brize Norton and this is an unscheduled deviation. Wait for me, please?' And he was gone, the car sliding easily down the drive heading out of Oxford.

Stunned and shivering slightly Nicola stood spellbound as the night air wrapped its darkness round her. The book had lost its appeal so she just sat in the darkness trying to compute what had happened. Had it really happened. How did he know where she lived and why had it taken so long for him to get in touch? Yes it really had been Lucas. But wait? For what and for how long? Completely at odds with her emotions Nicola sought the comfort of the dim light in her bathroom and drew out her red penknife. A shadowy figure moved beside the bath and Nicola waited for him to grab her hand. But Jamie didn't move.

'I'm not going to help you anymore, Nicola,' he said. 'You have to make peace with yourself and stop cutting. A window has opened for you and a path leads to Lucas. You must take it.'

For a long time Nicola stared at the scars on her arm and stroked her skin with the cold blade. It felt so good, so in control but she needed Jamie to go away from her. She couldn't drive the sharpness through her skin and into her flesh to make the red line glint with satisfaction. She couldn't do it with her conscience watching. But she had to do it now that Lucas was camping out in her brain again.

It was May and the end of the university Eights Week on the river before she heard anything. Unable to stand not knowing anything she had phoned Sulei in April but his mobile seemed to be permanently switched off. Dressed in shorts, Nicola was cleaning the flat when there was a rap on the door. Expecting to hear from Kate, she flung the door open.

'Coffee?'

But it wasn't Kate. A tall willowy figure stood out against the morning sunshine. A whirl of colour flashed at her.

'Nicola. It's Gellie. Can I come in?'

Startled, Nicola stood back as Gellie moved soundlessly into her sitting room and turned to face her. It was Gellie but a different Gellie. The crowd of colour was still there but it was more muted and the black curls had been cut short to frame an older face. There was a brief awkward moment and then Gellie flung her arms round Nicola.

'Oh Nicola, I've missed you so much. And Maggie, though I don't think she'll ever forgive me.'

Gellie paused and stood back. 'Have you forgiven me? It's important.'

Nicola swallowed unable to process all this. 'Was there anything to forgive, really?'

'Well, I suppose finding out about…you know, …about,' Gellie straightened and then said all at once 'about Charlie and me and about Lucas being my son.'

Nicola shook her head slightly. This was all a bit too much. She had never thought about Gellie being Lucas' mother especially since he was adamant about not wanting to have anything to do with her.

'I know you're in love with Lucas. That's why I'm here. He needs you.'

It was a wild dream. It must be and any moment now she'd wake up and be at her desk at KS Publishing.

'Nicola,' Gellie said her name very softly like Lucas did and drew her gently to the sofa.

'You'd better sit down. I've a great deal to explain.'

'Lucas has been on some crazy mission in Somalia with Sulei. There was a gun battle. Lucas was shot in the arm and the force fractured his collar bone. He had it all bound up and some medic managed to remove the bullet but the stupid boy carried on. The wound became infected and it wasn't until he collapsed that someone had the sense to get him out of there and get him home. He's just up the road in the John Radcliffe Hospital. I have been there giving blood. He's in an induced coma, thank goodness, as doubtlessly if he'd known they were planning to use my blood he'd have refused and discharged himself.'

Gellie paused and looked at Nicola who had gone very pale.

'He's not going to, you know, die? I mean he will get better won't he?' the thought of losing another person she truly loved was almost too much to bear.

Gellie reached out and touched Nicola's arm. 'My son is the strongest, bravest person I know. Of course he's going to get better.'

This was too much for Nicola and she fell backwards into a black hole. How dare Gellie call Lucas her son when she'd given him away after he was born. How dare she talk like that when Nicola hadn't had that option with Julia. Gellie had had it all. She'd given Lucas away but then stolen him back by being the fantastic aunt while he was growing up. She still had Charlie around to love and support her. Nicola had had none of that, forgetting, of course, that Gellie knew nothing about Julia. One thing became crystal clear in her mind as she floundered around in the mill stream of whirling thoughts. Lucas was hers and she was going to make sure that she didn't let him go.

Stonily she faced Gellie. 'When can I see him?'

Gellie was taken aback by this cold response. She thought Nicola would be happily forgiving her and hugging her.

'That's why I'm here. The doctors are going to bring him out of the coma this afternoon and they would like someone close to him to be there when he comes round. Of course they suggested that it should be me,' Gellie decided to hit back at Nicola, 'but seeing how he refuses to see me, I thought perhaps you might be the best option.'

Now it was Nicola's turn to be shocked. Honestly, she thought she was close to Gellie.

'I'll just change and be right with you.' She said to Gellie.

'Oh, I'm not going back to the hospital just yet. I'm on my way to Caroline's in Summertown. I'm sure you can find your own way, just look for signs to ICU and ask for Lucas at the nurses' station. I'll find my own way out.'

With a swirl of muted colour, Gellie was gone leaving a stunned Nicola staring at the door.

The bus journey gave Nicola a break to consider Gellie's visit, but it didn't help. She deeply regretted being horrid but it was too late to undo the damage. She couldn't take it back so she'd just have to hope that a damage limitation opportunity hauled into view very soon.

Lucas was lying propped up in bed amid a mass of hissing and ticking machinery. The whole of his left arm was punctured with crazy stitching and tubes draining noxious looking liquids. A nurse guided her to a chair on his good side and, as she sat down quite suddenly, Lucas' bed started to wobble. She reached forward and took his hand in hers wondering what one was supposed to do in these situations.

'I'll get you a cup of tea,' said the nurse and disappeared.

'Lucas. It's Nicola. I'm here and this time I'm not going to leave until you tell me that you love me.' She found herself ranting on about how much she loved him and that of course she'd marry him. That was all she ever wanted and so he had to get better immediately. Looking up she saw the nurse hovering with a cup of tea.

'That's just the sort of thing he needs to hear,' she said smiling at Nicola. 'Far more effective than modern medicine and it always works. Now I need to ask you to move to the waiting room as the doctors are waiting to examine him. He's nearly there. He should be awake very soon.'

'Don't worry,' she added, seeing the alarm on Nicola's face. 'He's doing really well. We'll have him walking down the aisle in no time.'

Nicola blushed deeply and scuttled out of the ward.

The waiting room was a no man's land hovering between the land of the sick and the rest of the world. It was beige. Everything was beige as though the use of colour would be rude and inappropriate. A young couple sat welded together in misery hardly glancing up as the door banged behind Nicola.

'Sorry,' she mumbled but got no reaction.

Locating herself as far away as she could, Nicola sat staring at the wall. She constructed a life equation for Lucas where the letters represented his injuries, as far as she could list them, and numbers the likelihood of recovery. The final summation was Lucas' chances. Actually she had to admit it looked good even though she may have been slightly biased in equating his ability to survive. Love was certainly colouring her judgment. She glanced at her companions. Their life equations didn't seem to be going too well. It seemed like hours before they told her she could go back to

Lucas.

She stayed beside him all night watching the nurses and doctors monitoring Lucas and his machines and holding onto his hand as if he might disappear if she let go. The night shift was leaving when she eventually let her head drop onto his bed and she fell asleep.

'Hey, wake up and talk to me.'

Nicola looked up and saw Lucas gazing at her. Her first reaction was to fling her arms round him but it wasn't possible so she just gazed back at him.

'Lucas?' she said stupidly.

'Nicola. I'm going to be fine. Just a couple of flesh wounds that got out of control. I've had plenty of sleep and now ...' The colour drained from his cheeks and a monitor bleeped ominously. Several nurses rushed to the bedside.

'Miss Cowan, would you mind leaving us for a moment? We'll call you as soon as you can come back.'

On her return, Lucas was propped up smiling at her but very pale. His breathing was labored.

'I'm going to be fine. Out of here in no time.' A nurse popped her head round the door.

'No talking,' she said sternly. 'Listen to your girlfriend instead.'

Nicola sat down.

'How did you find me? I swore Sulei to secrecy. Obviously he can't be trusted.' Lucas still hadn't learnt to obey orders.

Nicola dodged that one.

'I waited Lucas. How did you know where I lived when you turned up on my doorstep?'

Lucas smiled and whispered, 'Of course I knew you were in Oxford living in Kate's flat. And I saw you in Tackley End Road looking at our house.' He grinned weakly.

'So why didn't you come over to me when you saw me in the road?' Nicola could hardly believe she was having this conversation.

Lucas looked sheepish. 'I was going to. That's why I came outside but I completely lost it.'

He turned slightly to address the ceiling.

'You've no idea the number of times I so nearly came to your flat. But I couldn't, not after the way you just rushed off and left me in Africa.'

Nicola looked down at her hands.

'You could easily have written a letter to Joe dumping him, explaining all about us. Then we could have stayed in Africa, at Swala, forever. Leaving all this shit behind. It wouldn't be the first time someone has been dumped by letter.'

Lucas sank back onto his pillow and a loaded silence walled up between them.

Nicola looked down at the floor. 'I owed it to Joe to see him face to face, to explain why I couldn't marry him but not to tell him I didn't love him. He didn't need to know that. I walked away from Joe, from my scholarship, from my research and came to Oxford to a dead end job in a bar. And all because I fell in love with you. Not in Africa but well before that.'

There she'd said it and burst into tears. Without looking at her Lucas pushed a white cloth in her direction.

'We'd better make sure nothing splits us up again,' he whispered softly as a nurse came in and shooed Nicola out.

The next day Lucas was moved to a ward and Caroline and Dermot had arrived looking nervous and anxious. Nicola wasn't sure what her position was now that his parents had arrived and Dermot seemed to be taking over. Caroline found her getting a cup of coffee.

'Nicola, my dear. Lucas is going to be fine and might be able to leave hospital tomorrow. We'll be staying in our house in north Oxford so that we can be close to the JR and you must come and visit as often as you like. I know how important you are to Lucas.'

Summer was slipping into autumn before Lucas could hold a cup in his left hand.

'At least I can still shoot to kill,' he told Nicola as they sat in the small back garden.

'You are not seriously considering going back to before?' said Nicola horrified.

'No chance of that. I have been grounded and it will be a desk and a lap top for me somewhere safe in the UK. I don't know whether I'll be to settle down to do that.' Lucas spat the words out. Nicola sighed, she seemed to be spending more and more time with Mr Grumpy. Thank goodness she went to work every day.

The physiotherapy was tough and when he wasn't in the gym someone, usually Nicola when she was around, had to throw tennis balls endlessly at his left hand. Apart from a few hugs and holding hands, his right, there had been no real physical contact between them. Nicola didn't know where she stood with Lucas and was too afraid of a monstrous row if she asked. His physio was obviously feeling the strain of not being able to fashion an instant cure and came up with a plan. He suggested a month at an army boot camp in the north of Scotland focusing on getting Lucas back to his prime fitness in the hope that his arm and shoulder would follow suit. If it isn't working, he told Lucas, we'll bring you straight back to Oxford. Lucas couldn't wait.

The night before he left he held Nicola very close.

'I want you Nicola. I want you so much. But I can't, not yet. I hate my broken body and I don't want you to see me like this. Can you wait, again, please…my love?'

'Of course. I'll wait for as long as it takes. I'm not going anywhere.' But she wasn't quite sure.

Communication was not Lucas' best attribute but he kept texts and emails flowing back to Nicola without much news apart from the fact that he was still alive and enjoying the challenge.

Nicola used the break to summon up courage to tell her parents about Lucas. Maggie already knew but was sworn to secrecy. Her parents suspected, and hoped, that she'd met someone because her visits to Frampton had become very erratic and quite sparse over the summer which had previously been a time Nicola loved to spend in the Cotswolds. So when she said she had something to talk about they waited in eager anticipation.

'Do you think it is someone local, someone we know? Or someone she's met in Oxford?' hazarded her mother but Andrew refused to drawn.

'We'll just have to wait and see,' was his reply.

It was a warm early October morning at precisely 11.00am that Nicola arrived. Her mother had made coffee far too early and was just on the point of making more when Nicola walked into the kitchen. Her father leaned back against the dresser for support. The air crackled in anticipation.

'Darling, how lovely to see you.' A kiss on both Nicola's cheeks. 'We've missed having you around over the summer. Coffee?' There were question marks hanging all over the ceiling.

Once they were settled round the kitchen table, Nicola cradled her coffee and went for it.

'I've been seeing someone over the summer. Lucas Smith Owen. It's quite serious between us.'

Her parents exchanged worried glances as they absorbed the information.

'Have we met Lucas? He's Julian's brother isn't he?'

Her mother looked at Nicola rather pointedly understanding that there was a great deal of history behind this relationship.

'You've probably met him at one of the Willstone's parties and he's actually Julian's cousin.' This was going to get messy.

'So,' said her father straightening his shoulders. 'What you are saying is that you're in a relationship with your dead boyfriend's brother, good as, and in between there lies a broken promise to marry a good decent guy who loved you.'

Silence.

So he continued. 'Have you any idea about the fall out round here caused by Lucas? A family torn apart, friendship's destroyed. And now you're trying to tell us you've sold your soul to the perpetrator. How long has this been going on?'

Nicola opened her mouth to reply but her mother got there first.

'Andrew, you're being too harsh. Charlie's affair with Gellie Crawford was hardly Lucas' fault even though he was one of the outcomes.'

But he was not to be deterred. 'How long? It has nothing to do, I take it, with why you broke up with Joe and threw away your scholarship and the chance of a doctorate in a subject you professed to love?'

How could Nicola agree that her father had got it in one and then mitigate some of the damage by explaining you took the honourable route out.

'You're right,' she said softly. 'I finally realised that Lucas was the man that I love and not Joe even though Maggie had been telling me for ages. But I walked away from Lucas because I needed to sort things out with Joe. Then I moved to Oxford on my own and I didn't see Lucas for ages after that.' She went on to explain how they finally got together.

'He's recovering well in Scotland. Really getting back to his old self.' Nicola smiled as memories of Swala flooded back.

Her mother had been watching Nicola's face closely and noted how her face shone with happiness. She reached over and gave her a hug.

'Well, whatever Lucas does for you it works. You look amazing. More coffee?'

After his month away Nicola got a text from Lucas.

Meet me at The Bricklayers 7.30. Love you L xx

Nicola nearly burst with happiness and rushed out to buy some new underwear and very expensive jeans.

Lucas was waiting for her at the bar and gave her a long hard hug burying his face in her neck.

Guiding her over to a small table he lifted his glass with his left hand and grinned.

'All mended. Back to full working order.'

He did look fit and well but lines round his eyes and faint shadows beneath them showed how hard he had had to work to regain his fitness.

'Now we'll go and get something to eat and then I'm taking you to Chico's. Remember?'

How could she forget? It was a lovely idea, like they were both starting all over again.

After dancing till well into the early hours they walked back up the Woodstock Road, Lucas' good arm draped over Nicola's shoulder, talking about Latin American dancing and how maybe they should go to classes. At the door to Nicola's flat, Lucas kissed her for ages then gently untangled himself and stood back against the moonlight.

No, thought Nicola, no, please don't just leave me here oozing desire and run off up to Summertown. Not after all this time, after all this waiting.

Lucas took a cautious step forward, looked at the ground and then straight at Nicola.

'Marry me, Nicola,' he whispered into the night air.

Nicola stretched forward not really believing she'd heard him correctly. The air pricked and crackled between them.

'Marry me…'

The sentence lay unfinished as Nicola rushed into his arms.

'Yes, Yes, Yes.'

Lucas picked her up and carried her into the flat. Even though the place was empty, Nicola kicked her bedroom door firmly shut.

The next day Nicola was sure she was dreaming when she woke to find Lucas beside her. But he was real enough. She traced a finger slowly down the scar on his arm. Lucas had always kept it hidden until now.

'Sulei's medic friend was not much of an embroidery artist but I guess he did his best,' said Lucas without opening his eyes. Nicola hastily wrapped her left arm in the sheet to hide her own scars but Lucas wasn't paying attention.

'Look,' he said, demonstrating a side plank movement with his weight on his bad arm. 'How's that for a massive improvement?' and then he collapsed on top of her.

'Remember? You promised to marry me last night. I hope you haven't changed your mind.'

Nicola kissed him hard in reply. Lucas searched among the hastily discarded heap of clothes on the floor and retrieved a small leather box.

'I'm sorry, I rather jumped the gun here. Once I'd decided I had to marry you I told Mum because I just couldn't keep it a secret. She said that if you said yes, and she said it like you might say no,' he paused to look at her, 'then she would like you to have her mother's engagement ring.' He snapped open the box and eased out a ring with three square cut emeralds separated by tiny diamonds. 'What do you think? Do you like it? The lads in Scotland said girls wanted single whacking great diamonds these days but I would like you to have this.'

All Nicola could do was gaze at the ring as Lucas slipped it onto her finger. It was a bit big.

'If you like we'll go into town and get it made smaller and have lunch in Georgina's to celebrate.'

'Hey,' he said wiping away two very large tears, 'I thought you'd be pleased.'

'I am, I'm so happy. The ring is amazing. Thank you. I love you.'

What to do about her parents was the problem. Nicola hadn't exactly relayed the conversation she'd had with them while Lucas was away. Lucas decided to go straight into battle and booked an appointment at the surgery as he was still registered as living at Mulberry Cottage

Andrew Cowan was rather bemused when he saw Lucas' name on his morning surgery list and even more so when a very smart looking Lucas walked in. They had decided a suit would be over the top but he had scrubbed up well.

Andrew had been looking at Lucas' notes on his screen. Normal childhood illnesses and trips to A&E but later years had been left blank.

'Good morning, Lucas. How are you today? Any problems?' Andrew was trying to act normal.

'I'm fine. In fact I feel wonderful.' Lucas grinned: Andrew frowned.

'I'm afraid this is probably totally irregular but I wasn't sure how to do this,' Lucas paused.

'Andrew, Dr Cowan, I would like to ask your permission to marry your daughter, Nicola.' With that Lucas eyeballed Andrew and poured in as much charm as possible.

This morning's surgery was certainly different. Andrew cleared his throat, buying time, and looked expectantly at Lucas.

'I'm afraid my prospects are not looking too good at the moment. I have been informed that I will be invalided out of my current employment but that a job will be found for me somewhere like GCHQ in Cheltenham. With my experience in the field I have a great deal to offer in areas such a terrorist surveillance. I speak French, Spanish, Swahili and Arabic fluently.'

Lucas felt he was in a job interview. Andrew hadn't offered anything.

'But above all,' Lucas shifted and increased the intensity of his eye contact, 'I love Nicola more than anything in the world and all I want to do is spend the rest of our lives together.' Lucas stopped suddenly remembering that Nicola told him not to overdo it.

A silence was broken by Andrew. 'Yes, well I see.' Nothing from Lucas.

'I presume, and this is just between me and you, this is a bit of a fait a compli. That you have already asked her, she's said yes and there is nothing either I or her mother can do about it.'

Lucas leaned back in his chair. 'Yes, but Nicola needs you to say yes before we tell anyone. She really wants you to approve. It's important.'

Andrew smiled. It was probably unusual in this day and age for a young man to ask for permission. He rather liked the fact that Lucas had made the effort. If he was able to dismiss Lucas' unfortunate background, he wouldn't hesitate. Lucas was sitting very quietly waiting for Andrew's reaction. With his training he would be able to maintain that position for several hours and he was quite prepared to do just that. Andrew gazed back at the immovable object.

'Where's Nicola?'

'In the waiting room.'

Andrew pressed his intercom. 'Please could you send my daughter in? She's in the waiting room.' He got up and shook Lucas' hand.

'Congratulations.'

Completely caught off guard, Nicola's mother went straight into compensatory mode. Champagne, the best cut glass, lunch booked in Stroud. She was desperate to get Andrew on his own to discuss how this had all come about and why he'd done such a complete about turn re Lucas. But that would have to wait and anyway it wasn't really important when she saw how deliriously happy Nicola was.

'When do you plan to get married and where? Everything gets booked up so quickly. Frampton Church?'

Nicola had already told Lucas she couldn't possibly get married anywhere near Frampton. Lucas had come up with an interesting solution, Lincoln College chapel. It had been Dermot's college as well as Julian's. Nicola hesitated because the College held such memories, but then decided it was about time she got over it.

'We could walk round to the Ashmolean Museum and have a reception there. It would be different. I've always wanted a feast surrounded by ancient Greek and Roman statues.' Lucas was very pleased with his plan.

Her mother was initially disappointed that she would not be organising a wedding at home but thinking about it she could understand Nicola's reasons and threw herself enthusiastically behind the arrangements for an Oxford wedding. Maggie was over the moon and wore an 'I told you I was right' look smeared across her face until Nicola told her to wipe it off or she wouldn't be her chief bridesmaid. Much to her disappointment, Kate told her she couldn't be a bridesmaid. And then she told her why, Kate and Archie's baby was due in July just three days after the wedding. Nicola screamed in excitement and asked if they were getting married too and then guessed that that would not be Kate's style. Lucas suggested Kalan and Leila's two daughters as Sulei was, of course, going to be his best man.

It was a beautiful summer's day in Oxford. The bride looked stunning in a simple long white dress with pearl buttons down the back, her shoulder-length hair held off her face by two white daisies. The bridegroom was in morning dress and the bridesmaids had dresses designed by Maggie which had the bride's approval but her mother still wasn't quite convinced even on the day. But the dresses did come out well in the photographs. Katie and Archie made the wedding with little Saul in a sling.

Bemused shoppers watched as the wedding party processed from the College down Broad Street and into Beaumont Street to the Ashmolean Museum led by a town crier in full ceremonial announcing the event at every corner. Dee and Charlie Willstone hadn't been invited because it all seemed so complicated but Charlie insisted on sending a large cheque on behalf of the Willstones. Caroline wanted Gellie to be there because after all Lucas was her son but Lucas was adamant. No Gellie.

Back in Watamu, the Arit Jinn were relaxing splayed out on the branches of the Tree of Forgetfulness. The lookout signalled when Sister Benny emerged from the convent building heading off to her garden with a letter in her hand and they all leaned forward to read it. It was a cause for celebration when they discovered that Nicola and Lucas had got married and one of them suggested a game of champion quoits. All their mischievous planning had produced a wonderful result. Meanwhile Sister Benny settled herself amid her calming lemon grass and opened Gellie's letter. Her worst fears were confirmed bringing back the fear that her dark secret might one day be discovered. At least if Nicola had married Joe the secret would probably have stayed dead and buried. She would write a positive cheery reply wishing the couple every happiness for the future, crossing her fingers under her dark robe that Charlie would not find it necessary to cease his regular direct debit contribution to the Convent's finances. Pausing under the Tree of Forgetfulness while on her evening rounds, Sister Benny gazed up its branches. 'You may think you've won but I am determined, somehow, to have the last laugh,' she threatened.

Over the next few months Nicola purred along on a wave of happiness. Lucas had moved into the flat and for once she appreciated his minimalist approach to possessions. Always on the move and often at very short notice Lucas brought very little with him but even with just Lucas the flat was cramped. Such was their complete absorption with each other they hardly noticed the lack of space. Nicola continued to work for KS Publishing and finally moved on from GCSE text books to more cutting-edge environmental science while Lucas travelled to London or worked from home. Idly flicking through the latest edition of *Nature* one lunch hour, Nicola found herself reading an article by Professor Joe Delaney. Curiosity got the better of her and skipping to the end of the article she read:

Professor Joe Delaney, Head of Environmental, Marine and Energy Research at the Ryan Institute, College of Science, NUI Galway.

I wonder if he ever married,she mused. Perhaps he's living in a cottage in Roundstone. Consigning her thoughts to history she went back to work.

ANNIE BOON

10

Nicola was six months pregnant with twins and getting up and down the steep steps to the flat in Oxford was getting increasingly difficult. Her parents were adamant that Nicola and Lucas should move and it was Dermot who came up with the perfect solution. Caroline refused to sell Mulberry Cottage but Dermot could never envisage them ever living there again. Too many memories and Caroline had difficulties exorcising its role as Charlie and Gellie's love nest. They offered to let the cottage to Nicola and Lucas who were delighted to accept but not until after the twins were born. Andrew told Nicola that is would be quite simple for her to move from the maternity hospital in Oxford to Cheltenham were one of his best friends was the consultant obstetrician.

'You will have the best possible care,' he told Nicola.

But Nicola wouldn't hear of it. She liked her doctor and was happy with the care she was receiving at the hospital in Oxford. More importantly she did not want her parents to find out that this was not her first pregnancy. She was terrified that one or both of the twins would have the same heart condition as Julia. Her consultant had assured her that the scans had shown two strong healthy hearts in very good working order. Needing to be constantly reassured Nicola wanted to stay close to a hospital that could fix things if it turned out that the consultant had missed something. It was great having Kate and Saul upstairs and she was determined to go on working at KS Publishing right up to the last minute. Kate was another of Monica's worries as she had always regarded Kate as a bad influence and this now included Kate's parenting skills. Nicola suffered from a deep dark depression in the latter stages of her pregnancy. Her father sniffed out the depression but could find no answers apart from a huge blast of hormonal imbalance. Nicola flushed all the tablets down the toilet as she knew what was going on. She was being dragged down by the misery and grief she thought was tucked safely away in a box. She would never recover from Julia's death.

Miranda and Alice arrived a week early on a sunny afternoon in July, a year after they were married. Nicola's memories of Julia's birth were quite hazy. She remembered weird dreams, lots of people rushing around and a great deal of pain. This time Lucas was with her every step of the way, the midwife called the doctor only at the last minute and the pain relief was wonderful. In no time at all Lucas was sitting beside her holding two swaddled bundles with masses of dark curls.

'I'm surrounded by beautiful women,' he said happily.

Andrew was slightly miffed at missing the event but as Monica pointed out the last thing you'd want when giving birth is your father at your bedside even if he was a doctor. And so Nicola, Lucas, Miranda and Alice moved to Mulberry Cottage with Nicola's secret still intact. Andrew and Monica were besotted with the twins making Nicola feel rather jealous. She couldn't remember her mother lavishing so much love and attention on her when she was small. Caroline, whose own children had been largely brought up by a succession of ayahs (nannies in Africa) and Gellie, was not much help practically, but made up for it by being surprisingly good company. Maggie took to knitting a family of bears which delighted the girls. They became her number one fans and squawked with glee whenever she came to visit.

Two years later Nicola was standing in her kitchen in the early morning light with an airmail letter from Sister Benny burning a hole in her dressing gown pocket. She had just reached a point where she was at peace with herself and her life when the bombshell arrived. As she waited for the kettle to boil Nicola absently stroked the now unmarked inside of her left arm.

Whichever way she looked at it, Nicola knew that she was trapped. It was this problem that had kept her awake all night.

'Damned if I do and damned if I don't,' she had murmured to herself through her tears. As if in reply, the early morning breeze smirked and billowed the drawn curtain as it flooded into the bedroom. It crept up over the duvet and paused to lift a corner of the airmail letter as though taking a quick peek at the contents. Jamie was sitting cross legged at the foot of Nicola's bed, his long black coat tucked around him even though it was early summer. Nicola, sitting upright at the other end of the bed, clutched nervously at the duvet. The letter lay between them daring them to discuss its contents.

'What should I do now, Jamie?' asked Nicola

No reply.

She rushed on, 'It is all such a shock that I'm having trouble getting my head round what has happened. Sister Benny is a nun for god's sake but she has hardly behaved like one. I feel so let down.' Nicola buried her head in her hands.

'Gently, Nicola,' said Jamie. 'Sister Benny did what she thought was for the best at the time. Don't over think all of this.'

Jamie reached out towards Nicola and as the breeze caressed her face she felt calmness creep into her soul.

'You have one opportunity to get this right. Whatever decision you make there will be no going back. You know that don't you? And the decision must be right for all of you. You are going to discuss this aren't you, Nicola?'

Nicola lifted her tear-stained face to look at Jamie and nodded. The prone figure beside her shifted slightly and pulled at the duvet. Jamie smiled at Nicola and moved fluidly off the bed.

'Don't be afraid, Nicola. You know what you have to do.'

Raising his hand giving her a high five, Jamie left the room letting the door click behind him. The black curls on the pillow beside Nicola stirred a voice, husky with sleep, broke the new day silence.

'Right, which one of the twins is it this time? It must be my turn.'

'Shush,' replied Nicola, 'it was the breeze rattling the door. Go back to sleep and I'll creep down to the kitchen and make some coffee.'

Stuffing the letter into her dressing gown pocket, Nicola left the room. It was the only way she could make some thinking time.

Back upstairs, she put the cups of coffee down and placed the letter on the bed. Playfully she put her cold hands on Lucas' warm back.

'Ouch. You're going to pay for that.' he said rolling over on top of the letter. 'What's this? It isn't my birthday. Have I forgotten a special occasion?' Serious now, Nicola carefully extracted the letter from its blue envelope.

'It's from Sister Benny,' she replied handing it to Lucas. 'Read it please, out loud'.

She sat back so that she could study Lucas' face and watch his reactions.

Dear Lucas and Nicola,
Thank you so much for the lovely photographs of your two beautiful daughters. They have been passed around everyone here at The Convent and we all send many congratulations and best wishes.

'But that was ages ago.' Lucas looked at Nicola's face and then returned to the letter.

Life here in our community continues to be challenging but at the same time, sustained by our faith, warm and rewarding. I do realise that I'm not getting any younger and that my arthritis is now limiting the pace at which I can work.

However I can now spend more time in prayer and reflection with the sisters. This has not been as restful as I had hoped as memories flood the light in my eyes darkening my attempts to find peace. Africa is a hard unrelenting place where death is an accepted way of life. As Sisters of our Lord we set out to save as many lost souls as we can which brings me to the purpose of my letter – my confession.

Nicola, my dear, I will never forget the day you came to my garden to tell me that you were expecting a child. I could see that you had no idea what was going to happen to you and how your life was going to change even before it had really begun. When Julia was born and diagnosed with heart problems I knew it was something you would not be able to handle. Another problem was that the Convent could not afford the medical bills and that Julia would in all probability die before her second birthday. I had to make a swift decision. A month earlier I had been approached by a young English couple living in Lamu about the possibility of adoption but there was no suitable child at that time as they particularly wanted a baby. Julia was my solution. Looking back now I realise that I had no authority to play God and to lie to you but Julia had all the necessary operations and thrived with the McCauleys. I had saved a child and my secret was safe. I felt I could protect you from the truth forever.

Lucas leaned over and gently wiped a tear from Nicola's face.

You never know what life is going to throw at you. Last month the McCauleys were killed in a road accident on the Nairobi to Lamu highway. They had no immediate relatives and Julia's godfather in America does not want to be involved. She is now living with us in the orphanage but it is not ideal. Julia is used to living in a beautiful house with an ayah. She is nine years old and very aware of her circumstances. She needs a new home with loving parents which is why I thought of you both. Would you be prepared to forgive the sins of an old nun and consider adopting Julia? I know I'm asking a great deal and you could be forgiven for seeing my plan as emotional blackmail but I only have Julia's best interests at heart.

You will not hear from me again until I receive your reply.
With the blessing of Our Lord, God, Almighty
Sister Benedicta.

'Phew,' said Lucas running his fingers through his hair. He lay back and stared at the ceiling. Nicola watched him silently.

'This is really serious. How do we know the old bat is telling the truth this time?'

'Lucas. She's a nun.'

'May well be but her track record as far as the truth is concerned is not great. We need to think about this before we get too emotionally involved. We're talking about your daughter and my niece. Family.'

'How can we find out? It's odd that she is still called Julia. A bit creepy.'

Back in Watamu the Arit Jinn stirred in the Tree of Forgetfulness. This was just the kind of mischief making they loved.

A loud bang and a wail from the next bedroom brought Nicola and Lucas back to their immediate present. Lucas pushed back the covers.

'Let's get on with today for a start. I'm going to phone Sulei after breakfast to see what he can find out.'

Three days later Sulei arrived in Lucas' office in London. He put his messenger bag down and pushed two photographs across the desk. Picking them up Lucas went white as he gazed into his dead brother's eyes laughing at him. The second photograph showed an older child with blond hair tied back in pigtails looking seriously into the camera. Again the eyes were a perfect match but this time Lucas noted the slight dimple on the square chin. Silently he passed the photographs back. Sulei then passed a dated medical photograph of a healing scar running down a child's chest. Underneath was written Julia Rose McCauley dob 10.02.03.

'Birth certificate lists father and mother as unknown but the birth date tallies. The adoption papers are all in order and Julia is registered as Julia Rose McCauley. No known relatives and the godfather in America checks out. Sister Benny keeps a register under lock and key known as *The Book of Lost Souls*. Julia's birth is recorded there with her mother given as Nicola Cowan and her father as Julian Smith Owen. Your birth details are also listed in the book.' Sulei smiled wickedly at Lucas.

'How on earth did you get your hands on that?'

'Anna, Sister Benny's PA is married to one of my operatives. Simple.'

'It is pretty convincing isn't it? I mean I can see Julian right there in front of me. So, where do we go from here?'

'A DNA test would be proof.'

'And how do you suggest we get that done without arousing suspicion?'

'Well, I happen to know that Julia has a hospital appointment next week in Mombasa. Just a routine checkup but I could arrange for a blood sample to be taken and sent to a discreet laboratory for analysis. Then you would have to persuade Nicola to take a blood test too.'

Lucas looked at his friend. 'How do you know all this?'

'Well I come from a large extended family with many wives and children. Sometimes it is necessary to settle disputes especially where large sums of money are involved.'

They both sat in silence for a while.

'How does Nicola feel about all this?' asked Sulei.

Nicola had been feeling everything from all points of the compass. Sometimes she felt truly elated at the thought of getting Julia back, her precious link with Julian. Would Lucas be comfortable with suddenly having his dead brother/cousin's child by the woman who was now his wife thrust upon him? Then she would feel anger at Sister Benny for the pain and anguish she had caused. Imagining Julia becoming part of her family was frightening. Would Julia ever be able to forgive her mother for abandoning her? Would she and Lucas be able to bond with Julia? How would the twins take it? Perhaps Julia wouldn't want to come and live with them in England and be part of a new family. Perhaps Julia would hate her forever. And she would have to explain the whole sorry tale to her parents and to the Smith Owens. The inside of her left arm had become quite sore from constant rubbing and sometimes she longed for the cool reassurance of the blade of her red penknife against her skin. That way she could purge herself of this problem and find a solution. But she was determined not to go down that route again. Jamie had not been in contact either and she felt so much alone. She and Lucas talked constantly but as two different people and she had no idea how he really felt. Physically he was there for her but he seemed to have taken a couple of steps back and she was reminded of the time he disappeared to Oman to hide with Sulei's family.

The problem for Lucas was that he did not know what to feel. It was all emotionally too much to absorb and he wanted to run away but he couldn't. In fact he wouldn't this time; he would stay and sort the mess out. If he was brutally honest with himself, if the DNA tests proved positive they would have to adopt Julia and make it work. The alternative of walking away and leaving Sister Benny to cope with a child who was their flesh and blood was not an option.

'Nicola will take a blood test,' he said firmly.

It was a two weeks before the test results arrived. It was positive. Lucas and Nicola spent a quiet day with the twins talking to each other but not listening. Lucas took the twins out for a walk while Nicola made lunch. Looking up from the fridge, Nicola saw Jamie leaning against the work top.

'It will all work out in the end, Nicola. You have to be strong as it won't be easy. Lucas wants to adopt Julia, you know that. You just have to get him to say that to you.'

Later that evening they sat outside the cottage on the terrace watching the sun go down. The air was heavy with the smell of roses and it was a quiet time of the day for them with the girls finally in bed, asleep. Lucas gently reached for Nicola's hand and they both tried to speak at once. Lucas put his hand on Nicola's lips and then kissed her.

'We'll do it,' he said. 'We'll adopt Julia.' Nicola felt she had never loved Lucas more than she did at that momentous moment in their scent filled garden. Everything they should have said to each other passed between them and they were together again.

The next day big decisions had to be made. Who to tell and in what order. Andrew and Monica came top of the list as they would have to be asked to look after the twins when Lucas and Nicola went to Watamu. Sitting in the sunny garden while the twins played on the grass they turned to Andrew and Monica.

'We've something very important to tell you,' said Nicola and then let Lucas explain.

Andrew and Monica were aghast; silent; and then Monica was furious.

'How could you,' she growled at Nicola. 'How could you be so careless in this day and age to get pregnant in the first place? How could you not realise that you were pregnant and how could you not tell us, your parents, and me, your mother? Why didn't you come home as soon as you found out?'

'What for?' replied Nicola angrily. 'So that you can be this angry with me? I didn't intend to get pregnant. It happened. I was young and had no idea that things would turn out like they have. I didn't want a baby but you can't exactly ask for an abortion in a convent. Sister Benny made it all sound so easy. But now you'll be pleased to know that it has all come back to haunt me but I – we – are determined to make it right.'

'And how do you think running off to Africa to find some poor child who has just lost her parents and dragging her back to England is going to make things right as you put it? What about the twins? Have you stopped to consider them? No I don't suppose you have.' Shock had pushed Monica into the unknown and she was very close to telling Nicola and Lucas her true feelings about the Smith Owens and the Willstones.

Sensing the danger Andrew cleared his throat loudly and tried a diversion.

'The DNA tests, absolutely conclusive?'

'Yes,' replied Lucas fishing in his bag and handing the paperwork to Andrew who hastily retired to his study. Lucas followed not wishing to be the filling in the Monica/Nicola venomous sandwich. Following further angry exchanges with her mother, Nicola decided that she was getting nowhere and scooping up her precious daughters walked angrily home. Later that afternoon, Caroline and Dermot turned up to receive the news. Caroline gave Nicola a big hug while Dermot sat and took it all in.

'I'm so sorry you had to go through all that on your own.' Caroline said.

'It all seems like a horrible muddled dream now,' replied Nicola wiping away a tear. She had done a great deal of crying lately. 'It wasn't until I had the twins that I realised quite how enormous those events had been. I can't understand why I didn't ask about Julia. I just accepted what Sister Benny told me. I should have contacted the hospital, made more of a fuss, asked to see Julia.'

'Darling, you were so ill at the time and so young. And you'd only recently lost Julian,' replied Caroline.

'So I am now determined to get Julia back and to make up for all the love I should have given her.'

Caroline and Dermot exchanged worried glances.

'Are you absolutely sure about that?' asked Caroline after a very loaded pause.

'Yes,' said Nicola looking at Lucas. He came to stand beside her and put a supporting arm round her.

'Yes, we're both absolutely sure.'

'Well in that case Dermot and I will back you every step of the way,' said Caroline.

The next day Nicola was sitting in the kitchen staring at the bottom of an empty cup of coffee when a shadow passed the window. A gentle tap on the back door and Monica walked awkwardly into the room. She sat down opposite Nicola.

'I'm so, so sorry about everything I said yesterday. It was the shock of finding out so much at once about my daughter who I thought I knew so well. I never ever expected to be thrown into that sort of situation.'

Nicola stared stonily at her mother. Was she expecting forgiveness for the deep wounds she had made? Nicola wasn't sure that she could ever forgive her.

'Nicola. Please. I love you and will always love you and if you wish to adopt this child then your father and I will support that decision.' Nicola noted that Monica didn't refer to Julia as her granddaughter but talked of her as a stranger. She shifted uneasily in her seat. 'You don't have to do this simply because you think I don't approve.'

'Mother. Lucas and I are going to adopt Julia and bring her up because she belongs to us. Above all she is our flesh and blood and we owe her so much.'

'I can understand how guilty you feel. I am just concerned that you are taking on too much what with the twins and everything. How are they going to feel? Have you thought of that?'

'Lucas and I have talked about all the problems we could be facing. We know it isn't going to be easy but we're determined to make it work.'

'So what can I do to help? Would you like us to look after the girls while you go to Watamu to sort all this out?'

'Yes, please. That would be fantastic.'

Nicola tried to smile at her mother as a sort of truce to end hostilities but she knew their relationship would never be the same again.

Nicola and Lucas were exhausted when they arrived at their hotel in Watamu. They had arranged to meet Sister Benny early the next morning. That night Nicola couldn't sleep. She slipped out of bed, careful not to disturb Lucas, heading for the bathroom and her penknife. The stainless steel blade was caressing her arm making weals without actually drawing blood. Just as she was about to press the blade harder into her arm she felt Lucas come up behind her. Roughly he grabbed the penknife and threw it out of the open window towards the Indian Ocean. Dragging her towards the mini bar he emptied the fridge of ice cubes and packed them along her left arm and then held her as tight as he could against his chest.

Nicola reeled from the pain. It tore up her arm and then coursed with alarming speed through her body. No way was she going to scream and give in as the agony invaded her brain and blotted out her world. To her amazement the intense hurt gave way to an almost surreal sexual desire. Reacting to the change, Lucas threw her onto the bed and although the sex was an act between them as lovers, it seemed to be almost selfish in its intensity.

'I have said it before but I really mean it now. Don't ever cut yourself again, Nicola. Nothing that can happen to you is worth that much self-harm. Now talk to me. Really talk to me about Julia.'

This time Nicola tried to empty her mind of all the doubts and recriminations she had about Julia. She talked for a good hour and when she eventually ran out of things to say Lucas made her sit up and face him.

'Nicola, you're over thinking it all. Not very far from here is a little girl whose world has fallen apart. As far as she is concerned her life has shrunk to the Convent and its orphanage. We have the power to change all that. And we have to do it because you are her natural mother and I am her uncle. Nothing can ever change that. It will not be easy but together we have to make it work.'

Nicola nestled into Lucas' arms and fell asleep. He had made everything sound so uncomplicated.

The next day they were dropped off at the Convent gates. The corrugated iron looked more battered than before and only one of the gates opened properly. They edged their way in and walked slowly past the Tree of Forgetfulness towards the big wooden door. The tree rustled as the Arit Jinn jostled for the best view of proceedings. They could feel something important in their grand scheme and were over excited at the prospect of a dramatic turn of events. Nicola and Lucas held hands tightly but each was lost in their own memories. The door opened and a smiling but smaller looking Sister Benny rushed out to greet them. The chatter from the classrooms ceased for a moment as the Convent held its breath and then resumed at a seemingly high pitch.

'My Dears. How lovely to see you both. Did you have a good journey?'

Sister Benny gave each a big hug and without waiting for a reply led them inside. The door closed firmly and the Arit Jinn sat back to await developments. Moments later the classrooms disgorged a wave of children all neatly dressed in blue and white, some barefoot the others with an array of largely ill-fitting shoes. Trailing behind the main group was a serious little girl with blond hair pulled back tightly into two plaits who walked slowly towards the baobab tree where she sat down in the shade of its branches to wait for Sister Gabriel.

Nicola and Lucas were in Sister Benny's study wading through mounds of paperwork and reading notes on Julia's life so far. Nicola was staring at a birth certificate setting out Julia's correct birth details. She wondered idly if this was a fresh certificate or whether Sister Benny had had it stored safely in case it was ever needed. She still could not quite get her head round the complicity that surrounded the whole affair.

'Why did they keep her name?' she asked.

'Well, Mary McCauley's mother was called Julia and David McCauley's mother was Rose and they loved the name.' replied Sister Benny.

There was a silence as Lucas continued reading. Sister Benny rose stiffly and made her way to a cupboard behind her desk. Unlocking the large door she hesitated before removing a heavy ledger. Carefully she opened *The Book of Lost Souls* at the first marked page and twisted the book round so that it lay in front of Lucas and Nicola. Silently she ran her finger over the page and stopped at a faded entry.

Lucas Sebastian Crawford. Born 29 June 1981 at The Convent of Our Lady, Watamu. Mother: Angela Louise Crawford. Father unknown.

Lucas let out a long sigh and touched the entry. Nicola froze.
Sister Benny turned over the pages to the second marker.

Julia Smith Owen. Born 10 February 2003 at The Convent of Our Lady, Watamu. Mother: Nicola Grace Cowan. Father: Julian Edward Smith Owen (deceased).

There was no mention of Julia's death two days later.
Sister Benny stood without looking at either of their stunned faces.
'So who is buried in Julia's grave?' asked Nicola bluntly.
Sister Benny shrugged her world-weary shoulders. 'Another little girl whose journey into this world was cut short. We called her Julia too.' Keen not to talk about the past, she continued, 'I think it's time you met Julia. She's in the visitor's room reading with Sister Gabriel. We've talked to her about your visit but haven't explained your relationship,' Sister Benny made her way towards the door.

'Ready?' asked Lucas squeezing Nicola's hand.

Nicola jumped to her feet. 'I'm sorry. Really sorry but I can't face this just yet. I need to think this one out again.' Nicola rushed out into the dim hall and sank to her knees among the old trunks and armoires with locked in secrets of their own. It was all too soon. Last night it was all simple and easy. Now in the heady mix of religion, memories and history Nicola just couldn't cope. She had to escape. Dragging open the heavy door she ran across the courtyard to the shelter of her old matiki hut and curled up in a corner of the verandah. Squinting through her fingers she saw the Arit Jinn had covered their tree with flags charting her time at the convent, displaying her memories for all to see. She saw Julia's birthday; Joe coming running up to her on her return from Mombasa; it was all there. Her face burned with guilt. How did she ever get into this position, hiding from her daughter now only feet away from her after all these years, how could she ever be a good mother to Julia? The whole plan was ridiculous and her mother had been right all along. Slowly she got to her feet and stared at the Tree of Forgetfulness. To her right she saw a tall figure with ginger hair wearing a long black coat stride towards the Tree. Without looking round he raised his hand which swiveled at his wrist to give her a high five as the tree trunk opened up and wrapped him into its bark. Jamie had gone. She was on her own.

Lucas gently walked up to Nicola, took her hand and walked her out of the Convent. Before she had time to think it through they were back to the western normality of their hotel fronting onto the beach.

When the sun set with its final curtain effect, the tropical storm made its move. Gathering energy from the warm Indian Ocean, it picked up speed and threw itself at Watamu in the early evening. As the lightening split through the sky and heavy drops of rain sploshed on the dry earth, Nicola finally cracked. She raged at her life from Julian's death to her inability to embrace Julia that afternoon. Her anguish rained down on Lucas who held her close and let her cry herself into oblivion.

'All these years I have carried my grief around with me in a mythical box. Sometimes the box would spring open and I'd cry my heart out over her loss. Now I have this one chance to make everything right, and what happens? I can't do it.'

Used to making decisions instantly and acting on them whatever, Lucas found all this soul searching and introspection quite foreign. He would have picked up Julia, told her the truth and then got on with it. But he couldn't do it without Nicola and he wouldn't want to. They had come a long way in their relationship and no way was he going to lose that.

By morning there was no sign of the storm as the sun gazed benevolently across the sparkling ocean. Nicola's eyes were red and slightly swollen but she managed to find some ice to calm them down. Inside she felt a serene peace creep through her soul and Lucas silently thanked God that maybe they had got through the darkness and could get on with the really difficult bit.

As their car approached the Convent the following morning, Nicola sat up and stared. Something was different, something had changed. People were streaming out through the battered gates carrying baskets, bags and pushing carts loaded with hastily chopped wood. A huge space stood empty in the middle of the courtyard. Sister Benny hurried through the small crowd to meet them.

'It was the storm last night,' she cried triumphantly. 'One bolt of lightning, a direct hit, and the old tree split down its trunk into the roots. One branch hit a classroom roof but apart from that, no damage. Isn't it a great sight? So much more light in the buildings.'

Standing alone Sister Benny had watched the lightening reduce the Tree of Forgetfulness to a tangled mess of branches and trunk fragments, ridding the convent of the mischievous spirits that had taunted her. But the Arit Jinn had a last goodbye waiting for her. As she left her office, Sister Benny found the trunks in the hallway turned upside down the armoires thrown open. Their memories and secrets had been raided by the Arit Jinn and borne off to goodness knows where. Sister Benny shuddered when she thought of how much trouble could be caused if the Arit Jinn ever managed to match their stolen hoard with people who could still be harmed. Thankfully her *Book of Lost Souls* was safely stashed in the office safe.

'I invited all our neighbours over,' Sister Benny's arms indicated a wide area equivalent to the whole of Watamu, 'and haven't they done a grand job in clearing up?' No way was there any chance of the Tree of Forgetfulness being reconstructed on another site. By nightfall most of it would have been burnt on cooking fires. Hesitating, Nicola gazed across the courtyard bereft of the great tree that had dominated it for so long. She remembered only yesterday, seeing Jamie being absorbed by the tree as the Arit Jinn claimed him as one of their own. She looked quickly over her shoulder but there was no sign of Jamie. Lucas nudged her forward and looked into her eyes with a question mark.

'It's nothing,' she said realising that her friend had gone forever and from now on it would be Lucas that she would turn to.

Julia and Sister Gabriel both stood up as Nicola and Lucas entered the room. The morning sunlight poured over Julia outlining her in a warm yellow haze as Nicola gazed into Julian's eyes. She stopped quite suddenly and then the moment passed as Julia stepped forward hesitantly and held out her hand. It was Lucas who broke the tension by asking about the book she was reading. Instantly Julia showed it to him and soon they were deep in conversation. Sister Benny exchanged an 'it's going to be alright' smile with Sister Gabriel After an hour a bell rang and Julia had to go back to her class.

The next day Nicola sat beside Julia in her classroom. It was obvious that Julia was struggling to fit in. She chatted in Swahili to her class mates but the class was held in English and Julia was far ahead of them all. Nicola could see that she was desperately trying to be part of the convent but that she never would. Could Julia adapt to living in England, Nicola asked herself but they would never know until they tried. Nicola and Lucas spent a week visiting daily and spending time together in Watamu going over and over the same old questions. Sister Benny also spent time closeted in her study with Lucas sorting the paperwork while Nicola struggled to bond with Julia. Finally Sister Benny decided it was time to ask the big questions.

Sister Benny asked Julia to walk with her in her garden where she explained that Nicola and Lucas would very much like to be her new parents. This would mean leaving Watamu, leaving Africa and going to live in England where she would have a family again and two little sisters to play with. Life for her would be more like it was before with a proper house to live in and a nice school to go to. Not really understanding but trusting Sister Benny to be doing the right thing Julia nodded.

'Julia,' said Nicola sitting down beside her surrounded by lemon grass, 'Lucas and I would love to have you come to live with us in England. We want very much to be your new Mummy and Daddy. We have two little girls, twins who are younger than you so you would be their big sister. Would you like to do that?' Together with Sister Benny, Nicola and Lucas had decided not to explain to Julia the finer details of her parentage. That could wait until much later. Fishing in her pocket, Nicola slowly pulled out a photograph of the twins. 'This is Miranda and that is Alice.'

Julia looked at the photographs and then up at Nicola. 'I would like that,' she replied.

Later that week they said a tearful goodbye to everyone at the Convent with promises to visit and started the long journey back to Frampton. Julia didn't say much and held tightly to her rucksack holding her few precious belongings. Nicola and Lucas were very careful to include her in all decisions like what she would like to eat so that she felt a part of everything. Julia had clung silently to Sister Benny on the steps leading up to the big Convent door for what seemed an age to her new parents. Not being able to cope with such an emotional scene Nicola turned away to gaze out over the courtyard and grasped at the inner calm that she'd found when the Tree of Forgetfulness had been destroyed.

ANNIE BOON

11

Three months later Nicola felt they had hardly moved on as a family. She was still convinced that adopting Julia was the right thing to do – the only thing to do – and she had known that it would be difficult but not this hard. Julia was polite, neat and tidy but very self contained. Nicola had no idea whether she was actually happy. The twins adored Julia and followed her everywhere gazing intently at her whenever she spoke to them. 'Lia, Lia,' they would call whenever she came into the room and broke into grins of delight. Julia was very patient with them so at least they had no problems there. Nicola had no idea how to deal with a nine year old. At the end of term Lucas and Nicola took Julia to visit her new school so Nicola had a chance to speak to her teacher and ask about what she should expect from Julia at that stage of her development. The teacher was very helpful but none of her suggestions broke through the invisible barrier between them. They decided that Julia should remain Julia McCauley until such time as they could explain about surnames. Lucas took time to talk to Julia in Swahili so that she did not lose her language skills but that only made Nicola feel more excluded as her Swahili had been minimal and she had forgotten most of it. Maggie taught Julia how to knit and Nicola suggested she made a rug for her bed by knitting squares from Maggie's odds and ends of wool and cloth and got a faint smile as a reward so at least they had a project to do together.

Her mother was really difficult. She continued to make a great fuss of the twins but rarely included Julia who stood to one side gazing intently at Monica as though willing her to include her. Nicola felt she couldn't say anything to her mother because she was afraid of destroying the uneasy truce that had developed between them. At night when she couldn't sleep, Nicola would wonder whether she was ever going to make a breakthrough. She and Lucas had often talked about having another child but that would not be possible if or until she felt that Julia had become a true member of their family. Times when she looked at Julia and caught glimpses of Julian she just wanted to hug her and hold her tight but that opportunity had not happened. Although Julia talked about them as her mother and father she had not called them Mum and Dad for their faces. She never referred to her previous life in Kenya but she did talk to Caroline. They would go for long walks together in the Cotswold countryside where Caroline would explain about fields and woods and the animals they saw. Julia ate everything that was put in front of her, suffered English colds without complaining but she didn't move on.

In August Nicola and Lucas took the children camping in Devon. As they unpacked and put up their tents Julia seemed to grow anxious. Lucas asked her what was wrong.

'Where are the guards?' she asked, 'And why haven't you brought a rifle?'

Lucas took her for an ice cream and explained that England was very safe so there was no need for guards and he didn't need a gun because there were no dangerous wild animals. This seemed to reassure Julia but she insisted on having a torch on all night in the tent. The sea was far too cold to swim in as far as Julia was concerned but she did paddle with the twins and built sand castles though hers looked more like a Masai encampment. Such a long way still to go thought Nicola.

At the beginning of September Julia started at the village school. Thankfully she was not the only new pupil in her class. There was a French girl who was going to find it equally strange. Nicola took her on her first day and went into the classroom with her.

'This is Julia McCauley who has come to join us,' said her teacher introducing her to the class. 'She lives in Frampton so I expect some of you have already met her.'

'I'm Julia Smith Owen now,' said Julia in a clear voice smiling at Nicola looking for confirmation. Nicola could have danced with joy at that point. The teacher looked at Nicola.

'Yes, that's right,' said Nicola firmly. 'Julia Rose Smith Owen.' She smiled at Julia but she was looking in the other direction. Nicola couldn't wait to get home to tell Lucas so she sent a text message.

School made a world of difference to Julia. To their surprise she made friends easily and soon Mulberry Cottage was buzzing with her clasmates at weekends. Julia enrolled for every after school activity possible so she was soon exhausted by all the extra curricula sports and clubs. Unintentionally a puppy and then a kitten joined the household. Monica pointed out that Julia reminded her of Maggie at that age, never happy unless there was an impossibly busy schedule ahead of her.

Somehow Julia managed to exist without calling Nicola 'Mum' or 'Mummy' or even 'Mama'. Any of those would have assured Nicola that they were actually coming together as a family. She sent positive emails to Sister Benny on a regular basis who was delighted to receive news of Julia's progress.

Monica and Andrew decide to host Christmas and Caroline and Dermot were invited to stay at Mulberry Cottage. Henry and Maggie were also invited so it would be a real family Christmas. Then a letter arrived from Gellie asking if it would be possible for her to drop in on Christmas Eve to meet Julia and the twins and to catch up with Nicola and Lucas. Lucas had not seen her since that fateful day in hospital and was adamant he never wanted to see Gellie or Charlie ever again. Nicola had never told Lucas about Gellie's life-giving blood donations or that she knew that Caroline met Gellie on a regular basis. They were sisters after all and they had always been close. Charlie, Gellie explained in her letter, was spending Christmas in the States with Jocelyn and her family so she would be on her own. Lucas was adamant. Gellie was not to be invited and actually he never wanted to see her ever again. Nicola thought this was a bit harsh and asked Caroline for advice. Caroline could not explain Lucas' behaviour which seemed so uncharacteristic but agreed that Gellie should be given an opportunity to meet her grand children at some point.

Just after Christmas Julia brought chickenpox home from school and of course the twins caught it too. If Nicola had had the forethought, she observed, she would have bought shares in the manufacturer of calamine lotion recommended by Andrew as the best thing to stop the violent itching. The twins soon bounced back to their rude health but Julia struggled. The spots had all faded but still she seemed listless and unable to keep up with all the activities she had previously enjoyed. Andrew prescribed various tonics but none of them were able to lift Julia's spirits. Nicola started to worry that she might be suffering from depression.

Lucas was another concern. The year previously he had moved to GCHQ in Cheltenham in order to avoid the long commute to London but he missed seeing Sulei and his other spying friends, as Nicola called them. Sulei was spending more time in Saudi and Oman as he prepared to take over the running of his family's business. Lucas missed catching up with Leila on her flying visits to London though she had been persuaded, once, to leave London and venture out into the (unknown) countryside to visit them with her two girls. Lucas never whinged but Nicola could tell he wasn't entirely happy. He was spending too much time at a desk and he ached to be back in the field 'spying for real.'

'We should have a holiday in Kenya,' he said one day to Nicola. 'Visit

Piers and Elodie, go to Watamu and see Sister Benny as she is not getting any younger. Take Julia to Lamu. She could do with some sun.'

With the current state of the Smith Owen finances, Nicola knew it was unlikely. Perhaps she should contact KS Publishing to see if they had any proof reading or editing that she could do from home so that she could start a holiday fund. Maybe a teaching job at the University of Gloucester? She could get a government grant to retrain as a teacher. These idle thoughts came to an abrupt end when Lucas pointed out that such things would only be possible if someone put some more hours into the day. He didn't tell her that Sulei had been wafting some very lucrative contracts under his nose which he had dismissed as being too dangerous now he had a family to consider.

The spring brought a surprise visit from Piers and Elodie and their two boys. Piers had some family business to deal with in Scotland and they decided to round off their trip to the UK with a week in the Cotswolds. Nicola and Lucas were delighted to see them and the children got on well from the moment they arrived. Julia and Fergus, the elder of the two boys chatted away furiously in Swahili, Jack the other boy tried to keep up while the twins tagged along looking bemused. Julia salvaged the situation by starting to teach the twins Swahili and they were soon chattering together in a wonderful mixture of their two languages getting verbs, nouns and tenses all mixed up. Nicola took Elodie shopping in Cheltenham and they had to buy another suitcase to hold all her purchases. Lucas and Piers spent the time deep in serious conversation on long walks. Nicola was having such fun with Elodie and the children she didn't really notice how much time Lucas and Piers were spending together. On their last night Nicola and Elodie were sitting in the village pub waiting for Piers and Lucas to join them for supper. Monica had bravely offered to babysit though Nicola thought it would probably be Julia in charge. When they finally arrived Nicola noticed that Lucas was looking happier than he had for a very long time. We should spend more time catching up with old friends she thought especially if it makes Lucas this happy. While they were waiting for pudding to arrive, Piers said he had something to discuss.

'My father is planning to retire but intends to go on living on his ranch at Borana. To cut a long story short he would like Elodie and I move up there to run the place and to develop his game conservation alongside the Wildlife Forum. That would leave a huge hole at Swala as we have no one there trained up to look after it for us. I have asked Lucas, Nicola, if you two would consider moving out to Kenya to live at Swala and to go into partnership in the Mongomerie family business.'

Nicola sat there stunned. No way had she seen this coming. Elodie by the look on her face already knew and that would explain Lucas' happy face. She had never ever considered living anywhere else, well, not if you discounted the possibility of Galway in another life. Piers broke the silence.

'Of course we don't expect an answer right now. That wouldn't be fair as you have a great deal to talk about. It would big step but Elodie and I would be delighted if you decide to join us. Lucas and I have been thrashing out heads of agreement etc. to see if it would be possible but we need to be sure that you are both committed 100 percent. It's over too you.'

'Why on earth didn't you say something, Lucas?' asked Nicola when they were curled up in bed. 'I had no idea you were thinking about moving to Africa.'

'Piers kind of sprung it on me soon after they arrived and I couldn't say anything to you until we'd worked out whether it would be possible. I wanted to have some hard facts to give you not airy fairy ideas about possibilities. So there is a plan downstairs for us to discuss after they have left. Before you see the plan I need your gut instinct and your true feelings. If you don't like it, we don't go.'

'Tell me first of all. What do you know about running a ranch?'

'Absolutely nothing.' Nicola felt Lucas grin happily in the darkness. 'But I wouldn't be involved in the day to day business. Josh, Elodie's brother does all that. Our job would be expanding the visitors and running safaris.'

Nicola paused to absorb that. Lucas took her hand and played his trump card.

'Actually, I think it's you that Piers really wants on board. He wants your environmental science skills on the Wildlife Forum. You could get down to the research you've always wanted to do.'

Nicola smiled enthusiastically. 'That would be wonderful,' she said.

'Of course we'd keep Mulberry Cottage so that we always had a base here in Frampton, you know if things didn't work out. And for holidays.'

Nicola felt her last reservations slowly melting away.

'You don't have to say anything yet. Wait till you're ready.' Just before he went to sleep Lucas murmured. 'Come on, Nicola, time for a big adventure.'

It was very hard to sleep while Lucas lay dead to the world beside her. Eventually she got up and looked in on the twins who were sleeping as soundly as their father. Then she stood in Julia's doorway watching her tossing and turning and winding her duvet round her like a swaddle. She crept downstairs and stood in the kitchen. She needed to talk to Jamie but she'd left him behind when he'd gone off with the Arit Jinn to god knows where.

'What should I do?' she asked the night's silence.

When she'd been with Lucas at Swala she remembered doubting that she could ever live in Africa like Piers and Elodie. But things had changed. Lucas wasn't happy trapped behind a desk and the Cotswolds, beautiful in their own way, were not wild and remote enough. Julia wasn't thriving and the twins were young enough to adapt. All reasons for saying yes. Her parents wouldn't like it one bit but her father would be retiring soon so they would have no reason not to visit regularly. Maybe, just maybe, she and Lucas could have another child. Nicola gave herself a hug, she'd made her decision.

Suddenly the whole Smith Owen household was galvanised into a flurry of activity. Dermot was called in as adviser and his connections at both embassies was a life-saver. Her parents, as predicted, were not at all happy but were slightly mollified when Nicola told them they could come and stay wherever they wanted and stay for as long as they liked. Julia was over the moon as far as her reserved demeanour allowed but her immediate concern was the dog and the cat. Back to the Cowans who agreed to have the cat and it was Maggie who wanted the dog.

'Another Bundle,' she said happily, 'and I shall move from my flat into a house. I needed a good reason to move and now I have one.' The twins just accepted the plans without a quibble. Caroline and Dermot who had always lead an itinerant life found nothing unusual about moving to another continent and were delighted to have another place to stay in Kenya to add to their list.

Nicola wrote to Sister Benny telling her about their plans and promising to visit with the children as soon as they were able.

Gellie was a problem. Caroline naturally told her all about Lucas and Nicola moving to Kenya and Gellie was very anxious to see her grandchildren before they were spirited off to another continent. Nicola tackled Lucas.

'I told you,' he said in a very low dangerous voice, 'that I never ever want to see her again.' Nicola was at a loss as to what to say next. But it was a big step to move to Africa and she felt that they least they could do was let Gellie see the twins. She tried to explain this to Lucas and to get him to tell her why he now hated Gellie who had been such a big part of his growing up even though he thought she was his aunt at the time.

'All right. I can see you're not going to let this one go. I'm going to tell you this once and I will never speak about it again. You're not going to like it.'

'I'm just trying to understand, Lucas. I can't imagine it can be that terrible.' Nicola snuggled up to him under the duvet. Lifting her hair gently away from her ear, Lucas whispered, 'Just remember how much I love you.'

Turning onto his back he addressed the ceiling in the darkness.

'Gellie was always the fun part of my growing up. Caroline was the disciplinarian. Thank goodness because Gellie would have been a terrible mother. I think Caroline spent more time in Headmaster's studies pleading my case then I did receiving punishments. Julian was always the good one but to give him his due he often claimed to be responsible because he was the eldest not because he was the perpetrator.' Lucas paused, Nicola waited.

'I was in my first year at Brookes Uni and living in the house in Oxford. Julian was living in College in term time and Jocelyn was in Brookes' Halls. We spent at lot of time together with Sulei. Caroline and Dermot were in Saudi so Gellie was in charge as it were. She often appeared in Oxford to take us out for meals or just to check up. One night the four of us had been out partying till late. Jocelyn was making a great play for Julian but he simply wasn't interested. It was late and I offered to walk Jocelyn home. Somehow we walked up the Banbury Road to mine and then things got out of hand and we ended up in bed together.'

Lucas turned to Nicola. 'It was really stupid. Honestly it meant nothing. Jocelyn just wanted to get at Julian.'

'I woke up to hear Gellie coming up the stairs yelling about breakfast. I grabbed my jeans and rushed out to meet her. It wouldn't have been the first time she'd caught me in bed with a girl. Anyway Jocelyn heard Gellie's voice and came out onto the landing wrapped in my shirt. I'll never forget looking into Gellie's eyes and seeing, just for a second, something like Picasso's *Guernica*. Complete mayhem. I never understood it as the next second she was back to being Gellie. All bubbly fun.'

'Then, when she was so ill in hospital, I'd just given blood and found out that she was really my mother, I went ballistic. I went out drinking with my friends who finally bundled me into a taxi which took me back to Sulei. He was seriously unimpressed and spent two days drying me out. It was that bad. Anyway, I started thinking about Gellie about it not being that bad, her being my mother. Then I remembered her catching me in bed with Jocelyn and I worked it out. Gellie had caught me fucking my sister. She never said anything. Nothing. What if it had got serious between Jocelyn and me? Not that it ever would have but she wasn't to know that.'

Nicola sighed. This was a bigger deal than she'd imagined. She searched her mind for anxieties but there were none. It was all such a long time ago before she'd even met Julian.

'It was a very long time ago. Can't you forgive her? I'm not asking you to get all close with her but I do think having grandchildren is a big thing for her and denying her seeing them is very harsh. Remember we've never explained the parentage issues to Julia and the twins because we decided that the time is not right. But when it is, how are Miranda and Alice going to feel about never meeting their real grandmother? Can you handle that one?'

Lucas rolled over and wrapped her tightly in his arms.

'You're such an honourable person, Nicola. How come you ended up with me?' he said smothering her with kisses to mask her reply.

'All right. You win. But it must be at the Oxford house with Caroline in charge. And don't expect me to be there.'

The girls always enjoyed visiting Caroline and were surprised to find that she had a sister who was such fun. Nicola leaned on the door and watched Gellie sitting on the floor producing scraps of wool and material from her pockets which she twirled into fantastic shapes. Alice jumped on this game and made the shapes into big patterns on the carpet. With their masses of curls almost touching, bending towards each other engrossed in their creation Alice and Gellie became one.

'So, so, alike,' murmured Nicola. It will be very hard keeping them apart when Alice is older, she thought, Africa won't be far enough. She'll be another Maggie hanging out in Gellie's shadow.

Elodie came to meet them in Nairobi and looked after Nicola and the children while Lucas did more paperwork before the short flight to Nanuki and the long drive to Swala. Julia had her nose stuck to the window for the entire journey while the twins slept. Piers and all the ranch staff were on the steps to meet them as they drove through the gates. Piers took Lucas off while Elodie led Nicola and the children to the cottage where they would live until Elodie and Piers moved out of the main house. As they approach the door opened and a young African girl emerged with Elodie's boys.

'Fergus, Jack,' shouted Julia. Then she stopped and put up her hand to shade her eyes from the sun. 'Agnes? It's Agnes I know it is.'

She grabbed a twin on each side and started running towards the bungalow. Elodie and Nicola stopped to watch.

'I hope you don't mind,' said Elodie 'I managed to track down Julia's ayah and asked her if she would like to come and work here once I knew you were definitely going to come and join us. She is very good with the boys and I know she'll love the twins.' She looked hesitantly at Nicola.

'You're such a star,' replied Nicola. 'That's just perfect.'

Having put the twins hands firmly in Agnes' Julia turned and ran back to Nicola. For the first time she threw her arms round her mother.

'Thank you so much, Mama, for finding Agnes,' and then she ran back. Nicola glowed with love for her daughter at long last.

There was a sound of unshod hooves on dry packed earth as Lucas appeared round the end of the cottage riding a chestnut and leading Mistral.

'Come on, Nicola,' he shouted 'I'm taking you out to dinner.'

Nicola looked at Elodie who was laughing.

'Go on. The children will be fine.'

Nicola ran towards Lucas and grabbed Mistral's reins.

'See you tomorrow,' called Elodie, waving goodbye.

ABOUT THE AUTHOR

ANNIE BOON, born in Austria of Irish parents, was brought up in the Cotswolds. She went to school in Bristol and university in Belfast, Liverpool and Oxford. She is married and lives in Oxfordshire. *Protecting the Truth* is her first novel.

14510399R00155

Printed in Poland
by Amazon Fulfillment
Poland Sp. z o.o., Wrocław